"IS THIS THE YEAR OF THE GREAT DYING?" ASKED CADILLAC.

"This is the year it begins," said Mr. Snow.

"When will the iron snakes come?"

Mr. Snow closed his eyes, breathed in deeply, and turned his eyes toward the sun. Eventually the answer came. "When the moon's face has turned away three times."

"And what of the cloud warrior the Sky Voices have chosen?"

Mr. Snow let the air out of his body with a long sigh and dropped his head onto his chest. His eyes fluttered open. "His journey toward us begins. He dreams the dreams of young men. Of feats of valor, of triumph, of power, of greatness." Mr. Snow raised his eyes and looked at Cadillac. "But like all young men, he thinks these things are gifts. He does not yet know how much the world pays for such dreams."

BY THE SAME AUTHOR

Fade-Out
Mission

PATRICK TILLEY

CLOUD WARRIOR

BAEN science fiction BOOKS

CLOUD WARRIOR

A Baen Book

Baen Enterprises
8-10 W. 36th Street
New York, N.Y. 10018

First Baen printing, August 1985

ISBN: 0-671-55972-9

Cover art by Richard Hescox

Printed in the United States of America

Distributed by
SIMON & SCHUSTER
MASS MERCHANDISE SALES COMPANY
1230 Avenue of the Americas
New York, N.Y. 10020

—— 1 ——

Cadillac sat on the ground near Mr. Snow and listened with half-closed eyes as the white-haired, bearded old man told the naked clan-children the story of the War of a Thousand Suns.

Cadillac knew the story by heart. It was the two hundred and eighth time he had heard it, and it was not new to the sixty young children of the settlement, who squatted in a half circle before them. It did not matter. The children sat spellbound, hanging on every word, just as they had the first time. Most of them didn't remember Mr. Snow telling them the story before. But then, most of them hardly remembered anything for very long—and never would.

But Cadillac could.

Cadillac remembered everything. All he had ever seen and heard, down to the minutest detail. That was why he had been chosen by Mr. Snow to learn from him all that had happened to his people from the beginning of the New Time. When Mr. Snow left them to go to the High Ground, Cadillac would take his place as the clan's wordsmith. It would then be

1

Cadillac's task to find a young child capable of memorizing the series of events that made up the nine-hundred-year history of the Plainfolk.

Before that, stretching back even beyond the reach of Mr. Snow's memory, was the uncounted span of years known as the Old Time, when the world trembled before the feats of Heroes with Names of Power.

Mr. Snow knew a few tales of the Old Time; when there were as many people on the earth as there were blades of grass. When huts were built on top of one another to form settlements that rose high in the sky like the distant mountains. When the crumbling hardways, which once ran across the land like veins along his arm, were choked with a never-ending stream of giant beetles that carried people from one place to another so that no one would ever find himself alone.

As Mr. Snow rippled his fingers up the length of both arms to describe how, in the War, the falling Suns had burned the flesh from every living thing, Cadillac stood up and walked away down the slope toward the settlement. The morning sun warmed his bare back and cast a slim, broad-shouldered shadow in front of him.

Cadillac took a deep breath to fill out his chest, stretched his arms out sideways, and then brought them together above his head.

His shadow did the same.

It never failed to fascinate Cadillac. The shape of his shadow pleased him. It was different from the shadows cast by most of the others in his clan. It had a sleek, smooth outline, with long, straight arms and legs, and the shadow's hands had only one thumb and four fingers—like the shadows of the sand-burrowers Cadillac had never seen but whom Mr. Snow had described.

The hidden enemy far to the south by the Great Water who sent out the iron snakes and the cloud warriors—from whom he must always flee.

Cadillac M'Call, now eighteen years old, belonged to one of the many clans of She-Kargo Mutes that roamed the central and northern plains. According to Mr. Snow, their ancestors had come from beyond the dawn on the backs of giant birds whose beating wings made the noise of a mighty waterfall.

They had landed at a place called O-Haya, by the side of a great lake. To celebrate their arrival, they had killed and roasted the birds and feasted on them all summer long; then, when winter came, they had used the frozen waters of the lake to build a great settlement full of towering pillars of ice that glowed with all the colors of the rainbow and whose tops were lost in the clouds.

In the War of a Thousand Suns, the city had melted and flowed back into the lake. Every living thing had perished except for an old man called She-Kargo and an old woman called Me-Sheegun and their children. She-Kargo had fifteen sons, all of them brave warriors, tall and strong as bears; the old woman had fifteen beautiful daughters. She-Kargo's sons and Me-Sheegun's daughters crossed wrists and bound their bodies together with the blood-kiss, and their children and their children's children grew strong and multiplied, and moved westward into the lands of the Minne-Sota, the Io-Wa, the Da-Kota, and the Ne-Braska, killing all who resisted them and making soul-brothers of all those who laid the hand of friendship upon them.

They triumphed because their warriors were braver, their wordsmiths wiser, and their summoners more powerful. And thus it was that the Plainfolk grew strong in number and gave thanks to their great Mother-Goddess, Tamla Mo-Town.

Cadillac went to his chosen place among the rocks at the edge of the plateau where the M'Call clan had set down their huts to wait out the growing time. From the ragged edge of the plateau the ground fell away steeply, ridged and hollowed as if clawed by the talons of a giant eagle. Lower down the ground evened out, flowing in a gentle curve to join the rolling, orange grass-covered plain that stretched toward the rim of the world. Beyond that lay the hidden door through which the sun entered each morning. The pale blue that had quenched the golden fire-clouds of the dawn was deepening as the sun climbed higher; small widely spaced clouds, like a distant slow-grazing herd of white buffalo, were beginning to form over the far edge of the plains.

Cadillac lay back against the warm rock face and let his eyes roam across the unbroken stretch of blue, searching for the telltale flash of silver light that he had been told would signal the presence of a cloud warrior. As Mr. Snow's chosen successor, Cadillac had no need to act as a sentinel. Over a hundred of his clan-brothers were perched on the hilltops that lay around the settlement; young warriors, known as Bears, were on guard day and night—some watching the sky for cloud warriors, others searching the ground for any marauding bands from rival Mute clans seeking to invade the M'Calls' summer turf. Some manned hidden lookout posts on the high ground, others patrolled the area around the settlement in small mobile packs that doubled as hunting parties.

Cadillac continued his search of the sky. Not because he felt threatened but because he was consumed with curiosity. As a Mute he had every reason to fear the sand-burrowers, the mysterious people who lived beneath the earth and killed everything upon it whenever they emerged from the darkness. Yet in spite of their awesome reputation, or perhaps because of it, he yearned to confront them; to challenge them.

So far, they had not ventured into the lands of the Plainfolk. But the Sky Voices had told Mr. Snow that the time of their coming was near. The first sign would be arrowheads in the sky; the bird-wings that carried the cloud warriors on their journeys. They were the farseeing eyes of the iron snake that followed, bearing more sand-burrowers in its belly. When they came, there would be a great dying. The world would weep, but all the tears in the sky would not wash the blood of the Plainfolk from the earth.

When Mr. Snow had finished telling his story to the children, he walked down to where Cadillac sat with his face turned up to the sky and squatted cross-legged on an adjoining rock. His long white hair was drawn up into a topknot, tied and threaded with ribbon; the aging skin covering his lean, hard body was patterned with random swirls, patches, and spots in black and three shades of brown—from dark to light and an even lighter olive-pink.

Mr. Snow had said that the bodies of the sand-burrowers were the same color all over. Olive-pink from the top of their heads to the soles of their feet. Like worms.

Cadillac's body was marked with a similar random pattern, but his skin was as smooth as a raven's wing. Some of Mr. Snow's skin was smooth, too; but in other places, such as his forehead, shoulders, and forearms, the skin was as lumpy as if it had pebbles stuffed underneath, or it was shriveled up like a dead leaf or the gnarled bark of a tree.

That was the way most Mutes were born. And many were different from Cadillac in other ways, too. As a young child, when Cadillac finally became aware that his body was different from those of his clan-brothers, he had felt ashamed; a grotesque out-cast. Some of the other children taunted him, saying he had a body like a sand-burrower. He became alien-ated from his peer group; ran away; was brought back; fell sick; refused to eat.

Black-Wing, his mother, had taken him to Mr. Snow, who explained that the things he hated about himself were precious differences that would, in the years to come, enable him to perform great feats of valor. That was why he had been made straight and strong as the Heroes of the Old Time, and had been given a Name of Power. Cadillac, then four years old, had sat listening wide-eyed as, in the flickering firelight un-der a dark sky heavy with shimmering stars, Mr. Snow had revealed to him the Talisman Prophecy.

From that moment, Cadillac knew, with a childlike certainty he had never lost, that everything that hap-pened to him had a meaning, and that his destiny was bound up with the greater destiny of the Plainfolk.

Cadillac gave up his search of the sky and turned to Mr. Snow. He had no need to tell the old man what he had been looking for. Mr. Snow, his teacher and guide since early childhood, who spoke to the Sky Voices, knew these things; knew everything.

"Is this the year of the Great Dying?" asked Cadillac.

"This is the year it begins," said Mr. Snow.

"When will the iron snakes come?"

Mr. Snow closed his eyes, breathed in deeply, and turned his face toward the sun. The sky had now turned a deep blue. Cadillac waited patiently.

Eventually the answer came. "When the moon's face has turned away three times."

"And what of the cloud warrior the Sky Voices have chosen?"

Mr. Snow let the air out of his body with a long sigh and dropped his head onto his chest. His eyes fluttered open. "His journey toward us begins. He dreams the dreams of young men. Of feats of valor, of triumph, of power, of greatness." Mr. Snow raised his eyes and looked at Cadillac. "But like all young men, he thinks these things are gifts. He does not yet know how much the world pays for such dreams."

2

The one hundred members of Eagle Squadron jerked back their shoulders and sat bolt upright in their desks as the Flight Adjudicator entered the briefing room. The Adjudicator surveyed them briefly with expressionless gray eyes, then scanned the list displayed on his videopad. "Avery?"

Mel Avery leapt out of her seat and snapped to attention, thumbs aligned with the side seams of her blue jumpsuit. "Sir!"

"Flightline Three."

Avery grabbed her visored helmet, saluted swiftly, and headed for the door at the double.

The Flight Adjudicator keyed in a box code against Avery's name and looked up. "Ayers?"

Ayers stood up, jaw squared, back ramrod straight. "Sir!"

"Flightline Five."

Ayers saluted and ran.

"Brickman?"

Steve Brickman shot to his feet, stamped his right

heel into line with his left, and braced his shoulder blades together. "Sir!"

"Flightline Six."

The Snake Pit.

Despite his tensed neck and jaw muscles, Brickman let slip a brief, involuntary gasp of dismay.

The Adjudicator's gray eyes fastened on him. "Anything wrong?"

"No, *sirr*!"

"Okay, get moving."

Brickman picked up his helmet from the desk top and saluted smartly.

The Flight Adjudicator's attention was already elsewhere. "Bridges?"

"Sir!"

Brickman cursed his luck as he ran along the corridor that led to the simulators and free-flight rigs. The end-of-course exam consisted of eight segments. Like all the other candidates, he had been hoping to warm up on one of the easier rigs. Instead, his first test was to be over the toughest hurdle.

The Snake Pit—as it had been christened by a long-dead generation of flight cadets—was described officially in the Academy's training manual as the Double Helix, and listed in daily orders as Flightline Six.

The rig consisted of two circular ramps wrapped around massive central pillars housed side by side in a sausage-shaped shaft. In elevation, they looked like two giant corkscrews with opposing threads—the left-hand ramp descending eleven full turns in a clockwise direction, the right-hand one counterclockwise.

As each ramp wound down the shaft around its central pillar, it created a rectangular tunnel of air space one hundred and thirty feet wide and ninety feet high. In the center of the shaft the two ramps touched rim to rim, enabling a pupil pilot aboard one of the Academy's Skyhawks to fly from one to the other, weaving his way up and down the shaft in an almost infinitely variable series of ascending or descending figure eights and tight right- or left-hand turns around the two pillars.

Runways for takeoff and landing were situated in flight access tunnels at the top and bottom of the rig and these were linked by express elevators able to carry two Skyhawks with their wings folded.

The overall height of the Snake Pit was some twelve hundred feet. The shaft containing the spiral ramps measured seven hundred by three hundred and fifty feet. Each flight access tunnel was one hundred and fifty feet wide, one hundred feet high, and a quarter of a mile long.

And the whole colossal structure, together with the other rigs and the rest of the Flight Academy, had been drilled, hammered, and blasted out of the bedrock several hundred feet beneath the desert sands of New Mexico near the ruins of a city that, in the prehistory of the Federation, had been known as Alamogordo.

Already rated above average, Brickman knew every twist and turn of the Snake Pit. He knew he would make it through to the finish line, outperforming the rest of the senior year in the process. But that wasn't enough. Brickman was intent on gaining the maximum possible points.

That was the difficult part. It meant his performance had to be faultless. Not only on the Snake Pit but on all the other rigs and flight simulators, too. For Brickman was not only aiming to finish top of his class; he wanted to rack up a perfect score. Something no wingman had ever achieved in the hundred-year history of the Academy.

Fate had ordained that the graduation date of Brickman's class coincide with his seventeenth birthday and the hundredth anniversary of the Academy. The traditional passing-out parade, during which the senior third-year cadets were awarded their wings, was scheduled to be part of the celebrations. When he had learned of this providential conjunction upon his enrollment as a freshman, Brickman had determined to provide the Academy and his guardians with something extra to celebrate.

Steven Roosevelt Brickman. The first double-century wingman. Leader of the class of 2989 with a ground-flight test score of two hundred and winner of the coveted Minuteman Trophy, awarded on graduation for the best all-round performance while under training.

Brickman paused as he reached the access door to the Snake Pit, took several deep, calming breaths, checked the alignment of the creases in his blue flight fatigues, then stepped through into the Rig Supervisor's office and logged his arrival by feeding his ID sensor card into the checkpoint console at the door.

As soon as he was cleared to enter the flight area, Brickman ran at the double toward the ramp where two Skyhawk microlites were being readied by six of the Academy's ground staff. Bob Carrol, the Chief Flight Instructor, stood at the edge of the runway talking to another of the ten Adjudicators who had been sent down from Grand Central to conduct the flight tests and award the marks.

Brickman thudded to a halt with perfect timing, cocked his elbow into line with his shoulder, and saluted, his arm folding like a well-oiled jackknife, fingers, hand, and wrist rigidly aligned, the tip of his black glove exactly one inch from the bar and star badge on his forage cap. "Senior Cadet eight-nine-oh-two Brickman reporting for flight test, sir!"

The Adjudicator gave Brickman a dry, appraising glance, then lifted the cover of his videopad and scanned the text displayed on the centimeter-thick screen beneath. He pursed his lips at whatever was written there, then nodded at Carrol. "Ah, yes—your star performer." Then to Brickman he said, "Okay. Hear this. Takeoff and landing will be from this runway. Your first turn will be to the left. The rest of your flight pattern on the downward and return leg will be indicated by course markers on each level. Lead time will be fifteen degrees of arc. Points will be deducted for course and altitude deviations, and"

—the Adjudicator paused—"you'll be flying against the clock. Overall flight time will be counted in the final pass mark. Have you got that?"

"Loud and clear, *sir*!"

"Okay. You roll on the green in fifteen." The Adjudicator returned Brickman's salute and walked away toward the Flight Control room.

CFI Carrol, a sandy-haired thirty-year-old leatherneck, eyed Brickman sympathetically. Like all the Academy staff, Carrol was a tough, demanding instructor, but if he had allowed himself to show favor to a cadet, Brickman would have been the recipient. "I had a hunch you might draw the short straw. How do you feel?"

Brickman, now standing at ease, allowed himself a brief nonregulation shrug. He knew Carrol; knew he wouldn't pick up on it. "Someone has to be first."

CFI Carrol greeted Brickman's reply with an ironic smile. "Yes, I guess they have. Okay—you'd better get moving."

Brickman sprang to attention and threw another faultless salute.

Carrol acknowledged it with what looked like a halfhearted swipe at a fly on his forehead. Discipline was one thing, saluting another. Confronted daily for the last five years by zealous cadets, his right arm had often felt as if it were coming off its hinges. "Good luck."

"Thank you, sir."

"And Brickman—"

Brickman froze halfway through a left turn. "Sir?"

"This is a cruel world. The good guys don't always finish first."

"I'll try and remember that."

"Do," said Carrol. "But don't let it stop you trying." He lowered his voice. "Take Number Two. The controls are smoother." He dismissed Brickman with a nod and watched him as he ran toward the parked aircraft.

The Skyhawk—the only aircraft built by the Federation—consisted of a small three-wheeled cockpit and power pod, with a cowled propeller and rudder at the rear, slung under a wire and strut-braced arrowhead wing measuring thirty-five feet from tip to tip. The wing covering was of fabric with a plastic lining that could be inflated like a bicycle tire to give it an aerofoil section. The motor ran on batteries. For underground training flights, none of which lasted more than thirty minutes, the static charge in the power pod was enough; when used overground, the Skyhawk's wing was covered with solar-cell fabric that, under optimum conditions, gave it virtually unlimited range.

Carrol lingered by the runway as Brickman carried out his own quick preflight check of the Skyhawk then strapped himself into the cockpit frame and started up. There had been many able cadets who had passed through his hands in the last five years, but Brickman was in a class by himself.

Watching his progress on the rigs, Carrol had concluded that the young Tracker had more than a feel for flying. He had . . . well, there was only one way to describe it—some strange sixth sense that told him what was going to happen.

Carrol was sure of it. When flying in the Snake Pit, for example, Brickman seemed to know which way the course marker lights would go before Flight Control flipped the switches. There was no other explanation for the fact that he was always correctly positioned for the required turn. And after only a few hours on the rig, almost always flying a perfect course. Right down the wire.

It was uncanny. But marvelous to behold.

Carrol had not confided this feeling about Brickman to anyone. The concept of a "sixth sense" did not form part of the official Tracker philosophy. Indeed, the term had not formed part of Carrol's vocabulary until he had been assigned to one of the Trail-Blazer expeditions charged with pacification of the overground.

Many veteran Trail-Blazers believed that the Mutes—the perpetual enemies of the Amtrak Federation—possessed a "sixth sense," but very few were prepared to discuss it. In fact, to do so publicly was a punishable offense. Trackers had no need to dwell on such dubious intangibles. It was their physical and technological skills that had made them masters of both the earth-shield and the overground. It was the *visible* power of the Federation, which sprang from the genius of the First Family, that had ensured their survival and had brought the dream of an eventual return to the blue-sky world to the edge of reality.

That was what it said in the Manual of the Federation; a comprehensive information/data bank known colloquially as "The Book." Videopage after videopage of reference and archive material, rules and regulations governing every aspect of Tracker life, plus the collective wisdom of the First Family: inspirational insights for every occasion. What The Book didn't mention was that as a wingman you also needed a generous amount of good luck to survive the required minimum of three operational tours, each of which lasted a year. Fortunately, luck was one of the few permissible abstractions that Trackers could dwell upon during a short life dedicated to the pursuit of excellence in a world where the practical application of brawn and brain took precedence over everything else.

Brickman, strapped in his seat, with the nosewheel of the Skyhawk poised on the center of the start line, was oblivious of Carrol's presence on the edge of the runway behind his port wing. Brickman's eyes were fixed on the runway control light mounted in the left-hand wall of the flight access tunnel, his hand on the brake lever as the motor behind him revved at full power.

All his senses were attuned to the flight ahead. And the extra one, ascribed to him by Carrol, had already hinted that the first course marker would probably indicate another tight left-hand turn around the pillar.

A lead time of fifteen degrees of arc meant that, when the right- or left-hand arrow lit up, a pilot had a little under two seconds in which to react and make the appropriate course correction. If he left it too late, he would swerve off the center line. When that happened, lines of photoelectric cells in the ramp ceiling recorded the deviation. A similar arrangement of cells in the shaft wall also recorded variations in altitude. To score the maximum number of points, a pilot had to fly within extremely tight limits down the middle of the flight tunnel from start to finish. To do so demanded a high degree of airmanship, intense concentration, and hair-trigger responses.

Brickman possessed all these qualities, plus an inexplicable ability to predict random events several seconds before they happened. As he sat there waiting, with total concentration, for the green light, he was confident that he would "see" the course marker lights one or two seconds before they were illuminated by Flight Control. This sixth sense only seemed to operate in moments of stress—as now. A fortuitous gift he put to good use without speculating on its provenance; without the slightest trace of fear or wonder. He just accepted it. In the same way he accepted, without question, the fact that he, Steven Roosevelt Brickman, was destined to succeed.

Forewarned that the green light was about to come on, Brickman released the wheel brakes as the current reached the lamp filament. The Skyhawk surged forward and was airborne in thirty yards. By the time he had reached the end of the flight access tunnel and gone into his first turn, Carrol, who had moved to the center of the runway, sensed that Brickman was on his way to establishing an unbeatable lead.

By the end of the fourth day, when all the flight times were in, Carrol's hunch had been amply confirmed. Brickman had not only flown a faultless pattern, he had completed it in a time that was destined to become par for the course. And from the Snake Pit, he had gone on to rack up a perfect score on all the other flight rigs.

Brickman also scored full marks in the tests of his physical agility over the grueling assault course, on the firing range and general weapon handling, and in the video question-and-answer sessions on general and technical subjects. When the Adjudicators began processing the results, it soon became clear that 8902 Brickman, S. R., with one test to go, was within reach of an unbelievable double century.

"A-ten-*shun*!"

Three hundred pairs of heels crashed together on the chorused command of the Cadet Squadron Leaders as CFI Carrol entered the main lecture hall followed by Triggs, the senior Assistant Flight Instructor.

The cadets, whose turn it was to be in charge of the three units that made up the senior year, about-faced, saluted, and reeled off the usual class report as the CFI mounted the dais.

"Condor Squadron present and ready, sah!"

"Hawk Squadron present and ready, sah!"

"Eagle Squadron present and ready, sah!"

Carrol responded with his famous fly-swipe and went to the lectern. AFI Triggs, a noted drill freak, positioned himself one pace back, and one arm's-length to Carrol's right, feet apart and angled symmetrically outward, stiff-fingered hands crossed in the small of his back with thumbs overlapping on the joints.

"Be seated, gentlemen."

Three hundred butts slid smoothly into place.

"Okay," said Carrol. "I've seen the provisional results. So far, so good. All that remains is your final make-or-break flight test. The big one. The real thing. At oh-seven-hundred hours tomorrow, you'll begin moving up—a section at a time—to Level Ten for your first overground solo."

Steve Brickman shared the surge of excitment and apprehension generated by Carrol's announcement.

"You've all seen pictures of it," continued Carrol. "You've all been briefed. You all know what to expect. Right?"

"Yess-*sirr*!" chorused the class.

"Wrong," snapped Carrol. "Everything you've experienced and everything you've been taught up to now is totally useless. Forget it. *Nothing* can prepare you for that moment when you lift off the ramp and catch your first glimpse of the overground. It's like entering a new dimension. The initial impact will overwhelm you, may even frighten you. That's okay. When you fly your first patrol into Mute territory, you're going to be scared, too. Anyone who isn't is an idiot. The important thing is to stay in control. Of yourself and your aircraft. Don't allow yourself to become disoriented. It's just like being in the free-flight dome—only bigger."

A lot bigger. Vast. Endless. Terrifying. . . .

"Some of you are going to breeze through. After the first few minutes, you'll be flying hands off—wondering what all the fuss was about. And some of you are going to hate every minute of it. You're going to want to ball up in your seat and close your eyes and hope it goes away. But you're going to fight that feeling. If you plan to graduate as wingmen next Friday, you're going to fly that blown-up bedsheet every inch of the way around the course that's been mapped out for you, and you're going to bring it back in one piece. And what's more, you're going to do it with a clean pair of pants."

This news raised a ripple of nervous laughter.

"No, don't laugh," said Carrol. "I'm not kidding. Your Flight Instructors are going to be on duty in the shower room. Right?"

Mr. Triggs nodded meanly. "Right."

Carrol eyed his audience. Remembering. "Two of my classmates freaked out when they cleared the ramp. One of them just rolled over on his back and went straight in from five hundred feet. The other took one look, made a one-hundred-and-eighty-degree turn, and tried to fly back inside. Came in at full throttle. Would have made it, too . . . but he was in such a hurry, he didn't wait for the ramp crew to open the door."

Brickman winced. The Academy staffer who had

briefed them on the overground had mentioned that the outer ramp doors to the arid desert above the Academy were colossal ten-foot-thick slabs of reinforced concrete.

The CFI concluded his cautionary tale with a grimace. "I trust that I can count on you all not to do anything in the next ten days that might, in any way, spoil the centenary celebrations."

The class gazed at him silently.

"Good," said Carrol. He turned to the senior AFI. "They're all yours, Mr. Triggs."

Despite Carrol's dire warning, the fail rate on this crucial solo flight was now almost zero. Since the days when the CFI had been a cadet, the psychological profile of the ideal wingman had been carefully reconstructed and each applicant was subjected to rigorous tests during the selection process.

In theory the psy-profile of successful candidates had to achieve a 75 percent match with the referent. In practice this was not always possible. In the thousand-year history of the Federation, as in the millennia preceding it, no one had yet found a way to endow the art of applied psychology with the mathematical exactitude of the physical sciences.

Which meant that, now and then, an aggressively normal bonehead would soar off the ramp and, after a few minutes aloft, agoraphobia would set in. The fear of open spaces that afflicted the majority of Trackers. The unlucky candidate would find that his hand on the control column had become palsied, and that his intestines were doing the shimmy-shake. And while he might master his fear sufficiently to fly the allotted course, it was the end of his career as a wingman. For during the crucial solo flight, each cadet was wired up like someone taking a lie detector test. Sensors fixed to his body and linked to a recorder monitored various functions that included such giveaways as heartbeat, brain activity, and skin temperature and humidity. The Flight Adjudicators from Grand Central did not need Mr. Triggs on standby in the shower room. With the sophisticated telemetry at their command, they *knew* when a student pilot had been scared shitless.

Brickman, who had begun mapping out his career at the age of five, was confident that he would pass this test—as he had all the others—with flying colors.

This is not to imply that success came easily to Brickman. It did not. Apart from his inherent flying ability, he was by no means the brightest or the strongest student in the senior year—but he was, without doubt, the sharpest. His intellectual and physical achievements in course studies and track and match events were the result of endless hours of hard work and unrelenting concentration; a total commitment to the task in hand.

Brickman's true talent lay in maximizing his potential, making the most of his natural assets. Which included a tall, straight-limbed body; a well-boned, honest, dependable face; and a pleasant, engagingly shrewd manner that was used, with good effect, to conceal a brain that functioned as precisely and dispassionately as a silicon chip.

Although the cadets assigned to Eagle Squadron traditionally regarded themselves as innately superior to the rest of the Academy intake (the Eagles had been overall champions in team events for fifteen out of the past twenty years), they figured third in the organizational listings. As a consequence, Brickman and his fellow cadets had a four-day wait before being cleared to Level Ten for the final test flight.

On the fifth day, the long-awaited moment finally arrived. Armed with their movement orders, Brickman, Avery, and the eight other cadets who made up the first section of A-Flight presented themselves at the Level Superintendent's office and rode the elevator to Level Five. From there they took the conveyor to the second Provo checkpoint on Six, then entered another elevator for the ascent to the subsurface: Level Ten.

It was the first time that Brickman had gone beyond

Five. Prior to joining the Academy, his whole life had been spent within the Quad. Levels One to Four.

The ground floor of Level One was fifteen hundred feet below the surface of the overground. Each level was one hundred and fifty feet high, subdivided into ten floors, or galleries. Thus, counting up from the bottom, One-8 was the eighth floor of Level One, and Ten-10 was the ramp access floor—the heavily defended interface between the Federation and the overground.

For reasons of security, only a limited number of subdivisions went all the way up to Level Ten. Most of the Federation's bases were located between Levels One and Four and linked with each other by interstate shuttle.

Stepping out of the elevator on Ten-10 gave Brickman a strange feeling. At first glance there was little to distinguish the ramp access floor from those below it, but Brickman could "feel" the overground. Even though it was still, at that point, some fifty feet above his head, it registered as an almost palpable presence.

Reporting to overground Flight Control, Brickman found he was listed number one to go. One of the ubiquitous Flight Adjudicators stood by as two medics taped the sensors to his body and checked the screened printout from a data recorder. Brickman then stepped back into his blue flight fatigues and fed the umbilical carrying the sensor wires through the flap provided.

In the Chart room, a second Flight Adjudicator handed him a map, a set of course coordinates, and the latest weather data. "You have fifteen minutes."

Gripped by rising excitement, Brickman choked back a smile that could have cost him valuable marks, saluted smartly, and went to work on one of the plotting desks. He was finished in under ten but spent the extra time checking his calculations a third and then a fourth time. Flying one of six alternative courses, the other cadets in his section, and the rest of the squadron, would be following him off the ramps at quarter-hourly intervals over the next two days.

From the Chart room Brickman was directed toward the northwest ramp, one of four lying at right angles to each other in the form of a giant Maltese cross. Reaching the ramp access area, he found a Skyhawk parked with its nose pointing toward the huge lead-lined doors. The delta wing was covered in a metallic-blue fabric into which were woven thousands of solar cells. Brickman carried out the usual preflight checks, donned his dark-visored bone dome, strapped himself into the cockpit, and plugged his mike lead into the VHF set and the umbilical into the on-board transmitter. From now until he stepped out of the cockpit, the data from the sensors taped to his body would be displayed on a monitor screen in Flight Control before emerging as a printout providing an indelible second-by-second record of his reactions.

The data transmitter was attached to the right-hand side of the cockpit by his elbow. Brickman reached across with his left hand and switched it on.

Flight Control radioed back immediately. "Easy X-Ray One, your data link reads A-Okay."

Brickman acknowledged the Ramp Marshal's wind-up signal and hit the button. The electric motor behind his seat whined into life. Brickman checked the movement of the control surfaces, then moved forward under the direction of the Ramp Marshal's batons until the nose of the Skyhawk was a couple of feet from the innermost ramp door.

With a swishing noise that Brickman barely heard above the thrumming engine, the fifty-foot-high wall in front of him slid downward into the floor. Following the orange batons, Brickman taxied over it toward the double outer doors, stopping on the parallel yellow line.

At this point the ramp access tunnel was one hundred feet wide, its sides sloping gently inward toward the ceiling. Brickman remembered from the briefing that the inner pair of doors opened sideways; the outer pair overlapped horizontally, the larger top section going into the roof, the lower section into the floor. This arrangement allowed the ramp crew to adjust the aperture to the size of the object passing through it.

Glancing in his rearview mirror, Brickman saw to his surprise that the huge door behind him had risen noiselessly, cutting him off from the Federation.

The voice of the Controller came over his headset. "Easy X-Ray One, this is Ground Control. Light balance will commence in five seconds. The doors will open in ten. Do not attempt to taxi through until you see the green. Once you cross the double yellow line, you are clear for takeoff. Transmit your call sign when you pass over the red, white, and blue beacon on your return leg. Over."

"Easy X-Ray One, Roger." Brickman's voice contained a tremor of excitement.

"Good luck," said the voice in his ear.

In the same instant, banks of neon tubes stretching along the walls from floor to ceiling and across the ceiling itself rippled into life, creating a glowing tunnel of light that grew progressively brighter toward the ramp door to match the intensity of the daylight that lay beyond.

Brickman lowered his visor. Five seconds later, the ten-foot-thick inner doors slid apart and the lower section of the outer door sank level with the ramp, presenting Brickman with a slot just high and wide enough for the Skyhawk to pass through.

Nosewheel on the center line, Brickman taxied out on the green, passing under the equally massive concrete curtain that formed the top section of the outer door. Rolling clear of its threatening bulk, he paused on the double yellow line that stretched from wall to wall and took stock of his surroundings.

He saw that he was in a concrete canyon with sheer, unseamed, hundred-foot-high walls. Ahead of him, the ramp sloped gently upward. Brickman knew from his study of the model that the walls now enclosing him angled out sharply, tapering down, as the ramp rose in the shape of a giant fan, to meet the overground.

The canyon was roofed with a flat expanse of brilliant blue.

With a sudden shock of recognition, Brickman realized that he was not looking at another illuminated ceiling—like those in the Federation's central plazas—but at the sky.

The ceiling of the world. "The wild blue yonder"—that heart-surging phrase from the battle hymn of the Flight Academy that had fired Brickman's imagination at the age of ten. Not wrought by concealed tubes of neon, but filled with a light of dazzling, almost overpowering, intensity that bounced off the bleached concrete and cast sharp, rich, dark shadows on the runway beneath the Skyhawk. The light of the sun—blazing down upon him so brightly that even his visored eyes could not bear to look at it directly, its raying heat piercing his body, making the marrow in his bones tingle with its warmth.

Willing himself to remain calm, Brickman took a deep breath of the fresh, oven-baked air, pushed the throttle wide open, and aimed the Skyhawk up the center line of the ramp and at the sky beyond. A wave of reflected heat floated the lightweight craft into the air unexpectedly. Brickman quickly adjusted the Skyhawk's trim. The enclosing walls fell away, and as the ramp beneath him shrank into a shimmering slice of concrete pie, Brickman caught his first glimpse of the overground.

And was engulfed by the vastness of the earth and sky.

For the past sixteen years and fifty-one weeks of Brickman's life, the most distant object he had gazed upon had never been more than half a mile away; the highest vaulted space, seven hundred and fifty feet above his head. He had seen video pictures of the recently completed John Wayne Plaza at Grand Central; a marvel of engineering a mile wide and nearly half a mile high. But even that was rendered totally insignificant by the vista that unfolded as the Skyhawk climbed higher. For now, Brickman could see for more than a *hundred miles*. A mind-blowing, eye-popping, heart-stopping panorama bounded by an impossibly distant, cloud-flecked horizon under the fathomless blue bowl of the sky.

Brickman's response to the overground welled up from the innermost depths of his being. CFI Carrol had been right. Nothing in his past life could have possibly prepared him for this moment. For years he had prided himself on his clinical detachment; his ability to control his reaction to any situation, investing his words and actions with exactly the required degree of emotion. No more, no less.

But not today.

For one brief instant Brickman let the mask slip, abandoning himself to the raw sensations that made his scalp tingle and his heart pound, that left him gasping for breath. He lay back and let the essence, the latent power, of the overground flood through his whole being; let its seductive beauty embrace him (had he known the phrase and understood its implications) like a long-lost lover.

Was reunited.

Heard voices.

Sensed danger.

Recovered. Regained control. Returned his being to the service of the Federation; purging himself of all feeling; crushing his newfound sense of wonder beneath the iron heel of his Tracker psyche.

Outwardly restored, Brickman throttled back for the climb to altitude, checked that he was on the correct course heading for the first leg of his flight, and turned his attention to the land below.

The overground. The despoiled birthright of the Trackers. Overrun by the shadowy, hostile Mutes. The blue-sky world that the First Family, in the name of the Federation, had vowed to cleanse and repossess.

Brickman consulted his map. The ramp above the Flight Academy from which he had taken off was situated some five thousand feet above sea level and halfway between two prehistoric sites called Alamogordo and Holloman AFB. All that remained of Alamogordo were a few jagged walls sticking up out of the ground in vague rectilinear patterns among the bright red trees. Holloman AFB, below his port wing, consisted of three enormous, overlapping craters partially filled with windblown sand.

Brickman turned his attention back to the giant cottonwoods.

Trees. . . .

Like the distant clouds, they were something else Brickman had only seen pictures of.

At this point, Brickman's altitude was twenty-five hundred feet and climbing, above terrain that had been described by the Academy's Chart Officer as "high plains country." Over his right shoulder, beyond the ramp, Brickman could see the towering summit of the Sierra Blanca, part of the mountain range barring the way to the east. Ahead lay the San Andres Mountains, which he would cross between Black Top and Salinas Peak. From here his course lay in a straight line over the Jornada del Muerto to the northern end of a large overground reservoir that formed part of a giant river cutting deep into the bedrock of the land as it snaked its way south.

The Rio Grande.

Despite all he had been told, Brickman found it hard to accept that the overground could be as deadly as it was beautiful. Yet he could not deny the firsthand evidence provided by his guard-father, who as a wingman had put in a double-six up the line and was now a shrunken shadow in a wheelchair, his body ravaged by the all-consuming sickness that lay in wait for all those who survived the allotted number of overground tours of duty.

The sky above, the land below, the crisp fresh air that now filled his lungs, was charged with lethal radiation that, even on this first sortie, had already begun its silent attack on his own unshielded body.

Every square inch of ground, every cubic inch of sky, harbored the kiss of death.

It was this ever-present danger, lying across the world like an invisible funeral shroud, that had caused the subterranean birth of the Federation; had kept it, for nearly a thousand years, from assuming its rightful place in the sun. Antiradiation topsuits did exist, but they were ungainly garments that were scorned by Trail-Blazers, who, like the pre-Holocaust American Green Berets and British Paras, regarded themselves as elite shock-troops—the cream of Amtrak. The standard-issue closed helmet with its air filtration system and "flak" jacket were considered an acceptable form of protection; antiradiation topsuits did not even form part of a wagon train's inventory. The refusal to wear them was viewed by Grand Central not as a breach of discipline but as proof of the Blazer's readiness to die for the Federation.

The cross-country course Brickman had been given to fly was in the shape of a roughly equilateral triangle and covered a total distance of two hundred and twenty-five miles. The first seventy-five-mile leg was angled northwest to the head of the Elephant Butte Reservoir; the second almost due south, running parallel to the Rio Grande and crossing it at another prehistoric ruin bearing the name of Hatch to reach the peak of the Sierra de Las Uvas. The return leg ran ENE, skirting the eight-thousand-foot peak that marked the high point of the San Andres Mountains, then across the dazzling, desolate expanse of White Sands and back to the ramp.

Aware that the Adjudicators might possess the means to monitor his flight pattern, Brickman flew a perfect course at the required cruising altitude of eight thousand feet, at a ground speed of seventy-five miles an hour. He searched the sky around him but could see no sign of any other craft.

Once clear of the mountains, he began losing altitude for his final approach. Ahead of him, he could see the thousand-foot-high, pencil-slim red-, white-, and blue-striped beacon balanced on its point as if by magic. Below him, the white sand, wind-shaped into curving lines, stretched away on all sides like a vast frozen sea.

The sea. . . .

Brickman had heard about it but had never seen pictures of it. He only knew that it lay beyond the southern horizon. He fought down a mad impulse to break away in search of it and continued his slow descent toward the southwest ramp. When he was some two miles from touchdown, he saw a tiny, tri- angular speck of blue rise from the takeoff ramp, becoming a flash of silver as it banked around and caught the sun. High in the sky to the southeast hung another microdot. Someone else on their way back in.

Brickman throttled right back and drifted down through the warm air with the tranquil ease of a seabird, putting all three wheels on the ramp three hours after takeoff—matching, to the second, the es- timated time he had filed with overground Flight Control.

A final, flawless performance.

As he taxied down the ramp, the converging walls seemed to leap upward, cutting him off from the overground; hemming him in; suffocating him. Within seconds, all that remained of the sky world was a flat slab of blue visible through the clear-view wing pan- els above the cockpit.

The ramp doors slid open noiselessly as the Skyhawk reached the double yellow line. The green light sig- naled he was clear to taxi in.

Brickman knew that the brightly lit tunnel beyond represented safety, offered total protection against the dangers of the overground; yet he found himself momentarily paralyzed, gripped by an inexplicable fear.

A fear of being buried alive.

With an involuntary movement he hit the brake pedal, holding the Skyhawk's nose on the double yellow line. One, two, three, four, five seconds. Six, seven—

A warning klaxon blared harshly. The Controller's voice spoke quietly into his ear. "Clear the ramp, Easy X-Ray One." The voice paused, then added, "Your data line is down but we have no malfunction signal. Check system, over."

Brickman moved his right arm back and glanced down at the data transmitter to which his body was wired. A chill shiver ran through him. It was switched off! Somehow he must have unwittingly knocked it with his elbow. Oh, Christopher Columbus! How could he have done such a stupid thing? And when?! He quickly flipped the switch back into the "on" position and berated himself silently. Oh, shit, shit, and triple shit. You bonehead! You've blown it!

The bland, disembodied voice of Ground Control cut across his mental confusion. "Okay, we have your data. Roll it in, Easy X-Ray One."

Willing an inner and outward calm upon his body, Brickman eased his foot off the brake and taxied in under the raised section of the outer door. As soon as he was inside, the lower section rose with a barely audible hiss and the inner doors slid out of the walls. As the bright rectangle of daylight in his rearview mirror shrank rapidly and disappeared behind the overlapping curtains of concrete, Brickman did his best to bury the strange, troubling feelings that had assailed him during the flight. Dangerous, treacherous sensations that he could not put into words; that would be better forgotten, but that he knew would haunt him for the rest of his life.

What Brickman had experienced was a sense of freedom. His inability to perceive this, or to put a name to it, was perfectly understandable. The word "freedom" did not appear in the Federation's dictionary. It was, of course, known to the highest ranks of the First Family, but officially the concept did not exist.

CFI Carrol waved the senior classmen back into their seats and took his place at the lectern. The six

AFIs led by Mr. Triggs lined up against the wall behind him.

"It's been a long haul," said Carrol, "but we've come to the end of the line. After home-base leave, you'll be shipping out on your first unit assignments. Between then and now you're going to be busy drilling for the big anniversary parade, so as this is probably my last opportunity to address you as a group, I thought I'd mark the occasion with a few farewell words."

Carrol paused and let his eyes range slowly over the seated cadets. "I've seen the results—"

The senior year reacted with a rustle of excitement.

Carrol held up a hand. "Hold it. The marks and places will be screened as scheduled tomorrow. However . . . what I can tell you is that there are no wipe-outs, and no retreads."

The news was received with total silence.

Carrol shook his head as if he couldn't quite believe it and turned to the AFIs. "Amazing. None of them look at all surprised."

The three hundred cadets, over a third of them girls, broke into laughter. They all knew no one would be choked for airing their teeth today. Not by Carrol, anyway.

"I know what you're thinking," continued Carrol. " 'Here it comes. The CFI's standard address to every graduation class.' Not so. I have to tell you that three years ago, when you joined the Academy, we thought we'd been landed with a bunch of zed-heads; but you all did well. Some better than others." His eyes rested briefly on Brickman. "In fact, you all turned in such terrific grades, the average pass mark is the highest ever in the Academy's history."

The class of 2989 gave themselves a congratulatory cheer. The six AFIs allowed themselves an impassive smile.

Carrol gestured soberly for silence. "Yes, I suppose I should congratulate you, but the truth is, you people have just made life more difficult for the rest of us. Because now Grand Central will expect us to do even better next year." Carrol looked over both shoulders at the AFI's. "Which means, gentlemen, that as of tomorrow, you and I are going to have to kick ass."

The six AFIs responded with mock resignation. "We could always put in for promotion," said Triggs.

Carrol cocked a finger at the senior AFI. "Good thinking." He turned back to the class, placed his hands purposefully on the upper corners of the lectern, and cleared his throat.

The class of 2989 straightened their backs and faces.

"Okay. Hear this. In a few days you'll have a badge pinned to your chests. You'll be wingmen. The frontline force of the Amtrak Federation. It's a great moment. Savor it. But don't think that life's going to get easier, that the hard work is over. You have another twelve months of operational training ahead of you when you join your wagon trains. And if you're smart, it won't stop when you swap your silver badge for a gold. You'll go *on* learning. Because it's the only way to become a better flier. Always remember that when the chips are down and you're fresh out of luck, it's the hot pilots who make it back to base." Carrol paused and ran his eyes along the rows of bright, eager young faces, his mouth tightening with a hint of regret. "Who knows? If you don't power down, or pull a trick, some of you could even end up making speeches to classes like this."

His audience greeted this with a dry, ragged laugh. To "power down" was Trail-Blazer jargon for a crash in hostile territory—usually with fatal results, like "buying a farm" or "going into the meat business," for it was well known that Mutes ate any prisoners they caught alive. To "pull a trick" was another euphemism for death, from what the Federation medical establishment had labeled a TRIC. A Terminal Radiation-Induced Cancer.

Most of the wingmen on the Academy's Roll of Honor had powered down or pulled a trick. Usually before they reached the ripe old age of thirty. Carrol knew that at least half of the young faces now fixed on his would never see the sun rise on their twenty-first birthday. His audience knew it, too. And didn't give a damn. Every year, the Academy was swamped with thousands of applications for the three hundred places available for Squabs—the derisive name applied to first-year cadets.

That, according to the Manual, was the great strength of the Amtrak Federation. The raw courage and dedication of the Trackers. Two of the Seven Great Qualities possessed by the founders of Amtrak. The Foragers and the Minutemen. Qualities now enshrined in the First Family and the members of the two elite companies that bore their name. "They died so that others might live." The message was emblazoned on wall surfaces throughout the Federation and every Tracker was encouraged, from birth, to emulate their example.

Without question.

When the examination results were screened, Brickman found to his amazement that after three years of dedicated, relentless effort, he had been placed fourth with 188 points, behind Pete Vandenberg from Condor Squadron, the cadet Brickman had judged most likely to come a poor second to his brilliant first. That was bad enough but there was worse to come. Gus White, a wingman in the same flight as Steve who had not even figured in his calculations, had landed in the number two slot, ahead of Vandenberg by one point at 190, Donna Monroe Lundkwist, another cadet from Eagle Squadron who Steve had thought might make the first ten, had come top of the heap with a score of 192 and had been nominated as Honor Cadet; winner of the prized Minuteman Trophy.

Brushing aside the congratulations of other A-Flight cadets in the crowd milling excitedly around the screens, Brickman retired to his shack, wedged the door shut, and spent two silent, solitary hours trying to come to terms with what had happened. He went over every move he had made in each of the tests and

found nothing that could have cost him marks. His
one error had been that fatal hesitation on the ramp
after landing but he could simply not believe that
those seven seconds had cost him not only the first
place he was convinced he deserved but also second
and third.

And to find himself trailing fourth behind a no-
hoper like Gus White, who had not even been close in
the monthly class tests! It just didn't add up. . . .

Admittedly there had been the additional problem
of the three-minute break in the transmission of data
from the sensors taped to his body, but he had talked
this through exhaustively with the Adjudicators and
Ground Control after landing and they had accepted
that the switch could have been moved inadvertently.
The data transmitter was not fitted to Skyhawks
when used operationally, and during his discussion
with the Adjudicators they had admitted that it was
positioned awkwardly. But despite their apparent understanding he had been savagely penalized.

No matter. One day he would even the score. With
Lundkwist, with Gus White, Vandenberg, Carrol, the
Flight Adjudicators, and the others—as yet unknown—
who had conspired to humiliate him. They would all
pay. It might take years, but that would only make
his revenge all the sweeter.

The decision did nothing to assuage his bitter dis-
appointment, but it filled his breast with a harsh,
cold joy. It enabled him to think clearly; to function.

Rising from his bunk, Brickman showered, put on
a fresh, neatly pressed jumpsuit, then sought out
Lundkwist and Gus White amidst the raucous celebration party in the mess and offered his congratulations, hugging each of them in turn with heartwarming
sincerity.

Faced with the astonishing results, CFI Carrol felt
obliged to commiserate with his star pupil. Brickman
put on an outward show of philosophical resignation,
but Carrol knew that he felt himself to be the victim

of a blatant injustice. Inwardly, Brickman was suffering. And would continue to suffer.

Which, insofar as Carrol could understand these things, was how those who ordered the affairs of the Federation wished it to be. For in addition to their luggage, the Adjudicators from Grand Central had brought floppy-disc files on all the candidates. No one at the Academy had been allowed to see what they contained, but in an unguarded moment Carrol had glimpsed an enigmatic notation on the cover of Brickman's electronic dossier.

It read: "This candidate is to be marked down."

3

Armed with a crossbow and a handful of the precious iron bolts fashioned in the Fire-Pits of Beth-Lem, Cadillac and Clearwater made their way down to the grassy plain below the settlement. Clearwater was the sixteen-year-old girl chosen by the clan-elders to be his soul-mate. They had not yet crossed wrists or exchanged the blood-kiss, but since the Yellowing of the Old Earth they had lain together, skin against skin, under his furs at each black moon. What was known to the Plainfolk as "sleeping between the wolf and the bear."

Underneath the swirling pattern of black, brown, and dark cream pigment, Clearwater's body was smooth-skinned, like Cadillac's. Her jaw was small, her teeth evenly set and concealed by her lips; her long hair was streaked with yellow and brown like the leaves blown from the trees before the White Death; her eyes were a brilliant pale blue like the morning sky that poured light into the lakes and streams, bringing them to life and making them good to drink. Hence her given name—Clearwater, blood-

33

daughter of Sun-Dance and Thunder-Bird, a great warrior who filled ten head-poles before falling at the Battle of the Black Hills. She was tall and straight-limbed like Cadillac, swift as an eagle, strong as a mountain lion, and her heart was warm and filled with goodness, like the Middle Earth at the time of the Gathering.

Cadillac and Clearwater journeyed eastward through the shoulder-high orange grass until the mountain that rose behind the M'Call settlement was no wider than the fingers of their outstretched hands. As the sun reached the head of the sky, they drank from a shallow, swift-running river and rested for a while in the cool shade of a large rock. The water rippled over worn pebble beds with a slapping noise like women throwing flat-bread at a clan-bake.

Cadillac climbed up onto the rock and cautiously scanned the ground beyond the river. The grass was shorter on the far side, and in the distance he saw the telltale flash of white hindquarters that indicated a herd of fast-foot—sharp-eyed reddish-brown deer that could outrun a mountain lion. They would require careful stalking, but if he could bring down one of the horned males it would be a highly prized catch that would give him standing with the Bears—and might even earn him a fire-song.

Cadillac slithered quickly down the rock to where Clearwater lay curled in its shadow. He touched her shoulder. "Fast-foot." He pointed across the river, then picked up his crossbow and cranked the lever that drew the bowstring onto the half-trigger.

Clearwater sat up and smoothed her boned and ribboned rattail plaits into place around her ears. "How far?"

"Two bolts," grunted Cadillac. Even with the aid of the lever, it required considerable strength to pull the bowstring back to the halfway position.

A bolt was one of the methods used by Mutes to judge distances, and was, as the name suggests, the distance a bolt traveled when fired from a fully cocked crossbow. Since the maximum range could vary considerably it was a somewhat imprecise measurement, but on average, one bolt equaled a little under four-fifths of a mile.

Clearwater climbed swiftly up onto the overhanging rock and searched the plain beyond the river. "I see them." She clambered halfway down, then jumped. Cadillac caught her as she landed at his feet. "Let us wait here. They will come to the river at sundown."

"Are we old ones?" said Cadillac. "Must we sit and wait until someone puts meat in our lap? She-ehh!" He breathed out sharply, making a short hissing sound—a sign, among Mutes, of annoyance. He turned away, picked up the crossbow, and moved to the water's edge.

Clearwater caught hold of his wrist. "We should not cross the river. The water marks the edge of our turf. If you would bring food, let us take fish."

Cadillac jerked his arm free. "Fish?! Where is the standing in that?!"

"You have standing," Clearwater said. "You are the one who will speak for us after Mr. Snow has gone to the High Ground. You have no need to hunt, or run with the Bears. That is the task of those born without pictures on their tongues."

"Need ... she-ehh! What do you know of my needs?!" said Cadillac. He laid a fist on his heart. "I would be as *they* are. Oh, I know I cannot be like my brothers in the strength and shape of my body. Like you, I was made from a different clay. But my heart is as strong and as brave as theirs. I paint pictures with my tongue, yes—but the colors are those of the brave. The flashing silver of sharp iron, the blood-red of victory. The history of the M'Call clan and the Plainfolk is the history of its warriors. The tales I tell are of battles won by Bears with Names of Power...."

"You, too, have a Name of Power."

"It is empty. I have no standing. My tongue is full of brave deeds but my knife-arm has never drawn blood. How many fire-songs will bear *my* name when I go to the High Ground?"

Clearwater's eyes blazed with anger. "Is that all that fills your mind? To be puffed up by praise like a marsh frog with a throat full of wind? How many times must it be said? You were born in the shadow of the Talisman. It fell upon *you*! Not upon Motor-Head, Hawk-Wind, Steel-Eye, Convoy, or the other Bears you long to run with, but upon *you*! When the Sky Voices call you to the service of Talisman, you will have to be braver than the bravest of your clan-brothers. More fearless than my father. Mightier than the mightiest warriors who have gone to the High Ground. When that moment comes you will stand at the side of Talisman, and there will be a thousand fire-songs that bear your name!"

"But when will that *be*?" asked Cadillac.

"Who can tell when, or how, the Talisman will enter the world?" Clearwater replied. "You must wait as we all wait. But you must prepare your heart and mind. You must listen to the sky."

"I *listen*. But I hear nothing. The Sky Voices do not speak through me."

Clearwater tossed her head. "She-ehh! You anger me when you talk as if you had nothing between your ears. How many times has Mr. Snow spoken of these things? You must hold yourself ready for whatever task is to be given to you."

"I *am* ready," said Cadillac. "But I am sick of waiting." He broke away and splashed across the pebbled bed of the river. Even at the deepest point, the rippling water barely covered his knees. Clearwater sighed, shook her head—and waded after him.

She caught up with him as he reached the far bank. "Cadillac . . . stop. This is not our turf. You swore to Mr. Snow to keep within bounds, to never put the gift of words in danger."

Cadillac laughed. "Where is the danger in a herd of fast-foot? Did you not say I was born in the shadow of Talisman? If it is true, then his shadow will protect us. Come. . . . "

The young fast-foot males were scattered around

the edge of the herd on picket duty, alternately grazing and nosing the air, their long necks arched, white-rimmed eyes sweeping across the knee-high grass. With the sun beginning to descend toward the mountains, the fast-foot were slowly moving closer to the river, where they would gather in the cool of the evening to drink at the water's edge—unless a careless movement by Cadillac or Clearwater stampeded them in the opposite direction.

Clearwater was tempted to make such a move, but she knew that Cadillac was determined to bring one down. There was no point in making it more difficult. She understood his feelings. "Standing," being able to "cut it," was of paramount importance within a Mute clan, and crucial to the self-respect of a young male reaching the age of fourteen—the age when he became a warrior. But as the next wordsmith of the M'Calls, Cadillac had no need of standing. The gift the Sky Voices had given him set him apart from the rest of the clan, and when he took Mr. Snow's place even the clan-elders would seek his advice; would defer to his opinions and judgment. Wordsmiths did not need the raw, hot-blooded courage of Bears. They needed to be calm, resolute. Cadillac could be both, but at other times he burned with a childlike impatience that made Clearwater doubt the wisdom of the Sky Voices that spoke through Mr. Snow; the all-seeing, all-knowing powers that guided the destiny of the Plainfolk. When they had poured her spirit into the belly of Sun-Dance, her mother, and shaped the course of her life-stream to flow alongside that of Cadillac, did they *really* know how difficult he could be? . . .

Moving downwind, Cadillac found a dry, shallow gully which snaked away into the plain toward the center of the herd where the capo—the dominant male—grazed surrounded by his retinue of a dozen or so females. Cadillac carefully parted the long grass and counted the branches on the capo's horns. Ten points. No Bear in the M'Call clan had brought in a fast-foot with more points in the lifetime of Mr. Snow. To bring down this capo would give him great standing in the eyes of his clan-brothers.

Squatting in the bottom of the gully, Cadillac and Clearwater cut tufts of the long orange grass and quickly wove them together to make a tall crown for their heads and a cape to cover their shoulders and backs. They tied the capes around their necks and waists with plaited ribbons of grass and put the tight-fitting crowns with their waving plumes of grass on their heads, arranging the strands that made up the deep fringe around their faces. Using their hunting knives, they unearthed a layer of damp clay which they smeared over their bodies to mask the smell of their flesh. Thus prepared, they crawled along the gully, working their way deeper into the heart of the plain, cautiously raising their heads from time to time to check the position of the capo.

He was still in the center of the herd, but masked from attack by the does in his mating group. Twice, as they crept closer, young fast-foot males leapt across the gully only yards ahead of them to continue feeding on the other side. Hardly daring to breathe, Cadillac and Clearwater inched along. The gully became shallower, forcing them to worm along on their bellies to avoid showing themselves above the rim. The carpet of knee-high grass had broken up into scattered tufts, interspersed with the short, sweeter red grass on which the fast-foot were grazing.

The gully angled sharply to the left around a large outcrop of rock, taking them away from the capo. Cadillac led the way around the bend and froze. A few yards away, the earth had been gouged out from under a rock by the floodwaters in the rainy season. A big rattle-tailed snake lay coiled in the shadow of the overhang.

Adopting the almost imperceptible movements of a stick insect, Cadillac peered over the edge of the gully. There was no long grass within reach. Three fast-foot were grazing some twenty to thirty yards away, tails lazily flicking flies from the long, heart-shaped white flash on their hindquarters. One of them raised her head and looked over her shoulder toward Cadillac, her jaw moving from side to side in a casual, ruminative manner. As Cadillac held his breath, she tossed her head sharply in a vain effort to drive away the flies hovering around her eyes then stepped forward to crop a new stretch of grass.

Cadillac sank slowly back into the gully and saw that Clearwater had been checking the other side. She pointed toward the sleeping rattler, indicating that Cadillac should go past him.

"What if he wakes?" Cadillac hissed.

Clearwater smiled. "You shall have a fine fire-song—telling how bravely you died. Go," she whispered. "He will not wake until we are ready. We will send him to the capo."

Brave as he believed himself to be, Cadillac had an unreasoning fear of snakes. But to have any standing at all, if it had to be killed, *he* would have to kill it. He regretted bringing Clearwater with him. He had done so to have an eyewitness of his hunting prowess. Now he would *have* to be brave. He took out his hunting knife, placed it between his teeth, and, pushing the crossbow ahead of him, edged forward gingerly with his back pressed against the right-hand slope of the gully.

Taking the knife-sticks from her belt, Clearwater inserted the tapered end of the first into the hollow handle of her knife and twisted the second into the tube of rolled hide that was bound to the end of the first—transforming her hunting knife into a spear with a strong four-foot shaft. She moved forward, knife-stick raised, poised on one knee, ready to skewer the rattler at the first sign of danger.

As Cadillac eased his chest past the snake he saw to his horror that its black beady eyes were open. He froze momentarily as the forked tongue began darting in and out less than two feet from his stomach, then willed himself forward, wriggling past with a minimum of movement. His heart was pounding as he drew clear and turned on his tormentor. Hurriedly assembling his own knife-stick, he aimed the trembling blade at the coiled bulk of the snake.

Clearwater reversed her knife-stick and gently prodded the rattler with the butt of the shaft. The rattler stirred, uncoiled the top half of its body, and hissed angrily. Clearwater's eyes fixed on the snake with an unwavering, hypnotic stare. Cadillac jabbed the point of his knife-stick against the rattler's throat as it flicked its head toward him, jaws open; then both recoiled simultaneously. The bones on its tail rustled ominously. Uncoiling the rest of its six-foot length, the rattler tried to slither up around the rock under which it had been sleeping. Clearwater quickly drove it back. Caught between the two prodding knife-sticks the rattler took the only avenue of escape, zigzagging out of the shadows onto the sunlit side of the gully and up over the edge into the short grass.

Cadillac took a tentative peek over the top. "Where has it gone?"

"Toward the capo," whispered Clearwater. Holding the knifestick in her two hands, she rested her elbows on the edge of the gully, pointed the knife blade toward the capo, put the butt of the shaft against her forehead, and closed her eyes.

"What are you doing?" Cadillac whispered.

"Don't talk," she hissed, closing her eyes even tighter. "Load your crossbow and aim for the capo."

Cadillac slithered quickly along the gully, pushed the camouflaged crossbow over the edge, and wormed his way into a patch of long grass. Reaching into the bag at his belt, he took out one of the barbed, ten-inch-long bolts and placed it against the taut bowstring, with one of its four vanes in the slot cut in the barrel of the bow. He parted the grass cautiously. The capo with its prized ten-point horns was about two hundred yards away. Well within the range of a Mute crossbow but a difficult shot for a relatively untrained marksman like Cadillac. He rubbed his palms in the earth to wipe off the sweat.

The female fast-foot masking the capo started nervously and skittered sideways as the rattler reached them. The capo backed away, stamping its right foreleg, nosing the ground, then tossing its great horns in the air. Cadillac came up on one knee and brought the crossbow hard into his shoulder, the elbow of his left arm locked against his raised thigh, hand supporting the barrel of the bow rock-steady. He sighted along the upright vane of the bolt, aiming at the chest of the capo, allowing for the distance the bolt would drop on its way to the target. The big fast-foot lunged forward, caught the rattler on the forward points of its horns, and tossed it high in the air. As the powerful neck arched backward, Cadillac fired at the base of the white throat. The capo staggered under the force of the impact, mouth open to the sky, emitted a brief, deep-throated roar of pain and alarm, staggered again, fell to its knees, and then toppled sideways, hitting the ground with a great thud.

Cadillac leapt to his feet with a whooping cry of triumph as the rest of the herd bounded away eastward across the plain; the young males, who had crossed the gully behind them, jinked crazily as they passed. Clearwater scrambled out of the gully carrying their knifesticks.

Cadillac danced around her gleefully as she ran toward the fallen capo. "Did you ever see such a fine head? Or such a fine shot?"

Clearwater knelt and examined the fast-foot as Cadillac strutted around it, his face glowing with excitement. The body of the deer quivered spasmodically as the nervous system responded to the last confused signals of the dying brain.

"Where did you aim?" said Clearwater.

"For the heart," Cadillac replied. "Where the throat joins the chest." He knelt beside the dead animal and ran his hand down its neck. He felt blood run between his fingers. "See ... here ... you can feel the end of my shaft."

Clearwater nodded gravely, then lifted her hand from the side of the capo. "Then whose bolt is this?"

Cadillac's mouth dropped open as he saw the vanes of a crossbow bolt sticking out of the capo's chest just behind the right foreleg. He pulled his knife from its stick-shaft and cut the bolt out of the dead buck. Clearwater wiped the blood away with a handful of grass. The pattern scored on the shaft in front of the vanes was not that of the M'Call clan.

"What is this, brothers?" said a mocking voice. "A coyote and a fox that feed off the meat of lions?"

Cadillac's and Clearwater's hearts faltered momentarily as four unknown Mute warriors rose from the grass around them. One of them, who to guess by his adornments was the gang leader, carried a crossbow; the others were armed with knife-sticks and stone flails. The strangers wore helmet masks of hardened buffalo-hide onto which were sewn bones and colored pebbles. They had stone-studded leather cuffs on their forearms, and their patterned bodies were shielded with similar thigh, chest, and shoulder plates, hung with feathers and bones that had been dipped in blood.

Cadillac and Clearwater rose slowly to their feet as the four Mutes took a menacing step forward. Cadillac slipped his knife into the sheath tied to his waistbelt and turned to face the heavily built gang leader. The Mute tossed his crossbow to the warrior on his right.

Cadillac offered the bolt to the gang leader on his outstretched palm. "I am Cadillac, of the clan M'Call, from the bloodline of the She-Kargo, firstborn of the Plainfolk. We have stalked this fast-foot since the sun was at the head of the sky. The bolt I fired lies in its heart." He gestured to the dead capo. "Cut it free and you will see I speak the truth. Yours was aimed too high to kill." He tossed the bolt toward the Mute, who snatched it out of the air with an angry gesture.

Clearwater's heart quailed at Cadillac's recklessness.

One of the other warriors knelt and examined the wound in the breast of the dead buck. He nodded to his leader as if to confirm Cadillac's claim.

"It does not matter," said the gang leader. "I fired first. It is our meat."

Cadillac flushed angrily. "He was already dead when your bolt struck!" He tapped his chest. "I made the kill!"

The gang leader filled his deep chest, flexed his shoulders, and treated Cadillac to a mocking smile. "You have a big mouth, coyote. But your tail will soon be between your legs."

Cadillac stood his ground. "A coyote does not fear the cawing of carrion crows with no name."

The gang leader swaggered forward until his nose was almost touching Cadillac's and folded his arms—a gesture indicating his total indifference to any possible danger from his opponent. "Listen well, coyote—while you still have ears. I am Shakatak, of the Clan D'Vine, from the bloodline of the D'Troit, mightiest of the Plainfolk." He indicated his companions. "These are my brother Lion-Hearts—Torpedo, Cannonball, and Freeway. We have chewed bone, coyote. A full head-pole marks the door to our pad. Your skull will sit well upon the second."

His three companions laughed and mocked Cadillac by yelping like frightened coyotes.

Clearwater moved to Cadillac's side and addressed Shakatak without any sign of fear. "By what right do you take the life of a soul-brother? Are we not all of the Plainfolk? Do we not breathe the same air? Let us divide the fast-foot between us and share the triumph of the kill."

Shakatak uncrossed his arms, holding his fists clenched against his thighs. "The D'Troit are not soul-brothers of the She-Kargo." He spat on the ground in front of them. "Your name is dirt in our mouths. We share nothing with those who invade our turf and steal the meat from our knives."

Clearwater could not restrain her anger at the insult. "This is no-man's land! Your clan have put down no markers!"

Shakatak flung out his left arm toward Cannonball

and snapped his fingers. Cannonball reached down into the grass and picked up a claim stick—an eight-foot pole hung with feathers and plaques of sculptured wood colored with dyes, which Mute clans used to mark the boundaries of their turf. Grasping the long pole with two hands, Cannonball lifted it high into the air and drove the point deep into the ground.

"We have now," growled Shakatak. He turned to Cadillac. "So, coyote—if you would take meat back to the stinking yellow cubs you call clan-brothers, you will have to show me how sharp your teeth are."

Cadillac stepped in front of Clearwater. "Sharp enough to tear your liver out," he snarled.

Shakatak smiled. "Hot words, coyote. Does your knife speak as boldly?" He pulled out his long blade and sprang back, dropping into the crouching, wide-legged stance of a knife-fighter.

Cadillac fumbled for his blade and stepped back, adopting the same fighting pose. His throat was dry. He had fought mock duels, wrestled and undergone trials of strength with his clan-brothers; his body was lithe and well muscled, his reflexes sharp, his mind alert. But up to this moment he had never faced anything more lethal than a sheathed blade. Now he found himself staring at a weaving eight-inch blade with a vicious, dished-top cutting edge and suddenly realized that he was about to get himself killed—very painfully. He imagined Shakatak's blade sinking into his groin and ripping upward through his bowels. His stomach became a ball of ice; the skin on the back of his neck quivered. If only he had stayed on the far side of the river. If only . . .

Once again Clearwater moved between them, thrusting a raised hand at the fearsome Shakatak. "Put up your blade! There is no standing in this fight. This is not a warrior you seek to kill, but a wordsmith!"

Shakatak paused, clearly surprised by the news.

"Are the Lion-Hearts of the D'Vine so weak that they must hunt down those who have not chewed bone?" Clearwater laughed, but there was a note of desperation in her voice. "That would make a fine fire-song!"

Shakatak growled angrily and looked at his companions, uncertain of his next move. Before he could reply, Cadillac hurled Clearwater aside and slashed the air in front of Shakatak's face with his knife. "Even a wordsmith who has not chewed bone is worth ten warriors from a clan like the D'Vine, whose name is dirt and whose bravery can be recounted without the taking of a single breath!" He spat on the ground at Shakatak's feet.

Shakatak's eyes almost popped out of his head with rage. He bared his teeth and jabbed a blunt forefinger at Cadillac. "You are going to eat those words, coyote—along with your scrawny little nutbag. Torpedo! Draw the circle!"

Cannonball and Freeway grabbed Clearwater by the neck and arms and dragged her to one side. Torpedo put down Shakatak's crossbow, reversed his knife-stick, and quickly drew a ten-foot circle in the earth around Shakatak and Cadillac.

Shakatak indicated the circle. "Each time you step over that line, Torpedo will take a slice off the fox. Do you understand?"

Cadillac replied by making another slash at the air in front of Shakatak's face. Torpedo threw his knife-stick aside and helped pinion Clearwater by the arms.

"Cut him slow!" yelled Freeway.

"Don't worry," Shakatak gloated. "I'm going to unpick this mother one stitch at a time. I'll leave his eyes till last so he can watch us grease the tail of that fox." His knife flashed from his right to his left hand with frightening rapidity and slashed forward under Cadillac's guard, slicing along Cadillac's rib cage with surgical precision.

Clearwater's scream was choked off by Cannonball's hands on her mouth and throat.

A spasm of pain shot up through Cadillac's chest as the blood welled out of the wound in his side. Shakatak's knife flicked forward again, this time in his right hand, slashing open the skin on the other side of Cadillac's ribs. They were the first two strokes in the ritual of wounding and dismemberment in single-handed fights to the death. Cadillac had seen the pattern on the bodies of his clan-brothers and marauding Mutes. Next would come the cuts on the shoulders and upper arms, weakening the opponent's knife thrusts. The deep jabs into the thighs would be followed by the cheek slashes; then the forehead stroke, causing blood to pour into the eyes; the second horizontal slice, across the belly; the upward rip through the groin; and then—if you were lucky—the plunging thrust into and across the throat that preceded the severing of the head. Those who were unlucky suffered further mutilation before choking to death on their severed genitals.

Cadillac's terrifying vision of what lay ahead lent wings to his feet as he bobbed and weaved around Shakatak. He could not run, could not abandon Clearwater; yet he knew that if, by some miracle, he managed to defeat Shakatak, his brother Lion-Hearts would take his place, either singly or together. He was going to die! It was unthinkable that he should, but there was no way to escape. He leapt backward as Shakatak's blade scythed through the air less than an inch from his navel.

Shakatak's knife thrusts were terrifyingly fast, but because of his heavier body he was slower on his feet. After the two opening cuts on his ribs, Cadillac's natural agility had kept him out of serious trouble; but this merely offered a temporary respite, it was no solution. He could not dance beyond the range of Shakatak's blade forever. He had to find some way to get under his guard and inflict a short, sharp, disabling thrust. But how?

Cadillac sidestepped as Shakatak lunged forward and ran behind him to the far side of the circle where he stooped down and scooped up a handful of dirt and pebbles. Shakatak turned, his face creased with a knowing smile. As Cadillac advanced toward him warily, Shakatak flung out his arm toward the three Mutes who held Clearwater and snapped his fingers. Holding on to the struggling Clearwater with one hand, Torpedo unfastened the stone flail looped through his belt and lobbed it toward Shakatak's outstretched hand. As his arm came up Clearwater kicked at it desperately, causing the flail to fall between Shakatak and Cadillac. Shakatak stepped forward, switched his knife into his right hand, fixed Cadillac with his glittering eyes, and bent to pick up the flail.

Cadillac knew it was his one and only chance. Hurling the handful of dirt at Shakatak's face, he threw himself sideways into the air above Shakatak's knife-hand with a tremendous yell and kicked out at Shakatak's head with both feet. His heels connected with a force born of desperation. The knife flew from Shakatak's hand as his neck snapped sideways. Cadillac felt a terrible jarring pain as his feet slammed into the stone-covered helmet. There was a fleeting instant when time seemed to suddenly stand still and he found himself praying he had not broken his ankles—then Shakatak crashed to the ground with Cadillac sprawling on top of him.

Cadillac kicked out wildly at Shakatak's face, knocking off his helmet at the same time he stabbed viciously at the thick, strongly muscled legs that thrashed around his own head. Shakatak roared with pain like a crippled bull-buffalo. Twisting around, Cadillac scrambled to his knees, fumbling to change his grip on the blood-stained knife so that he could plunge it deep into Shakatak's throat or between the stone and leather chest plates protecting his heart.

Before he could strike, Shakatak rolled into him, then jerked upright, his left hand flashing out to grasp Cadillac's wrist, staying the knife. Seemingly oblivious of any pain or the blood pouring from the deep slashes in his leg muscles, Shakatak smashed his right forearm with its leather and stone cuff against Cadillac's throat, knocking him backward onto the ground, half-dazed and choking for breath. Cadillac tried to roll aside. Too late. Shakatak still held his wrist in a grip of iron. Kicking out with his right heel, he hit both of Cadillac's thighs with paralyzing blows, then threw his whole weight upon him. Cadillac squirmed wildly, arching his body like a speared fish, clawing at Shakatak's eyes; but in a matter of seconds Shakatak was sitting astride his chest, with his knees pinning Cadillac's arms to the ground and with Cadillac's knife in his hand.

Shakatak grabbed Cadillac's hair, forcing his head back, and pressed the sharp edge of the blade under Cadillac's left ear. "You fight well, wordsmith," he gasped hoarsely. "Well enough to have earned the life I now hold in my hands. The D'Vine have no tongues that can pierce the mysteries of the world. The past is darkness. Our fire-songs are not remembered. If you would weave them for us so that the bright thread of our bravery endures, you and the fox shall have meat, shelter, and standing."

Cadillac struggled against the crushing weight on his chest and dragged air down his battered throat. "I would sooner have eagles tear out my tongue than poison the air with your name," he snarled, half choking on the words.

"So be it, coyote," said Shakatak. "I have no past, you have no future." He raised the knife high into the air. Cadillac saw the late afternoon sunlight flash off the blade as it hung, poised, ready to plunge into his throat. He suddenly felt drained of fear; was filled instead with a great sadness at leaving the world, at being parted from Clearwater. But it would not be forever. He would roam the sunset islands in the sky until his spirit was poured into a new earth-mother, re-entering the world in another skin to fulfill his destiny, sharing the triumph of Talisman's ultimate victory.

In the split second before the knife fell, Clearwater wrenched her head free of Cannonball's grip and let out a piercing cry; a blood-curdling half scream, half shout—the dreaded ululation that was the mark of a summoner.

In the same instant, Clearwater became the epicenter of a mini-tornado that hurled her three captors from her in a shower of dust, stones, and uprooted grass. The claim stick wavered, was wrenched from the ground, spun wildly up into the air, and drove itself through Torpedo's chest as he tried to strike Clearwater with the stone flail. Cannonball and Freeway crouched low, vainly trying to shield themselves against the shower of stones that rained on them. Cadillac was terrified, too. He covered his ears, but the intensity of the sound coming from Clearwater's throat grew, piercing his brain.

An instant later, the spiraling wind enveloped him and Shakatak, still seated on his chest, arm upraised. The power that Clearwater had unleashed seemed to imbue the knife he held with a life of its own. It vibrated wildly in Shakatak's fist, but instead of breaking free of his grip, the awesome force in the wind caused his fingers to lock tighter around the handle. Sensing the danger, the now-terrified warrior threw up his other hand in a desperate effort to force the knife loose; but as he touched it, his fingers closed around those already gripping the knife. Shakatak let out a howl of fear. The muscles on his neck and shoulders bulged as he strained to hold the knife above his head. The vortex of force increased in power, the swirling wind howled, drowning out Clearwater's wavering, unearthly cry. With one swift, unstoppable movement, the knife in Shakatak's hands curved downward in front of Cadillac's horrified face and buried itself up to the hilt in the warrior's solar plexus.

Shakatak gave a harsh, gasping scream and fell forward across Cadillac, his hands still clasped around the knife. Cannonball and Freeway scrambled to their feet and took off across the grass like stampeding fast-foot, closely followed by the howling twister. The sound coming from Clearwater's throat faded. She fell to her knees, eyes glazed as if in a trance.

Wriggling out from under Shakatak's lifeless body,

Cadillac stumbled across to Clearwater on his numbed legs and gathered her in his arms. Her body felt cold; drained of life. He laid her down gently and caressed her face, not knowing what to do, completely over-awed by the deadly nature of the power that had come from within her. A power he had not suspected she possessed; that she had never given the slightest hint of possessing.

After a few minutes the gray veil lifted from her eyes. He felt the warmth flood back into her body. She smiled at him, then a look of alarm crossed her face. She sat up quickly, then relaxed as she realized that they were both out of danger. Cadillac stood up, walked over to the fallen Shakatak, and turned his body over. As the dead warrior rolled onto his back, his hands fell limply away from the handle of Cadillac's knife. Clearwater joined him and they walked to where Torpedo lay transfixed by the D'Vine claim stick. Their eyes met over his lifeless body.

"Why did you not tell me you were a summoner?"

Clearwater shook her head in bewilderment. "I did not know until now. It was only when you were about to die that the power came upon me. It was sent through me. It used my voice to call the forces up from the earth, but I did not guide it." She paused and looked back at Shakatak's body, suddenly intimidated by the terrible violence she had unleashed. "I do not know if it will come again."

Cadillac nodded. "The door in your mind has been opened. If you call, the power will enter. Mr. Snow will teach you how to guide it."

Clearwater shivered and rubbed her arms. "It frightens me."

"Me, too," Cadillac agreed. "But it is a good power. Did you not save my life?"

Clearwater shook her head. "No. Talisman saved it. It was his strength that flowed through me." She gently brushed the wounds on Cadillac's ribs with her fingertips. "If I could have saved you with a single cry I would have struck down Shakatak before he drew his blade. But it was not to be. Talisman did not reveal his power until you revealed yours. You fought bravely, like a great warrior, and at the point of death you refused to dishonor your clan. You have standing. You have the heart and blood of a Bear and there shall be a firesong to mark this day—"

"I shall choose the words myself," said Cadillac, swelling with pride at the prospect and his newfound ability to ignore the pain that pulsed through his chest.

"—but only," Clearwater continued firmly, "if you hold fast to your oath to Mr. Snow. Never act rashly again. Never put the gift of words in danger."

Cadillac shrugged arrogantly. "If it is my destiny to be a great warrior—"

"Then the fire-song *I* sing shall tell how these Lion-Hearts *truly* died. Not under the hand of a brave Bear they called coyote, but by a single cry from the lips of a tame fox!"

"She-ehh!" hissed Cadillac. "For a tame fox you have sharp teeth."

Clearwater slipped her arms around his neck. "They bite softly enough in the darkness of the moon." She rubbed her nose against his cheeks, then kissed him on the mouth. "Come . . . let us prepare the fast-foot."

They gutted the carcass of the capo and strung it to the eight-foot claim stick. The weight of the dead beast made it sag dangerously and they could only shoulder it with great difficulty. To take it back unaided would mean abandoning the dead Mutes and their weapons.

Cadillac shed his end of the load. "You will have to get help. I will stay here and guard what we have won. Take the Lion-Heart's crossbow." He hauled back the lever with a gasp of pain, placed a bolt in the barrel, and offered it to her.

Clearwater did not take it. She was looking past him across the plain to the north; home of the White Death. "Running clouds," she said.

Cadillac turned, following the direction of her pointing finger. He saw a low dust haze hanging in the air above a distant rise—a sign that often meant a group of warriors on the move, running with the character-istic, loping gait that enabled Mutes to cover long distances, sometimes running for forty-eight hours without a break, sleeping on their feet as birds do on the wing, guided by some mysterious internal navi-gation system.

The running cloud drifted against the gray-blue shadowed land beyond, burning with orange fire as it caught the slanting rays of the sun. Cadillac hur-riedly loaded his own crossbow. "Could those two crows have flown to more of their brothers?" he asked anxiously. From his experience of Mr. Snow's powers he knew that if it left the summoner exhausted, it did not come quickly again. If those who now ran toward them were marauding Lion-Hearts . . .

"Make me tall and I shall tell you," said Clearwater.

Cadillac cupped his hands together so that Clear-water could climb up and stand upon his shoulders. He sucked his breath in sharply as her added weight compressed his slashed ribs.

Clearwater, like most Mutes, was blessed with re-markably sharp, almost hawklike vision; she quickly focused on the tufts of golden feathers on the side of the runners' head-masks. "They are Bears—" she waved vigorously, then leapt nimbly to the ground and faced Cadillac with a smile—"come to escort their warrior-wordsmith home in triumph."

The posse of M'Call Bears reached them some fif-teen minutes later. They were led by Motor-Head, the most fearless of Cadillac's clan-brothers. A pow-erful young warrior, heavily built like the dead Shaka-tak, he had filled not one, but *two* head-poles. With him were Hawk-Wind, Black-Top, Brass-Rail, Steel-Eye, Ten-Four, and Convoy, all of them bearing—as was the custom—Names of Power that had once be-longed to the Heroes of the Old Time. Each was dressed in the eccentric fashion of Mute warriors, their leather body plates adorned with trophies and emblems attesting to their prowess and courage, and they arrived carrying the limp bodies of Cannonball and Freeway slung like dead fast-foot from newly cut saplings.

Motor-Head circled the bodies of Torpedo and Shakatak, gave an approving nod, then walked over to Cadillac and threw an arm around his shoulders. "Good work, little sand-worm."

"Sand-worm" was Cadillac's nickname among this particular group of Bears, whose spirits had entered the world in the same year as his own, and he suffered it in silence.

Motor-Head waved toward the bodies of Cannonball and Freeway. "You must have frightened them mightily. Their running cloud was like a tower in the sky!"

Cadillac exchanged a sideways glance with Clearwater. She bit back a smile, then said, "He also brought down the capo."

This news brought grunts of approval from Cadillac's clan-brothers. Convoy counted the branched horns. "Ten points! No one has done better!"

Motor-Head added his grudging approval. "So, sand-worm . . . is wrestling with words not enough to fill your day? Would you also fight and hunt and run with the Bears?"

Cadillac faced up to Motor-Head's mocking gaze. "Does not the branch-worm become a leaf-wing? Why should a sand-worm not become a warrior worthy to bear his Name of Power?"

Motor-Head chuckled and planted himself before Cadillac with folded arms. "Your tongue strikes sparks, wordsmith. And now your hands have held sharp iron. You have cut down meat, and you have chewed bone." He turned toward the other warriors. "How say you, brothers—is he worthy to be one of us?"

One by one, Hawk-Wind, Black-Top, Brass-Rail, Steel-Eye, Ten-Four, and Convoy solemnly thrust out their right arms toward Cadillac, the fingers clenched, the thumb raised.

Motor-Head took off his feathered head-mask and

placed it on Cadillac's head. "Welcome, blood-brother Bear! May your arm strike hard and true, may your heart be strong, and your name be honored in the fire-songs of our people!"

"Hey-*yuh!* Hey-*yuh!* Hey-*yuh!!*" chorused the others. Clearwater's eyes glistened with tears of joy as she joined with the others, raising her arms as they shouted the traditional accolade.

It was a sweet moment of triumph, which Cadillac spoilt by fainting from loss of blood.

—— 4 ——

The joint centenary celebration and graduation ceremony was held in the Academy's giant free-flight dome. The bare rock from which it had been hewn was hung with flags and bunting, and crisscrossed with computerized colored laser beams that had been programmed to create dazzling, ever-changing patterns of light.

When the five thousand spectators had filed into their allotted seats, the nine squadrons of cadets and the Academy staff paraded to the stirring synthesized sounds of brass, fife, and drum, then lined up with geometrical precision for inspection by the visiting dignitaries from Grand Central. This was followed by squadron displays of marching and countermarching, weapon handling, assault training demonstrations, gymnastics, and quarterstaff combat drills.

The ground events, interwoven with highlights from the videorecord of the Flight Academy's history and achievements projected on a giant screen, were climaxed by a flying display in which Steve Brickman took a leading part.

After the ceremonial presentation of wings, prizes, a video address by George Washington Jefferson XXXI, the President-General of the Federation, and seemingly interminable speeches by members of the Amtrak Executive who had shuttled from Houston, the amplifiers boomed out the opening chords of "The Wild Blue Yonder," the Academy's historic battle hymn. Five thousand spectators rose to their feet and, with one voice, joined the two-hundred-strong choir in the verses and chorus that accompanied the final march past. Tears flowed unashamedly down the cheeks of veteran Trail-Blazers in the stands as the voices and music soared to fill the huge circular arena; the sound merging, as if by magic, with the rhythmic pulsing of the lasers, to create a heart, mind, and gut-gripping audiovisual experience—the crowning moment of a triumphantly successful anniversary parade.

As the final words of the last ringing chorus faded, and the tears were wiped away, the hymn was reprised in voiceless diminuendo. The first- and second-year cadets marched out of the arena to the sound of retreating drumbeats, and the three senior squadrons, now proudly bearing their newly won wings on their tunics, were halted and dismissed in front of the packed reviewing stand. After nearly four hours on the parade ground, the third-year cadets broke ranks with broad smiles of relief as their guardians and kinfolk—some of whom had traveled from the farthest reaches of the Federation—left their seats and streamed down the steps to greet their wards with hugs and handshakes and shoot off more videotape for the unit album.

"How ya doing, Wonder Boy?"

Steve ducked out from under the enthusiastic embrace of his kin-sister and smoothed his uniform. "Hey, Roz, come on. Grow up, will you?"

"I am grown up. I was fifteen last February, remember?"

"Sure, I remember."

"Could have looked in on me. Or at least sent a vee-gee."

"I forgot, Worm. Happy Birthday whenever. Okay?"

"And not a bleep from you when I passed my Inter-Med."

"Steve hardly ever looks in. You should know that," said Annie Brickman. Her voice was entirely devoid of malice or reproach. It was just a plain statement of fact. Annie, Steve's guard-mother, stepped aside as her kin-brother Bart Bradlee eased Jack Brickman's wheelchair through the crowd.

"I was gonna send a vee-gee, Annie, but it got kind of busy."

"We know that, boy." In the year since his last home leave, his guard-father's voice had faded to a husky whisper.

Steve lifted his guard-father's hands from the arms of his chair and squeezed them gently. Jack Brickman's fingers responded to the contact like palsied chicken claws. It was hard to believe that these hands, and the wasted body they were attached to, had once been packed with lean, hard flesh and enough muscle power to knock many bigger men clear across a room.

"Good to see you, sir. I really appreciate you taking the trouble to make the trip."

"If we hadn't brought him, he'd have gotten some-one to tie him to the chair and had himself shipped out as freight," said Bart. He patted Jack Brickman's shoulder. "Ain't that so, old-timer?"

The "old-timer" answered with a wry, gasping laugh. Steve's guard-father was thirty-four years old. Jack knew he would be dead from radiation sickness within a year. They all knew. But no one felt sad about it, or thought of it as tragic. His tenacious sur-vival thus far was little short of miraculous. Very few Trail-Blazers made it past thirty. Indeed, most Track-ers assigned to overground operations were dead long before that—killed in action or through pulling a trick or, more regrettably, executed before the TV cameras for a Code One default.

Undergrounders had a greater life expectancy, but even they didn't live forever. Annie, who was also thirty-four, and her kin-brother Bart, a twenty-nine-

year-old staff officer, had never been posted overground or suffered a day's illness; yet both would die
soon after their forty-second birthday. For despite
the spectacular advances in the life sciences over the
last three centuries, the secret of longevity still remained to be discovered.

The oldest Tracker on record had died at the ripe
old age of forty-five.

The oldest *ordinary* Tracker, that is.

The current President-General of the Federation
was—to judge from his video appearances—a vigorous sixty-five, and his predecessor had lived into his
eighties. No one had ever given Steve a satisfactory
explanation of why this should be so. That was the
way it was. The Jeffersons were the First Family
because they lived longer than everybody else. And
they lived longer than everybody else because they
had been born to rule the Federation.

That was what it said in the Manual.

Steve embraced his guard-mother. "I really did
work hard, Annie. Can you forgive me?"

Annie laughed. "For what—coming fourth?"

"I should have been first."

"Fourth sounds pretty good to me," said Annie.
"Jack wasn't even in the top twenty."

"The Eagles took three out of the top four places,"
said Bart. "Never been a squadron that done that
before."

Steve turned to Bart. "You don't understand, sir. I
should have been first. I should have been Honor
Cadet. I was shafted."

Bart's face muscles hardened a little around his
good-natured smile. "Now, that's a real bad thought
for you to have, Stevie. The system doesn't make
mistakes like that."

"No harm in the boy wanting to be best," said
Annie. "We trained him to think that way before he
could even walk. Roz, too."

Bart shook his head. "Wanting to be and being is
different, sure enough. But that's not what a girl and
boy should set their minds to. *Trying* to do their best,

that's something else. That's what's expected of each and every one of us. Just like it says in The Book."

Steve nodded respectfully. Bart held the powerful post of Provost-Marshal for the territory of New Mexico. Young men planning to make their way up in the world did not argue with Provost-Marshals. Even if they were kinfolk.

"I tried, sir."

Bart patted him on the shoulder. "That's all a man can do. It's all been worked out, boy. The Family's had their eye on you from the day you were born. Same way as they look after all of us. A Tracker doesn't need to question the order he's given, or the place he's been assigned to. The only thing he has to ask himself is, 'Am I trying hard enough? Am I doing the best I can?'"

"Amen to that," said Annie.

Jack Brickman waved a frail hand. "You passed. That's the important thing. The marks don't matter a damn. Combat is the only way a wingman can prove himself."

"Exactly." Roz linked arms with Steve and her guard-mother. "Now will somebody please shoot a picture before my brother gets too famous to talk to me?"

The rest of the afternoon was spent sightseeing. As with every annual passing-out parade, the Flight Academy complex was thrown open for inspection by the kinfolk of the senior classmen. Food and drink were freely available in the mess halls, where the first-year Squabs were on duty as waiters. Second-year cadets conducted tours of the classrooms and other training areas, giving practical demonstrations on the flight rigs, simulators, and weapon ranges. Steve took over control of his guard-father's wheelchair, but an hour into the tour Jack Brickman's face clouded over as the sharp-toothed serpent within him crept out of its secret lair and began to gnaw away at another part of his body. Annie gave Jack a couple of Cloud-Nines and cradled his head until the drawn sinews on his scrawny neck slackened and he fell into a drugged sleep.

Seeing what had happened, Chuck Waters, a buddy from B-Flight, invited Steve's kinfolk to join his own ten-strong bunch of Okies. Steve took Jack Brickman up in the elevator to the quarterdeck and wheeled him into his shack. Putting a pillow on the chair back, he gently eased the gaunt open-mouthed skull onto it, crossed the limp, wizened hands, then sat down on the stripped bunk and gazed impassively at the man who had raised him. The only sign of life was a thin, gasping sigh as air passed in and out of his guard-father's throat. Sometime next year, the sighing would stop. The bag-men would call, his body would go down the gaspipe, and his name would go up on the Flight Academy's wall.

Another good man gone.

Steve sat there a while longer, then got up and began packing his clothing and personal equipment into a big blue trail-bag.

"Okay if I come in?"

Steve looked over his shoulder. Donna Monroe Lundkwist, a slim, fair-haired wingman who had, in Steve's calculations, been his only serious rival for first place, stood at the door. The blue-and-white-tasseled Honor Cadet lanyard was looped over her right shoulder; the big metallic-thread Minuteman badge was sewn on her left breast pocket under the silver wings.

Steve folded the last of his shirts into the trail-bag. "What can I do for you?"

"Nothing special." Lundkwist sat down casually on the bunk next to Steve's trail-bag. "Just dropped in to say 'good-bye.' " She nodded toward Jack Brickman. "Your guard-father?"

"Yeah. . . ."

Lundkwist registered the two gold, double triangles on Jack Brickman's sleeve and gave a low whistle. "A double-six! Twelve tours and two White House lunches with the President-General. How come you never told anybody your guardian was an ace wing-man?"

Steve shrugged. "That kind of information is dispensed strictly on a 'need to know' basis." He zipped up the side pockets of his trail-bag and wedged some more of his gear into the middle section. "How was *your* lunch?"

"Oh—you mean with the Academy-General? Interesting. He gave me the inside track on my first assignment. I'm being posted to Big Red One."

"That's good," Brickman said flatly.

Big Red One was the popular name for the Red River wagon train. It was known throughout the Federation for the spectacular success of its many expeditions against the Mutes; its Trail-Blazer crew had an unrivaled combat record, and as a result of their renown the Red River wagon master was able to cream off the top layer of graduates from the combat academies and specialist schools. For the last twenty years, the top three cadets from the Academy had joined the Trail-Blazer team aboard Red River. Steve had planned to be one of them this year.

"I asked about you."

"And? . . ."

"You've been assigned to The Lady from Louisiana. She's based at Forth Worth." Lundkwist paused. "Gus White, too."

"That should make his day," grunted Steve. Service aboard Big Red One was traditionally regarded as the all-important first rung on the promotion ladder. He turned to face her. "Does he know yet?"

Lundkwist shook her head. "I thought you'd enjoy telling him."

"I will." Steve closed the long zip on the middle section of his trail-bag. As he moved the zip tag toward Lundkwist she laid a finger on the back of his hand and drew a slow, exploratory circle. Their eyes met.

"How about putting the bomb in the barrel?"

Steve ran the zip tag the rest of the way while he thought about it. "You mean here? Now?"

Donna Lundkwist's eyes flickered toward the sleeping figure of Jack Brickman. "You worried about him waking up?"

"Not really. He's on Cloud-Nine."

"So? . . ." Lundkwist looked at him expectantly.

"So . . . maybe some other time."

Lundkwist pointed to the sleeping Jack Brickman. "Listen. You are not going to be upsetting this guy. In twelve years on the wagons he must have walked past some heavy traffic. Right?"

Steve mulled the situation over.

Lundkwist tugged at Steve's parade suit, forcing him to take a step toward her. She closed her trousered thighs against his legs. "Come on, Brickman, I never made it with you. And after today, I may never see you again."

"Nothing I can do about that."

"Oh, yes there is." Lundkwist stood up, slipped her arms around his waist, and gently ground his genitals with the point of her pelvis. "Five weeks from now I could be on a wagon train heading into Mute territory. Six weeks from now I could cease to exist. Eight weeks before my seventeenth birthday. If I'm going to go into the meat business I want the satisfaction of knowing I've been with the best." Without waiting for Steve's answer she lifted his trail-bag clear of the bed, closed the sliding door to the shack, unzipped his tunic, swiftly peeled off her own uniform, and climbed onto the bunk.

Steve glanced at his guard-father. Jack Brickman's head was slumped sideways on the pillow, his open mouth accentuating the hollowness of his cheeks. He lifted his guard-father's hand a few inches, then let it go. It fell back limply onto his lap with the lifelessness that characterized deep sleep. Steve turned back to Donna Lundkwist and undressed in his own good time. He ran his eyes casually over her naked body. Neat. A strong neck and good square shoulders, well-defined muscles without that bunchy look that some of the guys went for. He lay down beside her.

Lundkwist ran an appraising hand along his shoulder, then down the side of his chest onto his hips. "I really get off on you, Brickman. How come we had to wait three years for this?"

Steve shrugged. "Busy, I guess. Okay, how do you want it?"

Donna teased his mouth with her tongue. "Every which way. The works." She turned around and backed into him. Underneath the deep UV tan, her shoulders were covered with freckles. Even though they had often been under the showers at the same time it was something Steve had never noticed before. He snaked one arm underneath her and up over her slim breasts. Donna grabbed his other hand before he had decided what to do with it and slid it down between her legs. "Oh, yes," she murmured. "Oh, yes!" She arched her neck and rubbed her face against his.

Steve closed his eyes and pictured her making it with that creep Gus White. And the other guys. Saying the same thing, reacting the same way. It was an accepted fact that by the end of the course almost everybody had made it with everybody else. It was no big deal. If you were that way inclined—and most guys were—you just went the rounds on a regular basis.

Brickman was not so inclined. Not because he was lacking any vital parts, suffering from dimensional deficiency, or bereft of the normal urges that come upon young people of his age. His voluntary celibacy merely reflected his pragmatic approach to life.

Brickman had not gone the rounds for the simple reason that, while it might afford some welcome relief, it was not part of the curriculum. There were no marks awarded for jacking up, or bombing, one's fellow cadets. It was not even regarded as a reliable way to make friends and influence people. Consequently, it figured lower than nowhere on his list of priorities. On the other hand, being Brickman, he could not bear the thought of doing anything badly, and now that he had allowed Donna to get to him, Steve wanted to do it right.

He held on like a limpet as Donna ground her rump into his belly. It felt like someone had lit a fire in his lap. It wasn't the first time, but it was the first time in years. He had buried the memory of how it had felt at the back of his mind. Now it came flooding back, warming his body, and for a while he forgot that his guard-father's wheelchair was parked less than two feet away and that at any minute the rest of his kinfolk might walk in through the door.

Half an hour, or maybe an hour, later, after they'd done everything but bounce off the walls, they lay alongside each other breathing deep and hard. Where their bodies touched the skin was tacked together by a thin film of sweat.

Lundkwist caught her breath and put her mouth against Steve's ear. "D'you wanna drop another one in?"

"Uh-uh," said Steve. "This is where I bail out."

"Okay." Lundkwist sat up and dropped her legs over the side of the bunk. "That was good. Right on the button." She ran a hand down her throat, between her slim breasts and onto her flat, hard stomach. "Need a shower, but, uh, somehow I think I'm gonna have to leave that till I get home."

Steve nodded. "Long ride to Wichita," he observed. Lundkwist came from the northernmost Federation base—Monroe Field in Kansas, opened up in 2900. Which also made it the newest. "Your kinfolk here?"

"Are you kidding?" said Lundkwist. "They brought the whole base along." She began to dress.

As Steve put his clothes on he studied Lundkwist and thought about what they had done. It had set his brain and body fizzing with feelings and desires he had long since put a cap on. Putting the bomb in the barrel with her had provided an undeniable moment of pleasure, but that was something he could live without. Allowing yourself to need other people in that way—to let them get that close—was a dangerous luxury. It made you vulnerable.

"So . . ." said Steve. "It's 'good-bye,' then."

"Yeah . . . we're booked out on the four o'clock

shuttle." Lundkwist checked her watch, then zipped up her parade tunic and adjusted the tasseled Honor Cadet lanyard.

Steve could cheerfully have strangled her with it. "Good luck and, uh . . . good hunting."

"You, too." Brickman established firm eye contact and smiled warmly as they shook hands. "And take it easy, okay? You made the number one spot. You don't have to prove it all over again to the Mutes."

He patted her shoulder as she turned away. Lundkwist looked back at him from the doorway with a tight-lipped smile. "You know how to make a guy feel good, Brickman, but underneath that whiter-than-white smile you really are one mean sonofabitch."

Steve eyed her steadily and continued dressing. "Part of my survival kit."

"You know what your trouble is?" Lundkwist didn't wait for him to reply. "You think you're different. You're so busy working at being number one you've got no time to be one of us. It frightens people. And that's bad, because one day you may need a friend."

"Anything else?" asked Steve imperturbably.

"Yeah," said Lundkwist. She tapped the Minuteman badge on the breast pocket of her tunic. "You and I both worked our asses off to win this. I just want you to know that whatever it was you did wrong, in my book you're still the top gun."

Steve shrugged modestly and zipped up his pants. "Time will tell. . . ."

"It will indeed," said Lundkwist. She stepped away from the door, then leaned back in. "Oh, by the way—happy birthday."

5

Two days after his triumph against Shakatak D'Vine, Cadillac went with Clearwater and Mr. Snow deep into the forest. They found a glade by the edge of a stream where they squatted cross-legged, facing each other on a carpet of red leaves. Behind them, on all sides, the black-brown trunks of the redwoods stood guard, like giant warriors. Here and there, rose-colored shafts of sunlight pierced the thick canopy leaves, casting bright pools of light on the sea of ferns that washed against the gnarled roots of the trees.

Cadillac listened attentively as Clearwater put questions to Mr. Snow about her newly discovered power, which, like Cadillac's prodigious memory, was a gift of the Sky Voices, sent with the blessing of their great Mother Mo-Town. Mr. Snow explained many things, emphasizing that the effort needed to guide the power and shape it to his, or her, will drained the life-force from the summoner. Thus, the greater the force unleashed, the greater the power needed to control it. Great power should only be summoned in extremis because it could, in untrained hands, result in the death of the one who sought to wield it.

This was why Clearwater had fainted when she had saved Cadillac from Shakatak; the summoner was left weakened after the power had passed through her body and had to wait until their life-force had been restored before the power could be used again. It followed that, in times of danger, the skill of the summoner had to be employed judiciously; otherwise he or she might find those powers depleted when they were needed most.

When it was Cadillac's turn to speak he said, "I am troubled that I do not hear the Sky Voices."

Mr. Snow smiled. "You will hear them when you are ready to listen."

"Then teach me how to listen."

Mr. Snow shook his head. "The heads of the young are filled with the sounds of the world. The trumpets of vainglory. The dark murmur of earth-longings. With age, your inner ear may learn to shut out such noises. Only then will you discover that the great truths are gifts that come wrapped in silence."

"I have a gift of which I have not yet spoken," Cadillac said.

"A pupil should not conceal knowledge from his master," said Mr. Snow.

Cadillac laughed. "Nothing is hidden from you, Old One."

"True," admitted Mr. Snow. His eyes twinkled. "Though I do not send my mind into your hut at the dark of the moon."

Clearwater put her hands over her nose and mouth, and eyed Cadillac over her fingertips.

Cadillac took a deep breath to avoid stammering from embarrassment. "I did not speak because I was not sure whether it was a true gift or nothing more than dream-stuff fashioned by a half-empty mind." He hesitated. "I see . . . pictures in the stones."

Mr. Snow nodded soberly. Clearwater listened, wide-eyed.

"Not all stones," Cadillac explained. "Only those which are . . ." He groped for the right word.

"Seeing-stones," said Mr. Snow.

"Yes." Cadillac reached toward the bank of the stream and picked up a smooth rock the size of a large apple. "This one says nothing." He ran a finger around its circumference. "The seeing-stones have a ring of soft golden light. I cannot always see it, but if I hold one of these stones in my hand and take its essence into my mind, I see pictures. Whether they are in the stone or in my mind I cannot tell but"—Cadillac shook his head and sighed regretfully—"I do not understand them."

Mr. Snow nodded again. "The power is difficult to master. The pictures you saw could have been from the past . . . or from the future. They are of the place where the stone lies. Stored memories, visions of things yet to come, sealed like reflections of the cloud-filled sky on the surface of the endless River of Time."

"Can you teach me to make sense of these things?"

Mr. Snow shook his head. "No. The art of seership cannot be taught. He who has the gift must learn to use it himself."

"So," said Cadillac, "I am wordsmith and seer. Might not the power of the summoner enter me in the days to come . . . as it has been given to Clearwater?"

"It might," Mr. Snow said.

Cadillac weighed up the old man and squared his shoulders. "The shadow of Talisman is upon me," he said boldly. "Am I to be the Thrice-Gifted One?"

Mr. Snow closed his eyes as if seeking guidance. Clearwater reached out silently and took hold of Cadillac's hand. Their eyes met briefly, then returned to Mr. Snow, but he did not reply or open his eyes for several minutes.

"That is not a question I can answer," he said finally. "I conceal nothing. I do not know. There have been many times when I have felt the finger of the Sky Voices pointing at you, but I now know that my thoughts were colored by my desire to see Talisman enter the world before I go to the High Ground and"—Mr. Snow chuckled—"the unworthy notion that I had been chosen to be his Teacher." He sighed. "You may be." He indicated Clearwater. "*She* may be. . . ."

"But she is not a wordsmith!" Cadillac cried. "Does it not say that the Thrice-Gifted One shall be wordsmith, summoner, and seer?"

"That is indeed the Prophecy," admitted Mr. Snow. "But six days ago, which of us knew of the powers that Clearwater possessed? And how long ago did you find your first seeing-stone?"

"Two or three years," replied Cadillac grumpily.

"Let me remind you of the Prophecy," said Mr. Snow. "Man-child or woman-child the One may be. And none will know who is the Thrice-Gifted One until the earth gives the sign."

Cadillac eyed Mr. Snow disappointedly. His voice was tinged with resentment. "Are you sure the Sky Voices have not spoken of this more directly?"

Mr. Snow threw up his hands in mock despair and gave them both a long-suffering look.

Clearwater smiled sympathetically.

"They have spoken, but the meaning of their words is clouded," replied Mr. Snow. "I cannot put your mind at rest."

"Let me be the judge of that," Cadillac said.

"Very well," said Mr. Snow. "They have told me that Talisman will be someone known to you."

Cadillac exchanged a look of surprise with Clearwater, then turned back to Mr. Snow. "Someone known to me now—or someone I will come to know?"

Mr. Snow uncrossed his legs.

"Wait!" cried Cadillac. "Does that also include me?"

Mr. Snow shrugged and got to his feet. "It means what it says. You are a wordsmith. Work it out."

6

Within minutes of arriving at his kinfolks' quarters, Steve fell into bed and slept for two whole days and nights.

The relentless pace of his last year at the Flight Academy, plus the extra adrenalin that had been pumped into his system during the final run-up to the exams and his overground solo, had put his mind and body into permanent overdrive. It was only when he finally slipped under the quilt with the knowledge that he would not be awakened by an electronic trumpet blast that the months of pentup fatigue were released. As he lay back, he felt the aching tiredness flood out of his bones and into the surrounding flesh, spreading out in every direction like a slow-burning brush fire until his whole body was suffused with a dull, prickly pain that penetrated every fiber; oozed out of every pore. At the point when it became unbearable, darkness enveloped him.

Roosevelt Field—the place where Steve had been reared and schooled and with which he was identified by his middle name—was the operational headquarters and home base of a ten-thousand-strong division of Trackers. Compared to Grand Central, it had the no-frills, homespun atmosphere of a frontier town, but it was nothing like anything ever built in the pioneer West. Roosevelt Field was a self-contained multilevel mini-city. An air-conditioned colony of human termites with TV in every burrow, situated fifteen hundred feet down in the bedrock under the pre-Holocaust city of Santa Fe. Like all the other once-great cities of the southern United States, this was now nothing more than a dot on the map of the overground, but its name had remained in use because it marked the geographical location of the Federation base in the earth-shield below.

The layout of Roosevelt/Santa Fe followed the standard concentric ground plan developed by Grand Central engineers in the eighth century. Basically, it consisted of a central plaza surrounded by two circular transit tunnels (ringways) at a radius of one and two miles. Eight more transit tunnels (radials) arranged like the spokes of a wheel linked the plaza with the first and second ringways. At each intersection there were huge vertical shafts (two-level rises or four-level deeps) with accommodation units, workshops, and community areas built into the sides—rather like skyscrapers turned inside out. The domed hub of Roosevelt Field was known as New Deal Plaza; Annie and Jack Brickman's quarters were on Level Three-8 at NE and Second, the shaft known as Tennessee Valley Deep.

Steve woke up on the morning of the third day. The aching tiredness had vanished, but in the process his bones had turned to jelly. He felt drained of all energy and did not need much persuasion from Annie to stay in bed. Roz, his kin-sister, brought him a breakfast tray from the Level Three mess deck, and put the remote control handset for the TV within easy reach.

The Federation provided Trackers with nine TV channels. Channels 1 and 2 gave access to the Archive/data bank; 3, 4, 5, and 6 provided study programs covering a wide range of subjects; 7 offered vocational skills; and 8 was a recreation channel offering a variety of combative video games, such as the popular "Shoot-A-Mute." Feeling he had earned a break from studying, and having trained for the last three years to kill Mutes, Steve selected channel 9—the Public Service Channel—something he rarely watched. PSC broadcasts were composed almost exclusively of inspirational programs, banal blue-sky balladeers, and the networked news from GC, interspersed with mind-deadening "local interest" items from the home-base station.

One such item was on the screen now. An on-the-spot report about Young Pioneer work teams. An earnest stringer from Roosevelt Field, who insisted on being called Ron, put the next of a series of penetrating questions to a sweat-stained, dusty, politely attentive thirteen-year-old group leader. "So, how many yards of rock do you think your team of boys and girls has dug out today, Doug?"

Thank you, and good night. Click. Steve ate the rest of his breakfast facing a blank, gray-faced screen.

After four days of virtual inactivity, Steve's natural energy level was restored and he began to feel restless. He would have liked to talk more with his guard-father, but Jack was unable to sustain a meaningful conversation. After two or three exchanges his voice would become faint with exhaustion and he would lose track of the subject under discussion.

Annie Brickman, in between looking after Jack, was working behind the counter on the Level Three south mess deck. With the exception of senior staff officers like Bart, everybody on a Tracker base, regardless of their qualifications, had to put in a fixed number of Public Duty hours every month. In theory, PD entailed anything and everything to do with the running of the base; in practice, it usually meant one hundred hours on a work squad assigned to repetitive low-grade tasks ranging from food preparation and laundry work to road sweeping and garbage disposal.

Steve wandered into his kin-sister's room. Roz was packing her trail-bag, glancing every now and then at the TV set on the table by her bunkbed. She was running a videotaped Inter-Med lecture on genetics.

Steve stacked up the pillows and made himself comfortable with his feet up on the bed. "When do you plan to pull out?"

"Tomorrow," said Roz. "Enrollment at Inner State U doesn't start for another week, but I want to take a look around Grand Central while I've got some free time."

"Yeah ... they say it's really something." Steve gazed idly at the colored diagram on the TV screen. The sound track was pure gobbledygook. "Is that what you're going to specialize in—genetics?"

Roz nodded. "It's the only area where there's still a chance to come up with an amazing discovery that could change the future. Can you imagine what it would be like if we all lived twice as long—till we were eighty? Wouldn't that be something?"

"Yughh—it would be terrible."

Roz smiled. "Actually, I've chosen genetics because the Life Institute is the only medical center with unlimited research facilities. Who knows? I just might make a name for myself."

"You just might," Steve agreed.

"Always provided I qualify, of course. The bottom third of each graduate year is automatically wiped out. That's it." Roz drew a hand across her throat. "No retreads."

Steve shrugged. "So what. You still have your Inter-Med. If you don't want to tap chests and prescribe pills in a base clinic, you can always join a frontline surgical team on one of the wagon trains."

"And end up like Poppa-Jack?" Roz wrinkled her nose.

"Maybe," said Steve. "But in the process, you might save your big brother, or some other guys like him."

Roz smiled. "You'll survive. From what I've heard, those Trail-Blazer expeditions are a cakewalk. Okay, maybe the air burns you up, the way it did Poppa-

Jack, but don't start telling me how dangerous it is to be out there fighting Mutes. You know what? When I see those pictures of 'em on the history programs and hear about the way they live, I feel sorry for 'em. They're as ugly as bugs and we crush 'em out of existence as if they *were* bugs—"

"They're no better than," interjected Steve.

"Okay, I accept that," Roz said. "And I step on bugs the way you do. But as my heel goes down, I sometimes ask myself if bugs ain't got the right to live the same as we do. If not, why are they running around in the first place? Maybe whoever it was who created the First Family made the bugs, too. And maybe they made the Mutes along with 'em."

Steve studied his kin-sister. "You know something? Since we've been raised together you've come out with some pretty weird ideas, but that has to be the weirdest yet."

"But it could be so, couldn't it?" insisted Roz.

"It could be," Steve replied. "But I'm not going to let it worry me. I've been training for the last three years to go out there and kill Mutes and that's what I intend to do."

"Go ahead," said Roz. "I know it takes courage to face the overground. The Federation needs people to push out its frontiers and put down way stations. There's danger in that—in just being out there—and I respect you for putting your life on the line. But just as I wouldn't feel sorry if you were to break your toe stomping on a bug, I am not going to treat you like a hero for killing a bunch of defenseless Mutes."

"What d'you mean, 'defenseless'?" Steve said hotly. "Those lump-heads kill people. Everybody knows what they do to dead Trail-Blazers. They cut their heads, hands and feet off. Plus all the other odds and ends. And if you're captured, they skin you alive, smoke you over a fire to keep you nice and sweet, then eat you slice by slice through the winter. 'Defenseless' . . . huh! They got weapons, Roz. And they know how to use them."

Roz gave a quick laugh. "Come on, Stevie. You

know that's just Trail-Blazer pep talk. Those lump-heads, as you call 'em, don't even know what day it is."

"Okay, I admit they're not too smart. But they aren't as dumb as you make out, either. I don't get it. What are you trying to prove? And what the heck! I mean . . . whose side are you on, anyway?"

Roz sat down on the bunkbed and fisted Steve's shoulder. "Yours, dummy. It's just that . . ." Roz grimaced sadly. "I don't know. It's just that . . . when you get into this business of genetics and you get right down to whatever it is that creates life, you start to think about things. Ask questions. And when you realize just how little we know about how life is created, and the incredible complexity of even the simplest type of cell—just one of billions that go to make up the human body—you can't help feeling that maybe we ought to ask ourselves if we're doing the right thing to send guys like you out to kill off more Mutes."

"But Mutes aren't people, Roz. That's not something I dreamed up. Jack spent years out there. Have you forgotten the stories he used to tell us?"

Roz shook her head and smiled. "Some of them still keep me awake at night." She got up, closed the door, switched on the TV with the aid of the handset, upped the volume, and sat down on the bunkbed.

Steve frowned and pointed to the TV. "Do we have to have that on?"

"Yeah." Roz moved closer to her brother. "Do you wanna hear some music?

Steve leaned back cautiously into the stacked pillows. "What kind?"

"The kind that gives you a real buzz. Blackjack . . . what else?"

"Are you crazy?" Steve hissed. "I wouldn't go within a mile of that junk. Shaft it, Roz. Get rid of it—fast." An alarming thought struck him. He sat up straight. "Where is it? Have you got it with you?"

"Of course not." Roz pushed him back against the pillow. "Relax. There's this guy—"

Steve put his hand to her lips. "I don't want to know about him, or it, or anything. Don't get involved, Roz. You know what the score is. Anyone caught tuning in to that garbage is in big trouble."

Roz smiled. "You could be right. The word is this guy only handles Code One material."

"Keep your voice down," said Steve. "And stop kidding around. It's no joke."

"Have you ever lugged any blackjack?"

"No. And I'm not going to."

Roz smiled. "Because it's against the rules?"

Steve eyed her silently then looked away.

"Have you ever asked yourself *why* it's against the rules?" Roz pulled his chin around, forcing Steve to meet her challenging look.

"You know why we have rules," Steve replied. "It's the only way people can live together." His mouth tightened as she sighed wearily. "Come on . . . that's page one stuff."

"I know what the Manual says. But it's not the *only* way," insisted Roz. "If people are given a set of rules to live by—limits they mustn't overstep—it means there must be a whole different way of living on the *other* side of the line."

"Sure," said Steve. "People tried it a thousand years ago. And what happened? Anarchy, disorder, chaos. The cities burned. The blue-sky world became one great poisonous hell-fire that spawned the Mutes."

"Yeah, I know how the history program runs," Roz whispered. "Something bad must have happened, but none of us knows what, or how bad, it really was. We only know what the First Family's seen fit to tell us. Maybe . . ." She hesitated. "Maybe, in some ways, life was better than it is now."

Steve snorted. "Are you crazy? Without the Jeffersons there would *be* no life! If the First Family hadn't laid down the rules for everyone to follow, the Federation wouldn't exist."

"Yes, but, Steve—"

"Drop it, Roz," hissed Steve. "I don't want to hear any more of this shit."

"Okay, forget it," Roz replied with a sniffy laugh. "Don't worry, I won't do anything to damage your career prospects."

"I was thinking about yours," snapped Steve.

Roz looked unconvinced.

"I'm not kidding," Steve said angrily. And to be fair, at least 20 percent of his concern was temporarily directed toward his sister. He took hold of her hands. "These wild ideas . . . this is renegade talk. You can't go jumping the rails like this once you get to Grand Central. What's gotten into you?"

Roz pursed her lips then tilted her head to one side as she looked down at their clasped hands. "Maybe I need my big brother to look after me."

Their eyes met and held each other fast.

"That can't happen, Roz," said Steve quietly. "I know I'm real bad about getting in touch but . . . I do think about you and . . ."

"How it was when we were in high school together?"

"Sometimes. Things change. People, too."

"I'm people, and nothing's changed." Roz leaned forward and gave him a long, tender kiss on the mouth then sat back with a sigh. "D'you realize after this week we may never see each other again?"

Steve smiled. "That's life, Roz. Crying won't change anything."

"I wasn't about to cry." Roz took a deep breath. "There was something I wanted to tell you." She paused hesitantly. "About us."

"Oh, yeah? What about us?"

"You and I are different. We are, uh . . . we're not like Jack and Annie. Or the others. I feel close to you in ways I can't explain. I don't mean how it was before you went up to the Academy. I mean in ways I don't understand. Haven't you ever felt that?"

Steve felt suddenly apprehensive. "I'm not sure. Give me a for-instance."

Roz tightened her grip on his hands and drew her teeth over her bottom lip. Finally she said, "D'you remember the day before yesterday when you finally woke up and I brought you breakfast?"

"How can I forget?" said Steve. "It was the first time ever in my whole life."

"Be serious," Roz snapped. "You remember later on telling me about going up to Level Ten for your solo flight . . . and how you felt when you saw the overground?" Roz lowered her voice. "Those things you felt inside you? The fear of coming back in?" She saw Steve's eyes widen. "Don't worry, I won't ever tell anyone about that. But do you remember me asking what day and what time it was you made that flight?"

"Yes," whispered Steve.

"And you told me. But you never asked why I wanted to know." Roz fixed her eyes on his. "Do you know why I asked?"

Steve gazed back at her. "Why don't you tell me."

Roz's answer came in a hesitant whisper. "Because I—I *knew* you were up there. I felt everything you felt—when it happened. I felt the same fear of being buried alive when you hesitated before taxiing back under the ramp door. I was in the path lab with the rest of my class. I suddenly cried out. I—I thought the ceiling was going to fall in and crush me. Everyone thought I'd gone crazy. I've never had that kind of feeling in my whole life before."

Steve tried to draw his hands away but Roz held on to him with unsuspected strength. The words came spilling from her lips. "I saw it all, Steve. The red trees, the mountains, the sun shining on the water, the clouds, the waves of white sand. I was up there *with* you."

An unknown terror sent Steve's heart pounding. "Did you try to speak to me through your mind? Was it *your* voice I heard?"

"It may have been. There were other voices, too."

"Yes," he whispered.

"Where do they come from?"

"I don't know," said Steve.

"Why is it happening to us?" Roz whispered urgently. "Why are we different?"

Steve felt giddy. There was a roaring in his ears.

He felt his lips moving; heard a far-off voice saying, "I don't know. I don't know. I don't know." But another part of him knew that the wave of terror that had swept through his body had been generated by the knowledge that the answer to Roz's questions lay locked within his mind. Behind a door that he dared not open. A door that had been locked by others because it concealed a secret that could destroy the Amtrak Federation.

Rising early on the following day, Steve went to the Provo office in New Deal Plaza, where—with the help of a phone call from Bart—he got his movement orders amended to allow him to accompany his kin-sister to Grand Central before reporting to the Trail-Blazer depot at Nixon-Fort Worth. Annie Brickman brought Jack down to the subway to see them off. The shuttle from Phoenix slid to a halt at the platform. Roz and Steve put their trail-bags aboard then turned and embraced their guardians.

"G'bye, Poppa-Jack," said Roz. She planted a kiss on his forehead and ran a hand gently through his hair. Jack's lips moved in response, but no sound came out.

"Good-bye, sir," said Steve. He went down on one knee by the wheelchair and threw an arm around his guard-father. Jack's trembling grip on his other hand suddenly became firm and strong. It was as if the dying man had summoned every last ounce of energy in his exhausted body for the last embrace; the one his ward would remember him by.

"G'bye, Annie." Steve and Roz embraced their guard-mother.

Annie's high cheekbones filled with color, and her usually firm jaw trembled. "Okay, you two—take care of yourselves. And always do what's right. You got that?"

"Don't worry, Annie," said Steve. "You're going to be real proud of us before we're through." He grasped his guard-mother's hand briefly and stepped aboard the shuttle as the air hissed into the rams that closed the sliding doors.

Roz bussed Annie hurriedly on the cheek and stepped inside the door of the compartment. Annie held on to the doors as they slid closed, letting go at the last minute. Roz shouted through the glass. "I'll look in on you tonight!"

Annie nodded, tight-lipped, and waved with both hands as the shuttle carried them away.

The compartment for which Steve and Roz had been issued tickets was only a quarter full. Most of the other passengers slept or watched one of the overhead TV sets, listening to the sound track through earphones plugged into their seats. Saddling the monorail track, and driven by powerful linear induction motors, the shuttle sped eastward through the close-fitting tunnel, whose gray blankness was relieved only by the regular flash of white as the mile marker bands flipped past.

Even though the nearest passenger was four rows away, and there was no possibility of being overheard, neither of them referred to the secrets they had exchanged on the previous day. Lacking any knowledge of telepathy and unaware that the word-concept even existed, Steve and Roz were more than a little frightened of the powers they had unwittingly unleashed—or become prey to. To be "different" in a society whose structure and values were based on a cloying conformity, cooperative group action, and monolithic unity of purpose could, if discovered, lead to undesirable consequences. Deviant behavior—the mark of a potential renegade—was a Code Two default that could lead to arrest and extended treatment, known as "reprogramming."

Neither of them wanted to risk that. Steve knew that Roz had her own plans and dreams for the future; was aware that success lay in jumping, like well-trained dogs, through the approved pattern of hoops. As Bart had said, the system did not make mistakes. Only people made mistakes. It was people who failed, not the system. Trying to buck it only led to trouble and, for persistent offenders, could even prove fatal. Steve was already a master at dissimulation. Indeed, he had understood at a very early age that in a society whose members were constantly encouraged to exhibit in every facet of their lives the Seven Great Qualities of Trackerdom (Honesty, Loyalty, Discipline, Dedication, Courage, Intelligence, and Skill), possession of an eighth quality—duplicity—was vital for anyone planning to claw their way to the top.

Roz was different. For a long time she had actually believed that the Seven Great Qualities, immortalized by the sacrifice of the Minutemen and the Foragers and now said to be enshrined in the First Family, were the guidelines by which everybody should live; that this, in fact, was the way everybody *did* live. But now even she had begun to bend the rules. She was learning. Fast.

Steve and Roz spent three days together going around the capital of the Federation. Everything was much bigger and grander looking than at Roosevelt Field, and even though he had now seen the overground, the sheer size and glittering magnificence of John Wayne Plaza made Steve gasp in wonder. The huge, deeply vaulted central dome—a mile across and half a mile high—opened onto five lofty tunnels, each a mile long, known as vistas. These ran out from the dome to form the points of a star—the symbol of Texas, the Inner State, founder member of the Federation.

The new deeps that were being opened up were different, too. At Roosevelt field, where functionalism was still the keynote, the accommodation units were built around the sides of the shafts; but at Grand Central—at the brand-spanking-new San Jacinto Deep—a huge, free-standing circular tower with staggered clusters of balconies had been built in the middle of a vast shaft whose walls had been carved to form a series of interlinked, landscaped terraces planted with evergreen trees, bushes, and lush foliage.

From the top of this vertical rock garden, water cascaded down over rocks, was gathered in pools, ran in streams, rivulets, and mini-cataracts between mossy banks, splashing and dashing its way down through the greenery into a small horseshoe-shaped lake wrapped around the cobblestone base of the tower. Access to the buildings on Levels Two and Three was via slim, arched walkways.

Steve gazed in open-mouthed wonder at the falling plumes of water that spilled over the cleverly arranged ledges, filling the rock pools which in turn overflowed into others below before making the final plunge over a smooth wall of stone into the foaming edge of the lake at his feet.

Roz started back from the water's edge as she saw several dark, drifting shapes make a sudden movement under the surface. "Steve . . . look! There's something in there!"

"Yes," said Steve. "Fish."

"Fish? Really? That's fantastic." Roz stared into the water as if mesmerized. "Oh, Steve, look at that big dark brown one!"

"Yes," Steve said. "That's a good one to eat."

Roz shuddered. "Uggh! Christopher Columbus! That is really and truly gross, Steve. Makes me feel quite sick."

"I was kidding," said Steve. He took her arm and led her off the bridge. As they walked back along the throughway toward John Wayne Plaza, Steve puzzled over what had prompted him to make such an outlandish remark. Like Roz, he had never eaten, or ever thought of eating, a fish before. In fact, he had only known what the moving shapes were from having seen pictures of fish during an Academy lecture dealing with the main types of overground flora and fauna. Fish had only merited a passing reference; the main point of the lecture had been a review of the dangerous snakes and various other beasts of prey that might be encountered on a Trail-Blazer expedition. Yet as they had stood looking down into the water, he had had the distinct impression that somewhere in the back of his mind was the name of that particular fish, plus the knowledge that under the dark spotted skin, the flesh was pink and tender ... and remarkably tasty when roasted over a wood fire.

Since their minds had not joined on this particular occasion, Steve decided not to say anything to Roz. She was still troubled by the shared sensations of his overground flight for which neither had any explanation. With the start of the grueling three-year medical doctorate course now less than a week away, his fifteen-year-old kin-sister had enough to worry about.

--- 7 ---

When you finally come face-to-face with a wagon train, the thing that hits you first of all is its size. They're enormous. They make the rail-based MX missile trains that provided shelter and transport for the founders of the Amtrak Federation look like those narrow-gauge miniatures that the kids used to ride on in pre-Holocaust amusement parks.

The Lady from Louisiana—which Steve stood gazing up at—was a space-age, multisection, articulated vehicle over *six hundred feet long!* It was believed to be another example of the genius of First Family design engineers, but it was not, in fact, an original concept. It was a direct development of the U.S. Army's experimental overland train prototypes built in the 1960s. The technical specifications and design details had survived the Holocaust because they were stored in the prodigious memory of Columbus, the giant computer that was the guiding intelligence of the Federation; the inexhaustible wellspring of twentieth-century science and technology from which the First Family drew their inspiration.

The Lady consisted of two command/fire control cars standing some thirty-five feet high to the roof of their raised cabs and situated at the head and tail of the wagon train, two power cars, and twelve weapon, cargo, and accommodation cars—all connected by flexible passways. Each forty-foot-long section was mounted on four huge low-pressure tires, twelve feet in diameter and twelve feet wide, capable of traversing most types of terrain. Hydrogen-fueled turbines mounted in the power cars produced electricity for the drive motors attached to each of the sixty-four wheels.

Camouflaged in black, brown, and two shades of red, the wagon train's molded SuperCon shell was lined with lead to provide protection against radiation. Each car had several small shielded periscope ports fitted with armored glass that could be uncovered in an emergency, but under normal conditions external vision was via clusters of remote-controlled TV cameras. Long-range surveillance was provided by a section of ten Skyhawks flown by wingmen like Steve. The train was also equipped with air guns, laser weapons, a variety of other electronic devices, and—for close-quarter defense—invisible, superheated steam jets that could blast human flesh straight off the bone in seconds.

Gus White joined Steve by the side of The Lady. He was still as mad as hell at not having been assigned to Big Red One, but he was doing his best not to show it. "What do you think?"

Steve shook his head in wonderment. "Even though we trained all year on a full-sized mock-up of the launch car and lived inside that simulator for a week, when you finally see it all in one piece it's . . ." Words failed him.

"Big," said Gus.

"You can say that again," Steve agreed. "No wonder the goddamn Mutes head for the hills when they see one of these things coming."

"Yeah." Gus grinned. "They call 'em 'iron snakes.' I can't wait to see their faces when this little ol' snake starts breathing on them with some of that super-heated steam."

Side by side, they wandered along the length of the train, noting the multibarreled weapon turrets mounted on the sides and the roofs of the cars. Squads of engineers were checking out the motors on the huge wheels and testing the movement of power controls.

Gus edged under the wagon train and glanced warily at the evil-looking nozzles on the sloping underside of the car that blasted out the superheated steam. "What a way to go," he muttered. He rejoined Steve and together they walked around one of the huge wheels, inspecting the interlinked slabs of tungsten steel that made up the tread on the massive tire.

"Can't be much fun getting run over, either," Steve observed.

"Hey—you two!" said a flat, hard voice.

Steve and Gus turned to find themselves looking down at a stocky, tight-lipped girl in a blue wingman's jumpsuit. She had dark, closecut hair and a smooth, oval, not unattractive face; the peak of her cap was pulled down over deep-set gray eyes that looked half-closed but missed nothing. She wore the triple red stripes of a section leader on her sleeve. Above her left breast pocket was a pair of golden wings with five gold stars underneath; the printed tag over her right breast pocket identified her as 7571 KAZAN, J.

"Finished your tour of inspection?" asked Kazan, J. in a voice that meant business.

"Yess-surr!" chorused Gus and Steve. They snapped rigidly to attention and saluted with synchronized movements. Kazan's return salute rivaled theirs for zeal and correctness.

As they stared blankly into the middle distance, Kazan read off their name tags and eyed them in turn. "White and Brickman. . . . Ahh, yes . . . the smart ones." She walked a slow circle of inspection around them but could not fault their turnout. "Where's Fazetti and Webber?"

"We haven't seen them, sir," said Steve.

"They weren't around when we booked in," Gus said.

"I'll tell you where they are," said Kazan. "They're in the briefing room where the wagon master is about to deliver his preembarkation address!"

"B-but sir," Gus stammered. "That's scheduled for ten-fifteen hours."

"It's been moved forward thirty minutes," snapped Kazan. "Don't either of you watch the screens?" She pointed to the nearest overhead TV monitor. An announcement about the revised time was being flashed on the screen in sync with the usual red prompt light beneath the console. Ordinarily, there was no way either of them should have missed it.

Steve and Gus stared at the monitor in embarrassment.

"No, obviously not," concluded Kazan. She adopted an air of bitter resignation and shook her head. "Three years at the Academy and all you can do is behave like kids on a junior school tour."

"It won't happen again, sir," Steve said. He allowed himself a brief smile. "I guess we were both kinda bowled over by The Lady."

"Save that pretty-boy charm for barreling Squabs, Brickman," snapped Kazan. "And you can put away those teeth. If I see 'em again, you'll be picking 'em up off the floor. Got that?"

Steve's face became a mask of stone. "Loud and clear, *sirr*!"

"Good." Kazan drew their attention to the diagonal rank stripes on her arm. "See these? They're to remind you of three things." She laid a finger on the top stripe. "First, that I'm your section leader. Second, when I shout, you jump. Third, I don't take any shit—especially from wet-feet. Comprendo?"

"Yess-*surr*!!" chorused the two wingmen.

Kazan dismissed them with a jerk of the head. "Okay. Get your asses over to Block Eighteen."

Steve and Gus gave Kazan another precisely synchronized salute and doubled away. "One of those," muttered Gus as they ran.

Kazan's voice floated after them. "Yeah! One of those!"

The two young wingmen reached Block Eighteen with one minute to spare. They paused outside the door to recover their breath, then walked in to join the crowd of nearly three hundred men and women who were settling down on the rows of chairs. Rick Fazetti leapt up and waved them over to where he and fellow graduate Webber had saved two seats for them.

"We just met our section leader," Gus muttered. He rolled his eyes as he edged past them.

"Did you see she had five stars?" hissed Fazetti.

"Yeah," Steve said. "One for each guy she's eaten alive." Each star, in fact, represented one twelve-month operational tour. One more would earn her a lucky six—a double golden triangle on her lower sleeve—a call from the White House, and lunch with the President-General.

As Steve sat down, Kazan walked in casually and took her place with the other section leaders in the front row.

"How old do you think she is?" said Webber.

Gus White shrugged. "Five tours . . . she must be at least twenty-two."

Steve stared through the rows of crew-cut heads to where Kazan sat with her back to them. "Anyone know what the 'J' stands for?"

"Jodi," Fazetti hissed. "Jodi Kazan."

Okay, Jodi, thought Steve. You want to play it tough. We'll see how tough you are. . . .

There was no doubt about the physical strength of the man who stepped up onto the platform at the front of the briefing room. He was a big, barrel-chested guy with hands big enough to squeeze your head like a lemon. He had a deeply tanned, aggressive face set on a powerful neck, yellow hair cropped close to the scalp, and he was dressed in olive-drab fatigues with one broad, diagonal red stripe on each sleeve and a Stetson bearing the star and bar badge.

The crewmen fell silent as the man positioned himself beside the lectern with his feet apart and his fingers around the ends of a short gold-topped switchstick. It looked like a deluxe version of the canes carried by DIs at the divisional combat schools.

The man surveyed the room. "So. . . we meet again. Mostly the same tired, old faces, I see." He pointed his stick at a nearly baldheaded man sitting a few rows from the front. "Tino's back again without getting his hair cut—"

There was a ripple of laughter from the veteran Trail-Blazers in the room.

"—and the rest of you are still laughing at my tired, old jokes. Keep at it. Flattery'll get you nowhere, but there's no harm in tryin'. However. . . since we have a batch of wet-feet shipping out with us for the first time, maybe I'd better introduce myself." He cast his eyes toward the back of the room and upped the volume a little. "The name is Buck McDonnell—sometimes referred to in the dead of the night as Big D. I'm the Trail-Boss on The Lady. The guy you come to when you've got problems. That's why I've got such wide shoulders. I've had so many people cryin' on 'em."

His speech was punctuated by a hollow laugh from the veteran crewmen.

"Play it by The Book and you'll find me a very understanding guy. Get on the wrong side of me"—he tapped his rank stripe with his switch-stick—"and you're liable to end up with a backful of these." McDonnell paused briefly to allow this threat to sink home. "My main job is to make sure that the orders of the wagon master and his execs are carried out—to the letter. And aided by your section leaders, I am also responsible for on-board discipline. Any wet-foot who thinks he can relax because he's not shipping out on Big Red One had better think again. You won't find a tighter train than The Lady, so keep your noses clean and your wagons trim—"

McDonnell caught a signal from a lineman standing by the door. He snapped his feet together, swept his switch-stick under his left arm, and grasped the gold top between the thumb and palm of his left hand, fingers extended rigidly along the axis of the stick. "Wagon train . . . *ready!*" he boomed.

Everybody jumped to their feet and braced their shoulders as Commander Bill Hartmann, the wagon master, entered the briefing room followed by his ten executive officers. All of them wore chrome yellow, long-peaked command caps and, with the exception of the Flight Operations Exec, olive-drab fatigues.

As they mounted the platform and Hartmann reached the lectern, McDonnell's voice boomed out again. "Wagon tra-a-i-nn . . ."

"Ho!!" chorused the crew. The ground shook as the three hundred men and women thundered to attention and punched their right arm upward in a clenched-fist salute.

McDonnell turned smartly toward Hartmann and brought his right arm up with jackknife precision to the brim of his Stetson. Hartmann's acknowledgment had a touch of CFI Carrol's famous flyswipe about it. Steve felt reassured. He didn't mind drills and the attendant bullshit as long as it was backed up by brains. It was hard to be sure at this distance, but the gray-haired Hartmann exuded an aura of thoughtful intelligence. He was a couple of inches taller than McDonnell, with a lean, square-jawed face whose most arresting feature was a large white mustache. Standing alone, one would have judged him to be well built, but juxtaposed with McDonnell's bull-necked bulk he looked positively anemic.

McDonnell turned to face the crew of The Lady. "Wagon train . . . *easy!*"

The men sat down, backs upright, their faces turned toward Hartmann. His execs formed two staggered lines behind him.

Gus leaned into Steve. "They call him Buffalo Bill," he whispered.

Hartmann laid his peaked cap on the lectern, placed

a pocket video memo pad next to it, ran a hand through his silver-gray hair, and smoothed his mustache. "Good morning, gentlemen." He paused and sized up his audience. "I see we have what looks like a full house, so it's obvious we gave you more than enough home leave. I don't know about you, but after two weeks I start to get the Trail-Blazer blues; after three I'm almost ready to volunteer for PD; and by the end of the fourth week I feel like calling in the bag-men."

There was a murmur of agreement from the audience.

"Fortunately, that's when I usually get the green line from the Tactical Plans Board. Once I get that roll-out date I'm as happy as a wet-foot with a head in each hand. But then"—Hartmann paused and ran his eyes over the first few rows—"you trail-hands have heard all this before. It's the new generation who must be wondering just what the hell I'm talking about."

Hartmann glanced down at his video memo pad, then aimed his voice toward the back half of the room. "I understand we have fifty replacement linemen and four new wingmen shipping out with us on this trip. I will have an opportunity to meet you individually later, so for the moment, I'll just say to you all, 'Welcome aboard.' Even though you've all undergone familiarization training on simulators, you will probably find things a little strange at first. You may know how it all works and where everything's supposed to be, but somehow even the best mock-ups can't duplicate the feel of a real wagon train. They can never re-create the atmosphere, for a start." The Commander's face creased into a smile. "Three hundred horny trailhands generate a lot of static—and it's not the kind that can be simulated electronically."

This got a big laugh from the old 'Blazers.

Hartmann held up his hand. "The same goes for combat drills. You'll find it feels a lot different when you're actually faced with killing—and being killed—for the first time."

"I can't wait," muttered Gus. Steve, too, felt a sense of anticipation. Sitting there surrounded by the rest of the three-hundred-strong crew he could feel an undercurrent of excitement flowing through the room; an electric force passing through their bodies, linking them together. Something that, in older times, had been known as "esprit de corps."

"I can see from your faces," continued Hartmann, "that you'd like to know where we're going. So here's the broad outline. The Lady will load and make fast in the next five days and roll out on the sixth, making a couple of supply runs to way stations in Kansas and Colorado. These first two sorties—which will be load-out/load-back—will provide the new crewmen with an opportunity to shape up under operational conditions. The second phase of our mission is where it gets interesting."

The whole room held its breath as Hartmann paused. Everybody was on the edge of their seats.

"The Lady has been selected to make the first deep-penetration raid into Plainfolk territory. We're going hunting, gentlemen: northward into Nebraska, Wyoming, and South Dakota—"

"Yeee-hh-haaa!!" The old rebel yell came simultaneously from three hundred throats as the crew of The Lady leapt to their feet, faces glowing. Steve, Gus, Fazetti, and Webber stood up with them, their hearts pounding.

Buck McDonnell stepped to the edge of the platform. "Who's for The Lady?!" he boomed.

"We are—*ho!!*" roared the crew. Three hundred right hands punched the air.

"Are we ready and able?!" boomed McDonnell.

"*Yay!!*" roared the crew, punching their right arms up again. "Let's go-go-*go!!*"

Hartmann and his execs responded to the men's cheers with the same exultant clenched-fist salute.

The next five days passed quickly, night blurring into day as the entire crew of The Lady worked round-the-clock shifts: switching weapon cars for unarmed cargo containers and loading them with materiel, stores, and bulk food concentrates for the way stations; filling the overhead and underfloor storage bays of the other cars with ration packs, equipment, ammunition, and other supplies needed by the wagon train; and checking and rechecking the range of onboard functions—communications, environmental, weapon, power, control, and emergency back-up systems.

Apart from their normal role in the above, the particular task of Steve's section was to check the twelve Skyhawks, two of which were reserve airframes, before folding their wings and stowing them in the flight car of The Lady. In addition to the nine wingmen under her command, Jodi Kazan was also in charge of ten ground crew, whose primary task was to help erect, launch, retrieve, stow, and maintain the aircraft.

Like the other graduates from the Academy, Steve had been trained as a ground crewman and flight engineer. He could service, repair, or—if necessary—rebuild an aircraft. In the event of an emergency, he could also function in a number of other categories, including ground-combat duties as a lineman.

Some of the specialist linemen grades also had this multirole capability. And given such a relatively simple aircraft as the Skyhawk, many more Trackers could have been trained as pilots. But learning to fly was not the problem. There was another reason why wingmen rightly regarded themselves, as CFI Carrol had said, as the elite force of the Federation. The thing that separated wingmen from other Trackers was their ability to act *independently* at long range, for days at a time if necessary. The wingmen were the highly disciplined lone wolves; the sole permitted aberration in a tightly regimented society that placed unceasing emphasis on group identity, group effort.

Linemen on Trail-Blazer expeditions were able to function beyond the reassuring confines of the wagon train as members of a combat group, but it should be understood that many of them had a residual fear of the sheer vastness of the overground. Isolated from his unit, or companions, an ordinary lineman started to come apart in a matter of hours. He would undergo progressive disorientation, and if isolated for twenty-four hours or more, his movements would become increasingly lethargic. He would seek cover in a cave, or a hole under a rock, and stay there—unable to move further. Linemen had been found after several days in a completely comatose condition. If not found, they simply died—from exhaustion or starvation. Trail-Blazer records contained reports of men having been found dead from thirst under rocks on the banks of rivers. In other instances, when no cover was available, it had been known for Trackers to bury themselves alive.

The work during the re-embarkation period was organized on a four-hour-on, four-hour-off basis, with each section divided into two work squads to allow specialist maintenance tasks and equipment tests to continue without interruption. The four off-duty hours were known as "stand-down"; the all-too-fleeting moment when crewmen caught up with their personal chores and grabbed some sleep.

It was also the time when Steve and the other wet-feet questioned the old trail-hands about what it was like "up top." Depending on your attitude to things military, it may be sad or reassuring to learn that, despite the Holocaust, soldiers have not changed since time immemorial. Steve and the other young wingmen were treated to the traditional bloodcurdling tales of hand-to-hand combat and the primitive savagery of their wily enemy—the half-idiot, half-magical Mute.

"D'you know what those lump-heads sometimes do if they catch you?" said one grizzled trail-hand, concluding a particularly hair-raising catalog of Mute atrocities.

The eight wet-feet who sat around him, most of them with open mouths, shook their heads silently.

"They carry you on a pole back to their village,

strip you off, and peg you out with your arms and legs apart, then they set this bunch of beavers onto you."

"What's a beaver?" asked Steve.

"A female Mute," the trail-hand said. "You never heard talk of bouncin' beaver?"

"No," said Steve. The others silently shook their heads.

The trail-hand eyed them all and nodded soberly. "I can see you guys have got a lot to learn. Anyway, five or six of these dick-eaters set themselves around you—right? And you're lyin' there lookin' up at these big jaws and big teeth some of 'em have got and you're prayin' that one of 'em's goin' to do you a favor and tear your throat out. But no. You know what they do? They take turns sticking their tongues in your belly button. True as I'm sittin' here, that's what they do. Then bit by bit, two of 'em start work-ing their way up to your shoulders and along your arms and two more work down to your feet. A lick here, a little nibble there. By the time the bottom two are kissin' your kneecaps you start thinking, 'Hey, what the hell? This ain't so bad after all,' and maybe you start to jack up a little."

By this time, his audience was leaning forward with rapt expressions, hanging on every word.

The trail-hand ran his tongue around his lips and continued, his voice growing softer. "That's what they've been waiting for. One of 'em sits on your chest with her ass in your face, and brings you up real good. 'Oh, mother!' you say to yourself. 'How come this ain't in The Book?' That's when the four of 'em grab a hand and a foot and start bitin' off your fingers and toes. And you holler, boy. Oh, Columbus! You hit high C. It hurts, believe me."

The trail-hand raised his hands and extended his fingers. Both the middle fingers had been severed at the second joint and the tips were missing on the third. "That's for openers. Just when you think you can't stand the pain, the one on your chest bares those big teeth and chews your jack off—the way a mountain lion tears the leg off a buffalo. And while she's doing that, another beaver sneaks up behind your head, grabs you by the ears, and sucks your goddamn eyeballs out!''

Steve felt a cold shiver pierce his loins. Gus White, who had been sitting between Fazetti and Webber, went green about the gills, leapt to his feet, and was sick in the corridor outside. The story-teller, a Lucky Six known as Bad News Logan, turned to Steve with a contented grin. "You sure your friend is up to this trip?"

Thinking it over afterward, Steve was inclined to dismiss a large proportion of what he had heard, but he was intrigued by the *sotto voce* tales of Mute magic. Encountering Jodi Kazan when they were both on stand-down a couple of days later, Steve decided to risk asking for her opinion on the subject. To his surprise, he discovered that Kazan's belligerence dropped below boiling point when she was off duty. While she could not be described as friendly, she was, at least, approachable; her manner dry, her conversation laconic. She admitted that "some strange things have been known to happen" but was clearly unwilling to discuss the subject further. When Steve pressed her for details she held out her hand. "Gimme your ID." She got up from the table where they had been drinking java and, using his sensor card, called up the Public Archives on the nearest VDU.

Steve walked over and looked over her shoulder as she scrolled through the index of the historical section. "I've read everything in that," he said.

"Not everything," Kazan said. "There are different levels of access depending on where you are . . . and who you are. Didn't you know that?" She looked up at him. "Obviously not."

"You mean there's data in there that we don't know about?" said Steve, thinking back to what Roz had said. The possibility that more information existed had never occurred to him. A store of hidden knowledge! Kazan's casual announcement of the fact came as a startling revelation. "That's . . . incredible."

Kazan shrugged. "What you don't know you don't miss. You get access to another level when someone in the White House decides you're ready for it. When they do, they mark your card. Upgrade it." She keyed in a seven-digit call-code and brought up the reference she was looking for. She got out of the chair. "Make yourself comfortable."

Steve sat down and studied the printed extract on the screen. It was headed "922-854-6/MUTE MAGIC." "There are a couple of words I haven't come across before."

"Never mind," snapped Kazan. She sat with one leg up on the edge of the table. "Just read it out loud."

Steve took a deep breath and began. "Mute magic. From time to time it is rumored that Mutes possess paranormal . . ."

"Keep going," said Kazan.

"Paranormal powers of communication and the ability to control the forces of nature. This claim can be confidently discounted. Repeated investigations have proved that the temporary tactical successes gained by Mute clans in attacks on wagon trains and way stations are, without exception, due to the incompetence, or the failure of will, of wagon masters and their crews. In every case examined by the Assessors, the attribution of . . . mystical . . . powers to the Mutes has been found to be a device employed by defaulters to rationalize their own failure in the vain hope of avoiding punishment." Steve swiveled around to face Kazan. "The only force to be feared is that of the Federation."

"That's official," she said.

Steve wiped the text, retrieved his ID sensor card, and put it back in its protective wallet. "Yeah, but . . . is it true?"

Kazan's eyes narrowed. "I'll pretend I didn't hear that."

On the sixth day, the depot was crowded with the kinfolk of crewmen from nearby Nixon Field. Harried by Provos, they streamed in orderly fashion across the roads—the long, pillared bays where the wagon trains were housed—and pressed three deep against the crush barrier to watch the crew form up, section by section, alongside The Lady under the gaze of Hartmann and his ten execs.

On the booming command of Buck McDonnell, the crew snapped to attention and the flag-waving crowd fell silent as the familiar, heart-stirring fanfare for the First Family echoed through the depot's loudspeakers. The face of George Washington Jefferson XXXI appeared on the ubiquitous television screens and delivered a short, inspirational address in a firm, well-modulated voice—to which the crew of The Lady and the crowd responded with a thunderous *"Ho!!"*

On the command, "Mount wagons!" the crew climbed quickly aboard and took up their stations. The airtight hatches were locked down; the waving crowd became an electronic image on the train's visicomm system. Up in the saddle—the control center of the lead command car—Hartmann settled in the Commander's chair, called a systems readout, and spoke the eagerly awaited words into the mike. "Wagons *roll!*" The clusters of jumbo-sized turbines whined shrilly up to full revs. Power flowed through the drive motors. The giant steel-clad tires began to turn, easing the camouflaged, serpentine bulk of the wagon train out of its parking bay and past the crowd of flag-waving spectators.

On the screen above him, Steve saw the crowd break up and run alongside; heard them cheering; felt the glow of excitement as the music flooded through the depot and the wagon train; joined in the singing as The Lady from Louisiana began the long haul up the one-in-twelve gradient toward the overground to the echoing strains of the Trail-Blazer anthem, "The Yellow Rose of Texas."

8

Within a few days of the time predicted by Mr. Snow, a posse of Bears returned to the settlement and announced breathlessly that they had seen arrowheads in the sky. They pointed to the south; to that part of the sky where the dark rainclouds and the thunder were stored beyond the rim of the world.

"How far away were you when you saw them?" asked Mr. Snow, when the Bears faced the hastily gathered clan-elders.

"Two days running," said Mack-Truck, the leader of the hunting party.

"Does this mean that the iron snake comes?" Cadillac said. He sat in his appointed place, beside the silver-haired wordsmith. With the exception of those Bears manning the outlying guard posts of the settlement, the rest of the clan were gathered around them.

Mr. Show nodded. "Yes, this is the one predicted by the Sky Voices. The cloud warriors seek the best path for the snake." He paused, then added grimly, "They also seek us."

99

An awed murmur came from the squatting crowd of Mutes.

"Should we not run?" asked Long-Tooth, a clan-elder.

Mr. Snow shook his head. "We cannot outrun the cloud warriors. They can soar over mountains like eagles and can see as far. But we should hide our huts from the sky. We must move the settlement into the forest that lies four bolts north of where we stand."

Plainfolk Mutes did not like forests. They preferred to sleep under open skies. "It will be dark," said a warrior called Hershey-Bar. "I have seen this place. The trees are set close one upon the other and the branches press heavy on our heads. We will not be able to breathe."

"The darkness will hide us," Mr. Snow said. "And it is good that the trees stand close. The iron snake will not be able to enter. It is the fear of the forest voices that puts a tight band around your chest. You must master that fear. Make the tree spirits your friends and the forest will shelter and protect you. And you will soon find you can breathe as easily as on a clear mountain peak."

The clan-elders accepted Mr. Snow's advice. Drawing in the M'Call warriors from the hilltop guard posts, the clan quickly folded their small hide-and-timber huts, wrapped their pots and other possessions into mats made from plaited grass, and loaded everything on trucking poles—a contraption made of saplings and carried on the shoulders of four people like a palanquin. Within a couple of hours, the fifteen-hundred-strong M'Call clan was assembled in two long files with Bears stationed at the head, middle, and tail of the column. Rolling-Stone, the once-great warrior who was now the aging but alert chief elder, gave the order to move; the clan broke into a jog-trot, then opened their stride to assume the loping gait of Mutes on the move. At the rear of the column, Bears dragged branches to cover the tracks made by the two lines of runners.

When the M'Call settlement had been re-established

around a small clearing several hundred yards in from the southern edge of the forest, the clan reassembled, squatting around the clan-elders in their various groups: the warrior Bears, the males over fourteen years old; the She-Wolves, female warriors of the same age group who in times of extreme danger could fight alongside the Bears but whose main role was defense of the settlement; the Cubs, children of both sexes aged from six to fourteen, with their pack leaders; the den mothers, child-bearing women whose offspring were five or under; and the clan-elders, all those over fifty years old. Everybody—apart from the youngest children, who were carried—moved under their own steam, on their own two feet. Anyone over fifty unable to do so was left to die. In Mute parlance, to refer to someone as "legless" meant they were dead, or near death.

Mr. Snow sat to one side of the clan-elders, in case they should wish to consult him. Cadillac sat close behind him. His eyes sought out Clearwater, sitting with her clan-sisters among the She-Wolves.

The subject under discussion was how the clan should react to the imminent arrival of the iron snake on their turf. Iron-Maiden, a clan-elder, was speaking, advocating a hasty retreat. "It is said that the snake's breath turns men to bone. That sharp iron cannot pierce its skin. That it has eyes in its head and tail that can see in the dark, and—"

Motor-Head snorted and leapt to his feet. "Why do you fill our ears with the tales of faint-hearts, old woman?! Those in the south are not Plainfolk. They live under the heel of the sand-burrowers. Let us have no more of their yellow words. The names of their clans are dirt in our mouths!" He spat on the ground, the ritual gesture of defiance.

Mr. Snow held up his hand, staying Iron-Maiden's angry reply. "We should not condemn them. Even though they are not of the Plainfolk, many of our southern brothers fought long and hard with sharp iron—and died with the name of their clan on their lips."

Motor-Head planted his legs astride and folded his heavily muscled arms. "They do not fight as we fight."

"Hey-yah!" chorused the massed warriors.

Mr. Snow smiled. "No one fights like the M'Calls. That is a truth carved on the heart of the world. But those in the south who chose life know the darkness of dishonor. Their hands and feet are tied with iron ropes and they work under whips from sunrise to sundown like the tame buffalo of the Old Time."

"Oyy-yehhh. . . ." The clan groaned in unison, rocking from side to side in the traditional response to bad news.

Rolling-Stone, the chief elder, turned to Mr. Snow. "What do the Sky Voices say?"

Mr. Snow closed his eyes briefly as the gaze of the clan fell upon him. "They say there are two ways to go. We can withdraw into the high hills where the iron snake cannot pursue us, or we can stay and fight on ground of our own choosing. If we head for the hills, we will have to abandon our bread-stalks and the other earth-food we have planted. For if the iron snake reaches this place unchallenged, you can be sure that all we have sown will be destroyed before the Gathering."

"We cannot give up the growing places," said Buffalo-Head. "We need ripe seed to plant in the New Earth."

"Have we none in store?" Cadillac asked.

"A handful," she replied. "The rest has been fouled by the gray dust." Buffalo-Head was the chief among the women charged with organizing the M'Calls' food supply.

"Oyy-yehh. . . ." groaned the clan.

"But if we stay and fight," said Sting-Ray, another elder, "many of our clan-brothers will die."

"That is certain," agreed Mr. Snow.

"But if we move to the hills," Buffalo-Head said, "there will be nothing in our huts when the White Death comes. The Bears will have to raid other settlements. There will be blood on the meat. Our soul-brothers will not let us take the food from their mouths without killing."

This time it was Hawk-Wind who leapt to his feet. "We are not afraid to die," he cried. "But if we are to kiss sharp iron, we should do it over the bodies of sand-burrowers!"

"Hey-*yah!*" roared the warriors.

Cadillac rose. "My brother Bear speaks with the wisdom of a great warrior. We must defend our turf against those who have not laid the hand of friendship upon us, but if we cut down those we have made our soul-brothers, we are no better than the flesh worms that devour the dead. The Plainfolk will become as dust, scattered by the four winds across the empty land."

Mr. Snow nodded approvingly as Cadillac sat down again. "Well said. If this should happen, not even the power of Talisman could bring us together again. Our turf is sacred but we must always remember that the Plainfolk are brothers under the sky. Even those who are dirt in our mouths will one day stand at our side against the sand-burrowers."

"Those are good words," said Rolling-Stone, the chief elder. "Let us hope that day may come."

"But not before we have filled our head-poles!" cried Convoy from the rear of the massed warriors.

"Hey-yah!" replied the warriors, amid peals of laughter.

"You will all chew bone before the moon turns its face away," said Mr. Snow. "And if Mo-Town our Mother does not drink from your life-streams, your poles will be heavy with the heads of sand-burrowers."

"Hey-*yah!*" chorused the Bears.

Rolling-Stone exchanged a worried glance with the other clan-elders. "Is this the counsel of the Sky Voices?"

"The Sky Voices advise caution," replied Mr. Snow. "It will take more than the hot-blooded strength of our Bears to stop the iron snake. Cunning and magic are the weapons we must use."

"But can you still summon the earth-magic?" Long-Tooth asked.

"If Talisman wills it," said Mr. Snow. "But even if he strengthens my hand, many who now sit before us will not hear their fire-songs. This is the year that Mo-Town sits in the Black Tower of Tamla. Her heart is filled with love for the She-Kargo but her throat burns. She thirsts—and when she drinks, many streams will run dry."

"She will also have blood to drink from the necks of sand-burrowers," growled Motor-Head.

"Hey-yah," murmured the warriors, with the same low, throaty growl.

Rolling-Stone held up both hands for silence. "Enough talk. Let those who would head for the hills stand up and be counted!"

Nobody moved.

"The M'Calls have spoken," said Rolling-Stone. "We hold fast to our ground and fight the iron snake!"

Everyone, from the youngest child in Mr. Snow's story circle to the gray-haired elders, leapt to their feet joyously, arms raised, beating the air with their fists. The forest around them seemed to shake with their thunderous roar of assent. "Hey-*yah*! Hey-*yah*! Hey-*yah*!!"

In the evening of the same day, Cadillac knelt at the door of Mr. Snow's hut and asked permission to enter. Mr. Snow told him to come on in. They sat cross-legged, facing each other, on the mat of buffalo-skin. Mr. Snow filled his pipe with rainbow grass, lit it from his fire, puffed contentedly, then passed it to Cadillac. They had shared his pipe for a year now. The rainbow grass gave the things of the world colors that Cadillac had not seen before. Sometimes he saw pictures of a world that was not of the Plainfolk. Perhaps it was the sunset islands; perhaps another world beyond the roof of the sky . . . like the dream world he entered when his body slept. Often, when he drew the smoke from the rainbow grass into his body, his mind seemed to burst out of his head and float among the stars. When that happened, there was a timeless moment of great joy when he seemed to understand all things.

"Speak." Mr. Snow's voice came from a long way away. Like a call from a clan-brother floating on the air from the other side of a valley.

"I would run with the Bears in the battle with the iron snake," said Cadillac.

"Are you out of your mind?" Mr. Snow said.

Cadillac giggled at the question. "The grass gives my head wings but I speak from the heart. I would fight at the side of my clan-brothers."

Mr. Snow waved the smoke away from his face and shook his head vigorously. "No way, my son. The Sky Voices forbid it."

"But I have chewed bone," cried Cadillac. "My brothers have accepted me as a warrior. I have a pole with two heads outside my pad—"

"And Motor-Head has let you wear his hat," concluded Mr. Snow. "Why do you waste breath telling me things that even the hills know? Was your fire-song not sung loudly enough?"

"I was not boasting, Wise One. By talking of these things I hoped to persuade you to—"

"To ignore the Sky Voices?" interjected Mr. Snow. He took the offered pipe and drew smoke into his chest. "Not content with breaking your oath, you seek my help to break it a second time! Did not Clearwater remind you? Why do you now make me waste *my* breath, forcing me to speak to you as if you were like the others with nothing between their ears?! Their heads have no pockets to hold the past. Words trickle through the holes in their minds like water through their fingers. But you. . ." He stabbed the bowl of the pipe toward Cadillac's heart. "You are a wordsmith! Your brain is not a lump of buffalo cheese to be spooned out of your skull before it is stuck on the pole of some roving bonehead! It is a *jewel*—to be treasured, to be guarded night and day!"

"You use strange words," said Cadillac. "Jewel, trea-aured . . . what do these things mean?"

"They are words from the Old Time," Mr. Snow replied. "Jewels were stones dug from the earth and fashioned by those with the High Craft. They were small, like eyes, and glittered as if filled with the light of stars. Others were filled with red, green, and blue fire. Men and women of the Old Time loved them greatly and longed to possess them, for they were things of great beauty. They carried them tied around their necks and around their fingers. It was a sign of great standing."

Cadillac gave a perplexed frown. "They had standing because they carried stones?"

Mr. Snow shrugged. "They had many strange customs then." He paused and stared reflectively at the firelight flickering in the hollowed stone. "Clearwater is a jewel you must treasure."

Cadillac considered this, then nodded slowly. "I think I get the picture. Will you tell me more words from the Old Time?"

"Some other day," said Mr. Snow. "First you must show greater regard for the needs of the clan and less to your own."

"Your words bring me down," Cadillac said.

Mr. Snow smiled. "There is a saying that comes from the Old Time: 'It is hard to fly with eagles when you work with turkeys.' " He drew on the pipe, closing his eyes as he swallowed the smoke. When he opened them, he saw the uncomprehending look on Cadillac's face. "Forget it," he said, offering the pipe to Cadillac. "Let's hit the sky."

The next day, Mr. Snow and Cadillac went back to the plateau and sat amongst the rocks overlooking the plain while a group of clan-women tended the strips where the bread-stalks and the earth-food had been sown. Small posses of Bears watched the sky for arrowheads while pupil and teacher continued the conversation they had begun the night before.

"The M'Calls are a clan that have been favored by the Sky Voices," said Mr. Snow. "Consider this. The D'Vine have no wordsmiths, yet we have two! But my stream will soon run dry. That is why you must never join battle with the sand-burrowers, or challenge the warriors of other clans, why you must never, ever, put the gift of words at risk. You are the guardian of the clan's past and the light of its future. Your brain must serve those who have nothing between the ears. When Buffalo-Head forgets what the seeds of bread-stalks look like and when they should be planted, it is *you* who must remind her. With the help of the Sky Voices, you are their guiding spirit. Since Black-Wing brought you to the door of my hut, I have poured my mind into yours." He tapped Cadillac's forehead. "Nine hundred years of Plainfolk history are stored in that little bone box. You know all that I know—"

"Not everything," said Cadillac quickly.

Mr. Snow waved his hand airily. "What I have not told you, the Sky Voices will. The great secrets of the earth cannot rest in the hot, bubbling brains of young men. They will only enter when the passing years have brought a calmness to your thoughts. When the mind lies open to the sky like the darkly mirrored surface of a deep mountain lake, still and unruffled by the winds of desire. Only then will the great secrets enter, alighting like white waterbirds in the cool of the evening."

His eyes fixed on Cadillac with a sudden intensity. "These are the birds of wisdom. Their wings have the power to move heaven and earth. Be ready to receive them when they come."

"I will be."

"And be patient, also," said Mr. Snow. "These things are not given to all men, even those with such gifts as yours."

"What of Clearwater?"

"Ahh, yes . . ." murmured Mr. Snow. "She, too, has a precious gift that Mo-Town, the great Mother of the Plainfolk, has given into the hands of the M'Calls. As you can never be a true Bear, she can never be a true She-Wolf."

Cadillac frowned. "But she has great power. Is it not the task of a summoner to aid the clan in battle?"

"Yes," Mr. Snow said. "But like you she was born in the shadow of Talisman. The Sky Voices that spoke at her birth told me that she was linked to the Thrice-Gifted One. Just as your life-stream runs alongside hers, both merge with the great river from which Talisman draws his strength. The elders, your clan-brothers and sisters, know this. Know that you are among the Chosen Ones. That is why you have no need of standing. Even though Motor-Head may mock your manhood, he and the other warriors are ready to lay down their lives for you. Every man, woman, and child in this clan is prepared to die to protect you."

Cadillac sat back on his haunches, stunned by this revelation. "I did not know this. Talisman! Is that the truth?"

"I never speak anything else," said Mr. Snow.

"These words are heavy," Cadillac muttered.

Mr. Snow smiled. "You have strong shoulders. You will learn to bear them."

"But . . ." Cadillac wrestled with this new burden. "What must I do?"

Mr. Snow held up his left hand and counted off his fingers. "Listen to the sky. Seek wisdom, not glory. Act prudently. Love your brothers. Be worthy of their sacrifice."

They gazed silently at each other for a moment, then Cadillac nodded toward Mr. Snow's raised little finger.

"And the sixth thing?"

"Go easy on the grass," said Mr. Snow.

When night fell, the moon-glow did not reach the forest floor, and few stars could be seen through the treetops. This enveloping, suffocating darkness was something that the Mutes feared. Perhaps it was a race memory of a distant time when many of their ancestors had been entombed after the War of a Thousand Suns. Whatever the cause, most of the Mutes abandoned the huts they had set up amongst the huge trees and crept to the edge of the forest where they could look up and see the sky. There they slept, wrapped in their furskins, the children snuggled against their blood-mothers, all of them secure in the knowledge that Mo-Town, the Sky-Mother of the She-Kargo, watched over them, shielding them from danger with her star-studded cloak.

Cadillac was one of the few who, like Mr. Snow, did not go to the edge of the forest. He did not fear the whispering, rustling language of the trees, or the sudden shrill cries of the nightbirds. He lay under his skins and watched the wavering patterns of light and dark thrown on the roof of his hut by the firelight. Mr. Snow had told him that in the Old Time people used to sit in huts made of stone that were too heavy to move and had no doors. They sat in these houses day and night and watched pictures of the world outside that they kept in a box. A magic box made of frozen water, that glowed with colors and was filled with the sound of music.

Cadillac's thoughts turned to his duel with Shakatak and his renewed promise to Mr. Snow to avoid risking his life in the coming battle with the iron snake. He had shown he possessed courage that had not failed him even at the point of death, but he could not avoid the knowledge that it was the power summoned by Clearwater that had killed the two D'Vine warriors whose pierced heads now sat on the pole by the door to his hut. Despite everything that Mr. Snow and Clearwater had said, he felt that his manhood was diminished by his enforced noncombatant status. Fate might have set aside a place for him in Plainfolk history, but what Cadillac wanted more than anything was to prove himself a hero.

Not at some indefinite time in the future, but right *now*.

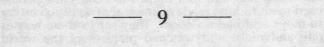

9

Two hundred and fifty miles to the south of the forest in which the M'Calls now lay hidden, The Lady from Louisiana neared the pre-Holocaust state line between Colorado and Wyoming. Catapulted from the wagon train, Steve Brickman soared up into the late afternoon sky followed by Gus White and their section leader, Jodi Kazan. Their task was to scout ahead of The Lady, searching the ground for hostiles before "circling" the wagons for the night. Steve and Gus had flown regular patrols during the two resupply runs, but from here on in they could not afford to make a mistake. The Lady was about to enter Plainfolk territory to begin the eagerly awaited second phase of her mission: hunting Mute.

During their patrol, the three wingmen roved independently in wide sweeps on either side of their allotted course, keeping in contact with each other by radio. Apart from scattered herds of buffalo, deer, and antelope, they saw no movements across the overground. Square mile after square mile of the vast plains that they had half expected to be dotted

110

with fearsome groups of Mutes massing to repel The Lady contained nothing more hostile than bright red buffalo grass. Even so, Steve's sixth sense told him that the seemingly innocent emptiness below was unnatural. He had the distinct impression that the overground—and its denizens—lay crouched like a stalking beast, lying in wait for them.

As they approached the pre-Holocaust site that had borne the name of Cheyenne, the three Skyhawks converged to fly in loose arrowhead formation with Kazan in the lead. She called up The Lady to get a check on its latest position.

The wagon train had been trying to follow the route of the old Interstate 25 highway running from Denver up through Fort Collins in Colorado to Cheyenne and Caspar in Wyoming. On the Navigation Exec's maps, these names were printed in capital letters, but the ground sites were nothing more than uneven hummocks of earth which the prairie grass, scrub, and trees had reclaimed and held for nearly a thousand years. Interstate 25 had long since crumbled into dust, and the wagon train's progress has been slowed considerably by the unchecked eastward expansion of what had once been known as the Roosevelt National Forest.

Steve was constantly amazed by the number of population centers marked on the pre-Holocaust maps they now had access to. If they had all been as densely packed as a Tracker base, or one of the larger way stations, there must at one time have been tens, perhaps *hundreds*, of millions of people living in America. Looking down at the emptiness below the Skyhawk's wheels, Steve found it difficult to imagine it crammed with people; teeming with life. The history videos called it the greatest country in the world. The *only* country in the world.

Since joining the wagon train, he had learned that America lay surrounded by sea on a spinning globe that sailed through space, circling the sun once a year. To someone like Steve, whose horizons up to his overground solo had been limited by the dimensions of a world carved from what was known as the earth-shield, the idea that behind the sky there was even *more* space that went on forever was absolutely mind-blowing. Even though he had now been flying the overground for three months, his mind and body still welcomed each sortie with the same secret, guilty pleasure. He resented the hours he was forced to spend in the confines of the wagon train, but he could not, dare not, share this feeling with his crewmates. They regarded it as a safe haven. A home away from home to which they returned with relief after the awesome vastness that stretched away on all sides.

Jodi Kazan circled overhead while Gus and then Steve lined up on the wagon train and lowered their arrester hooks. Throttling back to twenty miles an hour for the final approach, Gus skimmed along the rear section of the train, engaged the arrester wire, and touched down on the roof decking of the flight car. The plump rear tires flattened under the impact, then the nose wheel hit with its usual jarring thud as the aircraft rolled forward nose down under the braking action of the arrester wire. As Gus cut the motor, five ground crewmen scrambled up from the side platforms, unlocked and folded the wings of the Skyhawk, and went down with it as the front lift section of the flight deck retracted into the car beneath. The Skyhawk was rolled clear and stowed; the lift came up smoothly on cantilevered rams and locked into the deck; the second group of ground crewmen crouched on the side platforms in what were known as the "duckholes," ready to receive Steve. He skimmed along the tail of the wagon train, "landing-on" just ninety seconds after Gus's arrester hook had engaged the wire. Behind him, Jodi Kazan's Skyhawk angled in on the final approach.

The three wingmen went forward to the lead command car for the usual debriefing session with the Flight Operations Exec—a dry-mannered, stubby guy called Baxter. Steve told him he had seen what looked like crop patterns about fifty miles to the northwest of the wagon train's present position. The three of them checked their own maps against the bigger one on the plotting table in the Ops room. Gus's general line of flight had been too far to the east, but Jodi confirmed Steve's report.

The FOE marked the agreed location on The Lady's battle map and reported the find to Commander Hartmann. The wagon master came down to the Ops room with his Navigation Officer, senior Field Commander, and Trail-Boss Buck McDonnell. Hartmann and the two execs took a quick look at the map, noting the contours of the terrain around the position marked by the FOE on the southwestern flank of the Laramie Mountains.

"Did you see any settlements?" asked Hartmann.

"No, sir," Steve said.

Gus also shook his head. "It's hard to spot anything from fifteen hundred feet. If we'd been allowed to go lower . . ." Both wingmen had taken care to stay above the minimum altitude Kazan had given them before beginning the patrol.

Hartmann nodded understandingly. "You'll get your chance to cut grass."

"It can't come soon enough for me, sir," said Gus.

"They're down there," Kazan said. "When Brickman called me up to report those cultivated strips, I went on over and took a closer look."

Steve groaned. "Are you going to tell me that there were huts as well?"

"No, but there had been," said Kazan. She favored him with a tight-lipped smile. "You can see a lot more when you're six feet off the ground." She turned to Hartmann and the execs. "Whoever was there moved out in a hurry. An attempt was made to clear the campsite, but it wasn't good enough. There were dozens of post holes that hadn't been filled in and there was quite a lot of ash and charred firewood scattered around. When southern Mutes move camp they usually bury all that along with the camp refuse. There were also several long-handled wooden tools lying by the side of the crop-fields. In my experience Mutes don't throw tools away. They're too valuable. I think someone failed to cover them up properly." She paused, then added, "Those crops are still being worked."

"So they're still around," said Moore, the senior Field Commander.

Buck McDonnell leaned forward. "Any idea of numbers?"

"Hard to say, sir," Kazan said. "A few hundred, certainly. It was a big settlement. The crop-fields are quite extensive."

"Which is an indication that the clan is a strong one," said Hartmann.

Kazan nodded. "Yes, sir. Those recent intelligence reports indicated we could run into clans able to field a thousand warriors."

Gus White nudged Steve. "More than enough to give everybody a piece of the action."

Kazan tapped the map with her finger. "I have a hunch they could be holed up in these woods." She checked off the distance with the plotting ruler. "Two miles . . ."

"Close enough for them to run for cover when they see us coming," said the FOE. He saw Steve's frown. "Mutes have terrific eyesight," he explained. "They can pick up a Skyhawk at over five miles."

"Which means," said Kazan, "that they're off and running before you get anywhere near them."

"So how do we catch 'em?" Gus asked.

"With great difficulty," said the FOE.

"You've got to draw them out," growled Buck McDonnell. "You've got to lay ground bait. A downed Skyhawk. A patrol that looks like it's lost its way. You sucker them out into the open, get around the back of 'em so they can't run, then you hit 'em hard."

"We may be in luck with this batch," said Kazan. "It's too late in the year to start in with new planting. A few fire-bombs should bring 'em out into the open."

The FOE nodded in agreement. "Right." He turned expectantly to Hartmann.

The wagon master looked carefully at the map and weighed up the options open to him. He didn't take long to reach a decision. "We'll begin a search and destroy operation in the area of Rock River tomorrow morning—starting with a napalm strike on those crop-fields *and* the forest." He turned to Baxter, the Flight Operations Exec. "The attack on both targets will be made simultaneously using all nine aircraft."

Baxter stiffened to attention. "With your permission, sir . . ."

"Yes?" Hartmann said.

. "I'd like to fly one of the reserve aircraft and take part in the attack."

Hartmann eyed Jodi Kazan and saw there was no conflict. "Very well. Five aircraft under Section Leader Kazan will make the attack on the crop-fields. You will lead the others against the forest."

Baxter saluted. "Thank you, sir."

"Sonofabitch! This is it!" crowed Gus. He pummeled Steve's arm.

Buck McDonnell, the Trail-Boss, straightened up from the table and slapped Gus hard across the face. The force of the blow snapped his head sideways and rocked him on his heels. Recovering, he leapt to attention, his swelling lips drained of color. Steve braced himself at the ready.

McDonnell poked the polished gold top of his switch-stick under Gus White's trembling nose. "This is the Operations room of The Lady from Louisiana, Mister—not some third-rate base canteen full of zed-heads! Don't ever let me catch you mouthing off like that again in front of the Commander! D'ya hear me?!" he thundered.

"Loud and clear, *sah!*" cried Gus, in a cracked voice.

As darkness fell, the wagon train turned around on itself, parking nose to tail with its sixteen cars forming a circle. Secure behind The Lady's formidable defenses, the crew pulled down their folding bunks and went to sleep. A small guard detail in the front and rear command cars manned the TV screens linked to the wagon train's electronic sensing devices.

Despite their sophistication, they did not reveal the presence of Mr. Snow and a large posse of M'Call Bears studying the wagon train from the stony ridge of the nearest high ground.

Mr. Snow turned to Motor-Head. "The iron snake sleeps. We will go south. Bring Cadillac."

Motor-Head nodded silently and disappeared into the darkness with eleven of his clan-brothers.

Taking care to avoid high ground, Mr. Snow and the rest of the posse made a wide detour south and then westward until they picked up the trail left by the giant steel-clad tires of the wagon train. They found some cover and squatted patiently until Cadillac arrived with his heavily armed escort.

Mr. Snow took Cadillac by the arm and led him to the trail left by the wagon train. "This is the path of the iron snake. Walk along it and search for a seeing-stone. If you find one the snake has passed over, take it into your mind and tell me what you see."

Cadillac wandered up and down both sets of tracks. Mr. Snow followed at a discreet distance. After sighing heavily several times and throwing up his arms in supplication and to express varying degrees of despair, Cadillac found a seeing-stone. He picked it up and showed it to Mr. Snow.

The stone, which had—as far as Mr. Snow could see—nothing to distinguish it from those around it, was about the size of a baby's head. Mr. Snow examined it reverently. "Is this really ringed with a golden light?"

Cadillac took the stone back. "Don't mock me, Old One."

"I was never more serious," said Mr. Snow. "This is a great power that you have. One that I have longed for all my life. Let us hope that you will master it quickly and become skilled in its use. What knowledge does the stone hold?"

Cadillac knelt on the ground between the tracks. He closed his eyes, cupped the stone in his hands, and placed it against his forehead. After a while he lowered the stone, letting his hands rest against his thighs. "What knowledge do you seek?" he asked in a faraway voice. His eyes opened but they were blind to the outside world.

"I would know the iron snake," said Mr. Snow. "Tell me how it is fashioned. Tell me what lies within its belly."

Cadillac closed his eyes and gripped the stone tightly. "Many things," he said, distantly. "Strange things. I have no words to say what they are."

"Use the words you have," said Mr. Snow. "The Sky Voices will help me see beyond them."

Motor-Head and the posse of M'Call Bears split into two groups, one on each side of the trail, and crouched alertly, their eyes and their other heightened senses probing the enveloping darkness.

Cadillac stood up and retraced his steps up and down the track of the wagon train, the seeing-stone clutched tightly in his hands. Mr. Snow followed. Cadillac stopped and looked upward with unseeing eyes, lips drawn back over his teeth, his face contracted with fear. "The iron snake passes over me. It is full of hate . . . death . . . its belly is full of warriors who thirst for our blood."

"How many warriors?" asked Mr. Snow.

"A great number. They lie in every part of the snake."

"Count them," Mr. Snow ordered.

Cadillac frowned. "It is difficult. I cannot—"

"Don't argue," said Mr. Snow. "Just do it."

Cadillac knelt again and pressed the stone against his forehead. "I can see nothing. The stone is clouded with the blood of our southern brothers."

"Wash it clean and start again," Mr. Snow said patiently. He squatted down beside his pupil.

Cadillac sighed heavily. He lowered the stone and held it level with his waist, gazing at it fixedly. After several minutes of silence, punctuated by sighs of frustration, he said, "The chief warriors sit in the head and the tail of the snake."

"Find me the capo," Mr. Snow said quickly.

"I see him," said Cadillac. "He has pale hair under his nose."

"Fix his face and his soul in your mind," said Mr. Snow. He moved around on his knees until he was facing Cadillac.

"I hold him," Cadillac said.

Mr. Snow reached out and placed his hands on either side of Cadillac's head. "Give him to me. Pass the image of his being into my mind." He closed his eyes and breathed deeply. "Good. Well done." He dropped his hands and gripped Cadillac's shoulders briefly. "You have true power. Read the snake. I would know more."

Cadillac's sightless eyes rolled up under his lids. "The snake has two bellies filled with pipes that roar with hunger and are full of flame. These are also at the head and tail of the snake where the chief warriors live. The sand-burrowers feed gray dirt to the snake. It turns into bad air and is sucked down the pipes through rows of red-hot flashing teeth. These flame-pipes are also its heart. They send power through its veins to make its body work. A power like the white fire from the sky. It gives life to the snake, it makes its eyes see, and turns its great iron feet."

"Wheels," said Mr. Snow. "Probably powered by electric motors."

"I do not know of these things," Cadillac said.

"More words from the Old Time," muttered Mr. Snow. "Don't worry about them. Just keep going."

"The snake has eyes on all sides of its body. Some for looking at things close by, some for far-seeing—like eagles. The sand-burrowers have many boxes of frozen water that show them pictures of what the snake sees." Cadillac paused to decipher a new set of images. "There are both men and women in the snake's belly. The women are like our She-Wolves. They also thirst for our blood. They have . . . strange sharp iron. Things that throw bolts like our crossbows but filled with a great wind. Not bows . . . hollow reeds that spit out bolts like iron rain. At the head and the tail of the snake there is more sharp iron. Things which send out long shafts of sunlight that burn like the white-hot brands at the heart of a fire.''

"Look again," said Mr. Snow. "Do they use these things to make the darkness like day?"

"No," Cadillac replied. "They have no need. They have lanterns that send out red light, which we cannot see but which fills our body and draws our image into their magic picture boxes."

Even though he knew many things of the Old Time, Mr. Snow did not understand Cadillac's attempt to describe the infrared night-scopes carried by The Lady. Undeterred, he kept plugging away until Cadillac had sent his mind's eye into every part of the wagon train and come up with a head count of the crew.

Three hundred sand-burrowers. Mr. Snow considered the problem. The M'Call clan could field over a thousand Bears and She-Wolves. But that combined total would include everyone, from fourteen-year-old fledgling warriors who had not chewed bone to the elders aged fifty and over. The courage of the very young would not compensate for their inexperience, and despite their agility, Rolling-Stone and the other elders would no longer be the equal, in singlehanded combat, of the warriors in the belly of the iron snake.

Pressed for more information, Cadillac described the deadly, invisible breath of the snake that hissed out of holes in its belly, and the strength of its molded concrete skin, impregnable to Mute crossbow bolts. The hatches in the underbelly and sides were sealed from within and protected by the all-devouring breath of the snake. Mr. Snow was forced to admit, as his southern brothers had already found out, that a wagon train was a tough nut to crack.

Cadillac pulled more pictures from the stone. This time of the arrowheads: the twelve Skyhawks, neatly racked with folded wings in the flight compartment; and, in the adjacent car, the ten cloud warriors and their ground crewmen.

"It is strange," said Cadillac. "Their faces are shrouded in darkness. All except one. Him I see. His face and heart are strong, but Death sits on his shoulder. Is he the cloud warrior the Sky Voices prophesied?"

"He may be," Mr. Snow replied. "If you have been shown his face when those of the others around him are hidden, the vision must have some purpose. Mark him well, then break your bond with the seeing-stone and return to the time of this present earth."

Cadillac appeared to make an extra effort of concentration then his head sagged backward. His fingers opened limply; the stone rolled forward over his knees onto the ground. Mr. Snow picked it up and examined it again but could see nothing. He tossed it aside with a frustrated sigh, stood up, and hauled Cadillac to his feet.

Cadillac's eyelids fluttered open. He seemed unable to focus on his surroundings; his legs were like rubber. "What happened?" he gasped, making an unsuccessful attempt to stand upright.

Mr. Snow got his shoulder under Cadillac's left arm and held him around the waist. "You did well. You drew many pictures from the stone."

Cadillac smiled unsteadily. "Truly?"

"Why do you keep asking me that?!" snapped Mr. Snow. "When you were a child, you accepted everything I said without question. Now you believe nothing and you make me repeat myself. At my time of life I don't have time to fill my mouth with empty words."

"I am sorry, Old One."

"And don't start saying 'sorry,'" grumped Mr. Snow. "That's an even bigger waste of time."

"My tongue wanders, Old One. The stone has loosened the bond between my mind and my body."

"It happens," Mr. Snow said. He patted Cadillac on the back. "Take it easy. For the first time out that was a good trip, but you are going to have to work on it."

"What must I do?" asked Cadillac, sagging in Mr. Snow's arms.

"Well, it's no good waking up and asking *me* what

happened," said Mr. Snow. "I may not always be here. *You're* the one who sees the pictures. From now on you're going to have to try and remember them."

"It is difficult," said Cadillac.

"It's never been any other way," Mr. Snow replied.

Motor-Head strode over to them. "It is time to run, Old One. The sun wakes under his gray sleeping furs by the eastern door."

"Okay, let's move," said Mr. Snow. "Can you carry your clan-brother?"

Motor-Head hoisted the unprotesting Cadillac into the air and dumped him over his shoulder like a side of beef.

"The stone has drained his strength," explained Mr. Snow.

Motor-Head snorted disdainfully. "Magic! . . ."

"Don't knock it," Mr. Snow said. "If that Mother in the sky delivers, it may save your gravelly hide."

When Steve and the other wingmen awoke with a tingle of anticipation to the electronic bugle blast at 6:00 A.M. they found that there had been a radical change in the weather. In contrast to the clear, heat-laden skies of the previous weeks, the temperature had dropped sharply overnight. A heavy mist now surrounded the wagon train, cutting visibility to less than thirty yards.

Hartmann unwound The Lady, parked her in a straight line ready to begin the advance north, then called Kazan and the Flight Operations Exec up to the saddle.

"What do you think, gentlemen?"

Jodi Kazan grimaced. "It's not good, sir. I've been up on the flight deck. You can't even see the front and rear command cars from the middle of the train. It's really weird. I've seen mist this thick but never at this time of year. On the other hand—"

"We've never been this far north before," interrupted Baxter.

"Local variation, perhaps?" Hartmann suggested.

You weren't supposed to shrug in response to questions from the wagon master but Kazan let one slip. "It's just possible that it could be some kind of off-beat temperature inversion. But . . ."

"Weather is weather, right?" Hartmann said.

"Right," agreed the FOE. He knew what Hartmann was getting at. Three hundred years of meteorological data had been fed into Columbus since overground operations began. The computer's vast memory bank also contained a pre-Holocaust model of global weather patterns. By observation of the terrain and the prevailing atmospheric conditions it should always be possible by reference to the stored data to come up with a reasonably accurate forecast. Experience told them that heavy morning ground mists at this time of the year usually burned off as the sun's heat built up.

"We'll give it an hour," grunted Hartmann. He told the First Engineer to hold the turbines at tick-over, ordered a half-watch, and put the rest of the crew on make-and-mend. Steve, and the other new wingmen, all of whom had been unable to sleep properly because of the excitement, fretted at the delay. Gus White's face now sported an ugly bruise where McDonnell's backhander had caught him. The old hands in Kazan's section quietly checked their survival equipment. The ground crew tested the operation of the racks fitted to either side of the cockpit that would each carry three canisters of napalm.

An hour later, The Lady was still enveloped in thick mist. Steve and Gus went up onto the flight deck with Jodi Kazan. The air was cold and damp on their faces. There was no sign of the sun. The wagon train was enveloped in a leaden gray nothingness; the camouflaged hull was coated with a thin beaded film of moisture, which ran in dark rivulets down the steeply sloping sides.

Kazan put on her visored crash helmet and ad-. justed the strap under the chin guard so that it fitted comfortably. Wingmen's "bone domes" resembled the helmets worn by pre-Holocaust racing drivers and motorcyclists. All that had been added were earphones, two small mikes inside the chin guard, and an antiradiation air filter. Like the others, she was dressed in black, brown, and red camouflaged flight fatigues and lightweight combat boots.

On the forward section of the deck, her Skyhawk stood hitched to one of the two steam catapults with its engine running. A three-barreled high-velocity .125-caliber air rifle that could be switched from triple volley to full auto hung from the flexible mounting above the cockpit. A ground crewman checked the two racks inside the cockpit filled with 180-round magazines, which Kazan had loaded herself. It was a tradition among wingmen. That way, if you got a jammed round at a vital moment, you had nobody to blame but yourself.

Kazan fastened the neck strap of her helmet. "I'm just going to check how thick this crap is. If it's halfway flyable, we'll put up a forward patrol." She jabbed a finger at Gus. "Tell Booker and Yates to stand by."

Gus snapped to attention. "Yess-*sur!*" He saluted, then leapt off the deck into one of the duck-holes— the balconies built into the sides of the flight car around the access hatches.

Booker and Yates were two of the five wingmen already serving aboard The Lady when Steve and the other wet-feet had joined it at Nixon-Fort Worth.

Kazan caught Steve's questioning look as she turned toward the Skyhawk. "What's bugging you now, Brickman?"

"How will you find your way back?"

Kazan pointed fore and aft. As if in response to her gesture, a pencil-slim shaft of red light shot vertically upward from the roof of the lead command car; a similar beam of green light appeared from the roof of the tail car. "Soft lasers," she explained. "They go up to twenty-five thousand feet. All you have to do in bad weather is head toward 'em and spiral down around till you hit the deck."

"Got it," said Steve.

Half an hour later, Kazan hooked on to The Lady

and reported to Hartmann. The blanket of mist wrapped around the wagon train went up a couple of hundred feet. Above that was a heavy overcast; the cloud base was down to four hundred feet. Kazan had climbed to thirty-five hundred feet before breaking out into clear sky. Climbing higher, she discovered that the area of mist and low cloud extended over a ten-mile radius around the wagon train. Beyond that, the sky was clear and the weather conditions matched those of the previous days.

Hartmann exchanged a loaded look with his chief exec and ordered Kazan to launch a forward patrol. She told the FOE that she would go up with Booker and Yates. Like her, both wingmen had considerable experience with bad-weather operations.

As two more Skyhawks were lifted onto the flight deck, Steve and the other new wingmen listened while Jodi Kazan briefed Booker and Yates. When she'd finished, Steve jumped in with a question that had been bothering him. "I heard one of the guys say that you don't allow wet-feet to fly if the cloud base is below four hundred feet. That still gives us plenty of air space—so how come?"

"It's because of the danger from Mute ground fire," said Jodi. "The field reports from the forward way stations in south Colorado indicate that at least one in ten of the Plainfolk Mutes may be armed with a crossbow. In some clans it may be as high as one in four. That's a lot of sharp iron. One of these days, we're going to find out where they're getting them from. They're too dumb to make 'em on their own. But until we get a lead on that, we stay high— especially you, silver-wings."

"You mean unless the terrain allows us to fly low with an element of surprise," said Steve.

Jodi eyed him narrowly. "What I mean, Brickman, is that you follow orders. If I catch you pulling any stunts, I'll have your ass in a sling. And it'll be *me* that'll put it there. I don't need Big D to keep you guys in line. These Mute crossbows may have a lousy rate of fire, but in the hands of a skilled marksman they're deadly. Don't ask me how they do it but the best of 'em can shoot a barbed ten-inch bolt with pinpoint accuracy up to a range of a thousand feet."

"Is that why we were told not to fly below fifteen hundred?" asked Steve.

"Yeah," Jodi replied. "But don't think you can sit back and enjoy the scenery. One of those bolts is still traveling fast enough to kill you at two thousand feet—if it hits you in the right place."

"Thanks," said Steve. "Shouldn't you have told us this before we set out?"

Jodi grinned as she stepped past him. "I didn't want to spoil your trip."

Kazan's Skyhawk was catapulted into the clammy gray blanket of mist. Booker followed seconds later from the starboard catapult, then Yates's aircraft was rolled forward and locked onto the port ramp as steam hissed through pipes and vents, building up the pressure that would launch him into the air at forty miles an hour.

Watching the screens in the command car, Hartmann saw Yates's Skyhawk lift off and fade into the mist as he passed overhead. The NavComTech manning the radio established contact with Kazan. Hartmann gave the command, "Wagons *roll!*" The Lady moved off in a northwesterly direction past the now-vanished site of Laramie, toward Rock River and Medicine Bow. Like Laramie, they were just names on the map, nothing more than reference points for finding one's bearings.

After traveling fifteen miles, The Lady was still enveloped in dense mist. Kazan, Booker, and Yates, circling at five thousand feet around the line of advance, reported that the pancake-shaped blanket of low cloud and mist had *moved with the wagon train*. The NavComTech acknowledged Kazan's message, routed it through the voice-print converter, and keyed it through to Hartmann's signal screen. The wagon master read the signal and hit the relay button, which put it up on the station screens of the execs positioned around the saddle. Buck McDonnell was the first to swing around and meet his eye. The others were quick to follow.

Hartmann surveyed their tense faces. He knew what they were thinking. "Interesting," he said. "Anyone got an explanation?"

Nobody said anything. Nobody dared. They realized, as Hartmann realized, that there was only *one* explanation for what had happened. The Lady was facing a clan armed with the Mutes' secret weapon— magic. The Mutes' ability to manipulate natural phenomena was something that the Federation refused to acknowledge. Indeed, any public reference to the subject was a punishable offense. Yet everyone facing Hartmann believed that the mysterious summoners *did* exist and were, reportedly, to be found among the Plainfolk.

"Do you want to put up more Skyhawks?" asked the FOE.

Hartmann drew the ends of his mustache in toward his mouth and weighed his reply. "Not yet. I think we ought to wait until the weather improves."

The FOE got the message. So did everyone else.

"Tell Kazan and her two wingmen to circle the edge of the cloud cover and report any movement of hostiles," continued Hartmann. "I have a hunch that someone may be planning to pay us a visit."

Buck McDonnell, the square-shouldered Trail-Boss, straightened up expectantly as Hartmann swung around in his chair.

"Batten down the hatches, Mr. McDonnell. I want everyone in battle order, all weapons cocked and ready. Put ten rounds through each turret."

McDonnell swept his gold-topped stick under his left arm and saluted. "Yess-*sah!*"

Hartmann ordered The Lady forward at a cautious five miles an hour then turned to the exec charged with the organizing of the close-quarter defense of the train. "Pipe steam, Mr. Ford."

The exec activated the system that blasted the invisible jets of superheated steam out of the nozzles in the outer skin of the wagon train, then checked each car, triggering a five-second burst. The lethal shafts shot out some fifteen feet before materializing as a searingly hot cloud that merged quickly with the clinging mist.

Throughout the night, Cadillac had sat by Mr. Snow while the old man prepared himself mentally for the moment when he would attempt to summon up the earth-forces. In the eerie light of predawn, when the watching eyes that studded Mo-Town's dark cloak began to fade, Cadillac had been amazed to see the mist gather around the iron snake and the layer of gray cloud form overhead.

No chilling sound had issued from Mr. Snow's throat as it had from Clearwater. He had simply squatted cross-legged as he often did, hands resting on his knees, face turned to the sky, his sight turned inward. Now and then his breath came in gasps. The sinews of his wiry body tightened, and he clenched his jaw and fists as if trying to contain some inner force that caused his whole body to shudder violently.

Around dawn, he was shaken by a particularly violent spasm that caused his back to arch and finally toppled him over. Cadillac pulled him into a sitting position and cradled his head. After a few minutes, Mr. Snow's eyelids fluttered open.

"Are you all right, Old One?" Cadillac asked anxiously.

"Sure," said Mr. Snow. He breathed deeply. "Clouds are easy."

Jodi Kazan flew at a height of five hundred feet around the ragged, circular edge of the cloud that sat obstinately on top of the wagon train. She altered course constantly, zigzagging from side to side, occasionally turning back into the cloud, emerging at a higher or lower altitude and on a different heading, so that even though she was dangerously low, it was virtually impossible for a Mute crossbow-man to draw a bead on her.

In her skilled hands, the Skyhawk was like a kite

jinking on the end of a line in a stiff breeze. This was where her accumulated combat experience came into play. Maneuvering the aircraft was now totally instinctive in the same way that her body drew in breath without conscious effort on her part. The Skyhawk was as much part of her as the lungs and heart within her chest. All her attention was directed toward the ground, searching it with the sharp-eyed concentration of a bird of prey; the fingers of her right hand curled lightly around the pistol grip of her rifle, ready and able to bring down a running Mute in midmaneuver with the aid of what the First Family weapon designers proudly termed an "auto-ranging laser-powered optical sight," which threw a red aiming dot on the chosen target.

Any wingman who flew in a straight line and took more than ten seconds to line up on his target was liable to find a ten-inch crossbow bolt spoiling his digestion. If they didn't go straight through you, the barbed points made it impossible to pull the bolt out without tearing yourself apart. They had to be cut out, preferably by a field surgeon, and it was said that they were often dipped in some kind of shit that caused a nonfatal wound to turn gangrenous.

Jodi had been shot at during punitive actions against groups of runaways from Mute work camps. Where they got their weapons from was a mystery. There had been unconfirmed reports that small bands of Tracker renegades were involved, but to Jodi such stories did not make sense. With overground radiation levels still dangerously high, why would any foot-loose Trackers waste time setting up a trading operation when they would not survive long enough to enjoy any benefits that might accrue? And what could they possibly hope to gain?

Despite the ruthless pacification of the overground above the Inner and Outer States of the Federation, none of it beyond the guarded perimeters of the work camps and way stations could be regarded as 100 percent "safe." Even though Trail-Blazer expeditions might have killed everything that moved several times over, groups of hostiles kept infiltrating the fire-zones, where, despite the danger, they stayed holed up, waiting for an opportunity to make a sneak attack on a way station or a lightly armed wagon train on a resupply mission.

Acting on an inexplicable hunch, Jodi cut the motor and sideslipped silently out of the low cloud. She was startled to see two large groups of Mutes break from the cover of the tree line. They were moving in the direction of the wagon train. Jodi yanked back on the control column, pulling the Skyhawk into a steep climbing turn. Her one thought was to reach cloud cover. No crossbow bolts followed her into the cold, damp grayness, but that was no guarantee she had not been spotted. Mutes rarely wasted their precious crossbow bolts. The Field Intelligence reports she had read all stressed this point. The bolts were greatly prized and in desperately short supply, like the crude but highly efficient bows that fired them.

Back inside the low layer of cloud, Jodi switched on her motor, flying at the slowest (and quietest) speed she could without losing altitude. She called up Booker and Yates and told them to join her above the northern edge of the cloud bank, then radioed a brief report to The Lady. Hartmann told her to hit the Mutes before they could mount an attack on the wagon train. Hoping that the thick cloud would muffle the noise of her motor, Jodi pushed the throttle wide open and climbed southward through the murk. Breaking out into the clear, brilliant-blue sky above, she made a one-hundred-and-eighty-degree turn, cut the motor again, and glided back toward the advancing Mutes. Below her, away to the left, she saw a tiny arrowhead silhouetted against the white cloud tops. It was Yates, converging on the rendezvous point.

The Skyhawks, with their inflated aerofoil section wings, possessed excellent glide characteristics and, in optimum weather conditions, could soar on a rising current of air, staying aloft for hours without using their motors. Silent soaring flight offered a measure of tactical surprise, but speed and direction were dictated by the prevailing weather, and the thermals were not always where you needed them. It was best suited to long-range, high-altitude patrols. When you were contour flying, hugging every rise and fall in the ground, shooting from the hip, you needed maximum revs and then some. What was known to wingmen as "melting the wires."

As Jodi circled over the northern edge of the pancake cloud covering The Lady, Booker and Yates angled in toward her, the metallic-blue solar-cell fabric atop their wings glinting in the sun. They closed up on her, Booker tucking himself just under her port wing tip, Yates to starboard. They wheeled silently in arrowhead formation, keeping the same precise distance; close enough for Jodi to recognize the smiling faces under the raised visors of their red-and-white lightning-striped crash helmets—the mark of wingmen from The Lady. Both sat strapped into blue cockpit pods slung from rigid struts under the Skyhawk's wing. On the nose of each pod was the red, white, and blue star and bar insignia of the Federation, followed by a white aircraft number.

Flying like this in tight formation, banking through the cool, clear air above the clouds, was something that Jodi never tired of. It gave her a constant charge; awakened feelings inside her that she savored without attempting to analyze or put into words. Like Steve on his first flight, Jodi did not know that she was responding to the beauty of the skyscape, the overground world; an overwhelming sense of freedom. She only knew it felt good.

Almost as good as killing Mutes.

10

With Jodi in the lead, the three Skyhawks flew in a silent descending curve that took them over the line of the Laramie Range. Jodi's intention was to come around behind the advancing Mutes, firing a lethal burst into their unsuspecting backs before slamming the throttle forward and jinking away under full power, returning from different directions at low level to pick off the remainder. In previous actions against the southern Mutes she had found that they were as terrified of "cloud warriors" as they were of the "iron snake" and, if subjected to a determined, vigorous attack, usually turned tail and fled for cover.

Like the execs to whom she had reported, Jodi had not allowed the idea that Mutes might possess magical powers to take root in her mind. The interaction of earth-forces—ground and air temperature, humidity, atmospheric electricity, and the movement of air masses over differing terrain—were part of a logically constructed system of cause and effect that could be recorded, analyzed, and understood. Like Hartmann and his officers, Jodi had found it strange—and slightly unnerving—that the mist and low cloud that had formed overnight around and above the train should still persist several hours after sunrise. And not only persist; actually appear to move *with* the wagon train when it had begun its advance. Jodi was not an expert, but she preferred to think that there was a simple, rational, meteorologically sound explanation for what had occurred.

Back in Nixon-Forth Worth, she had been irritated by Steve Brickman's probing questions about the rumors of so-called Mute magic. Odd things had happened in the past, but when the facts were considered carefully and coolly—as in the incidents investigated by the Assessors—it was clear that most of the things people claimed had happened either hadn't happened at all, or were nothing more than strange coincidences. A haphazard conjunction of events which, in the heat of battle, had seemed extraordinary. What everyone carefully ignored was the fact that many hardened trail-hands stoked up on illicit caches of Mute "rainbow grass." It was a Code One offense, but that did not appear to deter the users from getting blocked out of their skulls—usually before making an overground sortie from the wagon train. Given the hallucinogenic effects of the grass it was not surprising that some trail-hands had weird experiences. And since they could not own up to smoking it, what better than to claim they had been victims of Mute "magic"? The idea, and the lurking fear of it, was a real morale-sapper. It was little wonder that it had been ruthlessly stamped on by the First Family. In the world they had labored unceasingly to create, all was explained and inexorable logic prevailed. Despite the odd, occasional doubt, Jodi had clung stubbornly to the official viewpoint. She refused to consider the possibility that "summoners" really existed. The idea that the Plainfolk clans had people who could manipulate the weather at will was clearly ridiculous.

As this thought passed through her mind, Jodi heard an ominous rumble of thunder. She looked up through the clear-view panel in the wing. The sky was clear. But it had been hot and humid for days. When that happened, you often got a buildup of pressure and static, and then . . .

Jodi checked the movement of the rifle mount and the ease with which she could pull the weapon into her shoulder and take aim, squeezing off imaginary shots on the uncocked trigger at rocks on the slopes of the mountain below. Satisfied, she stretched out her arms and pointed three times at Booker and Yates. They veered away obediently, opening out the formation to fly three wingspans from their section leader. As they assumed their new positions and turned their faces toward her, Jodi raised her right hand and brought it down in a slow chopping motion over the nose of her Skyhawk. It was the signal to go into what was known as a free-firing attack. Jodi brought her dark visor down over the chin piece of her helmet, grasped the pistol grip of her rifle, and pulled the butt into her shoulder. Booker and Yates did the same.

With their propellers windmilling silently behind their backs, they swooped down over the western flank of the Laramie Mountains like three giant birds of prey. The tops of the forest of red trees that carpeted the lower slopes rushed up to meet them.

To the south, The Lady continued to advance cautiously, still blinded by the heavy mist. Unknown to Hartmann, the wagon train had wandered two or three miles off course. What he took to be the eroded remains of Interstate 80, which had once run from Cheyenne, through Laramie and then westward to Rawlins, was actually a dry, shallow river bed. As they followed its winding course northwestward, Hartmann noted that the ground on either side was rising steadily. He made his second mistake of the day in thinking that they were passing through a cutting.

From the hour before dawn when the mist had formed around the wagon train, a small group of

Mutes camouflaged with scrub had been trailing it, sending reports of its progress to Mr. Snow by runners at regular intervals. Mr. Snow knew of Hartmann's navigational error. Indeed, with the knowledge Cadillac had given him, Mr. Snow had reached into Hartmann's mind and had created the confusion that had made the mistake possible and then prevented the wagon master from realizing what he had done. The rumble of thunder that Jodi had heard when she turned west over the mountains had been a trial blast by Mr. Snow, clearing his throat for the big event.

Escorted by ten Bears, Mr. Snow ran, Mute-fashion, some way behind the two large groups that Jodi had spotted. Cadillac and Clearwater had been ordered to stay hidden in the forest with the She-Wolves, the M'Call elders, the den-mothers, and the children. The remaining Bears were moving under cover of the trees to a point nearer the wagon train. This much larger group constituted the clan's strategic reserve and would be committed to the battle as conditions required.

The whole of Mr. Snow's remarkable mind was concentrated on the task he had set himself. He had produced the cloud and sown a degree of confusion in Hartmann's mind, but he was worried about his ability to summon, control, and ultimately survive the immense power he was about to draw from the earth and sky. As a consequence, the soundless volley of rifle fire that mowed down the running warriors around him came as a complete surprise.

A bullet struck him in the head, sending him sprawling to the ground. Miraculously, the needle-pointed round hit a cluster of knuckle-bones threaded on one of the plaited loops of white hair. The force of the impact drove them against his skull, shattering two in the process, and knocking him temporarily senseless. As his body rolled onto its back amidst his wounded and dying escort, he saw the three blue arrowheads flash overhead.

You dumb bastard, he thought. Darkness overcame him.

Jodi and her two wingmen achieved a similar surprise when they caught up with the advance groups lead by Motor-Head and Hawk-Wind. Both were running, on an almost parallel front, in open formation, glancing every now and then at the sky. In their case, however, the operative word was "up." They did not look directly over the ground behind them and thus were caught in mid stride as the three Skyhawks soared into view from a dip in the ground, slammed on full power, and swept through them, wing tips clipping the grass, guns firing right, left, and center.

The stream of bullets from their three-barreled rifles cut a deadly swathe through the mass of startled warriors. For Jodi and her wingmen, there was no heady smell of cordite or blazing barrels—only a harsh, staccato *chu-witt-chu-witt-chu-witt!* that was never heard by the quarry when flying at altitude and was now drowned by the shrill whine of the motors.

The leading wave of Bears, untouched by the attack, turned back, their faces twisted in expressions of incredulity and anger. A volley of crossbow bolts fired from the hip hummed past the Skyhawks as they climbed away, banking in different directions. A couple of bolts passed through Booker's port wing, deflating a section of the aerofoil; a third went through the clear-view panel above his head. Yates's aircraft took a bolt in the nose of the cockpit pod. It punched through the thin metal, passed under his raised legs, and tore a gaping hole in the other side. Yates's stomach went cold at the thought of the screaming pain he had so narrowly avoided. A couple of inches higher and it would have passed through both knees . . . .

Jodi flew through the first volley unscathed. She pressed the transmit button on the control column and spoke to her wingmen. "Stay up, keep moving, start picking them off. I'm going down to roast their fannies."

Booker and Yates wheeled and side-slipped across the sky in unpredictable flight patterns that made them difficult targets to aim at. With a comparatively high rate of fire of one hundred and eighty rounds a minute, they were able to direct an almost continuous rain of nickel-coated lead at the Bears below, and, like all wingmen, they excelled at snap shooting.

Diving away to one side, Jodi banked low behind a line of trees then flew back up the slope at zero feet. The M'Call Bears armed with crossbows were firing at Booker and Yates; the others stood their ground, stabbing the air defiantly with their knife-sticks, or brandishing stone flails, seemingly oblivious of the clan-brothers falling dead around them.

Approaching the battleground, Jodi pulled the control column hard back and over to the right. As her aircraft went into a steep climbing turn she released the three small napalm canisters from the port rack in quick succession, lobbing them over a wide arc. The canisters flew lazily through the air, tumbling end over end, then fell amongst the Mutes, erupting in an explosive burst of flame that spurted forward from the point of impact, engulfing the unwary warriors in their path and sending searing tendrils of flame out on both sides. Motor-Head and his clan-brothers, most of whom had somehow remained untouched by the guns of the circling arrowheads, stared aghast as the ball of flame and thick black smoke rolled toward them. They broke and ran for their lives, with the screams of their brother Bears ringing in their ears.

It was at this moment that Talisman, or the Sky Voices, or whatever power it was that plots the course of the world and the men who serve it, brought Mr. Snow back to his senses and gave him the earth-forces to command. Swept by a terrible premonition of danger, he staggered to his feet; then, as the strength flooded back into his limbs and his mind cleared, he ran forward, down, and up over the rise, reaching the crest in time to see the three napalm canisters burst

among the M'Call Bears, the flame blossom and un-
fold like the black-edged petals of a giant flower,
heavy with the scent of death. A jolting current
galvanized his leg and stomach muscles; made him
gasp for air. He became rooted to the earth as the
forces flowed through him. He flung out his arms,
fists clenched at the sky, and a blood-chilling ululating cry burst from his throat.

The response was almost immediate. A shrill, whistling, rushing sound built up to a frightening crescendo. It was if the whole sky had become the mouth
of a giant sucking in air, then expelling it with terrible force. A mighty wind swept down from the mountains behind Mr. Snow, tearing at the tops of the
trees. It whirled and screamed around his head, then
swept upward, sending Jodi's Skyhawk cartwheeling
across the sky like a kite that has snapped its string.
As she fought desperately to regain control, she heard
a sharp, dry, cracking sound like a felled tree tearing
itself loose from its almost severed trunk. The sky
exploded with a terrifying ear-splitting roar; was filled
with blinding light. As the Skyhawk whirled around,
a searing image burned itself into Jodi's brain like a
night scene suddenly revealed by a photographer's
flashbulb. A great shaft of lightning ripped across the
heavens, divided in two, and struck Booker and Yates.
The split-second horror was slowed by Jodi's brain
into a gruesome slow-motion sequence as the two
Skyhawks burst apart like ripped bags of confetti,
then were immediately engulfed in an explosion of
flame as their load of napalm ignited. Two great
splashes of orange were suddenly smeared across the
blue canvas of the sky, incinerating the pilots and the
falling debris. The bits that remained were scattered
by the driving wind, like flurries of sparks from burning pine branches.

A new blast of wind hit Jodi, this time from the
west, creating a maelstrom of turbulence as it met
the storm-bringer from the east. Clouds built up at a
terrifying rate, and, in what seemed like a matter of
minutes, a towering anvil-head of cumulonimbus rose

to blot out the sun. More lightning forked out of the sky. Jodi quickly pulled the lever that would jettison the three napalm tanks she was still carrying and tried to fly her way out of the bad weather. It was a losing battle; some malevolent force seemed to be drawing her into the heart of the storm.

Down on the ground, the thunder and lightning that had destroyed Booker and Yates and put Kazan in peril had been heard, but the noise had been muted by the multiwalled skin of the wagon train. The persistent layer of mist and low cloud also prevented Hartmann and his execs from being aware of the storm clouds forming over the valley. They did, however, detect the onset of the rain. And it was at about the same time that Hartmann began to take increasing note of the steepening river banks and decided to check their position on the map with the Navigator, Captain Ryder. Hartmann was also worried about the sudden increase in radio static, which had rendered transmissions from Kazan virtually unintelligible.

A few moments' intensive study of the route taken by Interstate 80 showed no match with their present position, and the rapidly growing feeling that they were rolling along a dry river bed was reinforced by the growing stream of water now washing around the bend ahead and between the sets of huge wheels. Hartmann realized that he could quite easily go into reverse. Both command cars had the full range of controls. Like many prehistoric streetcars, the head and tail of the "snake" were interchangeable. Hartmann decided instead to press on. It was, arguably, his third mistake of the day. What he was hoping to find around the next bend was a break in the bank through which The Lady could climb out and get back on course.

The wagon train nosed around the next bend and was met by a shrieking, howling wind that ripped away the mist, replacing it with driving rain that hammered along the length of The Lady like an unending fusillade of bullets. Hartmann pressed forward for another mile. The rain poured down relentlessly; bolts of lightning split the sky, to be greeted almost simultaneously by earth-shaking thunderclaps: a sign that the raging storm was directly overhead. The depth of water rushing beneath the wagon train increased rapidly. It was no longer a stream; it was a river—and one that Hartmann was suddenly anxious to get out of. Rounding another bend, he found the right-hand bank less steep than before. He sent The Lady rolling up it. The tires of the command car skidded wildly. The rain had turned the slope into a mud-slide. This in itself was not an insurmountable problem. As long as there was 25 percent traction, the wagon trains could usually push or pull themselves over most obstacles and out of trouble—rather like a centipede. All wheels, however, have certain limitations, even those designed by the First Family— especially in mud.

Urged on by Hartmann, The Lady angled up the bank, the skidding lead cars pushed by those at the rear. A few yards from firmer ground, the wagon train began to slip sideways. The helmsman turned the wheels, Hartmann called for full power. The huge cleated tires spun wildly, sprayed mud, slipped even farther to the left, then shuddered to a halt as the left front wheel sank into a hole. Hartmann told the helmsman to straighten her up and tried to roll her out using front- and rear-end traction. The offending wheel merely dug itself in deeper, blocked from going forward by something immovable—probably a rock. Hartmann cut the drive to the front-end wheels and tried again. The Lady edged foward a few feet and stopped again. The First Engineer got a red light from the strain gauge on the front left axle.

"We're going to have to back down and take another run at it," he told Hartmann. "Otherwise we're going to tear that wheel off."

Hartmann cursed under his breath and passed control of the steering to Jim Cooper, the deputy wagon master, stationed in the rear command car. Cooper eased The Lady off the slope, ran her two hundred yards downriver, and gave her back to Hartmann. The wagon master was determined to roll her out, mud or no mud. He took her out of the deepening river up on to the shallow slope at the foot of the steep left-hand bank so that he could curve around across the bed of the river to hit the mud slope at a better angle.

And that, although he couldn't really help it, was his fourth mistake of the day. As The Lady moved back across the river with the body of the wagon train angled over on the slope behind him, he and the rest of the crew became aware of a low, rumbling roar that built up rapidly into a thunderous crescendo.

It was a flash flood.

An angry, foaming, twenty-foot-high, mud-colored wall of water crashed against the outside bank of the upriver bend, then careened crazily down toward them, carrying trees and boulders in its wake. The raging torrent exploded against the exposed flanks of the first five cars in a great cloud of spray, then swept over and around them to engulf the rest of the train. Huge trees swept downriver, slamming, like floating battering rams, into the sides of the lead cars with tremendous force, causing branches as thick as a man's body to crumple like matchwood. The Lady reeled under the repeated blows. The lead cars tilted over and stuck at a crazy angle as boulders carried along the river bed by the current became wedged underneath the wheels, held in place by the unbroken branches of the trapped trees. Startled trail-hands in the lead cars picked themselves up off the floor. Buck McDonnell's voice boomed through the train, telling everyone to hold fast and stay at their stations.

Up in the saddle, Hartmann hauled himself upright. The execs around him balanced awkwardly on the sloping floor and ran through the well-rehearsed damage-control procedure. Conditions were verging on the chaotic, but nobody lost their cool.

"We're jammed fast," yelled Barber, the First Engineer. "All wheels are underwater, rear end has only ten percent traction, and we've got a ruptured pass-way between cars five and six!"

"Is that where we've angled over?" Hartmann asked.

"Yessir !"

"Any radiation inflow?"

"Not enough to show on the dial," Barber said. "The hatches on both sides close automatically when the air seal is broken."

Hartmann nodded and put himself on the visicomm circuit to address the crew. "Now hear this. A course error caused by the thick mist we woke up has put us in a dry river bed. What began as bad weather has gotten worse and we've been caught in a flash flood. The Lady has taken some superficial damage and we have lost traction due to a buildup of flood debris. But the worst is over. This storm will soon blow itself out and then we'll get The Lady back on the road. So sit tight and look chipper." He grinned. "This command has never had a wagon train sink under it yet."

His words brought a smile to Steve's face. He looked around him and saw that the tight, strained faces of the other crewmen had also cracked open.

Just as Hartmann finished speaking, the NavCom-Tech picked up a low-strength call from Jodi Kazan sandwiched between several bad bursts of static. "Have attacked Mute ... broken up ... Booker and Yates have gone down ... hit by .. Request ..." There followed the warbling tone of the automatic Mayday distress signal.

The NavComTech responded by switching on the fore and aft navigation lasers. He left the red beam on the lead car pointing vertically upward and put the green on what was known as "sweep and creep." This caused the beam to rock back and forth, quartering the sky, north, south, east, and west, from horizon to horizon, then repeating the same pattern, "creeping" around in a clockwise direction at five-degree intervals. The laser was, in effect, performing a function similar to that of the rotating beam in a pre-Holocaust lighthouse. And if Kazan picked it up—as she was bound to if she was within range—all she had to do was fly down the beam toward the source of the light.

Baxter, the FOE, sounded the alert in the flight car, told the crewmen of Kazan's imminent arrival, and ordered them to prepare for landing-on. Buck McDonnell, who had wriggled through the emergency hatches on either side of the broken passway, passed through the flight car to check that the weapon turrets in the rear cars were correctly manned. He buttonholed Steve and the other wingmen and told them to take their rifles up top to cover the ground crew waiting to receive the incoming Skyhawk. "It's blowing a storm out there, so it may take all of you to hold her down. The guns are in case some Mutes decide to hitch a ride." He passed through to car nine.

Steve hurriedly donned his helmet, took his air carbine out of the rack, checked the magazine and the compressed air bottle under the barrel, packed a few more mags into his breast pockets, and went out through one of the starboard hatches. Inside the cars, the sound of the storm had been muffled. Now he faced its full fury. The wind tore at his clothes, made him gag as he tried to draw breath, and pinned him to the balcony rail. Below, the floodwaters swirled past at breakneck speed, sweeping broken trees and bushes downstream. Ahead, he could see the lead cars of The Lady curved across the torrent, twisted over like the broken wall of a dam. She rocked violently in a burst of spray every time she was struck by another uprooted tree.

Gus tugged at his sleeve. "Here she comes!" he yelled. He pointed across the flight deck.

Steve peered through the rain-swept murk and saw two disembodied lights; the landing lights of Jodi Kazan's Skyhawk. She appeared to be about a hundred yards away on the port side of the wagon train, heading upriver into the teeth of the gale. As she crabbed nearer, Steve was able to make out the aircraft more clearly; its swept-back wings rocked wildly from side to side. Now he could see the red-and-white dot that was Jodi's helmet in the slim cockpit pod undernath.

"She's never going to make it," Steve yelled to the grizzled crew chief, who was crouched on all fours on the deck above him. The wind was gusting from seventy to over ninety miles an hour. What the hell was she going to do? The maximum speed of the Skyhawk was eighty-five miles an hour. Simple arithmetic told him that Jodi was going to end up flying backward. A conventional landing over the rear cars and onto the flight deck was impossible.

Jodi had evidently come to the same conclusion, and, in the few vital seconds when the wind speed slackened, she edged ahead of the wagon train. She evidently planned to drift in sideways at full power, letting the wind carry her back level with the flight deck.

Steve suddenly understood what she was trying to do and was quietly appalled at the prospect. It would mean standing up on the exposed flight deck in the teeth of a howling gale that threatened to blow him off his feet and into the water. It would mean reaching up and literally grabbing her out of the air as she drifted across. The Skyhawk was not heavy—half a dozen guys could easily handle it—and her ground speed would, with luck, be virtually nil. But her motor would be turning at full revs. If they weren't careful, someone was going to be shredded by that goddamn propeller. . . . Steve blotted the gruesome image from his mind and leapt up onto the deck, leaning into the wind beside the crew chief and his men.

"This could be tricky!" yelled the crew chief. He had broken out some lengths of rope and the ground crew stood ready to lash the Skyhawk down. But first they had to pull her out of the air.

Gus White clambered out of the duck-hole and grabbed Steve's arm. Like everyone else, he was drenched to the skin. "Shee-yitt!" he screamed. "She's still loaded with nap!"

Steve stared through the lashing rain at the bucking Skyhawk. One of the containers was still clipped to the starboard rack.

Gus pulled at his arm. "If she hits hard and that goes up! ..." He took a step toward one of the duck-holes.

Steve grabbed the neek of Gus's fatigues and hauled him back. "Stay right here, you yellow bastard!"

Gus tore himself free angrily and stood his ground, stung by Steve's accusation. "Why the hell'd she come back now, anyway?! Why couldn't she have ridden this out and come back when it was all over?!"

There was no time to reply. Jodi Kazan's Skyhawk swept in toward them on a level with the flight deck. When it was about twenty yards away, the wind suddenly slackened. Instantly Jodi cut the motor. She'd obviously thought about that, too. The Skyhawk rocked from side to side, slipped backward, and lifted, putting the three wheels six feet off the deck.

This was it. There was only one bite at this cherry.

Steve, Gus, and the ground crew leapt up and dragged the Skyhawk out of the air. Somehow Steve managed to get his hands over the edge of the cockpit, oblivious of the fact that his left elbow was resting on the racked napalm canister. He hauled downward, adding his full weight to the aircraft. Gus got one arm over the nose. As their heads came level with the edge of the cockpit they saw why Jodi had come back now instead of waiting. Her flight fatigues were soaked in blood that seeped out of a hole above her right breast pocket.

Steve had little more than half a second to register the scene. He glimpsed the barbed point of a crossbow bolt sticking out through the back of her seat. To judge from the angle, it must have come up through the floor between her legs. Jodi's head lolled forward. With the dark visor of her helmet clipped shut it was impossible to tell if she was still alive. . . .

The ground crew struggled to lash the Skyhawk down. A howling, shrieking, demonic blast of wind lifted it off the deck, tore it from their grasp, turned it over, and slammed it upside down against the roof of the car behind. Steve and the others stared horrified and helpless as the wings crumpled under the impact, struts sheared, and the cockpit toppled sideways, crunching like the pendulum of a disintegrating clock into the side of the wagon train. A great burst of orange flame streamed back along the car as the napalm canister exploded; then, an instant later, the wind swept the blazing wreckage into the raging waters.

And she was gone.

"Smokin' lump-shit. . . ." murmured Gus. The wind tore the words from his mouth.

Steve and the other crewmen crouched on the deck in a state of shock at their narrow escape, staring in disbelief at the smoke streaming from the heat-blackened, blistered skin of the next car; the only sign that Jodi Kazan had been there, just seconds before.

"We had her," muttered the kneeling crew chief. He pounded his fist against the flight deck. "We *had* her!"

Overhead the thunder roared for the last time. Steve felt it sounded like a triumphant, faintly mocking finale.

To what his sixth sense told him was merely the overture.

Motor-Head—who was the leader of one of the two groups attacked by Jodi, Booker, and Yates—gathered the scattered survivors and brought them to where Mr. Snow sat. The storm had subsided. The dark clouds that had gathered had been torn apart by the wind, washed white by the rain, and dried by the emerging sun into fluffy, soft-edged shapes that faded into the blue sky as they drifted westward.

The Bears from the other group, under the command of Hawk-Wind, joined them. Many of the warriors had suffered splash burns, some had been burned more extensively. All bore the pain stoically, as was the custom among Mute warriors, but it was clear to

Mr. Snow that several would not survive their silent ordeal. He could do nothing to help them. They needed surgical skills that exceeded those he possessed as the clan's medicine man.

"I need a drink," he whispered painfully.

Motor-Head sent a warrior to fill a skin-bag with water from a nearby stream. The Bears squatted patiently in a half circle before Mr. Snow while the water was brought to him.

Mr. Snow swallowed the bagful without removing it from his lips. He wiped his mouth and throat, then let out a long, world-weary sigh. His head still hurt. He felt the bump gingerly and addressed Motor-Head and Hawk-Wind. "How many of your warriors kissed sharp iron?"

"Four hands plus one," said Motor-Head.

"Six hands," said Hawk-Wind.

Sixty-one dead. It could have been worse, reflected Mr. Snow. If the arrowheads had managed to drop all their fire-eggs . . . It was unfortunate that Cadillac had not found pictures of these things in the seeing-stone.

"Convoy and Brass-Rail, my clan-brothers, fell to the cloud warriors," said Motor-Head. His eyes glistened with tears. While it was not worthy of a warrior to yield to pain, it was perfectly acceptable to express grief. "I would be revenged."

"Now is your chance," said Mr. Snow huskily. His throat felt as if it had been reamed out with red-hot fish hooks. Every bone, every fiber of his lean, hard flesh ached, burned, felt consumed by the power that had passed through him. "The iron snake is trapped in the Now and Then River." He pointed down the slope in the direction of the lower line of trees. Three columns of smoke rose where the grass still burned from Jodi's napalm strike. "The sand-burrowers in its belly must come out to free the snake. That will be the killing time. But you must be wary. They have sharp iron that strikes long blows with the speed of a rattler's tongue. You must be brave but not foolish.

You must hunt them as you would a fast-foot—quietly and with great cunning."

Motor-Head leapt to his feet and crossed his arms angrily. "Sheehh! Are the Bears to hide when their blood runs hot?!"

"Hey-*yahh!*" roared the warriors. Even those with burned faces and raw swollen lips joined in the traditional response.

Mr. Snow rose painfully to his feet, steadied his aching legs, and jabbed a warning finger under Motor-Head's nose. "Listen, numbskull! There is to be no fancy, toe-to-toe knife-work. I didn't just give this my best shot to have you all mown down! This is not a rumble over a piece of turf. We are taking on an iron snake full of sand-burrowers. They don't fight the way we fight. There's no stand-off. They are not going to wait while you spit on the ground." He swept his eyes over the rows of squatting warriors. "The moment they see the end of your nose they are going to try and blow your heads off!" He waved an arm in the air. "The way the cloud warriors struck from the sky! That's the way you must fight today! You must be as brave as Bears, but you must strike like coyotes! We have to wear them down. Pick them off, one by one."

"Heyyy-yaahhh. . . ." The response came as a reluctant growl from the warriors' throats. It was clear that they, like Motor-Head, were not happy at the prospect, but Mr. Snow's authority could not be challenged when expressed in this forthright manner.

"Go . . . quickly!" Mr. Snow ordered. "The river runs dry. And remember: the sand-burrower is not a man, but an animal. You do not fight animals. You hunt them." He stretched his left arm toward them, his hand extended, blessing the path they would take to the river. "Go! May the great Mother guide your arm. And may she drink the blood of our enemies and not from your cups!"

"Hey-yahh!" cried the warriors. They leapt to their feet and shook their weapons at the sky."Hey-yah! Hey-yah! Hey-*yahh!!*"

Mr. Snow watched them lope away toward the trees and the Now and Then River that lay in the valley below. A party of clan-elders summoned by a runner from the settlement's forest hideout joined him, and together they set about the doleful task of dispatching the dying. This was done with the aid of a narcotic shag, the dried shredded fragments of a psychedelic mushroom the Mutes called Dream Cap. Taken onto the tongue and swallowed, Dream Cap quickly induced a state of anesthetized euphoria. When it could be obtained, it was used in the crude bone-setting operations and basic surgery performed by some medicine men. Its purpose here was not primarily to ease the pain of dying but to loosen the bond between the warrior's spirit and his earth-body.

The elders gave the drug a few minutes to take effect; then, aided by Mr. Snow, they killed the hideously burned warriors with a quick knife thrust through the heart.

It fell to Mr. Snow to dispatch Little Feet, a young, fourteen-year-old Bear whose left leg had, in places, been burned through to the bone. He placed his hand on the boy's forehead and put the point of his knife on the slim chest. His hand trembled. His eyes glistened with tears.

Little Feet's drugged eyes fluttered open. He made an effort to focus on Mr. Snow. "Will I go to the High Ground, Old One?"

"Yes," said Mr. Snow. "When the sun goes through the western door, you will walk the golden islands in the sky and when you are rested you will come again to our people as a child of the earth and do mighty things in our name."

"But I have not chewed bone," Little Feet said. "I have no standing."

"In the eyes and the heart of Mo-Town, our great Sky-Mother, you have great standing," said Mr. Snow. "She has told me this. You have braved the fire of the cloud warriors and are truly a great Bear."

"I would have standing in my eyes also," said Little Feet. "Let me die with my hands on sharp iron."

Mr. Snow took the boy's hands and placed them over his own on the handle of the knife. Little Feet gripped his hand and wrist tightly. "Now!" he cried, pulling hard on the knife. "Drink, sweet Mother!"

Mr. Snow thrust the long blade swiftly and cleanly into Little Feet's heart. "Mo-Town drinks," he said quietly. He sat back on his heels and watched the boy's life ebb away. And wished yet again that, with the help of the Sky Voices, he might truly understand why the world was ordered thus.

11

The storm that had swept over the wagon train cleared with the same mysterious rapidity with which it had developed.

Less than an hour after the flaming wreckage of Jodi Kazan's Skyhawk had plunged into the raging floodwaters, the Now and Then River had been reduced to a narrow, ankle-deep stream linking a chain of muddy pools, leaving The Lady from Louisiana high and dry, its lead cars lying tilted across the river bed, trapped amidst a crazy tangle of trees, boulders, and sodden vegetation.

Hartmann, the wagon master, was relieved to see clear skies overhead, but he, like Steve Brickman, sensed that The Lady's ordeal was far from over. He ordered Colonel Moore, the senior Field Commander, to dispatch his linemen to form a defensive perimeter around the wagon train while Stu Barber, the First Engineer, took a party out to inspect the flood damage.

Steve had a word with Ryan, the wingman who had been made acting section leader following the loss of Kazan, then sought out Buck McDonnell and asked permission to take a small party downstream to look for Jodi.

The big Trail-Boss turned him down flat. "She was skewered, roasted, then drowned in mud sauce, mister. Nobody walks away from that. Besides which, we don't waste wingmen on bag jobs. Get back to your post and get ready to fly."

Wearing sealed helmets fitted with armored glass visors, molded face plates, air filters, and two-way radios, and clad in flexible body armor that gave them the fearsome anonymity of warrior ants, the linemen ran down the ramps dropped from the belly of the train and formed quickly into eight-man combat squads. Each man was armed with a three-barreled air rifle and bayonet. Spare magazines, six canister-type flame-grenades, a machete, reserve air bottles, and rations were carried in belt packs and pockets on the chest and thigh.

The force was led by Captain Virgil Clay, the junior Field Commander. They were followed out of the wagon train by Barber, Buck McDonnell, and the twenty-strong damage-control party. Clay, known by his radio call sign "Anvil Two," sent two squads upstream, two downstream, and sent three more squads up each bank to cover the open ground on each side. Aboard The Lady, the rest of the crew manned the weapon turrets, or stood ready to reinforce the groups on the ground, should the perimeter come under attack.

They didn't have long to wait. Ginny Green, the first lineman to clear the mud-slide on the right-hand bank, took a bolt through the chest. The impact of the ten-inch-long missile lifted her clean off her feet. Arms outstretched, her body did a sloppily executed back-flip and hit the ground like a sack of rivets. The seven linemen behind and on either side of her hit the deck, shoved their rifles out in front of them, and peered cautiously over the top of the bank. The first guy to poke his head up got a bolt through the back of his neck.

"Shit!" cursed the squad leader. He ducked below the top of the slide and flipped the transmit switch on his helmet from the squad channel to the Field Commander's. "Anvil Two, this is East Side One. We have struck out twice and are taking fire from both banks. Advise. Over!"

Clay's voice came back through his earphones. "East Side, this is Anvil Two. Mow the lawn. Stand by to jump off. Out."

"Mow the lawn" was lineman jargon for an extended, heavy burst of outgoing fire in which a stream of bullets was pumped into every hummock of grass, every bush, or each piece of scrub in the fan-shaped area that formed a group's immediate front. Anything that could furnish cover for a Mute warrior was riddled with lead.

Stu Barber moved under one of the wagons and spoke to Hartmann via one of the outside TV cameras fitted for that purpose. Buck McDonnell, toting a three-barreled air rifle, stood guard beside him.

"It looks like a real mess," he reported. "But apart from a few dents and that broken passway seal, we don't appear to have suffered any structural damage. The big problem is the debris that's piled up under the wagons. We're not going to be able to move until that's cut away and I reckon it'll take a good six hours. Maybe more. I'm going to need at least a hundred men out here if you want The Lady back on the road by sundown."

Hartmann chewed over his reply. "You've got twenty out there now. I'll give you another forty. If Clay's force is sufficient to contain this attack, I'll release more men later. Mr. McDonnell, will you come aboard and organize the work party?"

"Right away, sir!" McDonnell stepped up to the camera. "Uh, I don't know whether you've noticed, but these river banks are a mite too high for comfort. We don't have a clear horizontal field of fire from the top turrets to back up our perimeter defenses."

"I'm aware of that, Mr. McDonnell," replied Hartmann. "But we are facing an undisciplined, lightly armed enemy. Individually brave and tenacious, but without any overall military organization. I'm sure our men can hold the line until we dig ourselves out."

"Yessir!" McDonnell threw a salute at the camera and hurried aboard. Another screen picked up the Trail-Boss as he ran up the ramp into the wagon train.

A few minutes later, Big D entered the saddle. He was just in time to hear Anvil Two come on the air with the news that they "had hostiles wall to wall." Both up- and downriver sections had reported incoming fire and the men on the east and west banks were pinned down. Five linemen had been hit, three fatally. As yet, no visual contact had been made with the enemy.

"I thought these lump-heads were supposed to stand up and fight," muttered Colonel Moore, the senior Field Commander.

"Maybe we have to stand on their toes first," said Buck McDonnell. He turned to Hartmann. "Our boys have got to storm those banks and break out, sir," he urged. "We mustn't let 'em pin us down in the river while we're trying to move The Lady."

"The thought had occurred to me," Hartmann said dryly. He hit the transmit button. "Anvil Two, this is Lady Lou. Message. Over."

Clay responded instantly. "Anvil Two loud and clear. Over."

Hartmann leaned toward the mike. "Push on, Mr. Clay. I want a secure five-hundred-yard perimeter around The Lady by midday at the latest."

"Anvil Two. Roger. All groups wilco. Out."

Hartmann turned to the Trail-Boss. "Pick forty strong men, Mr. McDonnell."

"I tapped them on the way up here, sir," said the Trail-Boss.

"Okay." Hartmann looked toward the TV image of his engineering exec. "Put them to work with your damage-control party, Stu, and let's get this train back on the road."

Barber reached up to lower the visor of his helmet. He looked distinctly unhappy. "Are you sure you can't spare any more hands? Sixty is nowhere near enough. The more men I have, the sooner—"

Hartmann cut him short. "Just do the best you can, Stu. Put everybody on the rear end. If Coop can take four or six wagons downriver and up onto either bank, it'll give us the firepower we need to cover the spade-work."

"On my way," said Barber.

Hartmann broke the connection with the external monitor screen that Barber was watching and swung back to the Trail-Boss. "Drive 'em hard, Mr. McDonnell."

Urged on by Captain Clay, the combat groups on the river banks charged over the top with their rifles switched to full auto. Several more men went down before both elements reached a stretch of undulating ground that provided some semblance of cover, but as they threw themselves down, Mute warriors leapt out of shallow, grass-covered holes in the ground behind them and attacked them with knife-sticks and stone flails. The hand-to-hand fighting was short, sharp, and bloody. Several linemen fell to the lightning-fast knife-work of the Bears, but in the end the firepower and the disciplined cohesion of the Tracker combat squads triumphed.

The suicidal attacks by small numbers of Mutes on the flank units continued. Harried by a constantly retreating enemy, the linemen were drawn farther and farther from the river bank. Captain Clay, whose own small command group had been trying to coordinate the action while killing its own share of M'Call Bears, was slow to realize that the lead flank elements had overshot the five-hundred-yard-radius perimeter line ordered by Hartmann. Thus, when the main force of Mutes hit and overwhelmed the two eight-man upriver squads and swept down the winding muddy bed toward The Lady, the bulk of his force was spread all over the landscape.

Hartmann and his two Field Commanders had not

fully appreciated the danger of an all-out attack from this direction. The relief they had felt at having weathered the flash flood, combined with their unshakable faith in The Lady's impregnability, had caused them to overlook the fact that with The Lady lying curved across the river bed, only the port-side gun positions of the first five wagons could be brought to bear on an enemy advancing downstream. But of the ten revolving, six-barreled weapons pointing in the right direction, only three possessed their normal field of fire. The movement of the other seven was partially or totally blocked by piled-up flood debris that had also collected around the port-side TV cameras. The other eleven wagons lay in a line downriver, close to the steep lefthand bank and below the level of the ground on either side. And because of the angle at which the front five wagons were tilted over, the guns in the turrets on the wagon roofs could only be depressed to within seven degrees of the horizontal and were, consequently, useless—as was the considerable firepower on the unaffected starboard side.

Reacting with commendable swiftness, Moore led the rest of his combat squads down the ramps in an attempt to hold a line upriver of The Lady. Hartmann called up Clay and told him to fall back to the river banks, where he could support Moore with enfilading fire and cut off the Mutes' line of retreat. Hartmann turned to his execs with an exultant smile. Once that was blocked it would be like shooting fish in a barrel.

Captain Virgil Clay contacted his scattered combat squads on the east and west banks of the river and told them to fall back toward The Lady. The two south-side squads he had sent downstream had been pinned down by fire from hidden crossbow snipers and had then been badly mauled in hand-to-hand combat. Now down to half strength, they had nevertheless achieved a kill ratio of at least fifteen to one. Clay called up The Lady and requested additional firepower to be sent downriver to cover the fallback. The north-side group had earlier signaled that they were under heavy attack and had broken off in midtransmission. Clay had tried repeatedly to renew contact, but his radio messages had remained unanswered.

The M'Call Bears who had overrun and killed the two eight-man squads holding the line upstream did not have time to figure out how the Trackers' "long sharp iron" worked. Without Mr. Snow's help, it was unlikely they could have managed it in a week. To the warriors, the three-barreled air rifles were nothing more than odd-shaped clubs. The machetes, however, were a real prize. The belts and scabbards were quickly stripped from the fallen linemen and clipped around the waists of their proud new owners—of which Motor-Head was one.

The screaming charge down the debris-littered river bed was accompanied by the eerie howling noise made by wind-whips—perforated strips of wood tied to short sticks which, when whirled at great speed, emitted a variety of chilling tones or made harsh, dry, clicking noises like cicadas. To the raw wet-feet in the combat squads, the first sight of the M'Call Bears with their bizarrely clad, striped, and spotted malformed bodies—the legacy of generations of mutant genes—was like a vision of hell. A gut-shriveling eruption of primal savagery allied to mindless brute strength. A seemingly unstoppable threat to everything the Amtrak Federation stood for. The horror was increased, etched deeper upon the psyche, by the sight of the severed heads of their comrades, still encased in their helmets, bobbing on the end of stakes above the advancing throng.

The port-side gunners in the first five wagons swept the river bed as best they could with continuous fire and managed to cut down several dozen Mutes. The merciless hail of bullets failed to stop the advance. Dozens more unscathed warriors jumped unhesitatingly over the fallen bodies and surged forward. As Colonel Moore's linemen emerged confidently from under the train and fanned out, with their weapons at the ready, the running, leaping, screaming wave of

M'Call Bears burst upon them like the flash flood upon the train.

There was a fleeting moment when time stood still, when the brain froze. Then the months of rigorous training, the years of indoctrination from cradle to combat academy came on stream, transmitting red-alert signals to brain, eye, limb, and trigger finger; sending adrenaline surging through the system to line the stomach with steel; flooding the heart with cold, implacable hatred. What the linemen saw then were deranged travesties of humankind; the despoilers of the blue-sky world, whose poisonous presence filled the air with lingering death. Nobody faltered. Nobody flinched. Wet-foot and trail-hand gave vent simultaneously to an exultant rebel yell and charged forward into battle.

"Close the ramps!" yelled Hartmann.

The Systems Engineer responded instantly, sealing the belly of the train. In the whole history of Trail-Blazer operations no Mutes had ever succeeded in boarding a wagon train, but it still remained a nightmarish prospect that filled every wagon master with dread. The trains, and their sterile, air-conditioned interiors, were an extension of the Federation and, as such, were sacrosanct, inviolate.

Deafened by the buzz of chain saws and the noisy clatter of a small, tracked excavator, Barber and the sixty-strong party working under the rear wagons did not hear the chilling battle sounds made by the advancing Mutes. The first warning they had that fighting was about to engulf The Lady was an over-the-shoulder glimpse of Colonel Moore's linemen charging down the ramps of the wagons on either side of the flight section. The next sign that things weren't going too well was the reappearance, on the river bank, of Captain Clay and what was left of his perimeter force. Clay's squads had been obliged to fall back over open ground harassed by sporadic fire coming from both front and rear as Mute crossbowmen positioned behind the main force fired at them from the cover of the river bed. Barber kept levering away at the flood debris clogging the drive motors, but like the rest of his men, he found it difficult to concentrate when it became apparent that the four squads that had doubled downstream were covering the retreat of the force dispatched earlier. His concentration was further diminished when the driver of the excavator was blown out of his seat by a bolt that went in under his right armpit and came out between the collarbone and shoulder blade on the other side. Barber threw down his crowbar, grabbed his rifle, and took cover behind one of the huge, steel-clad wheels. The rest of the damage-control party did likewise.

Buck McDonnell ran under the length of the train to where Barber knelt and drew his attention to the pitched battle he had just left and which was raging less than a hundred yards upriver of the lead wagons. The Trail-Boss pulled the empty magazine from his rifle, threw it aside, clipped in a new one, then checked the reserve air pressure. The short bayonet fixed under the barrel was smeared with fresh blood. "These lump-heads are a bunch of real ballsy guys," he breathed hoarsely.

Barber's fingers flexed nervously around his own rifle. "Is Moore going to be able to hold them?"

Buck McDonnell replied with a grim smile. "If he doesn't, we may end up with stiff necks."

This grisly reference to the Mutes' habit of carrying the severed heads of defeated Trackers on stakes wasn't really the kind of thing the First Engineer wanted to hear.

Looking back downriver, Barber and McDonnell saw Clay's men on either bank launch a counterattack against a Mute force that was hidden from the wagon train by a bend in the river. They saw the orange flash from exploding flame-grenades and the rising plumes of black, oily smoke. Three wounded linemen stumbled back up the muddy river bed toward The Lady. One of them sank to his knees and pitched forward face down in a shallow pool. The Trail-Boss tapped three men and led them downstream, covering them while they picked up the prostrate lineman by the arms and legs and ran him back toward the cover of the train.

As they reached the rear command car, a Mute warrior leapt into view on the right bank, sighting down his crossbow. McDonnell, his reflexes honed by twelve years of overground combat, whirled around and dropped the Mute with a single triple volley. When the wounded had been passed up through an emergency escape hatch into the hands of The Lady's paramedics, McDonnell rejoined Barber in the shadow of one of the huge wheels.

Barber was close to losing his nerve. "This is murder. What are we going to do?"

"Well, these guys shouldn't be sitting here on their asses, that's for sure, growled the Trail-Boss.

"But we can't clear this shit while we're under fire," protested Barber. "It's impossible!"

McDonnell shook his head. "Not impossible. Just difficult. If we can free this tail end back to the flight section, we can roll right over these bastards." He pointed to the small excavator that had run driverless halfway up the steep slope of the right-hand bank before stalling, and slapped Barber on the back. "You drive, I'll ride shotgun."

First Engineer Barber swallowed hard, tightened his grip on his rifle, and doubled across to the excavator with McDonnell on his tail. They climbed aboard, the big Trail-Boss bracing himself behind the driver's seat, rifle at the ready. Barber brought the excavator's motor back to life and reversed down the slope. The tracks churned up the mud as he worked the levers to bring the machine around to face The Lady. It took him a couple of minutes to get his act together, then he lowered the shovel and trundled forward to clear another load of sawed tree sections and boulders.

McDonnell raised his visor as they neared the wagon train and waved vigorously at the linemen crouching underneath. "Okay, come on! Everybody back to work!" he bellowed. "Let's put some life in this Lady!"

Responding to their example, the linemen laid aside their rifles, picked up crowbars, shovels, machetes, and chain saws, and set about clearing the rest of the debris.

Up in the saddle, Hartmann fought a silent battle to clear the mental sludge that had clogged his brain since rising at dawn. He had no doubt about the ultimate outcome of the battle. The Lady would emerge the victor even if she lost most of the linemen now committed to battle. She would triumph because the Mutes did not possess any weapons that could cause her irreparable damage. The crew inside merely had to sit tight and ride out the attack with the aid of the wagon train's own defenses.

"Sitting tight," however, did not form part of the Trail-Blazer's combat philosophy. The most favored posture was one of aggressive pursuit of hostiles, in which the wagon train acted as a mobile firebase, giving close support to its linemen on their overground sorties. Ideally, the combat squads were used to flush out hostiles from unfavorable terrain, like beaters putting up game, and for mopping-up operations. The southern Mutes he had dealt with hitherto usually avoided pitched battles, and whenever a stand had been made he had always been able to bring the fearsome firepower of The Lady to bear.

It was for this reason that Hartmann was unhappy about the jam The Lady was in. The wagon master was convinced that the clan now attacking them possessed a summoner. The storm had been too swift and, like the cloying mist, too localized for it to be part of a larger weather pattern. There was also another disquieting factor. The tactical movement of the Mute warriors showed an unnatural coordination. From the secret talks he had had with other wagon masters, Hartmann knew of only one explanation for this: The Lady's attackers were being controlled by an over-mind—the mark of the highest-known grade of summoner. If so, he was facing an intelligent and highly dangerous opponent able to summon up immense and totally unpredictable forces.

It was this last thought that prompted Hartmann to order the Skyhawks to make the planned attack on the Mute crop-fields and forest hideout. The dawn raid, delayed by the weather, would create a diversion that would sap the morale of the attacking Mutes and might even cause them to break off the engagement, giving Hartmann's men a much-needed breathing space in which to right the battered wagon train. There was the further possibility that the attack might incinerate the summoner who was orchestrating the movement of the Mutes and was responsible for The Lady's present perilous condition.

The klaxon sounded in the two wagons that made up the flight section. Everybody turned toward the nearest overhead TV monitor. The head and shoulders of Baxter, the Flight Operations Exec, appeared on the screen. "Ryan?"

The senior wingman, who was now acting section leader, hit the button that put him on camera. "Sir!"

"Okay, hear this," Baxter said. "We have a green on the strike planned for this morning. Prepare to launch eight aircraft. You will lead the first group—consisting of Caulfield, Naylor, and Webber—against the forest. I will lead the other group and fire the crop-fields. Get Murray to rig and load one of the spare 'hawks for me."

Murray was the grizzled crew chief. He nodded and indicated to Ryan that it would be no problem.

"I want the first plane off the ramp in fifteen," concluded Baxter.

"Loud and clear, *sir!*" Ryan snapped.

The flight section erupted into a controlled flurry of activity. Ground crewmen hurried to ready the aircraft for lifting onto the flight deck; the crew chief ordered a detail to prepare a Skyhawk for Baxter, then called up the rear power car and asked for steam to power the catapults. Steve and the other wingmen grabbed their helmets, made sure the folded maps in the clear pockets on their thighs showed the correct section of terrain, and checked that their holstered air pistols were secure, their combat knives were firmly clipped in their scabbards on the outside of the right calf, and the zips on leg and chest pockets holding emergency water filters and survival rations were properly closed.

Ryan called them to attention. "Okay. Webber, Caulfield, you're numbers one and two to go. I'll follow, with Naylor on my tail." He turned to Steve, Gus White, and Fazetti. "Baxter will give you the lineup. Meantime, I want you and as many guys as Murray can spare up in those duck-holes ready to pump lead. This could be tricky."

It was. Webber and Caulfield were both hit in quick succession as their Skyhawks sat poised on the catapult ramps. Oblivious of the danger from the hidden Mute marksmen, Steve and fellow-graduate Fazetti leapt up onto the flight deck and aimed repeated volleys of fire up over the river banks while Murray and three of his ground crew freed the two pilots from their safety harnesses and lifted them out of the cockpit pods. The seventeen-year-old Webber had been killed outright. Caulfield was not so fortunate. A bolt had entered the side of his helmet just behind his left eye, driving the barbed point through his head and out through the matching spot on the other side. When the crew chief lifted Caulfield's visor to check if he was still alive, Steve glimpsed the full horror of what had happened. The shock wave generated by the bolt's impact had blown his eyeballs out of their sockets. While the battle raged around them, Caulfield sat, silent and uncomprehending, his grotesquely dislocated face streaked with blood. It was only when the ground crewmen attempted to move him that he began to kick and scream.

Steve helped hold Caulfield down while the crew chief tied his arms and legs together, then lowered him over the side to Gus White and the three medics sharing his duck-hole. "Get him to the Surgeon-Captain," shouted Murray. He returned dragging Webber's limp body. "And put this one in a bag."

Undeterred, Ryan climbed into the cockpit of Webber's Skyhawk and quickly satisfied himself that the controls were undamaged. Naylor, the remaining wingman in the first wave, tried to restart Caulfield's plane but failed. One of the ground crew found a vital lead that had been severed by a second bolt.

Naylor jumped out and helped pull the disabled aircraft off the catapult. "It's good to know they miss now and then!" he said, with a quick, edgy laugh.

Crouched on the deck to Ryan's right, Murray signaled him to wind the motor up to full power and swept his arm forward as the catapult was released. The Skyhawk soared into the air, climbed steeply to the right, rolled on its back at about two hundred feet, and went into a corkscrew dive. The sickening crunch of Ryan hitting the ground was obliterated by a muffled boom as his load of napalm exploded. Steve and the other people on the flight deck winced with horror but watched with morbid fascination as a searing burst of brilliant-orange fire ballooned outward from the point of impact, then rolled in on itself and lifted to become a mushroom cloud of black smoke, leaving the mangled carcass of the Skyhawk silhouetted in the middle of a circle of blazing grass.

Steve made an effort to swallow but his throat was dry. He was not squeamish at the sight of blood or ruptured flesh, and was confident of his ability to kill when the time came, but he could still not get used to the frightening rapidity with which someone like Ryan—a living, thinking human being, who had been there talking to him only moments before—could be transformed into an unrecognizable lump of charred meat. Jodi, Booker, Yates, Webber, and now Ryan. He recalled, with a flash of anger, his sister's words back at Roosevelt Field: "Don't start telling me how dangerous it is to be out there fighting Mutes." Roz should be here now, prizing what was left of Ryan out of the smoldering, twisted cage of struts up there on the river bank. She would realize that Trail-Blazer expeditions were not the "cakewalk" she had claimed them to be.

Hartmann, who had seen the slaughter on the flight deck and Ryan's death dive on the battery of screens in the saddle, quickly decided that to have three wingmen taken out of the air in under five minutes was an unacceptable loss rate. He put himself on the visicomm system and faced up with Baxter. "Put the air strike on 'hold' and call everybody in off the flight deck. We're going to try and break up this attack another way. Stand by to launch two and two. You're to stay on the ground. With the kind of luck we've had so far today I'm not prepared to risk the whole of my air force."

Baxter acknowledged the revised orders and halted the lift, taking Naylor's Skyhawk up to the flight deck. Naylor, who was already seated in the cockpit, steeled for his turn at Russian roulette on the catapult, unstrapped himself, and jumped out with evident relief. Baxter felt relieved, too. Like all pilots, he was prepared to face death in the air, on a mission; that was the constant risk all fliers faced. But nobody wanted to get himself killed sitting in a grounded aircraft. That was about as useless as a sailor tripping over the bathroom mat and drowning with his head jammed down the john.

Hartmann radioed Colonel Moore and told him to fall back with his men toward The Lady and form a new defense line beyond the five wagons jammed across the river bed.

"Anvil One, all groups wilco, out," said Moore. He understood immediately what Hartmann intended to do and hoped like hell that he would wait until his loyal Field Commander had gotten clear.

The wagon master then contacted Captain Clay and ordered him to pull his squads out of the main engagement so that he could reinforce and hold the downstream line. Finally Hartmann managed to get Barber in front of one of the external cameras and told him what was about to happen. "How's it going?" he asked.

Barber sounded exhausted. "The three tail cars are clear."

"That's not enough, Stu," Hartmann snapped. "I asked for six."

"We're doing the best we can," replied the harassed First Engineer. "I've got eight dead, another fifteen men wounded, and—"

Hartmann interrupted him. "Stu, I don't need statistics, what I need are results, okay? Just do it."

Clay's voice came over the speakers. "Anvil Two downstream and holding."

"Roger, Anvil Two," said Hartmann. "Just grind them down. No pursuit, over."

Clay came back on the air. "Anvil Two. Don't worry, Lady Lou. I wasn't planning on going anywhere. Too out of breath."

His words broke the tension in the saddle and brought grins to the faces of the execs.

"Stand by on one to eight, Mr. Ford," said Hartmann.

The Second Systems Engineer activated a bank of switches on his control panel and checked the readouts. "Head on eight."

Hartmann's throad felt constricted. "Put in the CQ's, please."

The fingers of the VisiComTech flicked nimbly over the line of switches, giving Hartmann a comprehensive picture of the underside of the train and the ground on either side of it. The wagon master and his execs could see Moore's combat squads falling back, locked in a running fight with the hordes of Mutes. Downstream, under the rear wagons, the damage-control party worked feverishly to clear the remaining debris. Hartmann recognized the broad-shouldered figure of the Trail-Boss perched behind the driver's seat of the excavator that Barber was now handling with confident ease.

"Anvil One moving back under the train."

Hartmann watched tensely as Colonel Moore and his four-man command group appeared on screen, firing from shoulder and hip as they passed under the lead wagons. The linemen followed in waves, each turning to cover the retreat of the one behind. Their passage under the train was not as smooth as Hartmann had hoped. With the Mutes hard on their heels, the battle continued as they struggled through the piled-up debris—a primeval swamp landscape of tangled branches and shattered tree trunks, clogged with mud and festooned with long sheaves of sodden grass interlaced with limp foliage; a grotesque web woven by a giant drunken spider, which trapped and hindered and which, as Tracker and Mute shot, hacked, stabbed, and killed one another, quickly became a Dante-esque vision of hell.

Hartmann waited a few moments more until the bulk of the Trackers had fought their way clear of the lead wagons. Several screens went blank as M'Call warriors smashed the external cameras with their stone flails. The remaining screens were filled with Mutes. "We'll try one to six, bottom line port and starboard, Mr. Ford," Hartmann said in a matter-of-fact voice.

"Head on six, bottom line," replied the Systems Exec.

"Pipe steam!"

The sound pierced the layers of lead, heat, and sound insulation that lined the molded shells of the wagons, and for those outside it was far more terrifying than the weird noises made by the Mute wind-whips. It was a chill, shrill, ear-piercing shriek. A hideous, ball-shriveling banshee wail that drilled into the brain, froze the heart. Invisible, laser-thin jets of high-pressure steam shot from the rows of nozzles along the curving undersides of the lead wagons, cutting through the air at supersonic speed with the keenness of a surgeon's scalpel and the irresistible, tearing force of a buzz saw.

The impact of the steam jets upon the Mute warriors surpassed the horror evoked by Dante and indelibly engraved by Doré. Caught completely unawares, locked in hand-to-hand combat with the last, unlucky linemen, and with escape hampered by the debris in which they found themselves entangled, a great mass of Mutes were blown apart. Skin, flesh, muscle were shredded, blasted from the bone; limbs were severed; bodies cut in half, their contents splattered in all directions; blood spurted onto some of the watching camera lenses, throwing a red curtain over the carnage.

Even those who escaped the pulverizing impact of this unseen fury were not totally spared. As the scything jets cooled to the point of visibility, the survivors were enveloped in clouds of scalding, blinding, blistering steam. The rear ranks of the M'Call Bears wavered, then turned on their heels and fled; those warriors who had been scarred by the breath of the snake but were still on their feet ran, stumbled, or tried to drag themselves to safety. Most were cut down by Colonel Moore's men and The Lady's gunners.

"Clear the screens," said Hartmann. He covered his face and pressed his fingertips against his closed eyes in a vain effort to wipe the bloodstained images from his retina. His fingers could not reach deep enough. What he had witnessed had already imprinted itself on his brain, had become another gruesome page in his own private war diary that would haunt his mind's eye in the darkness when sleep eluded him. He composed himself and addressed the Systems Exec. "Cap the line, Mr. Ford."

The Second Systems Engineer shut down the jets. "One to six, capped."

Hartmann called up Clay. "Lady Lou to Anvil Two. Report combat sit, over."

"Anvil Two. Remaining hostiles withdrawing northeastward under fire, over."

Colonel Moore came on the air. "Anvil One to Lady Lou. It's all over. They're on the run." His voice was shaky but exultant.

"Roger, Anvil One. Hold your position." Hartmann suddenly felt weighed down by the responsibility he carried as wagon master; yet, at the same time, he was also sharply aware of the advantages of his position. He had been able to wipe the horror from the screens, but there was no escape for his men out there on the ground. They had fought and died, had been subjected to the gruesome spectacle of a couple of hundred Mutes being turned into boiled mince right under their noses and were now faced with having to clean up the resulting mess before The Lady could get underway.

Hartmann put himself through to the flight section and faced up with his FOE. "How many 'hawks can we put up, Mr. Baxter?"

"Four, sir. Naylor, and three silvers. Brickman, Fazetti, and White."

Hartmann hesitated. "This'll be their first real operation. Will they be able to handle it? I mean, after what's happened?"

"They can't wait to go, sir," said Baxter.

"Okay. Launch the air strike." Hartmann cleared the screen and called up Lt. Commander Cooper, the deputy wagon master, stationed in the rear command car. "Mind the store, Coop. I'm going outside."

12

The four remaining wingmen climbed into their cockpit pods with expressions of grim determination and were lifted up onto the flight deck, where the ground crew unfolded the wings, locked them into place, and ran the aircraft in pairs onto the port and starboard catapults. Once they were hooked onto the slings, the catapult booms were cranked up fifteen degrees before hurling the Skyhawks into the air at a speed of forty miles an hour. Naylor led Fazette off the deck and set course for the forest; Steve Brickman followed Gus White toward the crop-fields.

Baxter watched them disappear with mixed feelings. In terms of casualties, it had been a catastrophic day. In previous operations against the southern Mutes, they had never lost more than two or three wingmen per six-month tour. Even if those now in the air returned safely, The Lady would have to make for one of the frontier way stations to off-load the wounded and await the arrival of reinforcements. Baxter wondered how the result of The Lady's first engagement with the Plainfolk would be received in

Grand Central. The Amtrak Executive showed little sympathy toward wagon masters who put their trains in jeopardy; costly tactical errors and failures in lead-ership were dealt with harshly. And it was not only wagon masters whose lives were at stake. If a team of Assessors came on board, nobody was safe. *Everybody's* performance was evaluated. Right down the line.

The scarred, defeated M'Call Bears straggled back over the hilly ground to the east of the Now and Then River. Reaching the comparative safety of the tree line beyond a steep escarpment, they flung themselves down in the shade. Some drank thirstily from a swift running stream while others, who had been scalded, splashed the cool water ineffectually on their raw, blistered skin. Slowly they gathered in dispirited groups, trying to estimate how many warriors had fallen to the iron snake.

Given the disparity between the weaponry of the Trackers and the Mutes it was a miracle that any of the attacking M'Calls had survived. But as many an old soldier can tell you, Lady Luck—or her shadowy sister, Fate—spares some in circumstances that defy comprehension, like the English infantrymen who survived four years of trench warfare in World War I, or the U.S. Marines who, against all odds, made it across the beaches of Guadalcanal and Tarawa in World War II.

Of Cadillac's clan-brothers, Hawk-Wind and Mack-Truck had fallen; Motor-Head had survived, along with Black-Top, Steel-Eye, and Ten-Four. Motor-Head had passed under The Lady seconds before Hartmann had given the order to pipe steam. A billowing cloud had engulfed him, searing his back and arms just as he faced sure and certain death under the guns of three linemen. His attackers had turned and fled. Terrified by the ear-splitting scream that obliterated the shrieking death agonies of his brother warriors, Motor-Head had run blindly through the burning clouds up onto the bank. There he had paused long enough to glimpse the hideous slaughter wrought by the breath of the snake, had hurled his stone flail at the nearest sand-burrower in a last gesture of defiance, then had run away.

Motor-Head was brave to the point of foolhardiness, but he had enough wit to perceive that the iron snake and its masters were strong in ways that the Plainfolk did not understand. Mr. Snow had given wise counsel, but in one respect he had been mistaken. The sand-burrowers were not animals. They fought valiantly, like men. Motor-Head knew that in single-combat the Plainfolk were the stronger, but the sand-burrowers had strange, powerful, sharp iron whose crafting and function he could not even begin to comprehend and against which the bravery of the Bears was like rain before the wind. The Plainfolk were the greatest people on the earth but they were not greater than the iron snake and its masters who lived beneath it.

Not yet. But there would come a time when the sand-burrowers would be defeated in battle. The time prophesied by Mr. Snow when Talisman, the Thrice-Gifted One, would assume the leadership of the Plainfolk.

Mr. Snow appeared, a pale, gray, wizened figure, moving with faltering steps and the aid of a long, knotted staff, among the trees. He moved among the exhausted warriors, greeting them with words of comfort, his face stricken with anguish at the sight of their raw wounds and scalded limbs, swollen as if balloons had been inserted under the skin. He sat down facing Motor-Head. "The Bears did well this day."

"Not well enough," muttered Motor-Head. "We ran from the sand-burrowers. We have lost standing." Tears trickled down his cheeks. "The Bears are nothing."

"The Bears have braved the breath of the snake, and the sharp iron of its masters," Mr. Snow countered. "Only the greatest of the Plainfolk could have done that. From this day you must learn a new kind of courage—the courage to face failure, yes, even defeat."

Motor-Head's eyes flared angrily. "She-ehh! Where is the standing in that?!"

"Listen to me," said Mr. Snow firmly. "Mark my words well. It takes great courage to fight bravely unto death. The Bears possess this courage. Our clan-mothers give birth to heroes. The M'Calls have strong hearts. Their fire-songs have sung of their greatness since the War of a Thousand Suns. But it takes even greater courage to taste fear, defeat, and shame and still remain strong! To face the power of the sand-burrowers with your warrior's pride unbroken, ready to fight again more bravely than before!"

Motor-Head eyed him stubbornly. "You told us we must have the courage of Bears but fight like coyotes. Must we also learn to run like fast-foot? Must we turn tail, as they do, at the first scent of danger?!"

"Times are changing," Mr. Snow replied. "The iron snake, the sand-burrowers. . ." He sighed. "How can I make you understand? This is a whole new ball game."

Motor-Head frowned. "You talk in riddles, Old One. The earth renews itself, yellows at the Gathering, and becomes old before the White Death. The clan-elders age, die, and are reborn in different bodies. But some things do not change. The love of Mo-Town, the great Mother, for her people. The courage of the M'Calls whose firesongs you guard within the head that we were born to defend. A warrior who shows fear, who runs from battle, is without standing. He must bite the arrow before he is worthy to bear sharp iron again."

"I accept that," said Mr. Snow quietly. "But you must also accept something. The old ways are finished. The Plainfolk must learn new ways to guard the earth until Talisman comes."

Clearwater was at the edge of the forest with a group of her sister warriors when the four arrow-heads were seen in the western sky. Mr. Snow had ordered her to guard the clan-elders and the den-mothers who had been persuaded to go deep into the forest with their newborn infants and all children under five years old. The She-Wolves—the young, female warriors—were dispersed at various points around the western edge of the forest, ready to defend the hidden settlement if it came under attack. Clearwater was worried by the sight of the distant arrowheads. She had seen the burnt warriors brought back by the elders and had learned of the deadly fire-eggs carried by the cloud warriors. If they should fall upon the forest . . .

Obliged by his renewed oath to stay out of the battle lines, Cadillac had helped to organize defense of the crop-fields. This task had been given to the Bear Cubs—the M'Call children aged six to fourteen—grouped under pack-leaders and reinforced by a sizable posse of She-Wolves. Since the clan's treasured stock of crossbows had been taken by the Bears to attack the wagon train, the remaining M'Calls were poorly armed. Cadillac possessed the only crossbow—the proud trophy he had won in his combat with Shakatak D'Vine; the rest were equipped with knife-sticks, slingshots, and stones, all virtually useless against an attack from the air.

Like Clearwater, Cadillac had seen the devastating effects of the fire from the sky. If the cloud warriors returned, there was little the Cubs could do to stop them. He and Mr. Snow had agreed that the clan's efforts should be directed toward limiting the damage caused by the fire. Neither had dwelt on the possibility that the cloud warriors might not fly away immediately after dropping their eggs. Cadillac had put the thought resolutely from his mind and had concentrated on teaching the Cubs and She-Wolves how to make longhandled flat brooms from bunches of red-leafed twigs and young saplings with which to beat out the flames. He did not appreciate that the carefully designed adhesive qualities of napalm would render such precautions totally ineffective.

The M'Call Cubs, their pack-leaders, and the She-

Wolves took up their appointed stations—some around the edge of the crop-fields, others at strategic points within it. The very young children ran from group to group, bringing more stones to add to the piles that lay ready to be hurled at any attacker. The mood was one of defiant bravado mixed with apprehension— not from any fear of the cloud warriors, but from the worry about how they would acquit themselves.

Snake-Hips, a young She-Wolf, flung a pointing finger in the air and called to Cadillac. "Look! They come!"

Cadillac turned and saw the arrowheads circling over the mountains to the east; saw the sun flash off their graceful wings as they dipped and swung around toward him. . . .

Gripped by a tense feeling of excitement, Steve Brickman and Gus White swooped down from the hills and banked low over the crop-fields. Gus dropped a smoke canister to check the strength and direction of the wind; Steve studied the layout of the fields, trying to determine the best place to lay down the napalm to cause maximum damage. They were met by a rising barrage of missiles. Most of the hand-delivered ones fell short; some of the slingshot projectiles bounced noisily off their cockpit pods or drummed against the taut wing fabric without causing any damage. One struck Gus White painfully in the side of the neck.

"Little bastards," he croaked to himself.

From his first low pass over the crop-fields, Steve saw that the hostiles were nothing more than a bunch of mainly unarmed kids who, despite their show of defiance, posed no threat. On the other hand, if they did not move from their present position among the orange cornfields, they stood a good chance of being barbecued when he and Gus dropped their loads of napalm.

Steve passed this observation to Gus over the radio and suggested that maybe they ought to try and scare the kids out of the fields first.

Gus's reply was swift and caustic. "They ain't kids, good buddy. They's little-bitty hostiles that grow up into big, mean mothers. We've got to stop'em now while we've got the chance. As my old guardee used to say, 'There ain't nothin' that smells better than southern-fried Mute.' Yeee-*hah!*" Gus signed off with a rebel yell, did a fast wingover, and fire-bombed the downwind corner of the Mute crop-fields.

Steve circled, stricken by a sudden reluctance to kill. He was conscious of being assailed by inexplicable, conflicting emotions as he watched the young children, some of them on fire, run from the spreading flames. Others began falling with an untidy flurry of limbs as Gus began picking them off with volleys from his air rifle.

Swallowing hard, Steve quickly regained his usual iron control and headed back across the target area, dropping his own load of napalm in an arc ahead of the fleeing children so as to cut off their escape.

"Look out!" yelled Gus over the radio. "One of those lumps has a crossbow! The sonofabitch just missed me by a whisker!"

Steve rammed the throttle wide open and went up in a climbing turn, searching the terrain below for the marksman.

Cadillac cursed himself for having missed the cloud warrior. He cast aside the bow and ran into the blazing cornfield to rescue a group of panic-stricken Cubs. Blinded by the rolling clouds of smoke and seared by the terrible heat, their earlier bravado had turned into a paralyzing fear, rooting them to the spot. Cadillac somehow managed to smother the sticky fire that was eating into some of their bodies and shepherded them through the waist-high corn. Despite his efforts, several of the children were gunned down by the wheeling cloud warriors as they reached safety. Seized by a terrible rage, and oblivious of the bullets that zinged past him like angry mosquitoes, Cadillac ran to where he had dropped the crossbow. He snatched it up and, with a strength born of his rage and desperation, tensioned the firing mechanism with one swift, brutal movement. With trembling fingers he scrabbled in the pouch on his belt for his last remaining bolt.

Gus White, in the middle of a steep turn around his port wing tip, spotted Cadillac loading the crossbow. Pulling his rifle into the shoulder, Gus brought the red aiming dot thrown out by the optical sight onto Cadillac's chest and pulled the trigger. Nothing happened. His gun had jammed. Gus uttered a string of obscenities, rolled quickly over to starboard, and began to jink across the sky in the manner of the late Jodi Kazan.

Steve heard the tail end of Gus's imprecations, followed by the news of his jammed gun and the location of the Mute crossbow-man. The vital details entered his ear while he was flying in precisely the opposite direction. Twisting around in his seat, Steve spotted Cadillac on the ground behind him. He threw the Skyhawk into a steep righthand turn. The last targets he had fired at had been to port, so his rifle, hanging on its overhead mount, was on the left side of the cockpit. He reached over and grasped the pistol grip to bring the mount and the rifle across and into his shoulder. The maneuver was only half-completed as he banked around toward his target.

In the vital second before Cadillac came into Steve's sights, Cadillac fired his crossbow. The bolt shot skyward with terrifying speed, punched through the upper part of Steve's raised right arm, and pinned it to his flying helmet. Entering the helmet at a steep angle above the ear, the bolt gouged through Steve's scalp, striking his skull a grazing blow, and came to rest with the barbed point poking out through the crown. Stunned by the force of the blow, Steve fought to retain consciousness. The world began to spin; became a blur as he lost control. . . .

In Unit 18, Gallery Three, on Level One of Inner State U at Grand Central, Roz Brickman, who had been filled with a sense of foreboding all day, tried to blot out yet another confused image of blood, broken bodies, and flames that threatened to engulf her. It was a losing battle. She felt a sharp blow on the head, and, in the same instant, a searing pain shot through her upper right arm, forcing an involuntary scream from her lips. The startled students working on either side saw Roz leap up from her seat in front of an electron microscope with her right arm folded across her head. She spun around, her eyes turned up under the lids, then collapsed, unconscious, hitting the floor before anyone could catch her.

Summoned from his adjacent office, the medical supervisor in charge of the class found that Roz was bleeding from a shallow scalp wound, which he assumed had been caused by her fall to the floor. He was, however, unable to account for the additional loss of blood which, when her lab coat had been removed, was found to be issuing from deep wounds in her upper arm.

Cadillac watched impassively as the arrowhead spiraled down and made a crash landing in the middle of the burning cornfield. Five hundred feet above, Gus White was still trying to unjam his rifle. He swore through clenched teeth as he tugged at the solidly locked breech but could not find a way to free it. Now that he had nothing to shoot with—apart from the air pistol that was part of his survival kit— Gus did not feel like hanging around. He knew it meant leaving Steve in the shit, but with a Mute marksman somewhere underneath him he stood to get a bolt coming up through his seat at any minute. In any case, Steve was probably dead.

Unaware that Cadillac had fired his last bolt, Gus jinked back across the crop-field to take stock of Steve's situation. "Blue Seven to Blue Three. Come in. Over."

After a moment's silence Steve came on the air. "Blue Three, have been, uh ... hit. Can you, uh ... can you ... cover me?"

"No chance, good buddy," Gus said. "My gun's still out. The only thing I can hit 'em with is a pair of

dirty socks and I can't get my boots off. How are you
fixed for taking out that lump with the crossbow?"

A long gasp preceded Steve's reply. "Can't reach
my rifle."

"That's tough," said Gus. "You hurt bad?"

"Yehh, but . . . as far as I can tell it's, uh . . . nothing
that Keever can't handle."

Keever was the Surgeon-Captain who led the medical team aboard The Lady.

Gus made a wide circle around the burning crop-
field. "Okay, listen. You hang on in there, good buddy.
I'll go get some help."

Out of the corner of his eye, Steve saw Gus rock his
wings in salute as he climbed away in the direction
of the forest. The anesthetizing shock of the bolt's
impact was beginning to wear off and Steve was now
increasingly conscious of the pain emanating from
his right arm. He also found it difficult to breathe.
He was lying on his left side, with his left leg twisted
at an odd angle in the crumpled wreckage of the
cockpit pod. Steve managed to undo his safety harness but found that any attempt to move his left arm
in any other direction generated an excruciating pain
in his shoulder. He could also feel blood seeping out
of the wound in his scalp. It was running down over
his face and neck. He managed to get his left hand up
far enough to unclip his visor, but he could not raise
it more than halfway. Its movement was blocked by
his pinned right arm. He began to fumble at the
helmet chin straps. If he could loosen the helmet and
somehow get it off his head he might then . . .

He stopped for a moment, breathing with short,
quick gasps, willing himself not to cry out in pain. It
was going to be all right. Gus would come back with
Fazetti and Naylor. He would come back and . . .

When it was clear that the remaining cloud warrior had turned tail and fled, Cadillac and several of
the She-Wolves plunged back into the burning cornfield to rescue more of the M'Call Cubs.

Hovering on the edge of unconsciousness, Steve
saw a straightlimbed Mute run past him without

giving him a second glance. The thought that he was going to be left to burn to death filled him with dread. He could already feel waves of heat from the approaching flames and was beginning to choke on the acrid smoke drifting over him.

Cadillac passed the broken arrowhead with a group of singed, smoke-stained children. They stopped and looked down at the trapped cloud warrior with expressionless faces.

Steve stretched his left hand out toward them in a pain-filled gesture of supplication. "Help me," he gasped. "Please. . . ."

The straight-limbed Mute eyed him for a moment then ushered the silent, dull-eyed children out of his line of sight.

Steve cursed them silently. Bastard, fucking lumpheads. His thoughts drifted back to his own predicament. What an end to all his high hopes! And what a dumb way to go—roasting in a fire that he had helped start! The irony of the situation did not escape him. He clung desperately to the hope that all was not lost. He could not really trust that yellow sonofabitch, but if Gus *did* manage to unjam his gun he might come back with Fazetti and Naylor. All it needed was someone with enough balls to land and pull him out while the other two flew cover. A Skyhawk without any ordinance could carry a passenger. It would mean a fresh-air ride on the external racks, but he was prepared to risk that if . . .

A searing wave of heat struck Steve. With his right arm pinned to his helmet he could barely move his head. He arched his body and succeeded in edging it around a few inches. A violent stab of pain shot up through his chest. Looking to his left through his half-raised visor he saw the flames begin to consume the corn around the port wing tip of the Skyhawk. The fabric started to smolder. Ignoring the pain in both his arms, Steve clawed frantically at his rifle, trying to pull it near enough to be able to shoot himself before the flames reached him. His efforts proved hopeless. He could not get a firm enough grip to free the gun from its mounting.

Steve took several painful breaths and, with increasing desperation, tried again. The straight-limbed Mute and two young lump-heads moved back into his field of vision.

Acting on the command of an inner voice, Cadillac leaned forward and forced open the dark head-shield of the fallen cloud warrior. The face beneath was covered in blood. Cadillac studied it carefully. It matched the one revealed to him by the seeing-stone.

Steve's hopes began to rise. He had not forgotten the horrific tales of Bad News Logan; he was just clinging, with total illogicality, to the hope that somehow, something would happen to save him. If he could just get out of the cornfield . . .

The straight-limbed Mute stepped back with a grunt. Steve's hopes plummeted as the Mute turned his attention to the air rifle. He tugged, heaved, fiddled with locking devices and finally managed to wrestle it off its mount. With blurring vision, Steve watched the Mute inspect the weapon cautiously, fingering the trigger, then looking down the three barrels. Steve let out a sobbing, painwracked laugh. Oh, Columbus, what a stupid world! *Brought down by an idiot who's going to leave me here to burn because he doesn't know how to shoot me. . . .*

The Mute tossed the rifle to the young lump-head on his right. The kid clutched it proudly across his chest, trigger guard up, barrels down. The other two Mutes moved out of sight. Steve felt someone tugging at the airframe. It was being twisted around and dragged away from the flames. The movement caused him to flop about like a rag doll. He let out a scream of pain. The straight-limbed Mute returned and leaned over him, a knife clenched between his teeth.

Oh, jeez, yes, of course, thought Steve, remembering his talks with Kazan. *Crossbow bolts are in short supply. This guy wants his back and so he's . . . going to cut my fucking arm off.* Great. Steve viewed the prospect with a curious detachment. Time seemed to have slowed down. The pain throbbing through his body was now so intense it had surpassed his capacity to react to it. His nerve endings had become overloaded. Nothing mattered anymore. . . .

Cadillac and his helpers had turned the arrowhead around so that the wings lay between them and the flames; but even so, they were uncomfortably close. He took the knife from his mouth and slid the point under the chin straps of the cloud warrior's helmet. The warrior shuddered as the blade touched his throat. Cadillac cut through the chin straps and slowly eased off the helmet and the arm pinned to it. The warriors's blood-soaked head lolled onto his left shoulder; glazed eyes wandering under half-open lids. Cadillac considered the problem of the bolt. It was stuck firmly through the helmet in two places. The helmet itself was crafted from a strange material, like polished bone, upon which his knife made little impression. Cadillac beckoned to Three-Son of T-Rex and told him to take hold of the cloud warrior's right arm. Three-Son gripped the arm on either side of the bolt and braced himself. Grasping the helmet firmly with both hands, Cadillac put a knee against the cloud warrior's chest and yanked hard, pulling the bolt with its sharp stubby fins through his arm.

It did not come out easily.

Steve's eyes almost popped out of his head. He bared his teeth, mouth opening wide, sucking breath into his chest to fuel a tortured scream.

It never came. He blacked out instead.

Having climbed beyond the normal range of Mute crossbows, Gus White switched radio channels and tried to raise Fazetti and Naylor. The net result, after several attempts, was a deafening silence. Circling the forest area at twenty-five hundred feet, Gus could see no sign of a napalm strike on the vast red canopy of leaves below him. He cut his motor and criss-crossed the area in a series of shallow glides, losing fifteen hundred feet of altitude before leveling out. Eventually he spotted a ragged patch of blue. On closer investigation, Gus saw that it was the tangled wreckage of two Skyhawks speared on the upper branches of one of the closely packed tall trees. He called up The Lady, reported the successful firing of the cropfields, then gave them the bad news: Steve's crash landing and his sighting of what looked like the wreckage of the Skyhawks flown by Naylor and Fazetti.

The reply from the wagon train was terse and uncommunicative. "Roger, Blue Seven. Return to base. Out."

Above the escarpment, where the surviving M'Call Bears had gathered, Mr. Snow saw the black smoke rising from the direction of the crop-fields. High above him, a lone arrowhead glided silently westward across the blue. Mr. Snow eyed it with a mixture of caution, envy, and cold hatred. He would dearly have loved to scramble the cloud warrior's brain and bring him plummeting down, but he was fresh out of magic. It would be several days, perhaps even a week, before he could summon up the powers of the earth again. He hoped it would be longer, for it was an ordeal he did not relish.

Two She-Wolf messengers reached him in quick succession. One had been sent by the small rear guard that had stayed to watch the iron snake. She reported that the snake had broken into two pieces. The tail had become a new head; half its body had crawled out of the river and was heading toward the escarpment, puffing out clouds of its burning white breath. Deep-Purple, the other She-Wolf, sent by Cadillac, brought the bad news that the crop-fields had been almost totally destroyed by fire. She also had a second message for Mr. Snow from Cadillac. The cloud warrior the Sky Voices had spoken of had been delivered into their hands.

With nearly two hundred and fifty warriors left dead and dying around the iron snake, plus those killed earlier by the cloud warriors, the fighting strength of the clan had been cut by over a third. A similar number had suffered injuries, some of which would need months of constant care and attention. Although seriously weakened, the M'Calls were still numerically stronger than many neighboring clans, but another full-scale assault on the iron snake was out of the question. If only Talisman would come! In the meantime, however, there was only one thing to do: head for the hills. They had to find a secure, sheltered base where they could heal the wounded and rebuild the shattered confidence of the Bears, and they had to find new stocks of food to see them through the White Death.

When Gus White reached the Now and Then River, he found that the rear command and power cars, plus nine of the wagons, had been freed and were now parked up on the east bank, where their guns could command the surrounding area. Gus buzzed the mobile element of the train, which included the flat-topped flight section, then turned and made a low pass back along the river. He saw Barber's men swarming around the front five wagons. They still lay across the river bed but were no longer tilted over. A few of the guys in the work party stopped and waved to him as he flashed past.

Gus called up Flight Control and got the green to land-on. Baxter met him as he came down on the lift. Gus pulled himself out of the cockpit of his Skyhawk and saluted. "Has the Chief transferred over, too, sir?"

"No," said Baxter. "He's outside giving the boys a hand." He led the way to the Ops room of the rear command car and put Gus through the normal debriefing procedure. Gus described the successful strike on the crop-fields and explained how his rifle had jammed at the crucial moment when Steve was hit and brought down.

"So you left him in the burning cornfield." Baxter's voice carried no hint of condemnation.

"I had no choice, sir," Gus said. "The place was

crawling with hostiles who were none too pleased with us for roasting their corn. Without my rifle . . ."

"Yes, sure. . . ."

"I figured if I could get Fazetti and Naylor to fly cover for me . . ."

"But you couldn't raise them."

"No, sir."

"Was Brickman alive when you left?"

"Just about. He didn't sound too chipper."

"Okay. We'll write him off." Baxter made an entry on his electronic note pad against Brickman's name. PD/ET/BNR: "Powered down in enemy territory. Body not recovered." Baxter added the date and keyed the fate of Brickman, S. R. into the pad's memory, leaving the small, flat, gray screen clear.

Baxter then listened as Gus reported, in greater detail, his sighting of the tangled wreckage of two Skyhawks in the forest. "Must be Fazetti and Naylor," he observed when Gus concluded his account.

Gus looked bewildered. "What happened?"

"We're not quite sure," Baxter said slowly. "All we know is we got a Mayday call from Naylor saying that Fazetti had flipped his lid and started shooting at him. The Chief told Naylor to shoot back."

"Columbus!" breathed Gus. "And? . . ."

Baxter shrugged. "Who knows? Naylor must have been slow on the trigger."

Gus gave him a stunned look. "But . . . I mean . . . why would? . . ."

"Good question," Baxter replied. "All I can tell you is that little item won't be reported to Grand Central. It'll just be a straight PD/ET entry like Brickman's."

"Wow. . . ." breathed Gus. "Nine Skyhawks down in one day. If the Federation's going to lick these Plainfolk Mutes into shape we're going to have to do better than this."

"Damn right we are." Baxter stood up from the table. Gus leapt to his feet. The FOE eyed him. "I should warn you that if that jam in your rifle turns out to have been caused by faulty rounds, you could draw a spell in the box. 'Negligence while on active duty.' "

Gus stiffened to attention. "Yes, sir, I'm aware of that, sir. It would mean that you'd be the only one aboard capable of flying forward air patrols."

Baxter's expression did not change. "I'll bear that in mind when I receive the armorer's report. Dismissed."

Gus saluted smartly, turned on his heel, and left.

In the forest, Clearwater watched with bated breath as a group of She-Wolves clambered up through the branches to the wrecked arrowheads. The bodies of the cloud warriors were cut free from their retaining straps and dropped unceremoniously to the ground. An attempt was made to dismantle bits of the aircraft. Various wires and control leads were ripped out, but the larger items proved difficult to dislodge. Most of the scavenging Mutes contented themselves with pieces of the metallic-blue solar-cell fabric.

Returning to earth with their trophies, they gathered around the two dead cloud warriors and watched as their visored helmets and clothes were removed. The pale, olive-pink bodies were almost hairless. A jostling crowd of spectators gathered to view the bodies; then the heads of the sand-burrowers were hacked off and mounted on stakes outside the hut Clearwater shared with three of her clan-sisters.

Ultra-Vox, the leader of the tree-climbing expedition, gravely presented one of the cloud warrior's helmets to Clearwater. It was a tribute, in recognition of the powers she had summoned forth to bring them tumbling from the sky.

Clearwater squatted outside her hut between the heads of the cloud warriors with the prized helmet cradled in her lap. She felt drained by the power that had passed through her, but this time she had not been weakened to the point of collapse. Even though Mr. Snow had said that the Sky Voices had chosen her to receive this priceless gift, she was still afraid of the mysterious strength that now lurked within her. She was also troubled by the striking resemblance between her own body, and Cadillac's, and those of the sand-burrowers. Their young faces, which now stared sightlessly from the stakes on either side of the doorway, had the same even teeth; the same slim jaw. It was if they had been cast from the same mold. She knew she should have felt elated by this victory but she did not. She felt saddened and confused. It was as if, with their deaths, part of herself had died. And the fact that she had fallen prey to such thoughts disturbed her even more.

Buck McDonnell, the Trail-Boss, led the cheers as the front wagons of The Lady eased up the now-dry mud slope onto the bank of the Now and Then River. Fifteen minutes later, the two sections were hitched together and she was ready to roll. With only one wingman to provide cover, over sixty wounded linemen, and another thirty-seven lying under the floor in body-bags, Hartmann decided to head back to one of the main way stations to seek assistance and await reinforcements. He ordered Captain Ryder, the Navigation Exec, to set course for Kansas.

When Roz Brickman recovered consciousness some ten minutes after hitting the floor, she found herself undergoing a detailed examination by the Assistant Chief Pathologist at Inner State U. Both wounds had ceased to bleed and the agonizing pain had been reduced to a dull ache. The ACP observed that the upper right cranium had been scored by a ribbed metal object and, by means of a probe, was able to establish that her right biceps brachii and the surrounding epidermis had been pierced laterally. Close inspection of the entry and exit points revealed that the wound had probably been caused by the passage of a pointed metal rod approximately one centimeter in diameter with four small vanes at the tip. A similar object could have caused the scalp wound.

Despite a thorough search of Unit 18 and a body check of the students and staff present when the accident occurred, no such object was found, nor anything else that might have caused a similar injury. The right sleeve of Brickman's lab coat was also found to be intact. Neither the Assistant Chief Pathologist nor anyone else associated with the preliminary investigation was able to explain how any object could have passed through Roz Brickman's arm without first passing through the woven fabric of the surrounding sleeve.

Three hours after collapsing, no trace of either injury could be discerned. Roz was hospitalized and kept under observation for twenty-four hours, and a confidential report on the incident was transmitted to the White House. The Amtrak Executive responded immediately by dispatching two special investigators, one male, one female. Despite skillful and outwardly sympathetic interrogation, Roz did not reveal the terrifying visions that had assailed her, especially the last one in which she felt herself falling out of the sky. After a final examination of her now-healed arm and head, the two investigators returned to the White House.

On the following day, Roz learned that the incident file had been closed. She was formally discharged from the intensive care unit and told to resume her course studies. When she rejoined her class, she found that, apart from asking how she felt, her fellow students were unwilling to discuss the incident. Roz didn't mind. She didn't want to talk about it either. It was too dangerous. Who would believe that she knew, with utter certainty, that her kin-brother had been hit by a crossbow bolt? Had crashed. Been injured, and was now in the hands of the Plainfolk. . . .

——— 13 ———

When Steve recovered consciousness, he found himself lying in semidarkness, wearing only his underpants, on a layer of furry animal skins. His air-conditioned sense of smell was immediately overwhelmed by the strange odors. He tried to close his nostrils to filter out the foulness that hung on the air but could not prevent it entering his lungs. He gagged silently; felt nauseated.

A small, lean-bodied Mute with long, braided white hair knelt over him, tending the wound in his scalp. Still woozy, Steve raised his head far enough to glance down at his body. His chest, both shoulders, and his upper arms were bandaged; his left leg was held, from thigh to heel, in a rudimentary splint. Beyond it, sitting cross-legged on a buffalo-skin, was the straight-limbed Mute who had pulled the bolt out through his arm. He met Steve's eyes with the same impassive expression he had worn when rescuing him from the burning crop-field.

Steve laid his head back on the furs. He let out a long sigh and coughed, trying to clear the rising bile from his throat. The environmental stink hung so thick on the air it seemed to have coated his tongue, filled every pore.

"Welcome back," said the old Mute.

The shock of hearing the Mute speak the same language in a clear, comprehensible voice brought Steve's senses back in a rush. Stung by the sudden realization of what was happening to him, he jerked his head away from the old Mute's ministering hands. It was an automatic reflex. All Trackers knew that Mutes had diseased skin which, if touched even briefly, caused your own body to rot.

The old Mute sat back on his heels with a patient sigh. "Don't you want me to fix your head?"

"There's no point," Steve muttered. "If you touch me, I'll die anyway."

The old Mute's weathered face creased into a smile. He chuckled into his beard then jerked his head at the straight-limbed Mute. "Hold this nitwit down, will you?"

Cadillac uncrossed his legs and knelt on the opposite side of Mr. Snow's patient. He placed one hand firmly on the cloud warrior's chin and the other on the crown of his head. The warrior's lack of self-control had been a great surprise. He seemed terrified, his eyes rolled wildly, but he was unable to put up much of a struggle because of his injuries. Were all sand-burrowers like this? Maybe, thought Cadillac, their courage has been swallowed up by their powerful sharp iron. If so, the Plainfolk had nothing to fear.

"I'll give him five threads of Dream Cap," muttered Mr. Snow. "That should quiet him down a bit." He addressed the cloud warrior. "You're a very mixed-up young man."

Out of the corner of his eye, Steve saw the white-haired Mute rummage amongst various bags and baskets, finally producing a small skin pouch from which he extracted a few short strands of a grayish-brown substance. He held them out to Steve. "Chew this."

Cadillac forced the cloud warrior's mouth wide

open. Mr. Snow inserted the shredded dose of Dream Cap, then Cadillac clamped the warrior's jaw shut.

"Okay, don't chew it," grumped Mr. Snow. "It makes no difference. You'll have to swallow it eventually."

Steve held out for about a minute then relented. He chewed the strands briefly then steeled himself to swallow them. The taste was strange but not unpleasant. Ahhgh, what does it matter? he thought bitterly. He was going to die anyway. The idea that he might somehow escape death, his confused appeal for help in the cornfield, had been part of a pain-filled fantasy. Someone, probably the old Mute, had tended his injuries with unsuspected medical skills, but it didn't make sense . . . unless they were saving him for the big event. The Annual Torture Stakes—which he was no doubt destined to win by a head. Terrific. . . .

In spite of such dire prospects Steve began to find that his anxiety was fading. The pain from the broken parts of his body was also gradually easing. He felt agreeably light-headed; weightless; could no longer feel the ground beneath him. He didn't feel like struggling anymore. He just lay back and let himself float.

Cadillac let go of the cloud warrior's head. He sat back on his heels and watched Mr. Snow carefully unwrap the bandage on his patient's right arm. He peeled off a mash of red leaves and examined the raw, gaping wound. "Hmmphh . . . he's lucky it was one of your bolts."

"Is it bad?" Steve asked in a faraway voice.

"It'll take a while to heal, but it's clean. Whether or not you'll recover the full use of your arm is up to you, but at least you'll have something to hang your right hand on. Okay . . . hold still." Mr. Snow used a sliver of wood to poke a fresh mash made from pulped herbs into both ends of the hole and bound up the wound.

Steve eyed the straight-limbed Mute. His attention was fixed on what the old guy was doing. Steve looked back over his head and saw, to his right, a yellow flame flickering in a small hollowed-out stone.

He took closer stock of his surroundings. The three of them were in a low eight-sided hut made out of wood and what he presumed were animal skins. The light poles that edged each panel curved over some four feet off the ground and sloped inward to meet its neighbors in the center of the shallow pitched roof. The poles fitted into a wooden ring that was open in the center and was evidently some type of flue, no doubt to provide badly needed ventilation. There were a number of untidy bundles and baskets piled around the inside edge, but nothing that Steve could recognize as furniture. Compared with the ordered, antiseptic layout of his shack on the quarterdeck of the Academy the hut was, frankly, a mess.

Steve could hear voices and sounds of activity coming from outside the hut. And music of a kind he had never heard before but that recalled the wind-whips used in the attack on The Lady. It had a strange, haunting quality that reached deep into his psyche, evoking a troubling response. He turned his attention back onto the young Mute kneeling by his left side and noticed that he only had four fingers and one thumb on each hand. Steve's mood was too detached to ponder deeply on the significance of this discovery, but it occurred to him that apart from his long hair, the only physical feature that distinguished the Mute from himself—or any other Tracker—was the random pattern of black, brown, dark cream, and olive-pink that covered his skin.

The old, white-haired, bearded Mute was a true six-fingered lump-head with an uneven row of tumorlike bone growths across his forehead. His varicolored skin was further disfigured by strange knotted patches on his arms and cheekbones; but contrary to what Steve had been led to expect, the old Mute's eyes sparkled with intelligence, as did those of his young companion.

"What's wrong with the rest of me?" asked Steve, as the old Mute completed his skilled inspection of Steve's injuries.

"You've got a simple fracture of the left shinbone,

a badly sprained ankle, at least three cracked ribs, severe bruising of the left shoulder, and a slight dent in your skull. You may have what used to be called a hairline fracture. In the Old Time there were things for looking through bones, but they don't exist anymore."

"X-ray machines," said Steve.

The old Mute nodded. "Is that what they were called?"

"They still are," Steve replied. "All the medical centers of the Federation have them. We've got all kinds of electronic scanning equipment."

"I see. Well, you're going to have to get by without all that," said Mr. Snow. "Not to worry. Your brain's still in one piece."

Steve lay on the furs, his body limp, unresisting. "Feels like it's leaking out of my ears."

"That's the Dream Cap," Mr. Snow said. "It's good stuff. Helps you to loosen up."

Steve nodded. "We have painkillers, too. Small pills called Cloud-Nines."

Cadillac looked surprised. "You have clouds in your burrows?"

"No, of course not. Clouds are part of the blue-sky world. And let's get one thing straight. We don't live in burrows. Those are for animals. We live on bases—like big cities. In clean quarters with plenty of room, light, fresh air." Steve waved his left hand limply. "A heck of a lot better than this lousy dump."

Mr. Snow had never heard the words "lousy dump" before, but he guessed their meaning from the tone of the cloud warrior's voice. "Tell me," he said affably, "do you have a name?"

"I've got a name and a number," answered Steve. "Number 29028902 Brickman, S. R. or, if you prefer to be less formal, Steven Roosevelt Brickman."

Cadillac repeated the number with awe. "Talisman! . . . That is a powerful number! More than all the raindrops in the sky. More than all the stars in Mo-Town's cloak." He looked at Mr. Snow. "Did you know there were so many people under the earth?"

Mr. Snow did not answer. He turned to Steve. "This number, and the names you bear. What do they mean?"

"I don't know what you're getting at," said Steve. "They're just names."

"No name is *just* a name," Mr. Snow replied quietly. "Every word has meaning. There must be a reason why you were given this number and these names."

"Ahh, I get it," said Steve. He continued to gaze up at the flickering light on the roof of the hut. "Well, 29028902 is my personal identification number. The number on my ID card." His hand went automatically to the appropriate chest pocket, then he remembered that he'd been stripped of everything except his underpants.

"ID card?" queried Cadillac.

"My identity card," Steve explained. "It's to let people know who I am."

"Do you not *know* who you are?"

"Yes, of course I do. The card is to prove I am who I *say* I am."

Cadillac's puzzlement increased. "But ... why would you say you were someone else? Are you not known to your clan-brothers and sisters?"

I'm talking to an idiot, thought Steve. "Look ..." he began, then gave up. "Forget that. The real reason we have a card is so that we can access the services controlled by Columbus. It's a big computer—"

"Computer?"

"A word from the Old Time," observed Mr. Snow.

"A machine that runs things," Steve explained. "With thousands of access points all over the Federation. That's why you need a number. You feed your card into a slot and the number and other magnetic data on it is passed to Columbus. That's how it knows who you are. With the help of the computer you can—depending on your credit rating—access all kinds of services: food, data banks, transit systems, video communications. Your number allows you to establish an interface. You can't exist without it."

Cadillac nodded thoughtfully. "So many strange words, strange ideas. I cannot get my mind around them."

"His world is not ours," said Mr. Snow. "It will take time to understand these things." He turned to Steve. "Tell us about your names."

"Steve—Steven is my family name, given to me when I was born by the President-General; Roosevelt is the name of the base where I live: 'Roosevelt Field'; Brickman is my kinfolk name. The name of my guardians."

"Guardians?" Mr. Snow raised his eyebrows. "Were you kept as prisoner on this . . . base?"

Steve replied with a wry laugh. "No. My guardians were the two people assigned to look after me when I was born."

"Do you not have an earth-mother and father?" Cadillac asked.

Steve did not fully understand the question. "My guard-mother carried me for the first nine months of my life. My father was the President-General. Head of the First Family. The father of all life within the Federation."

"President-General . . . is this the name you give to your chief elder?" asked Cadillac.

"No, that's his title. His name is George Washington Jefferson the Thirty-first."

"If he is more powerful, why does he have less numbers than you?"

Steve smiled. "It's a different kind of number. He doesn't need an ID card. He is the thirty-first Jefferson to head the Amtrak Federation. The Jeffersons have run things from the very beginning. They *were* the beginning. That's why they're called the First Family." The words tripped off Steve's tongue. "They gave us the light, and the air we breathe; they invent things, they design our cities; they can do anything. They taught Columbus everything it knows. They are our leaders, our teachers, our counselors, our guides on the path to the blue-sky world." End of lesson.

"The President-General is their chief elder. The top man."

"The capo di capo," murmured Mr. Snow.

"The what?"

"Capo di capo," Mr. Snow said. "Chief of the chiefs. The godfather. The top man. Do you not know all the words from the Old Time?"

"Not that one," said Steve.

Mr. Snow smiled. "Then perhaps you may learn something from us. As we hope to—"

Cadillac, impressed by the catalog of the Jeffersons' gifts, forgot his usual deference and cut in impatiently. "This great chief you speak of. You say he is . . . *your* father?"

Steve dropped his head back on the furs. "I already told you. He's *everybody's* father."

Cadillac gave Mr. Snow a questioning look. Mr. Snow raised his eyebrows. "Must be a busy man. . . ."

Cadillac looked down at Steve. "Which of your three names is your Name of Power?"

"I don't know what you're talking about," Steve murmured. His eyes wandered over the roof of the hut. He was finding it increasingly difficult to answer the pointless questions these two oddballs kept coming up with.

"You are a cloud warrior," explained Cadillac. "Do you not have a name that gives you the strength to fight?"

"I don't need one," Steve replied. "I've been trained to fight. Names have nothing to do with it."

"But you have just told us of your great chief. Is Jefferson not a Name of Power?"

"Not in the way you mean," replied Steve. "I could be called Pete, Dick, Jim, Larry, anything. It's just a handle. Whatever I was called I'd still be me. And so would the President-General."

Cadillac was perplexed by Steve's answer. He looked at Mr. Snow for guidance. Mr. Snow said nothing. Cadillac looked down at their prisoner. "But your name is the essence of your being. A Name of Power enables your spirit to draw strength from the earth and sky."

"Maybe for you," Steve replied amiably. "We don't need any of that garbage."

Cadillac raised his eyes to Mr. Snow. "Garbage? . . ."

"It must be another word from the Old Time," said his mentor. He whispered it to himself. "Garbage . . . mmmm, not bad. . . ." He made a mental note to ask the cloud warrior to explain its meaning.

Cadillac tried another question. "Do you not believe that there are powers in the earth and sky?"

"There are forces," admitted Steve. "Gravitational forces, geomagnetic forces, static electricity, wind and water power. The way it all works is very simple. We *know* how the world functions. But when you talk about 'essence, spirit, Names of Power,' I don't know what words like that mean. Ideas about there being something else, some invisible power, are a waste of time. It's all nonsense—like the magic you people are supposed to have. If you can't see it through a microscope or prove something works by the laws of physics, or whatever, then it doesn't exist."

"That's an interesting point of view," mused Mr. Snow.

"It's the *only* point of view," Steve muttered. He felt burned out by the effort needed to maintain a coherent conversation. He gazed up at the roof of the hut again. His captors squatted silently on either side of him. Steve got the impression that they were waiting for him to say something enlightening. He made an effort to focus on their previous conversation. "Roosevelt was a very powerful man," he ventured helpfully. "He was President of America. A great warrior who ruled the blue-sky world for a long time."

"Ahhh," said Cadillac. "Now I understand. *Roosevelt* is your Name of Power."

"If you say so," Steve replied. "It doesn't make any difference to me." He raised his head. "What are you called?"

"My name is Cadillac of the clan M'Call, firstborn of Sky-Walker out of Black-Wing."

"Cadillac . . . is that a Name of Power?"

"Yes."

"Cadillac. . . ." repeated Steve. "I never heard that word before. Interesting." He turned to the old, white-haired lump-head. "How about you?"

"My name is Mr. Snow."

"Is that on account of your hair? Or is that a Name of Power, too?"

Mr. Snow shook his head. "I am not a warrior. My name was taken from the words of an ancient song."

"From the Old Time," added Cadillac proudly. "Before the War of a Thousand Suns."

"I guess you must be talking of what we call the Holocaust. Nearly a thousand years ago. . . ."

Mr. Snow nodded.

"So what are you—the doctor for these people?"

Mr. Snow smiled. "Among other things."

"Like what?"

"He is a wordsmith," Cadillac said with a proud sweep of his hand. "The greatest and wisest of them all."

Mr. Snow shrugged modestly and motioned his pupil to be silent.

Cadillac, intent on extolling his teacher's virtues, pressed on regardless. "His tongue reaches back beyond the beginning of the Plainfolk to the world that was lost in the fire-clouds. He knows of ice-huts piled one upon the other until they touched the sky, giant beetles with men in their bellies, square baskets of frozen water full of music and pictures—"

"You mean television sets—"

"—and jewels!" cried Cadillac, flaunting his newly acquired knowledge. "All these things and more. Much more than even your President-General!"

"I doubt it," Steve countered. "Can he read? Can he type?"

Mr. Snow smiled. "You already know the answer. It is true that my eye does not know the signs for the words I speak, and that my hand cannot draw them in the earth. But we of the Plainfolk have other gifts. The wisdom of the Sky Voices is greater than all the words that lie buried in your dark cities. We pass on knowledge in other ways." He reached out to touch Cadillac's head. "This is the book in which I have made my mark. It has more leaves than the greatest forest."

"It's a book that can be destroyed," Steve observed.

"If Talisman wills it," admitted Mr. Snow. "Man, and the works of man, pass away like flowers before the White Death. This Columbus of which you speak and which knows so much is also the work of men. It, too, can be ground to dust."

"I doubt it," said Steve. "Columbus *survived* the Holocaust. It was built in what you call the Old Time and it's constantly being rebuilt—bigger and better than before. It will last forever."

Mr. Snow shook his head. "Nothing lasts forever. And when the day comes for it to return to the earth, the power you draw from it will pass through your fingers like the wind. But consider this: Your iron snake sent many of our warriors to the High Ground. It may return with others and succeed in killing us all. Our past may perish with us, but you will never destroy *true* knowledge. That is the gift of the Sky Voices—and they are beyond the reach of even *your* long sharp iron."

Steve felt a pang of remorse. He had been party to the killing the old Mute spoke of. Whatever his final fate might be, these so-called savages had not left him to burn. "Listen, before we go any further, I just want to say thanks for straightening out my leg and everything. After what happened back there in the crop-fields . . ."

"Mo-Town thirsts, Mo-Town drinks," said Mr. Snow quietly.

"Well, I guess you both know what I mean." Steve looked at each of them in turn then dropped his head back with a resigned sigh. "Are you guys going to kill me?" In his present mood of sedated euphoria, the prospect did not concern him unduly.

"Not unless there's a change of plan," said Mr. Snow.

"Great," Steve replied. He yawned sleepily. "Keep me posted."

The will to live is the crucial factor that enables certain individuals to survive in situations where others, in some cases their companions, quite literally "give up the ghost"; surrender without a fight. Jodi Kazan had that will—a tenacious, unquenchable spark of life that continued to glow feebly, against all odds, inside her burned and broken body.

When her Skyhawk had been blown off the flight deck, Jodi had smashed her fist against the quick release plate of the safety harness that held her in her seat. But when the cockpit pod crunched against the side of the wagon train, she found herself trapped by bent struts and crumpled metal. Despite this, and contrary to Buck McDonnell's belief, Jodi had not been incinerated by the exploding napalm. The shrieking wind that tore her Skyhawk out of the hands of Steve and the ground crew was also her unintended savior. The spectacular blast that appeared to engulf her had, in the same instant, been whipped away from the falling pod into a long fiery plume, a giant blowtorch whose searing heat had blistered the flanks of the rear cars.

Badly burned, Jodi then came close to drowning as the cockpit pod plunged into the raging current, sank under the weight of the rear-mounted motor, and was then carried along the river bed by the force of the waters, rolling and tumbling end over end until it finally tore itself to pieces. Choking and gasping, her lungs half-filled with water, Jodi finally surfaced and was washed up some three miles downriver from where The Lady had been trapped by the flash flood.

Jodi lay, half-dead, half-buried in mud and debris on the bed of the Now and Then River, for two whole days, unable to move. Her legs were trapped under a pile of debris, both arms were broken, her neck and chest had been severely burned, and the Mute crossbow bolt was still lodged under her right collarbone. The visor of her helmet had protected her face against the flames and subsequent injury, just as the tangle of branches under which she lay now protected her from the circling birds of prey. The coat of mud that covered most of her body dried out in the sun. She became part of the landscape. Insects swarmed over her, flies hovered, drawn by the smell of her charred flesh. When they began to feed on her, Jodi thought she would go mad. She fainted—from the heat, thirst, pain, and the screaming, itching horror of the bugs that threatened to devour her. The hours passed. Jodi hovered on the edge of consciousness, now and then sinking back into merciful oblivion.

On the second night a prowling coyote found her. He sniffed her mud-covered body cautiously, then nosed with obvious relish the raw flesh where the flies had feasted. When he began tugging at her camouflaged fatigues, Jodi set her teeth against the pain, reached down with the fingers of her right hand, and teased her air pistol out of its holster. Her fingers closed around the butt. In her weakened state she found the pistol incedibly heavy. To move it even an inch sent stabbing shafts of pain zigzagging from wrist to shoulder, across her chest, and up into the base of her skull. Jodi persisted, pushing and pulling the pistol onto her belly as the coyote seized her broken left arm in its jaws and tried to pull her from under the sheltering tangle of branches. Jodi almost fainted with the pain. A scream broke from her throat, a harsh, raw, animal cry. With one last desperate effort, she willed herself to remain conscious and took a firm grip on the butt of the pistol. Her fingers felt as if they were on fire. She pushed the pistol across her chest in the general direction of the coyote, summoned up her last ounce of strength to raise the barrel, and pulled the trigger. One, two, three. . . She lost count.

When she awoke at half light, Jodi found the coyote lying with its neck across her left arm. One of her shots had entered its skull just above the right eye.

The socket had already been picked clean. Two huge black crows were tearing at the coyote's exposed entrails. A third sat patiently on the broken branch above Jodi's head. She became conscious of the weight of the pistol that lay on her chest, her fingers still curled around it. It was like being trapped under a rock. She found it difficult to breathe. She could no longer move her right arm. The left lay under the dead coyote. When the sun came up, the insects returned; flies settled on her swollen, blistered neck and crawled over her visor, trying to find a way in.

On the third day, in one of her brief moments of lucidity, Jodi realized that her chances of being found by a search party from The Lady were fast approaching zero. She had been written off. Given the circumstances of her disappearance, it was not an unreasonable supposition. When the waves of pain built up to yet another unbearable peak Jodi began to seriously consider the idea of killing herself before the rest of the coyote pack came looking for their missing brother. She had the means—even if, at that moment, she did not have the strength—to turn the pistol on herself. She knew that if the decision were delayed too long she would be too weak to act upon it. Yet, in spite of the hopelessness of her situation, she hesitated. She simply refused to admit that death was the only option open to her.

Toward sundown, when Jodi was trying to focus her fading energy into the fingers lying limply across the pistol, she heard stealthy movements around her. The protective screen of broken branches was pulled away from her head and chest, and she found herself looking up into the craggy, weather-beaten face of a Tracker. But this was no Trail-Blazer. He wore a battered, wide-brimmed orange straw stetson with a ragged brim and his lean, square jaw was fringed by an untidy beard. The sleeves were missing from his faded red, black, and brown camouflaged fatigues, and they were covered in patches. Homemade bandoliers of the same material with pockets shaped to hold magazines and air bottles were slung over each shoulder. The only thing about him that did not look worn and shabby was his three-barreled air rifle. Its pristine condition told Jodi that this raggedy-ass was still a soldier; someone she could relate to.

The bearded Tracker laid down his rifle and knelt beside Jodi. His first move was to relieve her of her air pistol. When this was safely stowed inside his tunic he raised the visor of her helmet and studied her face. "How's it going, soldier-boy?"

Jodi tried to speak, but the words died half-formed in her throat. She rolled her head from side to side.

The Tracker carefully peeled back the charred collar of her tunic, lifted out her dog tags, and read off her name. "Ohh-kayyy, friend . . . ." He straightened up on his knees and cupped his hands around his mouth. "Hey, Ben! Roy! Come take a look-see!" The Tracker dropped back on his haunches, fingered the protruding tail of the bolt, then began to examine Jodi's arms and torso, whistling tunelessly under his breath. His touch was sure but gentle. He sat back and pushed up the battered brim of his Stetson. "Mmmhmmph. . . . You off that wagon train that got its ass kicked three days ago?"

Jodi signaled silently with her eyes and mouth that she was.

"Well, they took off, good buddy. Last we saw 'em they was headed Kansas way." He sighed and scratched his beard. "So unless you want to wait here for the Mutes or the coyotes, I guess that makes you one of us, Jodi."

"What you got, Beaver?"

Jodi could not see the owner of the voice.

Her bearded savior spoke across her. "We got us a woman, that's what we got."

"No shit. . . ."

Two other raggedy-asses peered down at her. One to her left, the other over Beaver's shoulder. Jodi guessed that they were Ben and Roy, though she didn't know which was which. The one on the left was wearing a wingman's bone dome. It had been smeared with mud to hide the bright blue-and-green stripes, but Jodi could see enough of the pattern to recognize it as once belonging to a crewman aboard the wagon train called King of the Pecos. The guy looking over Beaver's shoulder wore a crumpled yellow command cap. The long peak was frayed and the woven badge was missing.

"Are you sure?" asked Yellow-Hat.

"What kind of damn fool question is that?" Beaver looked up at Yellow-Hat and chuckled. "You think I've forgotten what they look like? Start moving that crap off her legs."

Yellow-Hat went to work. Beaver pulled the stopper out of his skin water bottle, eased Jodi's head off the ground, and tipped a little water onto her parched lips. Jodi licked them dry and opened her mouth for more.

"Thanks . . ." she wheezed.

"She don't look so hot," said Bone-Dome flatly.

"No. She's broke up pretty bad," Beaver admitted. "But she'll mend. Make no mistake, this is one tough lady."

"She'll need to be," said Bone-Dome. He seized hold of the dead coyote and flung it aside. "Okay, let's get her to Medicine Hat."

Jodi had been found by a scavenging party from a band of Tracker renegades. She'd known about them for years. As a youngster, she had seen several, who had been captured and brought back to the Federation for trial, confess the error of their ways before being shot on TV. Later, during her time as a wingman, she had also seen the bodies of about a dozen renegades killed by patrols from The Lady. Men and women that she had helped hunt down. Beaver and his two friends were the first live ones she had ever met face-to-face. Jodi remained conscious until they lifted her onto a makeshift stretcher, then she slipped into a coma. For a time, she knew nothing of the outside world, but deep within her subconscious mind the ordeal continued. Her inner eye was continually assailed by jagged, abstract images of pain; a limitless form of mental torture that drove her, screaming

soundlessly, to the edge of madness. Eighteen hours
later she emerged from the fevered coma to find herself in the hands of Medicine Hat. Someone holding a
clean, worn rag mopped her brow. She looked up at
the sky and took a deep breath, savoring the sweet-
ness of the air. Oh, Columbus! It hurt. Her whole
body burned from head to toe. It didn't matter. She
was going to *live!*

For Steve, the next weeks seemed to blur together,
making it hard to place specific events. He could
only remember being fed a thick soup twice a day
from a wooden bowl held by Cadillac, Mr. Snow, and
a number of female lump-heads who ranged from the
simply plain and unattractive to the hideously grotesque. At first the thought of eating Mute food filled
Steve with revulsion. He refused it for a couple of
days then became so hungry that he ate what he was
offered—and was promptly sick.

After several more days of mental and intestinal
discipline, he found he was able to keep the food
down without feeling nauseated and, eventually, began to look forward with growing relish to the next
strongly flavored dish. He did not, however, ask what
he was eating. His progress was rewarded with a
meal he could recognize—a fish with succulent pink,
flaky flesh, roasted over a wood fire. Exactly as in
that flash of memory he had had at Roz's side in San
Jacinto Deep. As he ate the fish, he wondered how he
could have acquired that knowledge. Perhaps, he con-
jectured, it did not stem from a memory of past
events but was a glimpse of the future. Perhaps he
had *foreseen* this moment, in the same inexplicable
way that he had often been able to predict the direction of the course marker lights when flying in the
Snake Pit.

Mr. Snow visited him from time to time to inspect
and dress his wounds. Sometimes Cadillac came with
him; at other times the straight-limbed Mute would
enter alone and squat silently by his side. Occasionally Steve would engage them in desultory conversa-

tion; desultory because he was given regular small doses of Dream Cap, which kept him in a state of drowsy euphoria. Twice, or maybe three times, Steve was vaguely aware of being lifted onto a stretcher of wood and skins, which was then carried through the darkness. He half remembered feeling the cool night air on his face; seeing the wondrous twinkling brilliance of countless points of light scattered across a black velvet sky. From the overheard snatches of conversation that entered his fudged brain, he understood that his Mute captors were moving camp under cover of darkness and lying concealed by day to avoid discovery by the arrowheads that now regularly crossed the sky.

Once, as he lay under a loose covering of branches, he saw, through a ragged gap in the leaves, two of the graceful Skyhawks dip and wheel across the sky; saw the white wing-tip panels and recognized them as coming from The Lady. Steve realized that she must have returned reequipped with a new section of wingmen to continue her thrust into Plainfolk territory. He wondered if Gus White were one of the pair now above him and whether they were looking for him, or whether they were just hunting Mutes. He felt a sudden pang of regret at being grounded then consoled himself with the thought that, against all odds, he was still alive and in one piece, being fed and cared for. If he could manage to stay alive, if his body mended, he could begin to plan his escape . . . provided his captors didn't find themselves on the receiving end of another napalm strike. Despite the fudging effects of the Dream Cap, this thought was a salutary reminder that he—Brickman, S. R.—was now one of the hunted. His fate was bound up with that of his captors.

After about a month, Mr. Snow stopped feeding Steve threads of Dream Cap. Steve found he was able to sit up without too much discomfort from his mending ribs. His left shoulder was still painfully stiff, but he was able to make limited use of his left arm. His right arm was still in a sling but the livid, gaping wound had closed.

Mr. Snow pronounced himself satisfied with Steve's general progress. "You should soon be ready to start moving around on that leg. I'll see if we can knock you up something to walk with."

"You mean a pair of crutches?"

"Yes, crutches," said Mr. Snow. "We must talk some more. You must know a whole lot of forgotten words."

"You must know a lot *I've* never heard of," Steve replied. "If you've got time, uhh . . . maybe we can learn each other's language."

"Maybe," said Mr. Snow noncommittally. "A lot of the words I use won't mean anything to you. You live in a different world; see things in a different way."

Steve shrugged. "You could teach me to see things your way."

Mr. Snow smiled. "I doubt it. What, for instance, do you mean by the word 'understanding'?"

" 'Understanding'?" Steve reflected for a moment. "Uhh, knowing what someone means when they give you an order. Knowing how something works, or what to do if anything goes wrong."

Mr. Snow nodded. "How about 'love'?"

Steve hesitated. "Is that a Mute word?"

"No, it's from the Old Time. It was a word that was constantly on people's lips. Not that it changed anything."

Steve shook his head. "Couldn't have been very important. If it was, we'd use it in the Federation. What is it—some kind of swear word?"

Mr. Snow let out a throaty chuckle. "I can see you've got a lot to learn."

Steve grinned. "Listen . . . Cadillac hadn't heard of 'television sets,' you hadn't come across 'crutches,' and I didn't know about 'love.' Maybe we can make a trade. Think about it."

Mr. Snow's eyes twinkled. "I will." He patted Steve on the shoulder and ducked out of the hut.

Now that he was no longer being fed Dream Cap,

Steve began to think more clearly and was quick to realize that his conversations with Mr. Snow and Cadillac could be his lifeline. He had been told about wordsmiths in the Field Intelligence briefing the crew had attended before their departure from Nixon-Fort Worth. In a race of idiots, the wordsmiths were the bright guys. Rare, gifted individuals who acted as the communal brains for the Mute clans that harbored them. It was known that Mutes could not read or write, and since most were dum-dums who didn't know what day it was, they were totally reliant on the memories of their wordsmiths. According to the three-man FINTEL team who gave the briefing, the cleverest of these guys carried up to nine hundred years of history around in their heads. They also possessed the ability to put chunks of it to music— what were known as "fire-songs"—*plus* retain a mental compendium of general knowledge that enabled Mutes to survive.

In the decimation of the southern Mutes in the centuries after the Break-Out many wordsmiths were believed to have perished. Those who escaped death during pacification and resettlement of the earliest New Territories had either moved north or were keeping an extremely low profile. They were believed to be more numerous among the Plainfolk, but not every clan had one and those that did guarded them well. Apart from the obvious advantages of owning a walking encyclopedia, it had become apparent that possession of a wordsmith gave a clan a vital edge over their rivals in other ways, ways that were still not fully understood. One thing, however, was clear: A definite correlation had been established—the more gifted the wordsmith, the more powerful the clan.

Having been told repeatedly from the age of three that Mutes did not take prisoners, Steve could not understand why his life had been spared. He longed to know the answer, but it was the one question he studiously avoided asking his captors. At the back of his mind was a lurking fear he might learn that their calendar included some bizarre festival at which the

entire M'Call clan solemnly dined on roast cloud
warrior. If that was what was waiting at the end of
the road, he preferred not to know about it. Steve
contented himself with expressing his appreciation
to all the Mutes who helped nurse him back to health
and congratulated himself on his luck at having been
shot down by Cadillac. Apart from being intelligent
and good-humored, he and Mr. Snow were insatiably
curious. Great. Couldn't be better. Steve was prepared to assuage their thirst for learning. He would
feed them the entire Tracker vocabulary one word at
a time, plus everything they wanted to know about
the Federation in the minutest detail. And what he
didn't know, he would make up. He would spin out
the material by getting them to tell *him* everything
they knew. As long as they felt they were on to a good
deal they would keep him alive. After all, who else
did they have to talk to?

In the long periods when he was left alone, Steve
dwelt on the possibility of escape. He wondered if the
wreckage of his Skyhawk had been abandoned or
whether any bits of the airframe or equipment had
been kept as trophies. It had not escaped his notice
that one of the female lump-heads assigned to bring
him food had blue-and-red electric cable threaded
through her plaited hair. Maybe someone had ripped
out the radio. Although normally powered by the
motor, it carried its own battery pack for use in an
emergency. There was also the survival equipment
he had been carrying: air pistol, combat knife, map,
food concentrates, flares, and a portable pocket-sized
emergency radio beacon that enabled the wagon train
to home in on a downed wingman. Steve had been
stripped of everything except his underpants, but he
had seen Cadillac wearing the top half of his flight
fatigues. The pockets had been empty. That meant
the goodies they held were probably stashed away
somewhere. If so . . .

Steve spent many happy hours devising elaborately
detailed escape scenarios—all of which ended in
triumph with a suitably thunderous welcome at Grand

Central. It was an agreeable fantasy. No Tracker who had fallen into the hands of the Mutes had ever lived to tell the tale. As the days passed and the strength gradually returned to his body, Steve became convinced that he was going to make it. He would be the first. His skill and daring would more than make up for his failure to gain top marks and the coveted Minuteman Trophy. His master plan would be back on course.

Set down outside Cadillac's hut for the first time in daylight, Steve discovered the source of one of the smells that had plagued him. The decaying heads of two Mute warriors were stuck on six-foot stakes set in the ground on either side of the doorway. Steve studied them with morbid fascination, noting the wide, powerful necks and lower jaws, the primitive helmets with their pattern of pierced stones, and the way the point of each stake, roasted iron-hard over a fire, had been hammered through the top of the skulls. Steve looked toward the other huts scattered under the nearby trees and saw that several of them had stakes outside the doors loaded with similar grisly trophies.

Around noon, Cadillac appeared carrying two freshly caught salmon trout. He used his flame-pot to kindle a fire, gutted the fish, threaded them on his knife-stick, and proceeded to roast them over the flames.

Steve's sense of smell had, by this time, adjusted itself to accommodate the appetizing aroma. His saliva glands began to work overtime. He noticed that Cadillac was wearing his digital watch—a calendar alarm model—strapped upside down on his left wrist. Steve twisted his head around in an effort to read the date, failed, thought about asking for the watch back, and decided to wait for a more appropriate moment. He drew Cadillac's attention to the head impaled on the stake to his right. Shakatak. "A friend of yours?"

Cadillac dropped his eyes onto the roasting fish, turning the knife-stick so that they cooked evenly. "He tried to invade our turf."

"So you killed him?"

"Both of them," said Cadillac. It wasn't strictly true, but to tell the whole story would mean explaining Clearwater's contribution. Mr. Snow had told him that the cloud warrior must not learn of her powers or her presence in the settlement.

"And if you kill somebody else, will his head end up on a pole, too?"

"It will join these," answered Cadillac. He broke up some more branches and fed them into the fire. "Each pole holds ten heads. A full head-pole is the sign of a mighty warrior."

"I see. . . ." Steve glanced at Shakatak's sightless head. "I guess that means you've got some way to go."

Cadillac responded with a quiet smile. "I am forbidden to run with the Bears. But in their eyes I have standing. I have chewed bone."

"Chewed bone?"

"Killed in single combat. Taken the head and eaten of the knife-arm."

Steve felt queasy. "Jeez. . . . You mean you ate the arm of this poor sonofabitch?"

"No," said Cadillac. "Our forefathers did many long years ago. The arm and the leg. Now, Plainfolk custom demands that on the first kill a warrior bite the fore part of the arm that wields the sharp iron through to the bone."

"Columbus. . . ." Steve shuddered and lapsed into silence.

When the fish were cooked, Cadillac slid them off his knife-stick onto a flat stone, cut off their heads, wrapped them in large red leaves, and handed one to Steve.

"Thanks." Steve took it in his left hand and edged his right hand up to help hold it. A sharp stab of pain pierced his torn biceps. He gasped, then inhaled the aroma of the roast trout, forgot about his sore arm and the artless savagery of his companion, and concentrated on assuaging his hunger. He brought his lips gingerly onto the fish. It was still too hot to eat. "Smells good. Did you catch these?"

"Yes." Once again, it was not strictly true. Cadillac had gone fishing with Clearwater and it was she who had gently stroked them into immobility and lifted them triumphantly by the gills from the rock pool.

Steve gave a quiet laugh. "It's crazy, you know. I've seen fish like this in the Federation. Swimming around in pools. But they're just decoration. No one would think of eating one any more than ..." He hesitated. "Than they'd think of eating someone's arm."

"A warrior who chews bone takes the strength of his enemy into his own body." Cadillac blew on the charred scales of his fish and bit into the pale, steaming flesh.

Steve replied with a hollow smile. "You don't really believe that, do you?" He shook his head. "I really can't work you guys out. You go to the trouble of pulling me out of the cornfield and putting me back in one piece, and at the same time"—he gestured toward Shakatak's impaled head—"you do this kind of thing and—"

Cadillac cut in. "The sand-burrowers have taken many heads from our southern brothers."

"Yeah, that's true," admitted Steve. "But it's not done all the time. It's a kind of initiation thing for wet-feet—linemen on their first trip, warriors who have not chewed bone—and the only reason it's done is because you started it."

Cadillac nibbled at his trout. "Do you not kill?"

"Yeah, sure," Steve replied. "We have to. We're trying to win back what belongs to us. The blue-sky world. But you guys kill each other." He gestured at the heads of Shakatak and Torpedo. "These fellas are Mutes, like you!"

Cadillac considered Steve's words. "In our world, all those who are not blood-brothers and blood-sisters of the clan M'Call are rivals. We must defend our turf. The M'Calls are descended from the ninth daughter of Me-Sheegun and the ninth son of She-Kargo. Many of the Plainfolk clans accept our greatness, for our seed goes back to the Heroes of the Old Time. But there are those who envy our greatness and wish to take it from us. If we are challenged, we must fight to the death or lose our standing. Without standing we are less than dust."

"Why? What's wrong in running away, then sneaking back later and nailing the other guy while he's asleep?"

Cadillac did not understand the question. He shrugged. "This is not the way of a warrior. If he is of the She-Kargo, he must follow the path laid down by Mo-Town, our great Mother."

That's your tough luck, thought Steve. "And where do we, uhh . . . 'sand-burrowers' fit into all this?"

Cadillac eyed him solemnly. "You are known by many names. The Beasts from the Bowels of the Earth, the Creatures of the Dark Cities, the Smooth-Skulled Worms that ride in the belly of the Iron Snake, the Death-Bringers, the Slave-Masters, the Evil Ones, the Servants of Pent-Agon, Lord of Chaos, and Scourge of the World."

Steve did his best to keep a serious face. "Fascinating. Back in the Federation we think *we* are the good guys. *You* are the ones who brought about the Holocaust that wrecked the blue-sky world."

"I know nothing about this Holocaust or the blue-sky world of which you speak."

"Oh, come on," insisted Steve. He swept an arm across the landscape. "This is the blue-sky world! You burned the cities and laid waste the land. That's what we call the Holocaust. It was you, the Mutes, who poisoned the air and drove us to take shelter within the earth-shield!"

"No, you are wrong," Cadillac said. "It was Pent-Agon who unleashed the War of a Thousand Suns through you, his servants. That war destroyed the earth and almost every living thing upon it. We, the She-Kargo and our soul-brothers and sisters now known as the Plainfolk, were spared. We were chosen by Mo-Town to grow strong in body and great in number, to guard the earth until the coming of Talisman."

"Look," reasoned Steve, "we both can't be right. I *know* what happened. It's all recorded in our archives. What proof have you got that what you say is the truth?"

"The proof is on the tongues of our wordsmiths. The history of the clan M'Call is sealed forever in the fire-songs of our people."

Steve laughed. "I don't believe it. I don't care if Mr. Snow *is* the greatest wordsmith of all time. Nobody can remember everything that's happened in the last nine hundred years! It's impossible. The Amtrak Federation deals in *facts*—billions of bits of verifiable data stored on silicon chips—not a collection of stories made up out of a mishmash of old folks' memories."

"You use many strange words," Cadillac said, "but my mind begins to grasp their meaning. Because of the war, many of our people are born without pockets in their heads. Their minds cannot hold the past or the knowledge needed for the high crafts, but to some, those we call wordsmiths, Mo-Town gave the power of a hundred minds and a thousand tongues." Cadillac squared his shoulders and lifted his chin proudly. "I, too, have been given this power. I know of the valiant deeds of the M'Calls, the history of the Plainfolk from their beginnings, and the workings of the world. I have learned these things from Mr. Snow, who speaks with the Sky Voices. You say you have this Columbus—a thing made with the High Craft—that holds the past of your people—"

"Yes, computer archives," interjected Steve.

"The words have a dead sound," Cadillac said. "No matter. If you remember nothing, how can you be sure of what these . . . computer archives tell you?"

"That's easy," replied Steve. "Computers like Columbus don't forget, and they don't make things up. A computer is a machine . . ." Steve paused. "You know what a machine is?"

Cadillac shook his head.

Steve searched their surroundings for something that might explain the concept. He pointed at Cadillac's crossbow. "You see that? That's a machine. It throws bolts. You could use your hand and arm to throw a bolt, but the crossbow throws it farther and faster. That's why we build machines. To do things better and faster than people can do them. Computers are machines that think. Mechanical brains that store information. 'Mechanical' means machinelike. You feed in the facts and they remember them. They also do all kinds of other things you wouldn't understand."

"Perhaps it is not necessary to understand these things," said Cadillac.

Steve smiled. "Are you kidding? When we started, the Amtrak Federation was little more than a hole in the ground. Now, thanks to the First Family and Columbus, we have twelve bases with more building, linked by linear-drive monorails. We have two-way video, geothermal power, hydroponic farms with automated weather systems, lasers, powered flight, the technological know-how to do whatever we want, and you—you're still in the Stone Age."

Cadillac smiled. "And yet, in spite of these marvels, here you are." It was the kind of observation Mr. Snow would have made and it pleased Cadillac immensely.

"A lucky shot," said Steve.

"And the other cloud warriors who fell?"

"Freak weather plus a few bad breaks. None of that makes any difference. It's time you faced up to the facts. No one can resist the power of the Federation. You've seen what The Lady can do. We have twenty wagon trains like that and we're building more all the time. Ten years from now we'll have a hundred. In twenty, we'll have way stations from coast to coast. We'll be unstoppable. We are the future. You are the past that's about to be swept away. You're living in a make-believe world—Sky Voices, Mo-Town, Names of Power. You've all been swallowing too much Dream Cap. I don't know where Mr.

Snow got his version of history from, but, believe me, it didn't happen like that."

"Are you not sand-burrowers?" countered Cadillac. "Do you not live in the Dark Cities beneath the Great Desert of the South?"

"They're not dark," Steve replied. "How many times do I have to tell you?! We have electricity. Neon tubes. Long sticks that give off light like the sun."

"They cannot banish the darkness in the mind," said Cadillac. "This is what we mean when we speak of the Dark Cities. The truth stands in the words of the Plainfolk. After the War of a Thousand Suns, Pent-Agon and his servants—you, the sand-burrowers—were buried beneath the earth as punishment for your crimes against the world."

"We must have been let off for good behavior," said Steve lightly. "It may not have come to your notice, but the Federation has had way stations on the overground for nearly two hundred years. And the way things are going, in another hundred the whole of America will be ours once again."

Cadillac shook his head. "It will not happen. The Sky Voices have spoken to Mr. Snow. The iron snakes will be defeated. You will be driven back into your burrows, and your Dark Cities will be crushed beneath the desert."

"Really," said Steve. "And when is this supposed to happen?"

"When the earth gives the sign," Cadillac replied. "The Plainfolk shall be as a bright sword in the hand of Talisman, their Savior."

Steve frowned. It was the second time this name had come into their conversation. "Talisman? Who's he?"

"The Thrice-Gifted One," said Cadillac.

Steve's curiosity was aroused, but his young bene-factor ignored his questions and left without offering any further explanation.

In the days that followed, Steve had a series of conversations with Cadillac and Mr. Snow. They questioned him endlessly about the Federation, how it was organized, what it was like to live in an underground city, what people did, what they wore, and what they ate. Steve, in turn, asked them about the history of the Plainfolk and how the M'Calls had come to be regarded as one of, if not *the* greatest of, the She-Kargo warrior clans, along with more practical questions about food supplies and how they survived the long months of winter, the period the Mutes referred to as the White Death.

Sometimes three or four, or as many as half a dozen, Mutes—clan-elders or Bears and She-Wolves—would gather around them and sit silently listening to their conversation. Now and then one of them would rise abruptly in midsentence to be replaced by a new listener. Steve got the impression that their audience did not fully understand what was being said; they were just listening to the sound of his voice and that of the two wordsmiths, letting the flow of conversation wash over them as one might sit listening to the rippling murmur of a mountain stream.

Mr. Snow was particularly interested in what the Federation termed its "pacification program" for the New Territories. Steve described in detail how the early Trail-Blazers had reconquered the overground above the Inner and Outer States. The resistance offered by the southern Mutes had been sporadic. The clans that had fought had been wiped out; those that had opted to surrender had been reduced to serfdom. The majority of the surviving clans had been relocated in work camps built around the semi-subterranean way stations; where this was impractical, they had accepted to pay annual tribute in the form of work gangs, or fixed quotas of metallic or chemical ores, timber, or other raw materials. These were ferried by wagon train to overground sawmill, smelting, and processing plants crewed by Mutes with Tracker overseers from the way stations; then they were hauled down to manufacturing plants within the earthshield. Mining operations located near

Tracker bases were accessed directly from the underground levels by groups of Young Pioneers, as they had been in the past before the Break-Out—the historic moment in 2464 when the Trackers opened up their first permanent interface with the blue-sky world.

Steve also told Mr. Snow about "yearlings." Following the Break-Out it had been discovered that now and then Mute females sometimes gave birth to a "straight"—a Mute child who, although multicolored, was smooth-skinned and otherwise free of the genetic malformations that characterized the normal "lump-head." For some unexplained reason straight Mutes were, without exception, males. Since any clan found harboring an undeclared straight faced immediate annihilation, all such children were handed over to the Trackers at birth.

In return, the fortunate clan was released from its obligation to supply its quota of ore, timber, or work gangs for a period of twelve months. Hence the name "yearling." The newborn Mutes were taken to a special center known as The Farm where, as far as Steve knew, they were subjected to various tests in connection with the Life Research Program and then disposed of.

"Have you ever talked with any of our southern brothers?" asked Mr. Snow.

Steve shook his head. "You can't *talk* to them. It's hard enough getting them to understand what work they're supposed to do. As wingman on a wagon train I was never close enough to 'em. But I must admit I never tried. First because if it's not your job, it's not encouraged; second because it's, well, uhh . . . not healthy to hang around them too long; third because it just wouldn't enter my head to talk to a lump—" He broke off with an embarrassed smile. "I mean, they're not like you and Cadillac. They're . . ."

"Stupid? . . ." volunteered Mr. Snow.

Steve shrugged. "If you want me to be honest, yes, most of them probably are. They don't know anything and they can't learn anything." Steve hesitated then concluded lamely, "Well . . . that's what we were told."

Mr. Snow nodded with an understanding smile. "How do you think they feel?"

"Feel? . . ." Steve looked puzzled, as if he couldn't quite grasp the idea that a Mute could *feel* anything; could have expectations of anything other than the life to which history had condemned him.

"Yes," said Mr. Snow. "How do you think they feel about working in slave camps?"

Steve pursed his lips and pondered the question. "I don't know. They're alive, aren't they? They get regular meals. They don't have to fight other clans."

"They are also bound with iron ropes."

"Iron? . . . Oh, you mean *chains*," Steve said. "Yeah, that's true. But not everybody. Only the trouble-makers."

Mr. Snow nodded then said quietly, "Why do you think they make trouble?"

Steve responded with a quick laugh. "I guess they don't like work."

"Maybe they have a different way of looking at the world."

"Maybe they have," said Steve. "What they have to learn to do is look at it *our* way." He smiled to take the hard edge off his words. "This is *our* world. This country belongs to *us*. The Mutes in those work camps are there beeause they lost out. They had a choice . . . and they chose not to die."

"Are those the only two options we have?" Mr. Snow asked. "Slavery or death? We think, we feel, we draw breath. Don't we have a right to exist?"

Steve chewed over his reply. "I don't know quite how to put it."

"Put it anyway you like. Shoot to kill."

"Then the official answer is 'no.' The First Family has raised us to think of you as being lower than animals. That it is our duty to wipe you off the face of the earth. But . . ."

"But what?"

"Now that I've met you and Cadillac I'm not so

sure. I'm ... well, kind of ... confused. I mean you talk like a ... real person."

Mr. Snow chuckled. "Thank you."

"And Cadillac ... If you ignore the color of his skin—"

"Looks like a real person. Yes, I can see the problem. Never mind." Mr. Snow patted Steve's shoulder. "I'm sure you'll work it out." He uncrossed his legs and stood up. He began to walk away then turned back. "What would you say if I told you that the ancestors of the Plainfolk were people from the Old Time—straight-limbed people, many of them with skins the same color as yours?"

Steve decided it was time to be diplomatic. "After meeting you I'd have to say that anything is possible."

Mr. Snow chuckled heartily. "You're a smart cookie, Brickman. You'll go far."

As he watched Mr. Snow walk away he had the distinct feeling that the old wordsmith and his heir apparent were stringing him along. Steve had always prided himself on staying one step ahead of the game and it annoyed him to be kept in the dark. It was Mr. Snow who was the smart cookie. It occurred to Steve that, just as he had been able to "predict" certain minor events a few seconds before they occurred, his two principal captors might also possess some means of knowing what was passing through his mind—such as his firm intention to escape at the earliest possible moment. Maybe that would account for the amused expression with which Mr. Snow listened to what he had to say. On the other hand, it was just possible that they actually *enjoyed* his company, despite the fact that he had made no attempt to curry favor. Steve was a survivor, but he was not by nature a groveler. So far, his robust approach seemed to be working. They did not seem to mind his outspokenness; in fact, they seemed to encourage it.

As a consequence, and totally against his better judgment, Steve found himself looking forward to his daily conversations—what the Mutes called "rapping." He could hardly bear to admit it to himself, but in an odd sort of way he was beginning to warm to his hosts. This was not, as so often in the past, a calculated act of deception; the feeling was quite genuine. He still viewed them as little more than primitive, misshapen savages who stank like an A-Level garbage line, but they had a relaxed life-style that was in marked contrast to the tightly structured Developmental Activity Program that had ordered his life within the Federation from day one. His Tracker psyche was being torn in two. One part chafing at the lack of discipline and vigorous organization, repelled by an alien way of life; the other part succumbing to the insidious attractions of overground existence.

Despite years of indoctrination some long-buried instinct had been aroused, was responding—as on his first solo flight—to the blue-sky world. It had, admittedly, been a privileged kind of existence thus far. He hadn't yet been obliged to hunt for food, or cook over open fires in pouring rain or a snowstorm. He had enjoyed room service and the attentions of a string of nurses, and the clan had not had to defend its turf since he had crash-landed amongst them. That said, compared to the Federation, it was still like living on a five-star dung heap.

But there was something else.

The one great discovery Steve had made as a captive of the M'Calls was the quality of stillness. An almost narcotic calmness had crept into his mind. There was noise, but it came from natural sources: the sound of wind through the trees, running water; from living sounds: the human voice in speech and song, children laughing, crying, being comforted with soothing murmurs. The haunting music made by blowing through wooden pipes, vibrant notes that hung on the air, created a disturbing resonance within him.

Such a simple device, yet something quite unknown within the Federation, where all music was produced electronically and—except for blackjack—under the total control of the First Family. But, above all, up among the Plainfolk there was no *hassle;* there was

no one riding herd on your ass; the eye and ear were
not being constantly battered by inspirational video-
casts. Yet, in spite of the complete absence of exhor-
tation from some central ruling body, there was a
unity of purpose; a cooperation in time of need without any overt sign of discipline.

A kind of togetherness. An unspoken kinship. An . . .
Awareness.

The word-concept came fully formed into Steve's
mind, catching him by surprise.

—— 14 ——

The day after Steve's conversation with Mr. Snow, Cadillac appeared with an elderly lump-head called Three-Degrees.

Both Mutes carried several freshly cut saplings and the lump-head was equipped with a machete, paring knife, awl, bone needle, and coarse handmade binding thread. Cadillac got Steve to draw the design of Federation-issue crutches in the dirt outside the hut. As these were made in metal, certain modifications were inevitable, and after some discussion Steve made a revised sketch which, although he could not know it, resembled the old split shaft model that had supported the wounded in the first half of the twentieth century. Steve watched with undisguised admiration as Three-Degrees wielded his primitive tools with skilled precision. Prompted now and then by Cadillac, he quickly fashioned a pair of crutches with firm, neat-fitting joints and armrests padded with fast-foot skin.

Cadillac helped Steve to his feet and stood by him as he took the first few halting steps with the aid of the crutches. His left leg could not yet bear any weight, his left shoulder and wounded right arm were still painfully stiff, but the pleasure of regaining a measure of mobility more than outweighed any discomfort.

Three-Degrees watched with a delighted grin as Steve got the hang of one-legged walking and began to move more rhythmically. "Is good?"

Steve nodded approvingly. "Terrific. You did a great job."

Three-Degrees looked at Cadillac uncertainly.

"A word from the Old Time," said Steve. "It means very good."

"Numero Uno," Cadillac explained. "Prima."

"Ahh, dig. Right on." Three-Degrees smiled broadly as he gathered up his tools. "Have a nice one." He patted Steve on the arm and ambled away.

One of the female Mutes who had brought Steve food on several occasions approached carrying his camouflaged flight fatigues rolled up under her arm. They had been washed and inexpertly sewn together where they had gotten torn in the crash. Cadillac helped Steve back into them. All the pockets that normally held his survival equipment were depressingly empty. It made Steve feel half-naked.

"How far am I allowed to go?"

"As far as you want," said Cadillac. "But for your own safety it might be better if you stayed within the bounds of the settlement." He smiled. "The overground can be a dangerous place."

Steve nodded. "Is that all?"

"No. Don't go into any huts without being invited, don't pick up any sharp iron or tools you might find lying around, don't take any food unless it is offered to you." He smiled again. "There are people here who would dearly like an excuse to put your head on a pole. Capeesh?"

"Terrific," Steve said, mentally filing "capeesh," "dig," and the other new words he had just heard from Three-Degrees. He had discovered that the Mutes had two distinct speech-modes. The first was a kind of ceremonial language with a curious elliptical syntax, in which the words were full of imagery. Mute songs were written in this style, probably the reason why it was known as fire-speech. It was the favored speech-mode of warriors when greeting people, in formal discussions, and in encounter situations. Cadillac, who seemed very concerned with status and protocol, had used it a lot in the beginning, but now he and the old wordsmith were conversing in a mixture of Mute and Basic—the language of the Federation they had picked up from Steve. The second, more informal, speech-mode, known as "sweet-talk," was closer to Basic and possessed the raw, juicy directness that characterized Trail-Blazer jargon. Sweet-talk also embraced a fascinating subset known as "jive," a semisecret warrior tongue that was almost impossible for a stranger to understand without an interpreter.

Steve adjusted the crutches comfortably under his armpits and set off on his first walk through the settlement. M'Call huts were scattered across a high wooded plateau where the days dawned crisp and clear. The adjacent slopes were thinly covered with the same dark red-needled trees; to the west, a farther range of hills rose even higher. Steve remembered being moved at least four times. From his general knowledge of the area gleaned from study of the maps aboard the wagon train, he reckoned that the clan had moved in a westerly direction. The trouble was, without a map he had no idea how *far* they had traveled, but the fact that many of the huts had been set up on open ground without any attempt to conceal them from the air implied that the clan now judged themselves to be beyond the range of the patrolling Skyhawks.

As he hobbled around the M'Call settlement, Steve began to discern the daily pattern of Mute activity. Each morning, posses of Bears and She-Wolves went out on hunting expeditions, returning soon after sundown with game of various kinds—mountain deer with thick curving horns, and, once, a buffalo. The

She-Wolves specialized in snaring birds and fish. Other mixed groups of warriors chosen for guard duty squatted motionless on high ground around the settlement or patrolled the limits of what the clan deemed to be their turf. Evading these sharp-eyed sentinels when he made his planned escape was yet another problem he had to overcome.

In between his exploratory walks, Steve sat in on several of Mr. Snow's classes for the young Mutes and admired the patience with which he dispensed the rudiments of knowledge. After a few sessions he realized that many of the lessons and stories were repeats of previous material. The long question-and-answer sessions with the two wordsmiths who, up to that point, had been his principal interlocutors had caused Steve to overlook this basic flaw in the Mute makeup. He was reminded again of their congenital forgetfulness when he ran into Three-Degrees on one of his walks. The old lump-head failed to recognize his handiwork and it was obvious that he only had a hazy recollection of who Steve was.

The young M'Call Cubs continued to regard Steve as an object of curiosity and source of innocent amusement. Like Three-Degrees, they seemed to have forgotten his role in the fire-bombing of the crop-fields. Steve found that a lot harder to forget, especially when the bodies of the children who trailed behind him on his walks were indelibly scarred by the napalm he had dropped with reluctant precision.

Some of the older children behaved more aggressively, jostling him as they ran past; dancing around him, pulling faces and jeering. Others played a boisterous game of tag wherever he happened to be walking, running into him at full tilt while attempting to evade their pursuer. Steve was "accidentally" knocked to the ground several times and once, as he was sent sprawling, two thirteen-year-olds grabbed his crutches and swung them wildly around their heads, smashing them together like quarterstaves. It was just another game, of course, but the intention was clear:

they hoped to break the crutches and send Steve crawling back to his hut on his hands and knees.

Fortunately, Mr. Snow happened by. He restored order and helped Steve back onto his feet. "Just high spirits. . . ."

"Yes, sure," said Steve. There was no point in complaining. He altered his exercise schedule so that his walks coincided with Mr. Snow's classes for the young Mutes and kept close to the hut he shared with Cadillac when they were out of school.

The majority of the adult Mutes—and that included everybody from fourteen up—treated him with a mixture of courtesy and circumspection. They didn't go out of their way to avoid him but neither did they seek out his company unless it was to eavesdrop silently on his conversations with Mr. Snow or Cadillac. A number of male and female warriors showed their hostility more openly by turning their backs on him whenever he approached. If they were sitting talking in a group, they fell silent until he was out of earshot. The classic cold shoulder. He was like a stray dog whose presence is tolerated but not actively encouraged; who is given odd scraps to eat but never becomes one of the family with his own bowl and a place by the fire.

His talks with the two wordsmiths continued on a more or less regular basis, but Steve found he was left to his own devices for the greater part of each day with very little opportunity to do anything except think and exercise his body. He concocted his own program of physiotherapy, spending up to six hours each day in strenuous physical workouts. As he sweated to build up his stamina and strength Steve continued to plan his escape, modifying various details as he gradually built up his knowledge of the clan's activities and the layout of the settlement.

As time passed Steve became increasingly certain that the M'Calls had no particular fate reserved for him. Roast cloud warrior was not on the menu. There was no Plan X. They were just waiting for something to happen. As a child of the Federation, Steve was totally baffled by the clan's attitude toward him. He could accept the undercurrent of hostility, but he could not understand the almost total freedom he was accorded. He was, after all, their *prisoner*, yet he was not shackled or guarded; he had no escort, no one asked him where he was going or where he had been, and the restraints upon him were minimal. On the face of it, if he wanted to escape, all he had to do was to walk out of the settlement. But how far would he get? It was this very lack of overt surveillance that led Steve to conclude that escape on foot would not be that easy. If there were no bars to his cage, it was because the M'Calls were confident that they could hunt him down as quickly and efficiently as they did the fast-foot and the buffalo.

Steve applied himself to his program of exercises with his usual diligence and was finally rewarded by being able to stand on his own two feet. Cadillac and Mr. Snow were on hand to applaud the moment when he cast aside his crutches and walked around the hut with a confident stride. Returning to where they stood by the head-poles bearing the decaying skulls of Shakatak and Torpedo, he punched the air exultantly with his right fist. As his arm snapped straight in the traditional Trail-Blazer salute, a stab of pain shot through the still-tender muscle, punishing him for such an arrogant gesture.

Steve concealed the pain beneath a tight-lipped grin and found the grace to thank his benefactors. "I'd like you both to know that I really appreciate what you've done for me." He paused and took a deep breath. "I may regret this, but . . . uh, I have to ask. Why have you gone to so much trouble to keep me alive?"

"Don't worry about it," replied Mr. Snow. "You'll find out soon enough."

Steve refused to let it go. "That sounds ominous."

Mr. Snow laughed quickly. "What can I tell you? Right now, the word is you're going to live. Okay?"

"But if you know what's going to happen . . ." persisted Steve.

Mr. Snow sighed patiently. "Look, young man, if I told you, you wouldn't believe me. You have a good mind. It has a great deal of potential but it is not open to the things of this world. You do not see it as it is, but as you *think* it should be."

"You've lived under the ground too long," Cadillac said. "Your eyes and your ears are full of sand."

Mr. Snow squatted in front of Steve and ran his hands gently up and down his left trouser leg between the knee and ankle, barely touching the fabric. "Mmm, feels good. . . ." He stood up, took hold of Steve's wrist, and flexed his right arm, checking the movement of the muscles as he did so. "I wish all my patients healed as well as this." Mr. Snow gave Steve's arm a friendly pat. "Keep on with those workouts. Another half-moon or so and you'll be ready to make the big break."

The old wordsmith chuckled at Steve's confused expression. He looked like a kid who'd been caught with his hand in the cookie jar. It was a saying from the Old Time that Mr. Snow had treasured ever since he had first heard it fifty-two winters ago. "Relax. It's only natural for you to want to get back to your burrow."

"The overground doesn't frighten me," Steve snapped, annoyed at being caught off guard.

"No, it doesn't," agreed Mr. Snow. "It should. The word from the south was that you people like to stay close to one another. Like a herd of fast-foot. But it doesn't seem to affect you. I wonder why?"

"I'm a wingman," Steve replied. "We're different. The pick of the bunch. We're trained to operate alone."

Mr. Snow nodded gravely. "I see. . . . Well, just remember that Cadillac and I can't protect you once you step off the edge of our turf. Capeesh?"

"Don't worry," Steve said lightly. "I'll let you know when I'm planning to leave."

"Good. . . . " The old wordsmith's eyes twinkled mischievously. "Let's get one thing straight, Brickman. I never worry." He turned on his heel and walked away, followed by Cadillac.

When they were out of earshot, Cadillac asked, "Was it wise to reveal that you know what he is thinking?"

Mr. Snow smiled. "In his case, yes. Our devious young friend is one of those people who thrives on a challenge."

When his leg felt strong enough, Steve added jogging to his exercise routine. Day after day, he gradually extended the length of his run, varying his route over the M'Calls' turf to build up his knowledge of the surrounding terrain. One particular day, while resting on a vantage point that gave him a good view over the slopes below, Steve saw a posse of Bears leave the main settlement on some errand. They set off with an easy, loping stride, running nimbly down the slope—and kept on running, for mile after mile across the plain below until they were lost from sight. Steve completed his planned circuit, returned to the same spot, and waited patiently. Five hours later, his vigil was rewarded. The posse of Bears reappeared, covering the ground with the same robotlike stride, running back up the slope as easily as they had run down.

Steve raced back to the settlement in time to see the Bears arrive. He expected them to collapse, red-faced and exhausted, but they weren't even gasping for breath. The runners strolled about, chatting unconcernedly with their families and other clan-members who had been on hand to welcome their return. Some even ran to join in a strange game in which two teams punched an inflated skin ball back and forth across a high strip of net strung between two poles. It looked like it might be fun to play.

Steve realized now why he had not been closely guarded. If he planned to make a break for it on foot he would not only have to be in top condition, he would also need at least a week's start on his pursuers. The discovery of the Mutes amazing stamina necessitated a drastic revision of his escape plan.

There was only one sure-fire way to evade his captors, and that was to *fly* out.

The notion had first occurred to him when he had been flat on his back, daydreaming about his triumphal return to the Federation. He had dismissed the idea then as totally impractical, but now he began to consider it as a serious possibility. The M'Calls had, after all, brought down at least three Skyhawks near their original settlement above Route 88 out of Cheyenne. His own in the cropfield; Fazetti's and Naylor's over the forest—the clan's presumed hiding place. In the several weeks he had lived amongst them, Steve had seen dozens of Mutes wearing strips of the blue solar-cell fabric and plaited lengths of cable. He had even seen instrument dials sewn onto some of the warriors' leather helmets and some of the kids had been rolling one of the small landing wheels around.

Steve had neither the hope nor the means of reconstructing a fullblown Skyhawk, but if the clan had hoarded enough bits of one or more of the basic airframes, there might be sufficient material to build a hang glider. Through his concentrated studies at the Academy, Steve had the knowledge and the technical skill to build something that would fly. But not without tools—and there was no way such an enterprise could be carried out in secret. He would need to make friends and influence people. That was no problem. If enough materials could be salvaged, he would offer Cadillac the chance of learning how to fly. The young wordsmith took himself very seriously and was obsessed with his status—what the lump-heads called "standing." He would jump at the opportunity. Through him, Steve would be able to get the help of M'Call craftsmen like Three-Degrees. Maybe there were others with abilities unknown to the Federation. Building the glider would provide an opportunity for discovering just how bright the Plainfolk really were.

Steve sauntered along one of the settlement trails, putting the final details together in his head. He could see it clearly, just as on a videotape. A craft would be constructed to his design, would need to be tested before instruction of his eager pupil could begin. His helpers would marvel at the faultless takeoff, would cheer as he swooped sleek-winged over their heads, would swell with pride as he gained height like a soaring eagle—blissfully unaware that his test flight would end a couple of hundred miles away at the nearest way station. He'd leave 'em standing, open-mouthed, like the idiots they were. Best of all, the two wordsmiths, who thought they were such wise guys, would be totally shafted. It was a good plan. It had style. And it was a hell of a lot better than trying to outrun a bunch of screaming lumpheads.

When Cadillac joined him for supper that evening, Steve used the opportunity to talk about his three years at the Flight Academy in New Mexico, culminating with an eloquent account of his first over-ground solo. Cadillac listened attentively. Afterward, when Steve had gone to sleep, he went to Mr. Snow's hut. They sat cross-legged on the talking mat and shared a pipe of rainbow grass.

"He wishes to build an arrowhead so that he may teach me to ride the sky like a cloud warrior."

"I know. . . ." The old wordsmith's voice floated through the smoke that curled lazily between them.

"Is there any reason why this should not be?"

"None at all." Mr. Snow pulled deeply on the pipe, inhaling the smoke. His face froze in a half smile for several minutes while his vocal chords waited for the air to clear. "He follows the path laid down for you by the Sky Voices."

Cadillac took the offered pipe and drew more smoke into his body. His head began to take wing. As a consequence, there was some delay before his brain managed to make contact with his mouth. "To help build an arrowhead will give me knowledge of the High Craft, and to fly like an eagle will bring me great standing. You are my teacher." He passed the pipe over. "It is not fitting that I should receive these gifts without them first being given to you."

"You go ahead," replied Mr. Snow. He waved the pipe in the air. "This is the only way *I'm* leaving the ground."

Steve was right in thinking that the clan had moved farther west, but he was not entirely correct about the reason for their retreat to the relative safety of higher ground. While the clan-elders were anxious to avoid further attacks from the arrowheads until they had learned to resist the fire from the sky and the long sharp iron wielded by the sand-burrowers, they had a second, equally pressing reason for moving westward. The elders wanted to avoid having to answer any challenge over the M'Calls' turf until the Bears had regained their standing. By running from the battle with the iron snake they had, like the Japanese samurai of old, "lost face." Without "standing," they were—by the unwritten laws of the Plainfolk—unworthy to bear sharp iron and engage other warriors in single combat. Since the M'Calls' turf was now threatened with incursions by the D'Vine, the clan to which the dead Shakatak and his three companions had belonged, Rolling-Stone had given the order to withdraw westward into the great mountains until the shamed Bears were ready to "bite the arrow"—the traditional proof of courage by which they regained their warrior status.

Steve was invited by Mr. Snow and Cadillac to sit in on the ceremony. Seeing the flames leaping from the big bonfire and hearing a rumbling background beat of drums, he thought he was finally going to hear one of the long-awaited fire-song sessions. Instead, he found himself watching a macabre ceremony of self-mutilation. Mr. Snow explained to Steve the reason why, since his capture, he had only heard solo voices, singing a keening lament, sometimes accompanied by a haunting melody played on reed pipes; the rousing fire-songs, which recalled the epic deeds of the M'Calls, could not be sung in honor of warriors who had lost their standing; they had first to bite the arrow.

Sitting beside Cadillac, Steve watched with morbid fascination as the first of the M'Call braves knelt before Rolling-Stone and presented him with an arrow. Each brave was required to make his own, whittling the straight shaft and honing the four blades of the iron head to razor sharpness. Rolling-Stone held the arrow above his head, flexing the shaft as he displayed it to the watching clan. This, Cadillac explained, was to prove that the shaft had not been weakened. The warrior then stretched out his arms toward two clan-elders who knelt facing him on either side and laid the palms of his hands on theirs, fingers stretched out and closed lightly together at shoulder height.

"Watch his hands," Cadillac whispered.

Steve fixed his attention upon them. The drumbeats and the clicking from wooden percussive instruments became sharper, more insistent, assuming an almost hypnotic intensity. They were joined by an unseen chorus in the darkness beyond the fire.

The kneeling brave filled his chest with air and let out a great shout. "Hey-*yahh!*"

With one swift movement, Rolling-Stone drove the arrow point through the left cheek of the brave and out through the right. Steve shuddered at the thought of how it must feel. He expected the brave's hands to ball into fists but he bore the pain stoically. His outstretched fingers quivered a little but his palms did not lift from those of the elders. The brave rose and turned to face the clan, arms still outstretched, his teeth clamped firmly on the shaft of the arrow. Keeping his elbows at shoulder height, he swept his outstretched palms slowly forward, then inward, and gripped the head and tail of the arrow. With a sharp downward jerk, he broke it between his teeth, pulled the two ends of the shaft out of his face, held them aloft with a showman's flourish, then stepped forward and spat the remaining piece into the bonfire.

"*Heyy-yahh!!*" roared the clan approvingly. Their chorus of approval merged harmoniously with the sonorous background chant.

Steve sat there, silently appalled.

One by one, the M'Call warriors who had been at the Battle of the Now and Then River stepped forward to bite the arrow. Motor-Head, Black-Top, and Steel-Eye, Cadillac's surviving clan-brothers, then Hershey-Bar, Henry-K, Average-White, Curved Air, Osi-Bisa, Seven-Up, Burger-King, Gulf-Oil, Camp-David, and the rest whose Names of Power Steve did not yet know.

After fifty or so braves had had their faces skewered, just as Steve was beginning to get a little bored by it all, he witnessed a new horror. Good-Year, a warrior Steve guessed was in his midtwenties (with Mutes it was hard to tell), crapped out. As Rolling-Stone plunged the arrow through his cheek, Good-Year balled his fists and half closed his outstretched arms with a convulsive jerk. The kneeling clan-elders on either side of him grabbed hold of his wrists, stood up, and pulled his arms behind his back, forcing his head down. Almost before Steve had time to realize what was happening, another clan-elder stepped out of the darkness behind Rolling-Stone, lifted a hefty stone hammer, and brought it down with tremendous force on the back of Good-Year's skull.

"Christopher Columbus!" breathed Steve. He grabbed Cadillac's arm. "Don't any of these guys get a second chance?"

Cadillac didn't answer. Four warriors who had passed the test with flying colors leapt up, grabbed Good-Year's body by the arms and legs, and threw it onto the fire. There was a shower of sparks and a hideous crackling noise. The flames leapt higher. The drumming, clicking, and chanting rose to fever pitch.

They are all mad, thought Steve. Or they are all so brain-damaged that they feel no pain? But then he cast his mind back to the river battle; to Trail-Boss Buck McDonnell standing up on the bulldozer behind Barber, the First Engineer, with crossbow bolts zipping around his ears; to Caulfield in his Skyhawk on the flight deck, a crossbow bolt through his temples and his eyeballs hanging down by his nostrils, yelling as they hauled him out of his cockpit, "Leave me alone! I'm okay, I'm okay. Let's go! Let's get at these bastards!" The M'Calls had summarily executed Good-Year for failing the test of a warrior; but Grand Central put guys up against a wall and shot them in front of the video cameras for crapping out on operations. It could even be happening to Hartmann, Commander of The Lady, right now. The smell of roasting human flesh assailed his nostrils. It was a salutary reminder that he himself had committed the same act in reverse. He had dropped bonfires made of napalm on the children of the people he was sitting with. We are all, thought Steve, as mad as each other.

Good-Year's body, blackened and charred, merged with the blazing embers as more wood was heaped on the fire and slowly disintegrated. The ceremony continued far into the night, with the clan roaring its approval as each Mute presenting himself for reinstatement as a warrior broke the bloodstained arrow held between his clenched teeth and spat the third piece contemptuously into the flames. The other two pieces, Cadillac explained, would be attached to a necklace; a badge of courage to be worn with pride.

Steve lost track of time. He was becoming tired. The incessant drumming and chanting had become, to his ear, monotonous, overwhelming. He longed to get up and stretch, to creep into the furskin bed he had been given and go to sleep, but he felt constrained to stay where he was. With the whole clan in a hyped-up state there was no knowing what might happen. Steve had an odd sense of foreboding. All it needed was for some of those Bears who'd been giving him mean-eyed looks to decide to have a little fun and . . .

He decided it would be safer to stick close to Cadillac and Mr. Snow.

Cadillac leaned into him and pressed something in his hand. "Take this," he muttered. "Just in case. . . ."

Steve glanced at his neighbors, but nobody appeared to have noticed the transaction. He brought his right hand casually up to his face, rubbed his nose with his thumb and forefinger, and glanced down at what Cadillac had put into his palm. It was shredded Dream Cap. Steve slowly rubbed his hand over his mouth and chin, scooped the drug up with his tongue, and chewed it discreetly. Something about the way Cadillac had passed over the Dream Cap suggested it was the best thing to do. But what did he mean by "just in case"?

Another roar of approval. Another M'Call knelt to have his cheeks pierced. The line of waiting warriors seemed endless. Steve let his eyes roam over the closely packed rows of lump-heads on either side of him. Male and female warriors, den-mothers, young Mutes. What, Steve wondered, did *they* make of all this? On the far side of the huge fire, partly masked by the rows in front, Steve unexpectedly caught sight of the most beautifully formed face he had ever seen. It came as a shock to realize that it belonged to a female Mute. It was hard to be sure in the flickering light but she looked smooth-skinned, like Cadillac. Her face was patterned with light and dark pigments but otherwise—even at this distance—Steve could see it was flawless.

And her eyes! Like two points of blue fire. . . .

When they connected with Steve's he felt an inexplicable surge of excitement. A shiver ran down his spine. He felt an insane urge to get up and make his way around to where she sat but did not dare move from his allotted place. As he had to look past Cadillac to see her, he averted his gaze so as not to reveal the true focus of his attention. He watched the next warrior break and wrench the arrow out of his cheeks, then slowly let his gaze drift around to where she sat. Her face was turned toward him; her eyes waiting to meet his.

This is crazy! Steve thought. Come on, get a grip on yourself! She's a lump-head. She's probably got a body like a sack of rocks. And even if she hasn't, what you are thinking is unthinkable. He tore his eyes away and silently berated himself. You're imagining things, Brickman. It's the Dream Cap. You've been a prisoner of these lumps so long, you're beginning to think of them as real people. Just keep cool. Hang loose.

Impossible. His body was tingling. He was in the grip of a sensation he had never experienced before and lacked the words to describe. He stole another look past Cadillac. Several Mutes blocked his view as they got up to take their place in the queue. When they had passed, Steve's heart sank. She had gone. Motor-Head, Cadillac's fearsome clan-brother, had taken her place. He glared at Steve with undisguised belligerence. Steve avoided his gaze and searched the rows of firelit faces in front and behind, but the Mute girl was nowhere to be seen.

Without warning, Cadillac got up and walked over to where Mr. Snow sat in the semicircle of clan-elders. Steve saw him squat cross-legged behind the old wordsmith's right shoulder. He laid his hands on his kneecaps, closed his eyes, and appeared to compose himself.

Once again, Steve was not prepared for what happened next. When the last disgraced Mute had bitten the arrow and regained his standing as a warrior, Rolling-Stone spread his arms wide and addressed the gathering. "The blood of our warriors flows hot and strong! They have proved themselves worthy to bear sharp iron in battle. The M'Calls are once again the greatest of the Plainfolk!"

"Heyy-*yahh!!*" roared the seated clan.

Mr. Snow and Cadillac stood up and moved to stand on either side of Rolling-Stone. The clan-elder spread his hands again. "Now let *us* bite the arrow to show we are worthy to lead the bravest of the brave!"

"*Yahh! Yahh! Yahh!*" chanted the clan.

I was right the first time, Steve thought. They are *all* fruitcakes. He understood why Cadillac had closed his eyes. He had been preparing himself mentally for the ordeal ahead. Interesting. Did that mean the Mutes had some way to switch off pain? That could be a trick that might be worth learning. No wonder they kept coming in spite of everything that the crew of The Lady threw at them. Too dumb to be frightened, and too numb to know they'd been hit.

Fort-Knox, a warrior whose own cheeks were streaked with blood, took the arrow proffered by Rolling-Stone and flexed it above his head for all to see. The old Mute knelt before him, his outstretched hands resting on the raised palms of two warriors. Just behind Fort-Knox, Steve could see Motor-Head curling his thick fingers around the shaft of the heavy stone hammer. Not that he needed it. He looked like the kind of guy who could stave your head in with his bare fist.

"Hey-*yah!*" cried Rolling-Stone.

Fort-Knox punched the arrow through the old lumphead's face. Rolling-Stone's hands never moved. Now one step removed from reality through the Dream Cap, Steve didn't even wince inwardly. The clanelder rose, turned, displayed his transfixed jaws to the assembled clan,then broke the arrow.

"Hey-*yahh!*" roared the M'Calls.

Well done, old man, thought Steve. I'm glad it's you and not me. It was no joke being head man if you had to go through the same performance every time the clan crapped out.

Mr. Snow and Cadillac both passed the test with flying colors. Their participation surprised Steve. They were too intelligent to get mixed up in such a primitive display of machismo. With a little thought they should have been smart enough to figure a way out . . . or to have invented some new rules.

Cadillac broke the arrow out of his face and spat the last piece into the fire. The clan roared its approval. Great, thought Steve, stifling a yawn. Now we can all go home. He began to get up then saw that everyone else was sitting tight. He sat back and crossed his legs and felt a chill ripple of fear run down his spine as Motor-Head fixed his glittering black eyes upon him. Grasping the stone hammer under its head, the square, heavily muscled Mute strode across the wavering circle of firelight and planted himself in front of where Steve sat in the fourth row.

Motor-Head flung out his right arm, pointing the hammer at Steve. "Now, brothers, what shall be done with this carrion crow?!"

Steve could feel everyone's eyes upon him. Black-Top and Steel-Eye moved through the crowd and stood behind him. Oh, boy, thought Steve dreamily. This looks like big trouble. Keep cool. Let Mr. Snow handle it. . . .

Motor-Head appealed to the assembled clan. "Did not this crow, before its wings were broken, destroy our crop-fields and kill our Cubs? Why is this carrion allowed to live in our midst? He takes the food from our mouths yet is allowed to fill his own. This wingless worm has no standing. I say he should taste the fire he let fall on others!"

"Heyy-yahh!" The response came as an angry growl. Not everybody answered, but it was clear a sizable number agreed with Motor-Head's proposition.

Black-Top and Steel-Eye grabbed Steve by the arms and hauled him to his feet. His head woozy from the Dream Cap, Steve struggled drunkenly in their grip. "Hey, come on, you guys, what is this?!"

Mr. Snow took a step forward. Like Motor-Head, his speech was slurred and wooden because of the fresh wounds in his cheeks. "Free him! He *has* standing. The Sky Voices spoke to me of this cloud warrior. The shadow of Talisman is upon him!"

Black-Top and Steel-Eye began to release their grip on Steve. Motor-Head stopped them with an imperious gesture. "The shadow of Talisman does not fall on the unworthy." Motor-Head turned to the clan for support. "Does a warrior lay waste to the fruits of the earth?! This carrion kills those who have not yet chewed bone. When Cadillac brought him tumbling from the sky he begged to be saved from death."

"Shee-ehh . . ." hissed the clan.

Motor-Head flung an accusing finger at Cadillac. "Is that not so, wordsmith?"

Cadillac hesitated, looked at Steve, then nodded gravely. "My brother speaks the truth."

Oh, terrific, Steve thought. Thanks a bunch. . . .

Black-Top and Steel-Eye dragged Steve out in front of the clan, twisted his arms behind his back, and forced him to his knees. Out of the corner of his eye, Steve saw Motor-Head heft the big stone hammer. His brain was fast losing its capacity to react. I don't believe this, he thought. He let his head hang down limply and slowly realized that it was becoming weightless.

Mr. Snow held up his hands. "Stay! His life was spared because Talisman willed it!"

Motor-Head paused with the hammer resting on his right shoulder. "I, too, have dreamed dreams, Old One." He pointed down at Steve. "This is the Death-Bringer. If it is Talisman's will that he tread the earth, let him take the spirit from this crow and put it in a braver body!" He gripped the gnarled shaft tightly and swung the hammer back over his head. As it arced forward on the killing stroke the stone head exploded with a terrifying boom. It was as if the hammer had collided head-on with an invisible bolt of lightning. The mysterious force that struck the hammer lifted Motor-Head off his feet and hurled him backward. Mr. Snow, Cadillac, Black-Top, and Steel-Eye reeled away, trying vainly to shield their faces from the shower of sharp splinters. Steve hit the ground nose first. By some metaphysical quirk, most of the splinters followed the line of the explosion, going behind Motor-Head and upward at an angle. Shocked and momentarily deafened but otherwise uninjured, they were helped up by the nearest of the startled spectators.

Mr. Snow walked over to where Motor-Head lay on his back, dazed and winded. "Perhaps that will teach you not to speak out of turn. You're lucky that didn't blow your head off." Motor-Head sat up groggily. Mr. Snow turned away to check that Steve was all right, then addressed the gathering. "There! You have seen for yourselves how Talisman protects those who walk in his shadow!"

"Heyyy-yahhh," murmured the awed clan.

Motor-Head leapt to his feet, his composure regained, and strode forward. Cadillac tried to hold him back but was brushed aside. "Brothers and sisters! Like you, I bow to the will of Talisman, but I still say this crow is unworthy to eat and drink and live as one of us. If he draws his strength from Talisman, let him prove he is a warrior! Let him bite the arrow!"

"*Heyy-yahh!!*" This time the vote was unanimous.

Steve swayed as the voices thundered in his ears. Mr. Snow and Cadillac grabbed him by the arms. "Hey! Hey! Come on! Stay awake!" whispered Mr. Snow urgently. "If anyone guesses you're stoked up on Dream Cap they'll call a postponement and thread your face when you're cold turkey."

"Does it hurt?" mumbled Steve.

"You won't feel too much," Mr. Snow said.

"Just switch off," Cadillac muttered. "Don't think about it."

They marched him over to the clan-elders. "Okay," whispered Mr. Snow. "Kneel down, stretch out your arms sideways, and whatever happens, keep your fingers straight and your palms flat on ours."

Steve nodded dreamily. "I know the drill."

Mr. Snow patted him on the back of the neck and hissed, "Head up! Keep your head *up*. Look sharp!" Mr. Snow and Cadillac knelt facing each other on either side of Steve and offered up a palm for Steve to lay his outstretched hands on. Rolling-Stone stepped up to Steve holding the unbroken arrow made by the luckless Good-Year. It was stained with blood where it had pierced his left cheek. The four-vaned head gleamed dully. To Steve's dislocated senses it looked huge. Far too big to pass between his jaws. In his mind's eye he saw it splintering his teeth, ripping across his tongue . . .

Rolling-Stone lifted the arrow above his head.

Breathe. He had to take a deep breath. Fill his

lungs with air to power the primal scream that would initiate his ordeal. Like the warlike cry he had been trained to use when delivering a blow in unarmed combat. How much would he feel? How much would it hurt? Steve had the impression he was both inside and outside himself. His mind was beginning to drift away. Again he could hear voices.

He heard a faraway echoing cry; dimly recognized it as the defiant Trail-Blazer yell. *"Ho!"* Oh-oh-oh-oh. He felt a violent blow against the left side of his face, just ahead of the jaw muscle. A harsh grating noise. Splayed fingers pressing against the right side of his face. Skin tightening, tearing. Something hard and thin pressing down on his tongue. Choking . . . mouth filling with blood. Rising. Turning, arms outstretched. Hands on his legs, steadying him. Look alert, Brick-man. Look sharp. Don't crap out. This is your big moment. Fold your arms slowly. Take hold of the arrow. Shit . . . driven the point into my hand! Okay . . . this is the bit these lump-heads have been waiting for. Bite the arrow. Shit. That *hurts!* Break, you bas-tard. Oh, sweet Christopher, it's tearing my fucking face apart! Bite harder. Bite through. Oh, boy . . . couldn't have made it without the Dream Cap. Still don't know whether I can . . . Hands are sticky. Got blood everywhere. Oh, boy! Think it's breaking. Going to have to . . . snap it . . . up . . . ward. Uh! *Uhh!*

"Heyyy-yahhh!"

The roar from the assembled Mutes washed over him like a great wave. His face throbbed. The inside of his mouth felt swollen, shapeless. Willing himself to stay erect, he walked stiff-legged to the fire and spat the piece of shaft into the flames. The rows of misshapen, firelit faces swayed, blurred . . .

The next thing Steve was conscious of was waking up inside Cadillac's hut. He was lying between his sleeping furs. Mr. Snow and the young wordsmith sat watching him. Both their faces bore the livid wounds made by the arrow. Steve sat up on his elbows. His face felt as if it were on fire. "How did I get here?"

"You walked," said Mr. Snow.

Steve touched his cheeks gingerly, measuring the extent of the damage with his fingertips. "Thanks for helping me out," he mumbled. "If it hadn't been for that Dream Cap . . ."

Cadillac pointed to Mr. Snow. "It was his idea."

Mr. Snow waved dismissively.

"I don't know how you guys managed without it."

Mr. Snow began to smile but it hurt too much. "The Mutes have learned to get used to pain." He leaned forward and gripped Steve's wrist. "Congratulations. You did well. Everybody was very impressed."

"Aww, come on," said Steve. "It was a total cop-out. I'm a fraud."

"True," Mr. Snow replied lightly. "But only the three of us know that." He saw Steve's face fall. "Don't run yourself down too much. Nor everyone could have gone through with it, even with the help you had."

"So welcome to warriorhood." Cadillac extended his palm.

Steve gave Cadillac's hand the traditional downward slap then offered his palm in return. "Laying on the hand of friendship" was the Mute equivalent of the Tracker handshake, but was not lightly bestowed on strangers.

"That bit with the hammer," began Steve. "The way it exploded just as Motor-Head was about to knock my brains out. You ran things a mite too close for comfort, but it was great timing. How'd you rig that?"

Mr. Snow exchanged a look with Cadillac before replying. "We didn't rig anything. These things happen."

"You mean . . ." Steve laughed woodenly. Like the others, his face was too painfully stiff for his mouth to open properly. "That stuff about me being in Talisman's shadow was for real? Does this guy actually exist?"

"Talisman has always existed," said Mr. Snow quietly.

"You mean he lives somewhere."

"Talisman lives everywhere."

"Wait a minute," Steve said. "Let me get this straight. Are we talking about a real live person?"

"Now and then, yes."

"What does that mean?"

Mr. Snow sighed patiently. "When the time comes for him to walk the earth, Talisman will manifest himself as a human being."

"Okay." Steve nodded. "Where is he now?"

The old wordsmith threw up his hands. "What a dumb question! What does it *matter* where he is?! He's around!"

"Around?"

"Yes! The way the sky is around the earth. The way heaven is around the stars!"

Steve considered this abstraction, trying to make some sense of it. "I see. He's like the other, uhh ... person you say lives in the sky—Mo-Town."

"He is greater than Mo-Town. She is the Mother of the Plainfolk. Talisman is Ruler of All."

Steve nodded again. "Got it. Are they, uhh ... related?"

"Yes," said Mr. Snow. "Talisman is both the Son and the Father of Mo-Town."

Steve frowned. "But that doesn't make sense."

"Not to you," Mr. Snow said. "Not now, anyway. But before you laugh off the whole idea just remember he saved your ass. Think about that."

"I will," said Steve, with as much sincerity as his wounded face would allow. He had already earmarked the conversation as eminently forgettable. How sad, he reflected, that two such amiable, ostensibly bright guys could cherish such batty notions. On the other hand, it made life a whole lot easier for the Federation. While the Plainfolk were waiting for their great Mother and Father in the sky to come to their aid on wings of thunder, the Trail-Blazers would proceed to take them apart with the aid of some good old-fashioned firepower. Still, it was *odd* about the way that stone hammer had exploded. . . .

Steve mentally pigeonholed the problem and turned back to the two wordsmiths. "Does the fact that I've got this . . . uhh, Talisman rooting for me mean that your friend Motor-Head will be off my back from now on?"

Cadillac shook his head. "Not necessarily. Now that you have both bitten the arrow it means that he can challenge you in single combat."

"He could not do that before," explained Mr. Snow. "In his eyes, you had no standing. But now you are a warrior. . . ." He spread his palms.

"Terrific," Steve said. "What are the chances of him pulling permanent guard duty at your furthest lookout point?"

"Slim," replied Mr. Snow.

"But . . . can't you tell him to lay off?" Steve said anxiously. "I thought you ran things around here."

"Ahh, Rolling-Stone is the chief clan-elder. There are certain areas where the clan seeks my advice, but . . ." Mr. Snow shrugged.

"So what do I do now?" asked Steve.

The old wordsmith savored his reply. "Well . . . you can either start practicing your knife-work, or start praying to Talisman. Preferably both." He uncrossed his legs, patted Steve on the shoulder, and got up.

"I'll see if I can get you a blade," Cadillac said. "Meanwhile it might be better to stay indoors." He followed Mr. Snow out.

"Make it a long one," Steve shouted, as they went through the door curtain. "Or give me my rifle back . . . if you've still got it." Some chance. Still, it was worth a try. Steve cursed inwardly. What a situation. After all he'd been through. All that mumbo jumbo, only to learn that the biggest ape on the campus was out there waiting for a pretext to jump on his bones. Christopher Columbus!

When they were safely out of sight of the hut, Cadillac and Mr. Snow slapped hands, pushed each other, and fell about laughing until tears of joy and pain ran down their wounded, swollen jaws.

"Did you see his face?!" choked Mr. Snow. He collapsed in a new burst of laughter, clutching his cheeks. "Oh, dear, this is doing me no good at all!"

"Do you think we ought to tell Motor-Head to lay off?"

"No, leave it. Let Talisman look after his own. Oh, dear . . . our Mr. Brickman takes things so seriously. And he's so *blind!* Do you think they're all like that?" Mr. Snow wiped the tears from his eyes with the back of his hand. "Yes . . . I'm going to be *really* sorry to lose him."

───── **15** ─────

With the aid of a daily application of Mr. Snow's antiseptic red-leaf mash, the wounds in Steve's face healed rapidly, leaving pale, cross-shaped scars. In the days that followed the ceremony, Steve found that many of the M'Cálls who had cold-shouldered him had adopted a more relaxed attitude. From being a despised, disarmed intruder he became an object of good-natured curiosity and for the first time began to attract a small crowd of followers, who, when challenged, revealed with an engaging shyness that they wanted to ask him questions. Not that, as it turned out, they were particularly interested in the answers, for they would soon be forgotten. They just wanted to hear him speak.

Along with this newly acquired social acceptability, Steve was accorded the additional privilege of an invitation to Mr. Snow's hut, where, in the company of Cadillac, he was introduced to rainbow grass. Because Buck McDonnell ran what was called a "tight train," the whispers about its availability and covert

247

use by some trail-hands had not reached Steve's ears
while aboard The Lady.

Steve accepted the proffered pipe and sniffed it
cautiously before taking an experimental puff. Despite the use of grass by Trackers on overground
expeditions, smoking was not a permitted social activity within the Federation; indeed, to most people,
the idea would have seemed absurd. Since cigarettes
did not exist, the need for them simply did not arise.

The first intake of smoke made Steve cough and
retch; the second, taken down into the lungs, nearly
choked him but induced an agreeable light-headed-
ness; the third turned his ears into wings; the fourth
prompted Mr. Snow to take the pipe away from him.

"Hey, hey, hey, slow down. What are you trying to
do—start a fire?"

Steve giggled lopsidedly. "Sorry."

"So you should be," Mr. Snow said severely. "You
and that other sonofabitch burned a good two acres
of this stuff. We're all still very sore about that."

Having a hole punched through his face produced
another, less desirable, side effect. Night-Fever, one
of the dozen or so female Mutes who took turns
bringing Steve his food, began to favor him with
hot-eyed glances. She had woven his broken pieces of
arrow into a necklace made of thin plaited strips of
buffalo-hide and, after presenting it to him, had taken
to squatting for hours on end outside his hut. Since,
in terms of looks, Steve rated her near the bottom of
an unprepossessing heap, her thinly concealed desires were an unwelcome development, which, added
to the lurking danger of an equally unwelcome attack upon his person by Motor-Head, should have
prompted him to put his plan for building a hang
glider to Cadillac. But he did nothing. He drifted,
gripped by a kind of mental languor, mesmerized by
the luminous eyes that had met his across the clearing. His waking hours and his dreams were haunted
by evanescent images of the face he had glimpsed in
the firelight; images that aroused feelings he was

unable to put into words because, like "freedom," they had been deliberately omitted from the Federation dictionary.

Escape was still Steve's ultimate objective, but all his plans and his Byzantine schemes to manipulate his captors had been put on the back burner. His primary task now was to find out who that face belonged to. He was plagued by an urgent need to assuage the feelings its mysterious beauty had inspired. Steve had, quite simply, fallen in love; but as he had not heard the word mentioned until his conversation with Mr. Snow and still did not properly comprehend what it meant in practical human terms, he was fated to remain—in the words of a song from the Old Time—bewitched, bothered, and bewildered.

Who was she? And where was she? Steve was pretty sure he had explored the whole area in and around the settlement and encountered, at one time or another, virtually the whole clan. But since the night he had bitten the arrow, he had not caught even a glimpse of his elusive quarry. Since being captured he had learned enough about the Plainfolk society to know that she was not a visitor. The fact that she was being kept apart from the other M'Calls must mean that she was either regarded as something special by the clan or that she was being kept hidden *because of him.*

Or both.

What was it the M'Calls did not want him to discover?

As he had promised, Cadillac duly furnished Steve with a long-bladed hunting knife. Not the usual Mute sharp iron, but standard Trail-Blazer issue. At first Steve thought it was his own, but when he took a closer look, he found the initials L. K. N. etched on the handle: Lou Kennedy Naylor, who had been inexplicably attacked by Fazetti and brought down over the forest. Steve's hopes that the M'Calls might also have kept bits of Naylor's Skyhawk and possibly his own received a fresh boost. "Thanks." He hefted the blade. "Aren't you worried I might kill somebody?"

Cadillac pursed his lips and shrugged. "Unless you killed in single combat your death would be inevitable, slow, and terrible. A wasted gesture. Where would be the profit in that?"

"When you put it that way, none, but ... " Steve hesitated. "Didn't Mr. Snow tell everybody that Talisman's shadow was upon me? Doesn't that mean I'm under his protection?"

"Yes, it does," Cadillac admitted.

"Then if he really exists and is as powerful as you guys say he is, nothing can happen to me." Steve flipped the knife jauntily into the air and caught it again by the handle. "He saved me from death in the crop-fields, and from Motor-Head's hammer, so ... "

Cadillac's eyes gleamed as he grasped the thrust of Steve's argument. "He may save you again, but only if you conduct yourself like a warrior."

Steve watched Cadillac walk away. There was no doubt about it, the two mouthpieces for the M'Calls had a whole bagful of great exit lines. They probably sat around rehearsing them in Mr. Snow's hut. He reflected on Cadillac's veiled warning. These guys and their gods. They tried to convince you that everything was already worked out, every move preordained by someone living way up beyond the clouds, but they always left themselves a way out in case things didn't happen as predicted.

There was only one power that worked. Manpower. And the Federation knew how to organize that. When they had won back the overground and wiped out the Mutes they would change the face of the earth. The forces of Nature at the heart of the so-called Mute magic would be observed, analyzed, understood, harnessed. The Sky Voices that supposedly gave Mr. Snow his marching orders would find that no one was listening; Mo-Town and Talisman would be reduced to a couple of laugh-lines in the history archives. Peripheral data. There would be no place for any of that crap in the new America the Federation was going to build. Just hard work and good living. That was the difference between the smoke-fueled fantasies of the Mutes and the vision that fired the Trackers. Thanks to the genius of the First Family, the blue-sky world was within their grasp, could be won by the strong and the brave. The bones of the Mutes would be buried under the gleaming cities that would rise from the empty, sunlit plains. Yes.

Still, it *was* odd the way that stone hammer exploded. . . .

Deciding that it was better to be prepared than spend his time trying to avoid the threatened confrontation with Motor-Head, Steve borrowed a machete and cut himself a quarterstaff, which he carried with him everywhere. He constructed a dummy opponent from branches and grass and practiced daily until he could wield the staff as effortlessly as he had in the Flight Academy. His use of the staff attracted the attention and interest of the M'Call Bears, and Steve soon found himself giving lessons to a class that grew rapidly to around fifty, and included the fearsome Motor-Head. The big Mute scorned the protective pads of wood and leather that Steve had insisted his pupils make and wear, and stuck with his own stone-decorated helmet and body armor.

In their practice bouts, Steve found Motor-Head fearless, apparently impervious to pain, and a fast learner. What he lacked in technique he made up for in speed and strength, and it was only Steve's arduously acquired superior skill and mental discipline that kept him out of serious trouble. His encounters with Motor-Head acquired an extra edge; became needle matches, which, despite Steve's rule that practice bouts should end after landing two strokes in the allotted "kill" zones, were only terminated when Motor-Head was brought, temporarily, to his knees. It was clear that the powerfully muscled Bear did not intend to give up until he had regained his position as paramount warrior and had beaten Steve into the ground.

Steve considered taking a dive to placate Motor-Head's pride, but on this occasion his stubborn streak won out over his natural guile. Since his capture, his corn-colored hair had grown out of its natural crew-cut shape and was hanging onto the nape of his neck and over his ears. Seized by an unreasoning defiance, he got Night-Fever to weave a thin plait in his hair interlaced with a strip of the blue solar-cell fabric, and each time he beat Motor-Head, he added another ribboned plait. Steve knew he was asking for trouble by baiting Motor-Head with such a provocative coiffure, but he was confident that his skill with the quarterstaff, allied with his superior intelligence and sixth sense, could outsmart this formidable but half-witted fighting machine.

His instruction of the Bears in the use of the quarterstaff enabled him to make a more objective assessment of their learning ability. Like all Trackers, Steve had been brought up to believe that all lump-heads were dummies. Since meeting Cadillac and Mr. Snow he knew this was not the case, but he had had first-hand experience of the average Mute's inability to remember. The mistake he and the rest of the Federation had made was in equating a Mute's faulty memory with low intelligence. Steve came to realize that his captors could not only absorb information, they could retain it. What was missing was the information retrieval system. Their brains were like computers that could be fed data but had no printout facility. The Mutes could put two and two together, but they couldn't always tell you the answer was four because the link between the memory center and the speech center kept breaking down. In some the link was so intermittent it was virtually nonexistent; in others, like Three-Degrees, the down time on the memory link was minimal, or limited to specific areas of knowledge. The old Mute had thus been able to acquire his woodworking skills and, as he went on to demonstrate, recognize Steve on some days but not know who the hell he was on others. The limited specific memory facility thus enabled the M'Call Bears to acquire and retain fighting and hunting skills; but even this, it appeared, was prone to the odd line fault. Which, Steve imagined, could be bad news if it happened in the middle of a rumble over your home turf.

There was a third memory factor that Steve had noticed but did not fully understand. When he had watched Three-Degrees make the pair of crutches, he had noted how Cadillac's presence had aided the old lump-head in his task. Somehow, through the odd spoken word or his physical proximity, Cadillac had helped complete the memory circuits when Three-Degrees' hands had faltered. Steve had already seen enough to convince him that the clan could interreact without the need for words. He had ascribed this ability to a sense of awareness—a word-concept that had come to him out of the blue. When he had smoked grass with the two wordsmiths his vision had been affected to the point where he'd begun to think he could see some kind of aura, or higher self, extending beyond the limits of their physical bodies. Steve's brain had begun to flounder among such unfamiliar concepts. Hallucinogenic drugs, heightened states of consciousness, and sensory distortion were totally unknown within the Federation. Did the two word-smiths play some shadowy role in which, with their superior intelligence, they acted as a kind of control mechanism for the clan? A group memory. A . . . Steve searched for the word, trying to reach for something he had been aware of during his trip along the rainbow road. A kind of . . . over-mind? Or were they merely the channel for a power that came from somewhere else?

Interesting ideas but also dangerous ones. He would have to observe his principal captors more carefully; more clinically. It would not enhance his career prospects to peddle such half-baked notions on his return to the Federation. Facts, Brickman. That's what they need back home. That's all that counts. Stay alive, note everything you see, score a few points for the guys who powered down, then hit the road.

But only *after* you've found that blue-eyed Mute. . . .

In the middle of all this, Steve awoke one night to find that Cadillac's sleeping furs were empty. The next night, the young wordsmith again slept elsewhere but joined him for breakfast in the morning as usual. Steve waited for Cadillac to say something, but the young Mute made no reference to the change in his sleeping habits. His silence on the subject merely served to arouse Steve's curiosity.

On the third evening after Steve had begun to note Cadillac's nocturnal disappearances, Steve received his second invitation to smoke some grass with the two wordsmiths. Later, after his mind had roamed the rainbow world, heard the same distant voices yet again, and understood many things, Cadillac helped him stagger back to the hut they shared. Steve mumbled his thanks as the young wordsmith rolled him into bed then opened his eyes just in time to see Cadillac slipping out of the hut. Pushing aside his furs, Steve shuffled quickly on his hands and knees over to the doorway and pushed his head out of the flap. He saw Cadillac, lit briefly by the glow from the dying fire, walking in the opposite direction of Mr. Snow's hut.

Summoning up his powers of concentration, Steve willed his brain back into one piece, rose unsteadily to his feet, and headed after Cadillac as he was swallowed up by the night. There was no moon. Beyond the last of the dying camp fires the darkness became impenetrable. Steve stopped, made an effort to listen, thought he heard Cadillac moving down a leaf-covered trail, followed, tripped over a tree root, crashed to the ground, and lay there—wondering with increasing detachment why he was so concerned by Cadillac's night games. Whatever curiosity he had started out with was gently wafted away on a roseate cloud of indifference. He fell asleep to awaken, some hours later, beneath a drifting blanket of ground mist in the deep purple grayness that preceded the dawn.

Chilled to the marrow, his face wet with dew, Steve stumbled back to the hut, frantically beating his arms and body. Sucking in breath through trembling jaws, Steve slipped gratefully between his furs. They were warm. His brain must have iced up because it took him a few seconds to figure out why. As the answer came, a bare arm snaked over his chest and a body that was hard in some places and soft in others eased its length against his. The owner's chin nestled against his shoulder; warm breath tickled his ear. Steve lay there not daring to look around, not daring to move in case he woke the intruder.

Filled with foreboding, Steve inched his right hand over and ran it lightly along the forearm that pinned him down, reading the distinctive pattern of crinkled patches with his fingers. He'd seen that arm enough times when she brought him his food. His bed-mate was Night-Fever.

Christopher Columbus! . . .

The skin on the back of his neck crawled at the thought of lying in bed with a naked female Mute. Luckily he was fully clothed. Moving an inch at a time, his ears strained to catch any change in her deep, slow breathing, Steve edged around so that his back was toward her. He held his breath as Night-Fever stirred sleepily, molding her body to his. Her mouth lay half-open against his jugular vein. Not a good scene. Night-Fever had fanglike lower canines set in a heavy jaw just like the claw-toothed bucket of an excavator. If she woke up and got excited and he said "no," he could end up with a permanently engraved windpipe. Ahh, what the hell. . . . Steve sighed resignedly. He had long since caught whatever he was due to catch and die of. Provided he stayed zipped up inside his flight fatigues and kept his back to her he couldn't come to much more harm. Steve was, above all, a practical young man: the fact of the matter was that despite the genius of the First Family, nobody had yet come up with a better way of keeping warm.

* * *

In addition to his exercise periods with the quarterstaff, Steve continued his self-imposed program of physical training. He was now able to sprint effortlessly, and could do fifty push-ups without feeling a twinge of pain in his right arm. He was back at the level of fitness he had reached on graduation from the Academy.

Striking off down a new trail on an afternoon run, Steve descended toward the plain. He wanted to test his stamina against that of the Bears by emulating their uninterrupted run back up the slope to the settlement. Reaching the plain, he ran out to one of the poles marking the edge of the M'Calls' turf then looped back to the foot of the slope about a mile north of the settlement. So far so good, but, as is always the case, the bluff he now had to run up looked a great deal higher than the one he had run down. Steve's resolve faltered momentarily; then, without breaking his stride, he began to zigzag back up the slope. His intention had been to angle southward across the slope to pick up the trail down which he had descended, but some rocky outcrops that he had failed to pinpoint on the way down barred the way. To clamber around them would have meant losing valuable momentum, so he turned north again, lost sight of the trail, and was forced to pick out a new route as he went along. The going got harder, and he wasted precious breath in a string of curses as he slipped and missed his footing, scraping his ankles painfully while crossing a sharp-edged patch of scree.

Two-thirds of the way up the slope, Steve realized that he was running out of steam and wasn't going to make it. Once again his formidable self-discipline came into play, driving him on. Looking up, he saw, to his right, a feathery plume of water cascading over a ledge of rock. The idea of running through it, letting it splash over his burning face, and catching some of it in his mouth to relieve the raw dryness in his throat, became irresistible. He altered his zigzag path toward the water course, his earlier nimble step becoming more leaden with each stride. His thigh and calf muscles were shot through with rods of pain, as if every vein were on fire. Every ounce of his willpower was now concentrated on reaching the pencil-slim waterfall. His heart slammed itself against his ribs like an angry caged animal; the pounding inside his head blotted out the thud of his feet against the rocky path; the air he gulped down burned and ripped through his gullet like red-hot sand. With a desperate weariness, Steve realized that even if he reached the plume of falling water, the top of the slope was another hundred yards away. It might as well have been a hundred miles. Stumbling across the rocks, he sank to his knees under the spray, fell forward onto his hands, then rolled over and gave up, content to let the cool mountain water cascade over him.

Twenty to thirty minutes later, when his heartbeat had slowed and the band of fever heat had been washed from his brow, Steve crawled stiff-legged out of the waterfall and peeled off his sodden clothes: red, black, and brown camouflaged trousers, combat boots, and blue flight T-shirt and underpants. He twisted the garments into tight rolls to wring on the bulk of the water, then beat them, Mute-fashion, against a flat rock to get rid of the remainder. The afternoon sun had sunk toward the western hills, throwing the slope into shadow. Steve rubbed himself vigorously with his damp T-shirt, then gathered up the rest of his clothes and clambered barefoot up the steep rock face that flanked the slim waterfall. Not the easiest way to the top of the slope but certainly the shortest.

Stepping into the warm autumn sunshine he spread out his clothes to dry, then sat down in a nearby patch of long yellow-pink grass. Behind him the ground rose in a series of undulating rocky ledges, carpeted with a profusion of grasses, ferns, and moss, until it met a wide bank of tall red trees. Concealed within it was the head of the stream that trickled past the spot where he lay before plunging over the smooth tongue or rock onto the slope some fifty feet below. Lulled by the murmuring passage of the stream and the warm earth at his back, Steve fell asleep.

When he awoke, the sun was setting behind the mountain, its last rays turning the edges of the gathering clouds into liquid gold. The Mutes had a quaint idea that the sun went through a door in the sky which, when closed, left the world in darkness until it entered again through a similar door set below the eastern horizon. Seized by a sudden chill, Steve hauled on his blue underpants, reached for his T-shirt, and stopped, hand outstretched. Eight small, black-skinned ovoid fruit, which Steve now knew to be wild plums, were piled neatly on a red leaf that someone had placed on the chest of his T-shirt.

Steve scanned the high ground quickly, then walked over to the edge of the slope. Nothing. No sign of movement. No dust trail. Nobody. He walked back, laid the leaf and its gift of plums carefully aside, and finished dressing. His clothes were still clammy but would soon dry off with his body heat. He tightened the laces in his combat boots, strapped the knife scabbard Cadillac had given him through the trouser loops around his right calf, picked up the plums, then—on a sudden impulse—set off cautiously along the line of the stream, eating them as he went.

As he bit into the juicy flesh, he speculated on the identity and motive of the donor. He felt sure he knew who it was . . . but why had she not awakened him? Was the gift inspired by the simple concern of providing food for an exhausted runner, or was it something more? A sign of her presence? A message saying, "I am here. I care. Keep looking." Confirmation that she, too, was consumed by the same ardent curiosity. Or had he totally misread the fleeting glances they had exchanged? Was it all in his imagination, or, worse still, was it some kind of trap? A wry smile crossed Steve's face. With his luck, it would be Night-Fever he would discover lurking behind the first tree. Or Motor-Head.

Steve smiled inwardly. If that mean mother had

found him exhausted and asleep he would not have made him a present of eight wild plums; he would have left eight rocks piled on his chest. No, this had nothing to do with him, but the thought of Motor-Head served to remind Steve that he ought to temper his curiosity with caution. Although Cadillac told him he could go wherever he liked, it might not prove too healthy to be caught prowling around in an area the clan regarded as being off limits. But on the other hand, without being told, how was he to know? Deciding that his momentary apprehension was primarily inspired by feelings of guilt, Steve shrugged it off and pressed on. In some perverse way, the inherent danger of the situation added spice to the strange but by no means unwelcome emotions that had assailed him ever since he had first seen her face in the firelight.

Working his way slowly through the tangle of ferns bordering the stream, Steve scaled the series of ledges toward the first line of trees. Every twenty-five paces, he squatted down and carefully checked his front, flanks, and rear. Holding his breath, he listened intently, hoping to pick up the sound of some human activity. Only the shrill chatter of an occasional bird cut across the constant background murmur of the stream trickling between the brown, lichen-covered rocks.

A hundred yards inside the tree line, the pines closed in on one another, creating a wall of loosely interwoven branches that began at knee height. Several, wrenched from their tenuous hold on the slope by the downward rush of water from melting winter snow, had fallen at awkward angles across the stream, blocking his path along its banks. He had to make a detour, but to go forward on foot meant cutting or crashing his way through the branches, making it impossible to proceed with stealth. The only other alternatives were to crawl under them or find a way around. Since he was unsure of what kind of a situation he was getting into, Steve did not want to risk getting trapped in a tangle of branches with his nose in the dirt. He was just about to give up and turn back when he caught sight of a broken yellow line up ahead. Cadillac had told him about the seasons of the overground year—the New Earth, the Middle Earth, the Gathering, the Yellowing, and the White Death. It was too soon for the leaves to turn yellow and fall from the trees. Steve suddenly realized that it was dead foliage that had been cut and arranged as a screen, and his uncanny sixth sense told him that behind it was what he was looking for.

Taking care to move as silently as possible, Steve circled away from the stream and crawled between the densely packed pines toward the suspect yellow foliage. As he drew nearer, he saw what appeared to be a long clump of bushes about eight feet high lying to one side of a grassy oasis; an irregular patch of grass, ferns, and chest-high undergrowth surrounded by the almost impenetrable wall of trees. Wriggling out from under the last branches, Steve cautiously stuck his nose above the undergrowth, checked what he could see of the clearing, then tunneled his way between the stems of a tall bank of fern until he reached the yellowing leaves. The "bush" in front of him was made of cut branches, loosely woven together.

Steve took another deep breath and lay there for a good minute, ears cocked, straining to catch the slightest sound of movement. All he could hear was his own heartbeat. Reaching forward, Steve carefully pulled out one of the branches that had been stuck in the ground. The end had been cut at an angle by a machete. Pushing it gently aside, he peered through. A Mute hut stood in a small clearing enclosed by a circular screen of leaves. The doorway to the hut faced a gap in the screen opposite Steve, making it impossible for him to see if the hut was occupied. There was no sign of smoke coming from the ring plate in the roof and none of the usual living debris scattered around. Even so, Steve was sure that someone was inside. Wait a minute! He *could* hear something. Was that somebody . . . humming a . . . tune?!

She was there! It had to be her. There was no one else it could be.

With rising excitement, Steve crawled around through the ferns toward the gap in the surrounding screen and stopped a yard from the opening. Moving with the utmost stealth, he eased another cut branch out of the ground and cautiously poked his head and shoulders in under a curtain of withered leaves. Steve found himself confronted not by the hoped-for view of matchless beauty but by the decomposing heads of Naylor and Fazetti spiked on poles on either side of the doorway. A large, dark bird of prey was perched on Fazetti's head, tearing a sinewy strand of flesh out of one of the gaping eye sockets. Steve recoiled in horror. The bird, startled by the sudden movement, flapped away with a harsh cry of alarm.

Steve swallowed hard and collected his thoughts. According to Mute tradition, the heads of his fellow wingmen were the battle trophies of whoever occupied the hut. But didn't Fazetti go bananas in mid-air? How could she, if indeed it *was* she who ... Another more pressing thought struck Steve. If whoever owned the hut *had* downed the two wingmen, maybe they had taken more than their heads. Maybe some of their gear was inside. Like a map, air pistol, flame-grenade, con-food pack. Useful things that someone planning to escape would need. Nerving himself to face his two spiked friends, Steve pushed his head back through the curtain of leaves. As he did so, the flap over the doorway, framed by the two head-poles, was pushed aside and the owner of the face that had haunted his dreams emerged, stood up, and stretched with the grace of a waking cat.

It was Clearwater. Steve, of course, did not yet know her name. But in the few seconds that she stood there in full view, Steve's eyes roved over every detail of her naked body: the long, straight-boned, supple limbs; the slim-hipped torso with its firm, rounded breasts, strong shoulders, and small waist; the smooth skin free of the disfiguring tree-bark patches and tumorlike bone growths that afflicted

other Mutes. Apart from the swirling pattern of pigments, her whole body was unflawed from head to
toe. Since art, in the generally accepted sense of the
word, did not exist within the Federation, Trackers
were not overly susceptible to such attendant qualities as the harmony of form and color, the graceful-
ness of line and proportion. But something deep within
Steve responded, made him aware that the Mute
female in front of him was an object of great beauty,
even though he could not express himself in those
words. He was seized simultaneously by two totally
conflicting emotions: an irrational desire to possess
her and a sense of shock, disgust even, at feeling
thus. In twentieth-century terms, his reaction was
akin to a founding member of the ultra-right wing
Afrikaner Broederbond—that bastion of white sup-
remacy—discovering within himself a secret predi-
lection for "dark meat." What passed through Steve's
mind in those few seeonds was unthinkable. Allowing Night-Fever to serve as a bed warmer was bad
enough, but to actively contemplate . . . Come on! he
urged himself. Snap out of it!

Clearwater reentered the hut. Steve heard a peal of
laughter; another voice, muffled but deeper; then
more laughter as the door flap was brushed aside
and Clearwater tumbled out backward, struggling
playfully in Cadillac's arms. The young wordsmith
was naked, too.

Not daring to move in case he betrayed his presence, Steve watched them with mixed feelings: dis-
appointment, irritation, toe-curling embarrassment . . .
and a dash of envy. They horsed around for a minute
or so, kissed briefly, got up, moved outside the circular screen, and began to gather big five-pointed pink
leaves from some kind of plant. In her search for
more, Clearwater moved nearer to where Steve lay
concealed. Looking up, Steve saw that the tangle of
ferns under which he lay contained several plants
with the same pink leaf. He had to move before
either of them came over. There was only one way he

could go—through the hole he had made in the screen of leaves into the clearing containing the hut. But supposing the leaves were to make soup with? Where would he hide if they came back in? Steve resolved to work his way around behind the hut. From there he could slip out through the first hole he had made. He wriggled under the screen just as the Mute girl walked over, leaned in, and began picking the leaves. Steve froze on the other side of the screen. Close! A couple of seconds more and she'd have tripped over him. Ooops! Surprise, surprise. Hey, fancy running into you guys! Steve ran through dialogue of discovery in his head. Don't get the wrong idea, folks. Walking around on my elbows is part of my physical fitness program. . . .

The Mute girl went on picking leaves until she had an armful. As soon as she turned her back, Steve began to wriggle around toward the rear of the hut. Luckily the grass inside the clearing was not too short. On the other hand it would not serve to hide him if they walked back in. Steve worked his way backward, pressing in under the fringe of leaves, conscious that his blue T-shirt stood out like a sore thumb against the orange grass and the yellow foliage. To his relief, Cadillac and the girl turned their backs on him and sauntered away from the hut hand in hand.

As the two Mutes went out of sight, Steve got up, tippy-toed over to the gap in the screen, and peeked through the leaves at the edge. His previous worm's-eye view of the area had been limited. From where he now stood, he could see a waist-deep rock pool that fed the stream he'd followed. Cadillac and the Mute girl were in the pool, and in between fooling around she was scrubbing his back with a handful of the pink leaves they'd picked. Dipped in water and rubbed on his back, the leaves produced a thin soapy foam. Bath night. Oh, well. . . . Steve, who would happily have swapped places with Cadillac, sensed that they would probably be busy for some time. Now was the moment to search the hut.

The entrance to the hut, the gap in the leaf screen, and the rock pool were almost directly in line, but on crouching down, Steve saw that a slight rise in the ground blocked the bottom third of the hut from the view of someone in the water. Hugging the ground, he crawled through the grass, circling behind Fazetti's head-pole and then in under the door flap. He had been with the Mutes so long, he no longer noticed the attendant smells. Steve got to his knees, peeked through the flap to check that Cadillac and the girl were still in the pool, then sat back on his haunches and surveyed the interior.

The hut was not as messy, or as crammed full of junk as Mr. Snow's, but there was not a lot of room to move. Several bundles of clothing, along with various-sized baskets with pot lids woven from dried orange grass, were stowed around the buffalo-hide walls; bunches of fruit, dried meat twists, and sweet-smelling flowers hung from the curved poles that gave the hut its squat, beehive shape. The furs on which Cadillac and the girl had no doubt been thrashing around lay in disarray. To his surprise, Steve saw two other sets of furs, rolled up—as was usual during the day. That meant the girl shared the hut, probably with a couple of She-Wolves. Now that he thought about it, it was obvious. If, for whatever reason, the girl was regarded by the M'Calls as a hot property, she would not be left unprotected. Her two hut-mates had obviously pulled out to avoid crowding Cadillac. Steve had discovered that Mutes accorded each other a greater degree of privacy in these matters than Trackers enjoyed, or expected. Which meant that the Mute's clan-sisters would probably not return until she and Cadillac had humped each other dry. But they might not be far away . . . and the area around the hut was bound to be regularly patrolled. Zip! Steve swore under his breath. He had totally ignored that angle when, on a sudden impulse, he'd set off upstream in the hope of finding her. Well, you've found her, Brickman . . . and she belongs to the guy you've been planning to get very friendly with. So forget the daydreams. All that was sheer insanity anyway. Start looking for those hidden goodies and get the hell out of here.

Steve checked out the bathing party again, then started rummaging through the lidded baskets. If he had to leave in a hurry, whoever came in after him would not immediately spot there had been an intruder. He found the pack of survial rations in the second basket and the water purifier pack at the bottom of the fifth. Steve kissed both items happily and slid them into the pockets provided on his trousers. Air pistol . . . Steve hurriedly ransacked the other baskets. Nope. Maybe that was too much to hope for. Map . . . That was the thing he *really* wanted. Where the hell was that?! He reached for the nearest bundle of clothing and stuck his hand into the loosely coiled layers of leather and fur to see if anything had been hidden inside. Nothing. He tossed it roughly back into place and grabbed another. A chill warning ripple ran up his spine. He threw himself forward toward the door flap, opened it a fraction . . . and saw the naked Mute girl walking toward the hut, pushing her wet hair away from her face and twisting it around on the nape of her neck.

For a split second, Steve lay open-mouthed, spellbound. Her skin was . . .

Tearing his eyes away, he looked past her to see Cadillac climbing out of the pool. Christopher! He was trapped! Steve looked over his shoulder and considered cutting his way out of the back of the hut by opening up one of the bound seams. But that would give the game away, and besides, he might not get out in time. Steve's mind went into overdrive. He looked desperately around the hut. Hide . . . But where? Under the furs? No . . . that's pathetic, Brickman. Not enough cover. Try and remember, you're a warrior now. Let's have a little dignity. It would not do to be discovered hiding under the bed—especially in the middle of some heavy action. The answer came.

Brazen it out. But wait! Get rid of the stuff! You
don't want to be caught thieving. Steve hurriedly
pulled the ration pack and the purifier kit out of his
pockets, crammed them into the nearest basket, threw
on the lid, reached up, grabbed a wild plum from a
bunch hanging from a hut pole, and dived onto the
bearskins.

The door flap was pushed aside and the Mute girl
entered. She went down on one knee and froze as she
caught sight of Steve lying there nonchalantly, legs
crossed, one hand behind his neck.

Heart pounding, Steve slowly extended his other
hand toward the Mute girl and offered her the plum.
"I saved one for you."

She didn't say anything. She just moved inside far
enough to let the door flap close behind her.

"Go on, eat it," Steve continued, trying to hide the
slight tremor in his voice. "The others tasted real
good."

The Mute just looked at him steadily. Now that she
was this close, Steve could see she was not just a
pretty face. This lump was no soft touch. The strong,
clear, ice-blue eyes set in the firm, well-boned face
had a surprising depth. They radiated not only an
unnerving intelligence but also a hint of danger . . .
the kind of shadowy menace you felt when looking
down the three barrels of a loaded rifle.

And her skin was now . . .

I don't believe it, thought Steve.

They gazed at each other for what seemed a long
time but in reality was only two or three seconds;
then the Mute took the plum from Steve's hand, ate
half of it, pulled the stone out with her white, even
teeth, and gave the other half back to Steve.

I'm winning, thought Steve. "Thank you. Listen . . .
your—"

As the words left his mouth, the basket he'd hidden
the gear in toppled off a roll of clothing and spilled
its contents onto a mat beside the Mute. She didn't
need to say anything. He knew she knew neither item
should have been in that particular basket. And she

knew he knew she knew. There was nothing else for Steve to do but go on chewing his half of the plum and wait for her next move.

The Mute girl slowly picked up the ration pack and the water purifying kit; then, quite unexpectedly, she placed them within Steve's reach. Putting a finger to her lips, she motioned him to remain where he was, gathered up two rolled grass mats, and ducked out through the door flap. Mastering his surprise, Steve grabbed the two packages and slipped them quickly into the thigh pockets of his trousers.

Fifteen seconds later, the Mute girl came back in, taking care not to throw the door flap wide open. Rummaging quickly through a pile of stuff at the back of the hut that Steve had not had time to search, she pulled out a folded wad of plasfilm and dropped it on Steve's chest.

Steve picked it up gingerly, hardly able to believe his good fortune. Fazetti's air navigation map! His return ticket home! In his excitement, he opened his mouth to let loose a rebel yell, but before he could utter a sound the Mute girl clamped a firm hand over his lips. Holding his head down on the furs, she leant across him and retrieved a rectangular, woven basket that lay against the skin wall of the hut.

Steve grabbed hold of her wrist and pulled her hand away from his mouth. "What's your name?" he whispered. "Tell me. I have to know!"

The Mute girl gazed down at him with the hint of a smile at the corners of her lips. Impossible to tell what she was thinking. "I am Clearwater, firstborn of Thunder-Bird out of Sun-Dance," she whispered.

Steve tapped the pocket containing the ration pack and held up the map. "These are great gifts. I shall not forget."

"These things are not from me. They come from the hands of Talisman." Her voice took on a new urgency. "You must go!"

"Yes, but how?" Steve mouthed.

Clearwater pointed to the door flap, swept her fore-finger around to the back of the hut, then put her hands together to form the wings of a bird taking flight. "When you hear me sing."

Steve nodded and stowed the map in another of his pockets as Clearwater went out through the door flap carrying the rectangular basket. It was one that he had opened during his hasty search. It contained six pots of thick, colored paste: one of them was black, the others were various shades of brown. His examination of the basket's contents had been so fleeting he had not understood their purpose . . . until now.

Steve got to his knees and inched his way over to the door and peeked through the flap. Cadillac sat with his back to the hut. Clearwater knelt behind him, painting a line of black dye onto his shoulder blade with a little stick. Steve stared at them, unable to accept the evidence of his own eyes. Cadillac's overall skin color was now a deep copper bronze; Clearwater's was a velvety olive-brown—just a shade or two darker than Steve's own sister, Roz. The random pattern produced by defective mutant genes that was the indelible mark of the Plainfolk and their southern brothers was, in the case of Cadillac and Clearwater, nothing more than a camouflage to enable them to merge with the rest of the clan. Physically and mentally, Cadillac was now indistinguishable from a Tracker. He was articulate, intelligent, and his memory was probably superior, even though, like Mr. Snow, he could not read or write. There had been no opportunity to test Clearwater's memory, but she had demonstrated a clear ability to think fast and was probably equally intelligent. It was incredible. They were . . . they were just like . . . *real* people!

Clearwater began to sing softly.

Thrusting all thoughts of this astonishing discovery and its ramifications to the back of his mind, Steve eased the door flap open, ducked out, and got to his feet with slow-motion movements. To his heightened senses the rustle of cloth against skin, of boot against grass, and the pounding of his heart against his ribs seemed magnified to deafening proportions. Cadillac *must* be able to hear him! Must *know* he was there! But no. Incredibly, the young wordsmith did not turn his head, did not budge an inch. He just sat there cross-legged, his upturned palms resting on his thighs. Clearwater glanced over her shoulder. Her eyes met Steve's briefly; then she turned back to her task. Running her hand up into Cadillac's hair, she bent his head forward and began painting the pattern of black dye up onto his neck. Hardly daring to breathe, Steve edged around to the rear of the hut, slipped out under the screen of leaves, crawled back through the ferns, and in under the low branches of the surrounding pines.

It was fortunate that the sight of the two extra bedding rolls in Clearwater's hut had reminded Steve that he should proceed with the utmost caution. Having gone to some lengths to prevent his learning of Clearwater's presence, the M'Calls were bound to have taken steps to guard her against unwelcome intruders . . . such as himself. And now that he had discovered the true nature of their prize exhibit he was in even greater danger from his shadowy adversaries within the clan. His impulsive actions had placed him in double jeopardy, for he knew he would not rest until he had seen her again. But before that could happen, he had to slip past any guards that might be around and get back to the settlement before sundown.

Trailcraft was not the Tracker's strong suit, but the extra adrenaline generated by his encounter with Clearwater raised Steve's level of awareness so that he was able to tune in to the sounds of the forest. His sixth sense functioned in a way it never had before. He heard the overground for the first time; was able to distinguish the rustle of leaves overhead from leaves being crushed underfoot; was able to differentiate between the shrill cries of birds and the birdlike calls exchanged by a patrol of Mutes; was able to discern their movement north along the slope toward him. When the trees opened out sufficiently for him to proceed on foot, he moved silently and swiftly across and away from their line of advance toward the stream. He planned to retrace his path down to the edge of the plateau, using the constant rippling cascade of sound to cover his progress along its bed, hidden by the wall of ferns on either side. At the tongue-stone, where it began its plunge onto the slope below, he would turn right and pick up one of the trails back to the settlement. After that, his biggest problem would be trying to pretend that nothing extraordinary had happened to him.

Reaching the stream, Steve turned right and paused, dropping down behind cover to check the ground to the south. Nothing moved. His adrenaline-charged senses noticed that a curious stillness had crept over the woods. There was no sign now of the Mute patrol. It was only when he was about to plunge through the tangle of ferns lining the bank that his plans started to unravel. As he rose and pivoted around, leaning forward from the waist, he felt a rush of cold air across the back of his neck and hear a loud *zzz-jjhonkk*. Glancing around, he banged his forehead against a crossbow bolt embedded in the tree he had been crouching against. Close! If he had been a fraction of a second slower in moving he would have been skewered through the neck. Steve didn't stop to see who fired the bolt; the fact that they had missed meant they were some distance away—and that meant he had a chance. He changed direction abruptly, dashed *up* the slope instead of down, leapt noisily across the stream, and went crashing through the ferns into the woods beyond. As he ran, he flailed his arms wildly in the hope of persuading his pursuers that he was fleeing in blind panic. Behind him, he heard the Mutes begin to whoop and whistle as they gave chase. Steve zigzagged northward some eighty yards, then turned sharp right, hurtled down the slope in a series of flying leaps and somersaults, turned sharp right again, and doubled back toward the stream, crawling on his belly through the undergrowth. He had put up some good times over the assault course during his years at the Flight Academy, but this was probably his fastest eighty-yard tiger crawl ever. Plunging headlong into the shallow water, he clawed his way frantically up over the stepped rock and loose pebble bed. Reaching a deeper section where the water covered most of his body, Steve wedged himself against the near bank under a loose fringe of ferns and broad-leaved grasses hanging in graceful curves with their tips dragging conveniently in the water.

His ruse worked. Keeping his head down with only his eyes above water he saw the whooping Mutes leap across the stream higher up the slope and race on into the trees on the other side. One, two, three Bears brandishing knife-sticks, the fourth carrying a crossbow, three She-Wolves. Seven . . . Zip! How many more of them were there? Another Bear carrying a knife leapt across the stream and ran after his companions. Eight . . . Steve knew he daren't hang on too long. If the lead Mutes didn't catch sight of him soon, it wouldn't take them long to work out what had happened. And then they'd be spearing him out of the stream with those knife-sticks . . . the way they did with trout. He was on his hands and knees with his back half out of the water when two more Mutes leapt across the stream with a shrill whoop almost directly over his head. Steve hit the bottom nose first. Christopher! He surfaced slowly and caught sight of a pair of She-Wolves crossing farther up. Twelve. Two hands. That had to be it. Move, Brickman!

Steve leapt to his feet and plunged down the bed of the stream, blindly leaping off the series of rock ledges without checking what lay below. Several times he lost his footing on the slippery moss-covered rocks and fell awkwardly, crashing against tree trunks lining the stream, bouncing off boulders, and sprawling headfirst in the water. His newly mended ribs took a terrible pounding; his elbows, knees, and chin were badly grazed. But he didn't stop to inspect the damage, and, amazingly he didn't feel any pain. He just picked himself up and pressed on, stumbling and weaving his way downstream like a drunken sailor in

San Diego on a Saturday night in the myth-shrouded years of the Old Time.

Reaching the tongue-stone he staggered sideways out of the water and sank to his knees. Finding that too painful he sat back, drew his legs up, and tried hugging them. That's when he found out that his elbows were on fire. He lay back on the ground in an effort to recover his breath and found that hurt even more. Sitting up, he pulled off his sodden T-shirt and combat boots, then stood up and stepped out of his camouflaged trousers and underpants, twisting and beating the water out for the second time that day. That hurt, too. Still, it was in a good cause. He pulled on his damp clothes, fixed the scabbard of his combat knife through the loops on his trouser leg, and stowed the map and the other items Clearwater had given him back in the thigh pockets. Great. . . . He put his right foot up on a nearby rock and buckled the side straps on his boot. With the sun now behind the far mountains the air had become suddenly chill. Steve swapped feet and began to buckle up his left boot, allowing himself a congratulatory smile at the way he had evaded the Mute patrol. He stamped his feet on the ground to settle them comfortably inside his boots and clapped his hands together happily. Okay. Time to hit the trail. It was at this moment that he suddenly realized that he had left his quarterstaff lying somewhere outside Clearwater's hut—together with its carrying sling.

Now that, thought Steve, is a real pain. . . .

Before he reached the settlement, Steve stepped off the trail, wrapped up the ration pack and water purifying kit in broad leaves, buried them in a hole between the roots of a tree, and cut a small blaze mark on the trunk with his knife. He had already decided that he would hide the map between one of the double-layered mats that served to make up the floor beneath his fur bedding roll. Satisfied that the ground showed no sign of having been distrubed, Steve blocked out the jabbing pain in his knees and headed for home at a fast jog.

*   *   *

Outside the hut hidden by the screen of yellow leaves, Clearwater labored lovingly to re-create the swirling body pattern that Cadillac had adopted as his mark. When it was finished, it would be his turn to paint her body. Although Clearwater's brain was not the equal of a wordsmith's, both she and Cadillac had received from Mo-Town the gift of a photographic memory, which included the ability to project a mind-image of the pattern onto each other's bodies. Cadillac's back was like a blank canvas on which Clearwater could "see" the exact area of every color. All she had to do was fill them in.

As she worked, Clearwater thought about the cloud warrior who had been sent to them by Talisman and who the Sky Voices, through Mr. Snow, had named the Death-Bringer. She had first seen his body when it had been brought in, broken and bloody from the cropfields. He had not seen her, for his mind slept, and she had been sent away before he awoke. The clan-elders had told her that she must live apart from the rest of the M'Calls while the cloud warrior was held captive. He was not to discover that she had been born with a smooth, one-colored skin like his. The body of a sand-burrower.

Like Cadillac, she had suffered as a young child because of her "otherness." It was they who, in their perfection, were the ugly ducklings, and it was their shared feeling of wretchedness that had brought them closer together. Although he was already weighed down with the task of absorbing Mr. Snow's prodigious knowledge, the young Cadillac had always come to her defense when she had been taunted by the other Cubs. She, in her turn, had aided him, hurling herself upon his tormentors and pummeling them with her tiny fists. When she was seven, and old enough to understand that there were other worlds above the blue roof of the sky and below the grass at her feet, Mr. Snow had explained that her body had been shaped thus because she, too, had been born to serve Talisman, the Thrice-Gifted One. She had accepted this and drawn comfort from it but had not *truly* believed until the recent unveiling of her powers as a summoner, and Cadillac's newfound ability to draw pictures from the seeing-stones. Mr. Snow *had* spoken the truth: the path of the future was already drawn. Most of the Plainfolk could only see that path one step at a time but Cadillac had the gift of seership. When his skill increased and his mind was ready, he would be able to pierce the time-clouds and see what lay ahead.

Mr. Snow knew some of these things already, because the Sky Voices spoke through him. They, the Masters of All, lived in a world whose horizons were bounded by the beginning and the end of time, on a mountain so high they could see below them all that had been and all that would be. The Sky Voices had told Mr. Snow that despite the wishes of the clan-elders, her path would meet that of the Death-Bringer. Never doubting his wisdom, she had done exactly what he had told her to do. Even so, she felt troubled at having to conceal her thoughts and actions from Cadillac. For had they not agreed to exchange the blood-kiss? Had they not been as one between the wolf and the bear? Was he—if not the strongest—the bravest, most valiant, and most stalwart of the M'Call warriors? And if he was not yet as wise as Mr. Snow, was not his tongue like sharp iron, and his head like a bright star? Did her heart not warm at the thought of him? Had she not pledged to guard him through all her days?

Yes. . . . All this was true, and yet she felt confused, guilty. Ever since she had gazed upon the cloud warrior across the firelit circle on the night he had bitten the arrow, her heart had been torn in two. She felt guilty because her mind harbored thoughts that the laws of the blood-kiss forbade: images of lying in the moon-dark with the Death-Bringer; images that brought her body to fever heat. Cadillac's eyes were dark; *his* were blue. It was like looking into her own eyes, reflected in the untroubled surface of a shadowed rock pool. Cadillac's shoulders were broad and square, but were not *his* broader, squarer? And was *he* not taller? Cadillac's hair was straight and dark as a raven's wing; *his* hair rippled like a field of bread-stalks in the wind. It shone like grass struck by the rays of the rising sun, and his voice ... Ah ... his voice was strong and smooth like deep running water. It made her heart tremble like the roar of a mountain lion and lit a fire in her belly that caused the bones in her thighs to melt like snow.

No one had seen her on the occasions when she had crept into the settlement under the cover of Mo-Town's starry cloak. She had crouched outside Mr. Snow's hut and listened to all they had said; had heard him speak of the Dark Cities under the earth. The word-pictures he drew had filled her with terror, but she could have sat there for days on end listening to the sound of his voice.

Some of her clan-sisters, who suspected nothing, had said he had the tongue of a viper, the smile of a coyote, and a heart of stone. Others had told her that they had sent Night-Fever to test his manhood and that he had spurned her. He fights well with a long stick, they said mockingly, but there is no sharp iron between his legs: only a broken twig. Clearwater had joined in their laughter but chose not to believe them. She did not care that his blue eyes were veiled and his spirit hidden. She had looked upon him and sensed the power within; had felt his heart quicken. And that was enough. The cloud warrior was, quite simply, the most beautiful being she had ever set eyes on.

By the tribal laws of the Plainfolk, Clearwater knew that she merited death at Cadillac's hand for harboring such desires; knew also that she would welcome death if it came to her while in the cloud warrior's arms. The guilt engendered by these feelings and the torment caused by their concealment had grown daily. Amazingly, no one seemed to have noticed, but she was sure that Mr. Snow knew, in the same way that he knew she and the cloud warrior were destined to meet.

Clearwater began to paint Cadillac's chest. As she charged the flat sliver of wood with more dye she looked into his eyes and saw they were focused on the horizon of a world beyond that bounded by the reddening sky. She traced two curving lines down the center of his chest and began to fill in the space between.

And she wondered if he knew that it was she who, hidden by the darkness into which she had retreated, had silently summoned up the power within her to save the cloud warrior from Motor-Head's hammer.

that again may easily be seen by passing the world which he would be able to see, in
...

16

On the day after Steve's encounter with Clearwater, he took the map from its hiding place and set off into the hills behind the settlement. After climbing for a couple of hours, he reached a point that gave him a panoramic view of the surrounding terrain. Orienting his map by the sun, he was able, by careful observation of various topographical features, to pinpoint his position with some degree of accuracy. His hunch that the M'Calls had moved westward was largely correct. From their original encampment north of Laramie, they had trekked some two hundred miles northwest to the eastern slopes of the Wind River Range from where Steve now looked down toward the head of the Sweetwater and Beaver rivers.

To the south, the line of the Rocky Mountains, of which the Wind River Range was part, opened out to surround the Great Divide Basin, an arid stretch of bare rock and sand dunes that looked as if they'd been shipped direct from the Sahara. From his map, Steve saw that the Rockies ran southward through Colorado. Proceeding on the improbable supposition that enough materials had been salvaged to allow him, with the help of his captors, to build a hang glider, his best bet would be to fly from peak to peak until he was within striking distance of the nearest way station—Pueblo, on the Arkansas River, in the southern quarter of the state. The steep slopes would provide a plentiful supply of updrafts and thermals, and if he had to come down, it would be better to land on high ground from which he could take off again.

Steve's flight map only covered Wyoming and Colorado, plus a narrow strip of Kansas, Nebraska, and South Dakota; so he could not work out how far he was from Grand Central. He did not even know the shape or extent of the American continent. It was not, and had never been, Federation policy to allow Trackers access to more information than they needed; not even Trail-Blazers. Each expedition was issued with the cartographical data covering its specific operational area, no more. Houston, in fact, lay some twelve hundred miles southeast of where he sat at that moment.

On his way back down the mountain, Steve mulled over how best to proceed and cursed himself for leaving his quarterstaff lying somewhere under the ferns at the back of Clearwater's hut. If it was found, it might blow his chances of enlisting Cadillac's help. He considered going back for it and decided it was too risky. With luck, it would remain undiscovered. The return visit he had inwardly vowed to make to the Mute with the blue eyes would have to be shelved. Indefinitely.

Steve's mixed-up feelings about Clearwater hadn't lessened, but his near miss with the crossbow bolt and the subsequent chase through the woods had been an all-too-sharp reminder that he was in enemy hands. So far he had not been challenged about the incident or confronted by his pursuers, but that didn't necessarily mean he was in the clear. Mutes didn't think the way Trackers did. There was no knowing what these lumps might be cooking up. He had allowed the regular meals, the good-natured discussions, and the general lack of restraint to lull him into a false sense of security. Worse, in his thoughts about Clearwater he had permitted himself to indulge in the kind of fantasy that the Mutes wallowed in all the time. Pipe dreams. . . .

In reality, his life was balanced on a knife edge. A knife that the two wordsmiths were holding between them. If he stepped too far out of line, the heat being generated by the head-hunters among the M'Calls might get to be too much for Mr. Snow. The old guy had come up with this great line about him being under Talisman's protection; he could just as easily arrange for Talisman to change his mind and declare him surplus to requirements. It could prove equally fatal to intrude into the relationship between Cadillac and Clearwater . . . especially in view of the cooperation he was about to solicit.

Steve's step lightened as he came to a firm decision. Even if it never left the ground, building a hang glider would provide an alternative focus for his thoughts and energy. It would also give Cadillac's mind something more important to latch on to than Steve's walk in the forest. If he and Mr. Snow put their weight behind the project, his own continued well-being was guaranteed until it was completed. Cadillac had not reacted in any positive way when Steve had first broached the subject, but he was pretty sure that the young wordsmith would not turn down the chance of learning to fly. At the back of Steve's mind lurked the idea that Cadillac might—just *might*—break his neck in the process. Steve banished such thoughts resolutely. The loss of Cadillac would be a double tragedy, for if the craft was wrecked in the process it would put an end to all hopes of escape. But on the other hand . . .

No. Forget it, Brickman. You can't afford to let it happen. The clan wouldn't let you get away with it.

Three more days went by. Cadillac didn't show.

It figures, Steve thought. Those patterns obviously

take time to apply. She has to paint him all over, and then he has to paint her. And so on. . . .

Steve found he didn't like to think about it. Jealousy was another word that had been omitted from the Tracker vocabulary. But, once again, Steve didn't know that. He only knew that he didn't like feeling the way he did. Back home, if you felt like putting the bomb in the barrel with one of the guys you just propositioned them. They either said "yes" or "no," depending on how they felt or whether they were busy. Either way it was no big deal. Nor did it matter who they'd been with or who you were planning to go with next. There were no ties, even when you decided to pair off with somebody and filed a bond application. That was primarily an administrative requirement relating to guardianship. Provided you and your partner performed that role adequately, you could both jack up whomever you liked. This was why Steve found himself tormented and confused by his feelings toward Cadillac and Clearwater. He did not like to think of them together; did not like the thought that Clearwater belonged to someone else. To someone who had saved his life and on whom his future well-being depended.

Steve's inner turmoil was compounded by the fact that he had begun to *like* the two wordsmiths; had actually felt stirrings of genuine warmth toward them; had experienced a very real but unsettling sense of kinship. And that was bad news. Such feelings corroded the armor plate he had riveted around his Tracker psyche. It made him feel vulnerable . . . and he didn't like that.

What Steve needed was something he had never previously contemplated: someone to confide in. He had been the confidant of his kin-sister, but even though they were close, he had always resisted the temptation to reveal his own secret thoughts or desires. With a supreme effort of will, he sought out Mr. Snow and found him perched cross-legged on a ledge above the settlement.

"I need to talk."

Mr. Snow studied Steve's face. "Okay, go ahead. Talk."

Steve squatted down beside him and gave the old wordsmith a hesitant and heavily edited account of how, in stumbling across the bathing party, he had discovered that Clearwater and Cadillac were straight Mutes. "It's amazing," he concluded. "There they were, right in front of me, but I just didn't see it! I suddenly realized that I wasn't looking at the color of their skin but at them as . . . uhh . . . as *people*."

Mr. Snow responded to Steve's confession with an indulgent smile. "It happens."

"Who is she?" asked Steve, with what he hoped was beguiling innocence. "What's her name?"

"Her name is Clearwater, first of three daughters born to Sun-Dance. Thunder-Bird, her father, was a great warrior who fell in the Battle of the Black Hills."

"What is her relationship with Cadillac?"

Mr. Snow patted Steve's knee. "Let me give you some good advice. Questions like that could be bad for your health."

Steve pretended he didn't understand. "Why? You've told me all kinds of things about the Plainfolk. I'm just curious to know why she is separated from the rest of the clan. What harm is there in that? Have they exchanged the blood-kiss?"

"Not yet. But a match has been made."

"What does that mean?"

The old wordsmith sighed. "They have been summoned before the council of elders. It is the clan's wish, with Mo-Town's blessing, that they bring forth children in their own image."

"The clan's wish?" Steve saw a possible loophole. "Does that mean the two of them didn't have any choice?"

"None of us choose what we will do or not do," Mr. Snow said quietly. "The exercise of what some call 'free will' is a cruel illusion. Happiness, contentment, stems from recognition of this fact."

It was Steve's turn to smile indulgently. "Ah, yes, I see. We're all marching to Mo-Town's music."

"Go ahead, laugh," Mr. Snow said. "You don't have to believe it. Maybe you're destined to have a difficult time on this trip."

Steve replaced the smile with an earnest expression that, this time around, was genuine. "What are you trying to tell me?"

Mr. Snow waved dismissively. "What can I tell a man who doesn't want to listen?"

"I'm trying," Steve insisted. "But you don't seem to understand. Some of the weird ideas you have about the way things work are . . . uh . . . well, they're kind of hard to take on board."

The old wordsmith eyed him. "Don't try and tell *me* how hard it is. I've been searching for answers ever since you and your guardfather were no more than gleams in your President-General's eye." He paused. "Tell me . . . is it really true he billies every would-be mother in the Federation?"

"The first President-Generals may have," replied Steve. "But now it's all done by artificial insemination. The real action takes place in culture dishes at the Life Institute."

"Sounds impressive."

"I'll explain it some other time," Steve said. "Let's get back to Clearwater."

"What is it with you, Brickman? Too much wax in the ears? I told you—forget you ever saw her. Oh, by the way . . ." Mr. Snow leaned to his left, pulled Steve's quarterstaff out from behind some rocks, and offered it to him with both hands. "She sent you this."

Steve stared at it for a moment, then took it from him and laid it by his side. He tried to hide his embarrassment. "Does Cadillac know?"

"Not yet. Have *you* told anyone else?"

Steve shook his head. "Who is there to tell?"

"Exactly. However, I think I should warn you—the word has gotten around. You were seen."

Steve felt the color flood through his cheeks under

Mr. Snow's piercing gaze. What was it with this guy?! He had always been able to hide things so easily before. "You mean in the woods?"

Mr. Snow didn't answer.

"Oh, yeah . . . I forgot to mention that," said Steve lamely. "I was on my way back, walking along minding my own business, when somebody with a crossbow tried to nail me by the neck to a tree. I didn't wait to ask who-what-where-why. I just took off."

Mr. Snow nodded. "In the circumstances I'd have probably done the same thing. My brother Bears were under the impression you had reasons for wishing to avoid them. Is there anything else you've missed out?"

Steve eyed him. "This is like being up in front of the Assessors." He gave a quick bitter laugh. "What can I tell you that you don't know already?"

"Not much," admitted Mr. Snow.

Steve decided that, whatever else she might have told Mr. Snow, Clearwater hadn't mentioned giving him the map, the food pack, and the water kit. "Look, okay, it may have been stupid to run away, but it was you and Cadillac who warned me that not all the natives were friendly. I don't know what their story is. I can only assure you that I haven't knowingly done anything I was told not to do."

Mr. Snow greeted this with an enigmatic smile. "I'm sure you haven't. Nevertheless your little jaunt yesterday has made things very difficult."

"In what way?"

Mr. Snow drew his hand down over his beard before replying. "There are certain people who feel that you should never have been taken alive . . . and that you now know too much."

Steve frowned. "How did they work that out? If you are the only person Clearwater and I have spoken to . . ."

Mr. Snow shrugged. "Certain assumptions have been made."

"One of them being that I must have discovered Cadillac and Clearwater are clear-skinned straights?"

"Yes, you could say that is their principal concern. They wanted to . . . ahh . . . question you."

"I bet."

"I advised them to wait until you came to talk to me about it."

Steve looked down at his quarterstaff, ran his hand along it, then looked up at Mr. Snow. "You *knew* I was coming. . . . How?"

"There's no mystery about it. I keep telling you. All things are known to the Sky Voices."

Steve tried to bite back a smile. "In that case you must have known what was going to happen yesterday."

"Not necessarily. I said, 'All things are known to the *Sky Voices*.' That does not mean that *I* know everything."

Steve breathed an inward sigh of relief. "Okay. But why should these zed-heads want to jump on me? 'The path is already drawn'—isn't that what you keep telling me? So how can whatever's happened be *my* fault? You can't have it both ways. If you guys are not happy with the way things are going, why don't you take it up with Talisman, or the Sky Voices, or whoever it is that's supposed to be running things up there?!

"Good point," Mr. Snow conceded.

"Here's another," continued Steve. "There's no need for anyone to get worked up about this, not unless they're deliberately trying to stir up trouble. If I had bumped into Clearwater on any other day I would never have known that she and Cadillac were straights. And even if, by chance, I *had* discovered the truth, why should it be such a big secret? You and I discussed this weeks ago. The southern Mutes have been trading in straights for centuries."

"Not female straights."

"True," Steve admitted. "I overlooked that."

It was a lie, of course. Steve knew perfectly well that ever since the Break-Out in 2464 when the Federation first learned of the existence of smooth-skinned Mutes and the first rare specimens were found, no female straight had ever been captured or handed over in lieu of tribute. Indeed, it was widely believed that due to some genetic quirk in an already flawed process, female straights simply did not exist. The M'Calls had not only produced one, they possessed a perfectly formed, highly intelligent, breeding pair! It was the kind of hard data that the Amtrak Executive would give their eye teeth for and was bound to earn him good grades at his next assessment. Always assuming there was one.

Steve thought back to something Mr. Snow had said in an earlier conversation. About the ancestors of the Mutes being straight-limbed people from the Old Time. Up to the moment of discovering the true color of Cadillac's and Clearwater's skin, Steve had believed that to be a grotesque lie. Since birth he had been taught that the Trackers were the only true descendants of those who lived before the Holocaust. The hell-fires that had consumed the blue-sky world had been ignited by the Mutes, who—according to the Archives—were *already* subhuman.

But what if Mr. Snow's version of history contained an element of truth? What if Cadillac and Clearwater proceeded to give birth to their own kind, and more like them amongst the other Plainfolk clans spawned succeeding generations of clear-skinned straights? Mutes would no longer be Mutes. The whole basis for the centuries-old conflict would disappear. Christopher Columbus! How would the Federation function if it had no one to fight? For over five hundred years, dispensing death had become the way of life for generations of Trackers. In every aspect of its organization—in thought, word, and deed—the Federation was geared to the conflict with the Mutes. Since the age of five his own life had been totally dedicated to learning how to kill lump-heads. What would wingmen like himself do without a war?

As the complications multiplied rapidly, Steve blocked off this alarming train of thought and switched back on to Mr. Snow. He found the old wordsmith watching him with an amused expression. "You've overlooked something, too. I'm your prisoner. You've ribbed me about escaping, but we both know I'm not going anywhere. Who am I going to tell?"

Mr. Snow shrugged. "Who knows? Things happen."

Steve wasn't sure what that meant but couldn't be bothered finding out. The old wordsmith loved to make things sound mysterious. Why not? Keeping people's attention was part of his job. "Tell me something—is Motor-Head one of the guys who've got it in for me?"

"He's not the leader, but yes, he's one of them. And you are right. Despite what I've told them about you being under Talisman's protection, they *have* been looking for an excuse to get rid of you. Your . . . uhh . . . how can I put it? Your interest in Clearwater could be the opportunity they've been waiting for."

"Who said I'm interested?"

"Come on, Brickman—it's written all over your face."

Steve felt his cheeks begin to burn again.

"Don't be embarrassed. It happens to all of us. It's nothing to feel bad about." Mr. Snow stopped and studied Steve intently. "I'm wrong. You really *are* upset. Is it because she's a Mute?"

"She's not a—" Steve bit his lip to keep from getting in deeper.

"Yes, I see what you mean." Mr. Snow nodded understandingly. "It must be difficult for you."

"Look," Steve said. "You're way off base, believe me. The fact that I now know Cadillac is a straight does not alter the way I feel about him. Clearwater is . . . well, another matter entirely. I can understand the clan wanting to keep her under wraps. Let's face it, she's . . ."

"Unique?"

Steve answered cautiously. "I wouldn't know about that. She's certainly a rare specimen. But then you know that. Just make sure you take good care of her."

Mr. Snow chuckled. "She can look after herself."

"This is nothing to laugh at," Steve insisted. "The

wagon trains will be back. Lots of them. It's only a matter of time before the Federation starts treading on your turf. When it does, the M'Calls may be glad of the opportunity to trade Clearwater instead of paying tribute. She's your greatest asset. Put her together with Cadillac and you'll be able to write your own deal."

Mr. Snow shook his head. "The Plainfolk have never paid tribute and never will. What you say is true: Cadillac and Clearwater are like bright jewels in the crown worn by a great king of the Old Time. But we possess something of even greater value. The greatest asset of the M'Calls is our readiness to accept our destiny. That demands a courage beyond your understanding."

"You're right," replied Steve. "I don't understand."

"You will one day."

It sounded more like a threat than a promise. Steve gazed at Mr. Snow in silence, then said, "So . . . what do you suggest I do?"

"Do?" Mr. Snow shrugged. "You play it as written. Life goes on. The Wheel turns."

"Is that all?"

"Not quite. I've taken the liberty of assuring the clan-elders that you will say or do nothing now or in the future that will harm Clearwater or her relationship with Cadillac. And that you will not attempt to approach her or converse with her except in the presence of others and *only* if requested to do so. Is that clear . . . and do you accept?"

Steve laughed. "What d'you think I'm planning to do—run off with her?!" He saw the old wordsmith's expression and wiped the grin off his face. "I'm sorry. Yes, of course I accept. I don't imagine I have much choice . . . right?"

Mr. Snow waved the question away. "I've also told them that you will never, under any circumstances, reveal the existence of either to anyone outside this clan. Unreasonable?"

"No, unlikely. As I already pointed out, I'm a prisoner . . . but, yeah, sure, I'll go along with that."

Since in biting the arrow Steve had gained the status of a warrior, Mr. Snow briefly considered asking him to swear the traditional blood-oath to guard the secret with his life. He decided such a pledge would be meaningless to an individual who scorned the ways of the Plainfolk and had no concept of honor. Such strange people, these sand-burrowers. And such consummate liars!

Steve's eyes wandered briefly over the random pattern covering Mr. Snow's body. "If no one is supposed to know their secret, why don't Cadillac and Clearwater just leave the dye on their skin and paint over it when it wears off?"

"It has to be removed at regular intervals to prevent their bodies from being permanently discolored," replied Mr. Snow.

"But . . ." Steve looked baffled.

Mr. Snow smiled. "Isn't it obvious? There may come a time when they will need to appear unskinned."

"You mean . . . disguised as Trackers?"

"I would not discount that possibility," Mr. Snow admitted.

Steve nodded. "Okay, then let me give *you* a word of advice, in case you've been picking my brains with the idea of breaking into the Federation. Forget it. Even if they managed to find a way in, they wouldn't get ten yards without an ID card. It's the key to everything—and it's nontransferable."

Mr. Snow digested this valuable piece of intelligence with a thoughtful expression. "Thanks for telling me."

A couple of days later Cadillac returned, sporting his new paint job. As far as Steve could tell, it was an exact duplicate of his previous body markings. He had even been rubbed down with something, probably a fine dust, to kill the fresh color. Steve greeted him casually and did not remark upon, or seek the reason for, his absence.

Shortly afterward Steve glimpsed Clearwater moving about the settlement accompanied by her two sisters, or in a group with other She-Wolves. Although he was never conscious of a deliberate effort by the clan to keep them apart, they somehow never managed to meet face-to-face. If their paths crossed it was always at a discreet distance. Despite his desire to get better acquainted, Steve held firmly to the promise he had given to Mr. Snow and contented himself with just looking at her whenever the opportunity presented itself. It was very seldom that their eyes connected, and for the most part her expression remained neutral; but from time to time he found himself on the receiving end of a brief, tantalizing glance which, had she been any closer, would have burned the soles off his boots.

Steve took care not to let his frustration hinder his growing friendship with Cadillac. He introduced him to the quarterstaff, and when the young wordsmith had once again demonstrated the ease with which he could acquire new skills, he put forward the idea of teaching him to fly. Cadillac's response was noncommittal, but two days later Steve emerged from their hut to find the dismantled remains of three Skyhawks arranged in several neat piles inside a large semicircle of seated spectators.

Curbing his excitement, Steve made a casual but beady-eyed inspection of the various bits and pieces. Some of the struts and wing spars were badly distorted, but most of the airframe components he needed were available. The crumpled, vandalized cockpit pods looked beyond repair. The sole surviving engine looked more or less intact, but it had a broken propeller.

Cadillac appeared at Steve's shoulder. "What do you think?"

"It's a possibility, no more." Steve's doubt was genuine. "I'm not sure we have enough wing fabric," he added, realizing he had torn up strips of the precious material to plait into his own hair. "But the biggest problem is the fact that we don't have any metal working tools."

"What kind of tools do you need?" Cadillac asked.

It took Steve several seconds to recover from his surprise. "You've got tools . . . *here?*"

"Some. We may be able to get others."

"Where do you get them from?"

"The people who make our crossbows. The iron-masters."

"Who are they—Mutes?"

"No, they are unskinned, like you. But like us in other ways."

Steve tried to make his interest sound casual. "Where do they live?"

Beyond the eastern door. In the Fire-Pits of Beth-Lem."

"Where is that exactly?"

Cadillac shrugged again. "No one knows. It is said that there are many lands beyond the eastern door, but the Plainfolk have never been there. We trade with the iron-masters when their wheel-boats ride the great rivers. The Yellow-Stone, Miz-Hurry, and Miz-Hippy."

Steve committed the names to memory. "When do they come?"

"Once, sometimes twice a year. Some years not at all."

"And what do you trade?"

"Bread-stalk seed, buffalo-meat, Dream Cap, men, women."

"You trade your own people?"

Cadillac smiled at Steve's reaction. "Only those who are prepared to go. Is that worse than staying and being killed because the clan has no sharp iron?"

"No, I guess not," Steve admitted. "What else can you tell me about the iron-masters?"

"Nothing."

"But why do they trade you weapons?" insisted Steve. "Why don't they use them to defeat you and the rest of the Plainfolk?"

Cadillac answered with a shrug. "Perhaps because they are too few in number."

"Okay, in that case why don't your people attack them, make 'em prisoners, and set 'em to work? Why trade valuable goods when you can make slaves of them?"

Cadillac smiled. "You're thinking like a Tracker."

"Come on," riposted Steve. "You kill other Mutes."

"Only in defense of our own turf."

"Yeah, sure. . . ." Steve realized that it would be a waste of time to argue the point further. He fisted Cadillac's arm. "Let's get to work. We need a screwdriver, something to drill holes with, a saw to cut this tubing, a flat file, a—"

Cadillac frowned. "What's a screwdriver?"

Steve sighed inwardly. "Just show me what you've got. . . ."

Aided by Cadillac, Three-Degrees, another skilled Mute with the apt name of Air-Supply, and a score or more of willing go-fers, Steve proceeded to construct a serviceable airframe. Throughout the process of rebuilding, Cadillac worked alongside Steve, helping him every step of the way. Once again, Steve was impressed by the Mute's agile brain and his mechanical aptitude. The young wordsmith had an almost instinctive grasp of aviation technology and the theory of flight. What Steve didn't know was that Cadillac's mental powers had enabled him to draw the knowledge and understanding of these things from Steve's own mind.

The wing fabric proved to be the biggest headache, but after sweet-talking the entire clan into handing back every usable scrap of fabric that had been ripped off by trophy hunters, two sets of panels were laboriously pieced together. The overlapping patchwork seams were bonded with pine resin and hand-sewn, and then the two layers were fitted over the wing spars and securely fastened together with parallel lines of stitching. There was no way Steve could re-create the inflated aerofoil section wing of the Skyhawk he had flown into captivity, but, amazingly, the solar-cell fabric still functioned. Using short strands of wire from multicolored power cable held in place with globs of resin, Steve connected the patchwork of panels in series. It was a slow, fiddly job, but finally the circuit was completed.

Lacking any proper measuring equipment, Steve was forced to improvise. He checked that he had a spark across the end of the wires then asked some Mute children to bring him a live fish from the nearest stream. They brought back a plump trout in a skin-bag and watched curiously as Steve stuck the ends of the wires into the water. The trout bent in the middle as if it were trying to bite its tail off then rolled over and floated to the surface. Satisfied that he had a modest amount of power at his disposal, Steve proceeded with the repair and installation of one of the electric motors for which Three-Degrees had proudly carved a new propeller from dark yellow wood.

Three weeks after picking up the first piece of tubing, a motorized, forty-foot-span hang glider—which they had named Blue-Bird—stood poised on head-high sapling trestles. Steve connected the cable, bringing the current from the wing panels to the motor, then everyone held their breath and waited for the sun to clear from behind a seemingly endless bank of dull gray cloud. After an interminable wait, the thin fuzzy shadow cast by Blue-Bird's wings darkened into a hard-edged arrow as the sun soared into a patch of deep blue and beamed down its warmth upon their upturned faces. Steve threw the switch. Nothing happened. He spun the prop. Nothing. Like churning mud with a stick. A disappointed sigh went up from the ring of spectators. Steve swore quietly and whacked the motor casing with the flat of his hand. The propeller turned obediently, blurring into a smooth disc of spun gold.

"*Hey-yaah!*" roared the clan.

Steve threw a double-handed kiss at the sky. "Oh, you sweet Mother!" he crowed.

"Will you have enough power for takeoff?" asked Cadillac.

Steve shook his head as he tightened one of the starboard rigging wires. "If the circuit holds, it will

help us stay up once we get airborne, but that's all."
But that's enough, he thought exultantly. With a zero
sink rate, I can wave good-bye to these lumps any-
time I choose. . . .

Blue-Bird was carried with great ceremony to the
top of a gentle slope, from where Steve made several
test runs, floating a few feet off the ground while
Mute children raced alongside him laughing and
shouting excitedly. The fear and pain caused by the
arrowheads over the crop-fields appeared to be entirely forgotten. Steve was pleasantly surprised to
find that Blue-Bird was inherently stable and responded well to shifts of the control bar and his
suspended body.

The first real takeoff from the top of a steeply
sloping bluff was perfect. As he hung in his harness,
riding the cool updraft, Steve experienced anew the
exhilaration of flight. It was like a rerun of his first
overground solo: the quickening heartbeat, the sharp-
ened senses, a new awareness. He banked around
toward the bluff and went into a series of climbing
figure eights over the watchers below. Above him the
sky was blue, with scattered white clouds.

Because of his stone-age circuitry, the solar-cell
fabric was delivering a fluctuating current that, from
the level of sound from the motor, Steve judged to be
between 30 and 50 percent of its normal potential.
While it did not enable him to climb, it produced
enough power to maintain altitude once he'd gotten
up there, by riding into the wind like a kite, or coast-
ing on the back of a convenient thermal. As the watching Mutes below shrank to antlike proportions Steve
realized that he now had a golden opportunity to
escape. The idea had been lurking at the back of his
mind from the moment his feet had left the ground
on the first test glides. Before taking off from the
bluff he had concealed the map under his fatigues.
He had not had an opportunity to recover the buried
ration pack and water kit, but that did not really
matter. He could survive for the few days it might
take to fly back to the Federation. He had been drink-

ing contaminated water and eating raw fruit for months now; he had also been breathing radioactive air and been in skin-to-skin contact with Mutes. Another week either way wouldn't make much difference. Since emerging from the days of semidrugged sleep way back at the beginning, Steve had gradually forgotten the invisible death shroud that still enveloped the overground. Now and then he remembered the constant danger with a sense of shock, followed by a moment of perplexity as he realized that despite his prolonged exposure, he had not yet suffered noticeable signs of radiation sickness. Steve knew it was bound to manifest itself sooner or later. There could be no escape. He would suffer the same fate as Poppa-Jack. But how strange! he thought. Maybe it's just being up in the air again, but it's been a long time since I felt as good as this.

Steve leveled out at an estimated altitude of three thousand feet—well beyond the range of any Mute crossbows below. If he was going to make a break for it, now was the time to do it. A seesaw battle raged inside him. Steve knew that if he chose this moment to fly away, he would be betraying the trust of Cadillac and Mr. Snow. And there was Clearwater. Despite his promises to Mr. Snow and to himself, his resolution was beginning to crumble. Steve wanted to get close to her again; to talk to her without being surrounded by a milling crowd of Mutes. He would stay, he decided. He would delay his flight to freedom until he found some way to meet up with her. Just once. Just the two of them. But that was crazy, too. He knew it was his duty to escape; knew that if he did not, he would inevitably fall sick and die. Yet . . .

Something was wrong. Something had happened to him. And Steve knew what it was: it was the same feeling that had gripped him when he had faced the open ramp doors after his first overground solo. The thought of returning to his life underground, a life that had once seemed the normal—indeed the only *possible*—mode of existence, now filled him with a strange dread.

Cutting the motor, Steve descended, shaving the mountainous rock face behind the bluff in a series of daredevil swoops; then, before landing, he made a couple of low-level passes over the heads of the spectators. To his surprise, he saw that Clearwater had joined Cadillac on the cliff top. Both waved to him as he swept past. Steve wondered how to handle the situation. Since meeting Clearwater and talking to Mr. Snow, he had not mentioned her name to Cadillac. How much did the young wordsmith know? Was he to pretend he did not know who she was? Play it by ear, Brickman. . . .

Steve brought Blue-Bird up into a stall and made a smooth, stand-up landing, coming to a stop after five paces. He quickly unbuckled his harness and, in response to a beckoning gesture from Cadillac, pushed his way through the excited crowd that surrounded Blue-Bird. Steve tried to keep his face in neutral as he came face-to-face with Clearwater. Cadillac made no attempt to introduce him but, on the other hand, did not act as if Clearwater weren't there. He congratulated Steve on his stylish performance then turned away briefly to tell the young Mutes not to tamper with the glider.

Steve took the opportunity to look deep into the Mute's blue eyes.

They blazed briefly as Clearwater returned his look, then became veiled. "I envy you. How does it feel to fly like a bird?"

"Fantastic. You get a wonderful sense of . . . it's indescribable. Each time I go up I never want to come down. In fact, the truth is, when I circled that peak, I very nearly decided to go home."

"I'm glad you didn't," replied Clearwater guardedly. Again her eyes flashed briefly.

"Oh, really?" Steve tried to keep all expression out of his voice and face as Cadillac turned back to them.

"Yes," said Cadillac. "You see. . . if you had tried to escape, you would have fallen out of the sky like a stone."

Steve looked at them both and laughed disbelievingly.

Cadillac touched Clearwater's shoulder. "Show him. Show our friend the power that, in the hands of Talisman, will drive the sandburrowers back into their holes and bury them forever."

The word "friend" carried a vague emphasis that made Steve uneasy. Cadillac *had* to know something. Probably knew everything. Steve tried to read their faces but neither gave anything away.

Clearwater closed her eyes and appeared to compose herself. Cadillac surveyed the ground nearby and picked up a rock about the size of a basketball. The sinews in his neck and chest drew taut under its weight. "Ready?"

Clearwater nodded, her eyes still closed.

Steve suddenly became aware that the crowd around Blue-Bird had fallen silent and had turned to watch what was happening. Cadillac tensed his arm and stomach muscles and, with a visible effort, heaved the rock into the air above their heads. As it went up, Clearwater's eyes snapped wide open and her right arm shot out, the first two fingers aimed at the rock. From her throat came a strange ululating cry that curdled Steve's blood. To his amazement, the rock did not fall. It hung there for a moment, then shot upward into the sky as Clearwater raised her arm higher. When it was some two hundred feet above them, the wavering, unearthly sound coming from Clearwater's throat stopped abruptly. The rock hovered, held in place by her pointing forefinger. As Steve and the others below watched raptly, Clearwater drew a circle in the air above her head. The rock began to move slowly around in a wide circle, as if it were on the end of an invisible length of string. Clearwater dropped her arm and turned with Cadillac to face Steve. Once again, incredibly, the rock didn't fall. Steve watched open-mouthed as it continued to circle around in the air behind them.

"Now make it fall," said Cadillac quietly.

Clearwater made a fist with her right hand and

brought it down sharply on the open palm of her left. The rock plummeted out of the sky and smashed to pieces on the rocky slope below the bluff.

"Heyy-*yaahh!!*" roared the watching M'Calls. "Heyy-yahh! Heyy-yahh! Heyy-yahh!"

"Now do you understand why the Federation can never conquer us?" Cadillac asked.

Steve looked at Clearwater, then at Cadillac, and back again, his mouth opening and closing soundlessly.

Clearwater gazed at Steve with a hint of sadness. "He sees but he does not believe."

Cadillac nodded. "His mind is still chained by the darkness below. He cannot understand because what he has seen does not follow the rules of his world." He smiled. "It does not compute."

Steve eyed them silently, then sat down on a nearby rock. Cadillac gripped his shoulder sympathetically, then walked away with Clearwater toward the settlement escorted by their clan-brothers and sisters. They began to chant a Plainfolk melody using a style of singing known as mouth-music, full of complex counterharmonies in which the voices were the instruments. There were no proper words, but Steve knew, as he sat there along with the abandoned Blue-Bird, that it was a song of triumph.

---

17 ---

Clearwater's unnerving mastery over the rock—the second manifestation of Mute magic that Steve had witnessed—blew away the last vestiges of disbelief, leaving him totally mystified and more than a little shaken. Anxious to know more but not wanting to play into the hands of the wordsmiths by appearing overawed, Steve pushed the incident to the back of his mind and proceeded to give Cadillac his first flying lesson. Barely a week later, he found himself watching the young wordsmith handle the glider with all the ease and confidence of a wingman graduating after three years at the Flight Academy. Steve should have been pleased, but he was not disposed to kid himself. He knew that as an instructor he wasn't a patch on Carrol, yet Cadillac had acquired his flying skill with chilling speed. It was uncanny. But no more uncanny than the power that Clearwater had revealed.

Steve began to understand why Jodi Kazan had been so evasive on the subject of Mute magic. Somewhere along the trail during the ten years she had been flying the overground she must have stumbled across the truth as he had just done. And if *she* knew, so did Grand Central—even though officially it had been decreed that Mute magic did not exist. Had he, by pure chance, uncovered another corner of a widespread conspiracy? The big brother of the plot that had prevented him from winning the top honors at the Academy? How many other things had the First Family, in its unchallenged wisdom, legislated out of existence? What were the untapped secrets guarded by Columbus, the Federation's computer? How high did he have to go to get the inside story? How many levels of access were there?

After Cadillac gained his "wings," he took Steve over to Mr. Snow's hut for a celebratory pipe of rainbow grass. It seemed like a good moment to seek an explanation for what had happened on the bluff. Had Clearwater *really* made a rock fly, or had he imagined it all? Both wordsmiths were remarkably forthcoming. They confirmed that what he had seen had actually taken place, but when pressed to explain *how* or *why*, neither was able to furnish a response that met the rational requirements of a mind shaped by the Federation.

Steve concealed his frustration and sought Mr. Snow's opinion on the questions that had begun to plague him regarding his search for the ultimate reality. Was it possible ever to *know* the true state of things? How high did he have to climb before he found this elusive Truth, with a capital *T*, that Mr. Snow had referred to?

"Climbing the mountain is not really the problem," observed Mr. Snow. "It's being able to appreciate the view when you get to the top. There are times during a man's life when he looks upon the Truth, but more often than not he fails to recognize it. The moment of understanding passes him by. It may take many years before he stands once again on the mountaintop; others less fortunate are not offered that second chance." Mr. Snow indicated Cadillac with a wave of his hand. "As I said to my able but headstrong successor shortly before you came to us, you must learn to ask the right questions. But your mind must also be open to understanding, like the deep waters of a lake in the still of evening. Only then will the great white birds of wisdom alight upon its surface. Until that moment arrives, I suggest for your own peace of mind that you simply accept that certain Mutes *are* capable of performing magical acts. By 'magic' I mean the power to manipulate the forces in the earth and sky—and they are given this power by Talisman.''

Steve listened patiently. ''It's amazing ... you really *do* believe this guy exists?''

Mr. Snow waved the palm of his right hand. ''Who else do you think split Motor-Head's hammer? It was *his* power that saved you, the same power that flowed through Clearwater and gave her mastery over that rock.''

Steve eyed both of them silently.

''Why do you find that so difficult to accept?'' asked Cadillac.

Steve answered with a shrug. ''Maybe because it's hard for us Trackers to believe that there are ... invisible people.''

''The world will see the Thrice-Gifted One soon enough,'' said Mr. Snow quietly.

''Thrice-Gifted? ...''

''It is the other name by which Talisman is known. Perhaps *you* may live to see that day.''

''And die regretting it.'' Cadillac smiled. ''Let him hear the Prophecy, Old One. Let him know why we do not fear the iron snakes, or the wrath of the Federation.''

''Prophecy? Oh, yeah, I forgot,'' said Steve lightly. ''You guys have got everything worked out.''

Cadillac's eyes flashed angrily, then died as he stifled all emotion.

Mr. Snow's calm remained undisturbed. ''You're wrong, Brickman. What *we* believe is that it has all been worked out *for* us. Some of us are blessed with an inner ear that can pick up the Sky Voices; a gift withheld from most of my clan-brothers. But they believe, as we do, that the pattern of future events is already drawn. The Cosmic Wheel turns, taking us along its eternal path, whether we want to go or not. You, too, despite your blindness, have a part to play. So thank your lucky stars *we* believe in prophecy, even if you don't, because it's the only thing that's saved your ass."

Steve adopted a chastened expression as the old wordsmith readjusted his cross-legged position.

"I was going to ask you to try and open up your soul to what I'm about to say, but"—Mr. Snow eyed him—"you don't understand."

"I don't even know what the word 'soul' means."

"Never mind. Listen well, and mark this. It was first transmitted through a wordsmith called Cincinnati-Red about six hundred and fifty years ago, and is known as the Talisman Prophecy." Mr. Snow began to speak in a rich resonant tone he had not used before.

When the great mountain in the west speaks
with a tongue of fire that burns the sky
and the earth drowns in its own tears,
then shall a child born of the Plainfolk
become the Thrice-Gifted One
who shall be Wordsmith, Summoner, and Seer.

Man-child or Woman-child the One may be.
Whosoever is chosen shall grow straight
And strong as the Heroes of the Old Time.
The morning dew shall be his eyes,
the blades of grass shall be his ears,
and the name of the One shall be Talisman.

The eagles shall be his golden arrows,
the stones of the earth his hammer,
And a nation shall be forged
from the fires of War.
The Plainfolk shall be as a bright sword
in the hands of Talisman, their Savior.

Then shall the cloud warriors fall like rain.
The iron snake shall devour its masters.
The desert shall rise up and crush
the Dark Cities of the sand-burrowers
for heaven and earth have yielded
their secret powers to Talisman.

Thus shall perish the enemies of the Plainfolk,
for the Thrice-Gifted One is master of all.
Death shall be driven from the air
and the blood shall be drained from the earth.
Soul-sister shall join hands with soul-brother
and the land shall sing of Talisman.

In some inexpressible way, the Prophecy touched an inner chord buried deep within Steve's psyche. Hearing it spoken for the first time in the flickering light of a fire-stone was an indelible experience, the impact of which equaled the discovery of Clearwater, and her remote-control mastery over the rock. Although Steve could not have described it thus, the poetic imagery contained in the lines opened up another world; gave him a whole new perspective on the people he had been trained to regard as subhuman. The wily, poisonous Mute. But what was truly astounding was the date the Prophecy was alleged to have been composed. It meant that the appearance of wagon trains and wingmen had been predicted by the Plainfolk some four hundred years before the Federation had envisaged their use! It seemed impossible, but if true—and if the other events that were predicted took place—the Federation's future looked distinctly unpromising.

"So tell me—is Clearwater a . . . summoner?"

"Yes," Mr. Snow replied. "As it says in the Prophecy, there are three gifts that are given to certain of the Plainfolk through the power of Talisman. The first is that of wordsmith, the second is that of summoner, the third is the gift of seership—the ability to read the past and future in the stones."

Cadillac squared his shoulders. "I have this gift."

Steve eyed him with evident disbelief. "Are you telling me that you can see pictures in stones?"

"Only certain stones," explained Mr. Snow. "Seeing-stones." He saw Steve's expression. "Don't laugh. It was Cadillac who read the iron snake through a stone it had passed over. That was how we knew you were in its belly."

Steve looked at each of them in turn. "Is this why you both went to so much trouble to keep me alive?"

"Yes. The Sky Voices had spoken to me of the coming of a cloud warrior whose destiny was linked to that of the Talisman. Your face was made known to Cadillac through his gift of seership. Fate drew your separate strands of existence together and the knot was sealed by the bolt from his crossbow. And when he looked upon you in the blazing crop-field he recognized you as the one revealed by the stone.

"And if I'd been just another Tracker?"

"We'd have left you to burn," Cadillac replied.

Steve thought about that for a moment, then asked, "Why is it that some of you call me the Death-Bringer? What is it that MotorHead, who fears nothing, has seen in his dreams?"

"He is a warrior. Perhaps the death he dreams of is his own," said Cadillac. He looked expectantly at Mr. Snow.

The old wordsmith smoothed his beard and fixed his eyes on Steve. "There are dreams that mirror the workings of the mind, dreams that reflect the desires of the body, and dreams that bridge the void between this world and that of the Sky People. It is true that over such a bridge certain knowledge comes, but, alas, I cannot say what Motor-Head's words may mean or know what he has seen. What I *can* say is that there will come a time when the role you are destined to play in the emergence of Talisman will be revealed to you." Mr. Snow paused, then added enigmatically, "At that moment you will discover not only *what* it is you have to do but also *who* you are."

The two wordsmiths watched Steve impassively as

he reflected silently on what he had just been told.
He lifted his eyes to theirs. "When is all this supposed to happen?"

Mr. Snow spread a palm. "When the earth gives
the sign."

"Yes, I know what the words say," Steve said with
a trace of irritation. "But when is that going to be?
You've been waiting six hundred and fifty years already! Maybe the Savior of the Plainfolk isn't coming. He may have decided that it's safer to stay where
he is."

Mr. Snow's calm remained undisturbed. "He will
come. Not in my lifetime, perhaps. But certainly in
yours—an event you may regret, for you are destined
to be a leader of your people."

"I, also, shall know the Talisman," said Cadillac,
not wishing to be left out of the discussion of such
great events. "The Old One has told me this."

Even though Mr. Snow's words seemed to confirm
his own belief that he had been marked out for greater
things, the conversation did little to ease Steve's inner turmoil. Even his basic instinct for survival, which
should have been telling him to head for cover, was
being torn in two. Steve remained insatiably curious
as to what his possible role might be but, at the same
time, was frightened by what he might discover. Despite his deep-seated responses to what he had seen
and heard, Steve's Tracker background with its emphasis on unquestioning obedience, military-style discipline, and rigorously applied logic made him shy
away from the darker side of the Mute persona with
its predictive visions and its manipulative magic.
The world of the Mutes was like a giant whirlpool
waiting to trap the unwary. Those foolish enough to
leap into the swirling currents in search of the answers to its mysteries were slowly sucked toward the
dark vortex at its center and disappeared without
trace. And yet ... and yet ... Steve felt himself
drawn back toward it, gripped by a shadowy power
beyond his control.

Escorted by thirty Bears, Mr. Snow and Cadillac left the settlement and, over the next three days, ran eastward, going far beyond the clan's turf markers into the middle lands of the Plainfolk. Twice during the outward journey they encountered the markers of other clans; on each occasion they altered course to run around the territory involved. Once they lay hidden until dark to avoid a large hunting party—not because they feared a confrontation, but because it was unnecessary. It would have involved a needless waste of life. After the battle with the iron snake, the clan needed to husband its strength in readiness for the next confrontation with the sandburrowers. Mr. Snow's purpose was to find a specific location, which the Sky Voices had indicated to him in a recent message. Eventually, after running nearly four hundred miles, his inner ear told him that they had reached the approximate location—the point where the great river whose course they had followed all the way down from the western hills met its sister coming up from the southwest. A point which on pre-Holocaust maps of the overground marked the junction of the North Platte and South Platte rivers in Nebraska.

Sitting down thankfully under the wide branches of a tree, Mr. Snow sent Cadillac to search for a seeing-stone. Motor-Head, who was charged with organizing their escort, ordered them to disperse in pairs to patrol the area around them. When Cadillac's search of the north bank proved fruitless, they crossed over onto the narrow strip of land where the two rivers ran side by side before becoming one. Then, when Cadillac again drew a blank, they tried again on the far side of the southern river.

It was here that they found traces of one of the ancient hardways along which giant beetles had once carried the men of the Old Time. The beetle, Mr. Snow explained, left a trail of sticky black slime—like snails and black horned worms—so it could find its way back again. This black trail gradually hardened, becoming thicker and thicker with each passing beetle—who for some reason liked to follow each other in long lines, jammed nose to tail. Once laid down, the hardway was used over and over again, because the beetles knew where they were going and could move faster.

Men of the Old Time, said Mr. Snow, were obsessed with speed. They had built a huge crossbow that had shot a bolt with men inside it all the way to the moon. They had other bolts with wings like huge arrowheads that could cross the sky faster than the sun. They were masters of the world, but they had never learned to love each other. And they had forgotten the Way of the Warrior. And so, through their ignorance and hatred, the world had died in the War of a Thousand Suns. Clans numbering more than the raindrops in the sky fell like shriveled leaves at the Yellowing, killed not by their equals in single combat but by strange secret words spoken by machines made with the High Craft, hidden deep within the earth—like this Columbus the cloud warrior had talked of. Sharp iron of unimaginable power wielded by men who had not chewed bone.

Cadillac pondered on these deep and tragic mysteries of the Old Time as he searched for a seeingstone. Eventually, as the sun sank toward the western door, he found one. Mr. Snow squatted crosslegged and watched intently as his pupil knelt, closed his eyes, raised the stone to his forehead, and began the process that caused the pictures from its memory to flow into his mind.

"Find me the iron snake," Mr. Snow said. "Go forward a little way through the time-clouds and find me a great battle."

Since his first attempts to make practical use of his gift at the urging of his teacher, Cadillac had gradually improved to the point where he now remembered much of what he had seen and spoken of while in contact with the stone. He had discovered that far and near memory could be distinguished by the intensity of the aura that surrounded them, and his inner eye had begun to recognize the difference between visions from the past and those of the future.

Still grasping the stone firmly, Cadillac lowered it to his knees. His face muscles tightened, dragging the ends of his closed lips back and down as he shied away from some fearful internal landscape of horror. "My mind flies forward, but I cannot yet tell how far I journey," he gasped, the words hissing out between his clenched teeth.

"Look for Clearwater," suggested Mr. Snow. "Look for yourself and the cloud warrior. Summon them with all the power of your mind. Perhaps, in this way their images will come to the fore and the others will remain sealed within the stone." The old wordsmith sat back patiently. Behind him, the wide waters of the two great rivers moved slowly eastward. Several minutes passed. Cadillac's head rolled from side to side and his body began to twitch and then was wracked by more violent muscular spasms. Mr. Snow made no attempt to prompt him further.

Suddenly Cadillac's spine became rigid. He turned his sightless face to the sky, his features contorted with anguish. "The iron snake stands over me!" he cried. "Oh, Mo-Town! Great Mother! It runs with the blood of our people!" Cadillac began to moan, a keening sound that became a harsh sobbing noise as he was shaken by another spasm. After a few moments, the convulsions died away. He slumped forward awkwardly, crushed under the weight of his grief.

Mr. Snow watched him in silence.

For several minutes Cadillac did not move, then he slowly sat up, drew his shoulders back, and turned his tear-streaked face toward Mr. Snow, gazing at him with great tenderness. "There is nothing but pain and sorrow in this stone." He cast it aside.

"The world is full of it, my son," Mr. Snow replied quietly. "It is the burden of the warrior. The dark side of existence that threatens to crush the soul. Only those strong enough to bear it can reach the light beyond where true happiness lies."

"Even so, I wish you had not brought me here."

"Why not?"

"Because this is the place of your death, Old One." Cadillac's eyes filled with fresh tears. He brushed them away angrily.

Mr. Snow grimaced and drew his hand slowly over his beard."When is it to be?"

"In less than twelve moons. Near the time of the Yellowing."

The late summer of the coming year. The old word-smith lowered his head and digested this news in silence, then raised his eyes and let them range over his surroundings: the rolling prairie covered with red buffalo grass that lay north of the river; the billowing towers of cloud advancing slowly from the eastern door like stately Spanish galleons under full sail—precious words, those, from the Old Time; to the south, a low band of dark gray rainclouds threw the long shadowed stand of tall, white-trunked larches into bright relief, their orange and yellow leaves aflame in the slanting rays of the sun; to the west, over his right shoulder, the blue, distant hills to which they must now return. Mr. Snow swept his hand around the horizon and beamed at Cadillac. "Come! Put away your grief and look around you! How can you be saddened by such beauty? This is a good place to die!" Slapping his thighs, Mr. Snow rose as if he had not a care in the world, threw his arms out wide, and drank in the late afternoon air.

Cadillac had seen many things in the stone at the joining of the two rivers. Some were too painful to talk of—even to Mr. Snow; but as they headed west on the return leg of their journey, he revealed that the cloud warrior would have to be set free, for it was his departure that led directly to the events he had foreseen, bringing fulfillment of the Prophecy one step nearer.

"It will not be easy to arrange," Mr. Snow observed. "Despite the sign at the biting of the arrow, some of our clan-brothers still seek his death. They will do all they can to prevent his escape."

Cadillac shrugged. "If he follows the path drawn by Talisman, the cloud warrior will overcome them."

Mr. Snow smiled. "Spoken like a true wordsmith. Even so, to stand any chance of success, the cloud warrior will have to take the arrowhead. Can you build another?"

Cadillac nodded. "If you desire it, yes."

The two wordsmiths exchanged a conspiratorial smile. Steve could not have picked a more apt pupil. Cadillac did not need to be "taught"; the act of instruction merely provided the young wordsmith with the opportunity to insert a mental plug into Steve's memory and make a duplicate record of everything that was stored in the files. Cadillac had learned to fly with consummate skill because his brain circuits now contained the same sensory data that had enabled Steve to perform so well at the Academy. And when presenting Steve with the "remains" of the three Skyhawks, the clan had taken care to conceal the wing fabric from Steve's own craft. Although split in several places and scorched at one wing tip, the panels were otherwise virtually intact. The M'Calls had also held back an undamaged motor and propeller. Unknown to Steve and his masters within the Federation, the Plainfolk now possessed, through Cadillac, the knowledge to build and fly a craft similar to Blue-Bird. It was a task Mr. Snow had secretly agreed to undertake on behalf of the mysterious iron-masters of Beth-Lem. They had asked him to deliver a cloud warrior and an undamaged arrowhead. In the event they would get neither, Cadillac's newly acquired flying skill and a reconstructed craft would serve their purpose just as well. And in return, the iron-masters—whose promises were always honored—would furnish the M'Calls with new and powerful long sharp iron. . . .

When they halted for the night, and while Cadillac slept, Mr. Snow stared thoughtfully at the glowing embers of the fire and considered how the cloud warrior's departure might be achieved. Steve had had the means and the opportunity to escape for nearly a month, but so far nothing had happened. After pondering the problem at length, Mr. Snow turned to the Sky Voices. With their help he understood that Steve's inertia was not due to his fear of Clearwater's powers as a summoner but because of his unrequited desire for her. It was the other, sweeter kind of death he longed to suffer by her hand. Allowing them to come together might, paradoxically, be the best way of securing his departure. It would be a minor betrayal of his young protégé and was totally contrary to the wishes of the clan-elders, but if this was the will of Talisman, then so be it.

Without disturbing the other sleeping warriors, Mr. Snow woke a young Bear called Death-Wish and told him to return immediately to the settlement. A run of three hundred miles—a day and a half's running. He was to bring twelve hands of warriors to meet them on the eastern edge of the D'Vine turf. He was also to take, in the utmost secrecy, a gift to Clearwater. Opening the bag slung around his waist, Mr. Snow handed Death-Wish a small pouch closed at the neck by a drawstring tied in a sealed knot around a knuckle-bone. Mr. Snow did not disclose its contents to his fleet-footed messenger, but inside was a thin, standard-issue chain necklace and dog tag bearing Steve's name and number, and a dozen threads of Dream Cap.

The next morning, when Cadillac discovered Death-Wish's departure, Mr. Snow explained he had been sent to fetch reinforcements to cover their crossing of the D'Vine turf. Cadillac accepted this without question. He had no knowledge of Mr. Snow's secret plan of action, but he was now aware, through his reading of the stone, of Steve's desire to possess Clearwater. He had already sensed they were drawn to each other but had not challenged either of them to deny it. His indecision on the subject was due to Mr. Snow. Ever since Steve's "confession," the old wordsmith had used his formidable powers to cloud Cadillac's perception in the same way he had fudged Commander

Hartmann's thought processes prior to the attack on the wagon train.

Unfortunately, Mr. Snow had not been able to beam out the same stealthy static while Cadillac searched the stone. As a result, the young wordsmith had been shaken by the unexpected intensity of feeling that accompanied the images of Steve and Clearwater. From his other delvings into the cloud warrior's mind Cadillac knew that his own friendship with him was based on genuine feelings; feelings that were in constant conflict with the dark, treacherous side of Steve's nature. Up to now he had viewed Steve's dilemma sympathetically, but the revelation of the full extent of his future relationship with Clearwater had a galvanizing effect on his psyche. When he emerged from his trance state, Cadillac's mind was stripped of its previous mental lethargy, and despite the renewed jamming operation by Mr. Snow it remained sharp and clear.

Up to that moment, Cadillac had firmly believed in predestination and the unquestioning acceptance of the will of Talisman. But now, pride, jealousy, a sense of outrage and betrayal made him a driven man. He felt a rebellious urge to *do* something; to be in *control;* to impose *his* will through some simple yet decisive act that would change the course of future events, would alter the direction of the River of Time so that the death and destruction he had foreseen would not occur. He was aware that in attempting to tamper with the preordained he was setting himself up as the equal of the Supreme Being who watched over the Plainfolk, and he knew it was wrong, but this did not deflect his growing resolve. It was a forgivable conceit he shared with numberless other young men—and many older ones, too—who had gone before him.

Toward sundown on the day that Death-Wish had been dispatched in the hours before dawn, Cadillac sought out Motor-Head during one of their brief halts. The heavily muscled warrior crouched in a stream splashing water over his face, chest, and arms. Black-

Top and Steel-Eye, his constant companions, lay sprawled on the bank eating yellow-fists—the Mute name for a type of large wild apple.

Motor-Head cupped his hands and splashed water over Cadillac as he hunkered down on the edge of the stream. "Your face looks heavy, sand-worm. You got something on your mind?"

"Yes. I would speak with my brother Bear of things I have seen in the stone."

Motor-Head stepped out of the stream and beckoned Black-Top and Steel-Eye to come and sit on either side of him. The three warriors squatted down facing Cadillac. Motor-Head snapped his fingers and pointed to Cadillac. Black-Top tossed him a yellow-fist. Steel-Eye placed another in his leader's outstretched palm. Motor-Head took a huge bite out of it. "What would you speak of?"

"The Death-Bringer."

Motor-Head spat the chunk of fruit out of his mouth, tossed the other piece away, then leaned forward with his wrists on his knees and fixed his jet-black eyes on Cadillac's face. His huge hands hung loose but his jaw was set, his neck muscles tensed, his killer instinct aroused by the subject of the cloud warrior.

"He plans to take wing," said Cadillac. "To return to the Dark Cities beneath the Great Desert of the South. And he wishes to take Clearwater with him."

Motor-Head glanced at his two companions, then studied Cadillac with narrowed eyes. "When is this to be?"

"Soon. It could be within two or three moon-risings."

"Does the Old One know of this?"

"He has not spoken of it to me," Cadillac replied. "Nor I to him."

Motor-Head's eyes glittered as he got the message. "What do you wish us to do—clip his wings?"

"Yes. But in a way that does not harm the arrow-head."

Motor-Head exchanged another look with Black-

Top and Steel-Eye and gained their silent assent. He turned to Cadillac. "We will make the run for home when the others sleep under Mo-Town's cloak. It will be hard. It is more than a day's running. We may not get there in time."

Cadillac offered the yellow-fist he'd been given to Motor-Head. "If anyone can do it, you will."

Motor-Head nodded with visible pride. "True." He gripped his knees and flexed the muscles in his arms and shoulders. "So ... this treacherous crow fouls the floor of those who feed him. Is he to be killed?"

Cadillac considered the idea very seriously. To delay the cloud warrior's departure was a decision that could be reversed; to order his death was an irrevocable act that might lead to an even greater disaster than the one he sought to avoid. It could also render him totally unworthy in the eyes of Mr. Snow. "No," he said. "Don't kill him or cut him. Just ... keep him on the ground."

Motor-Head's mouth turned down sharply. "You disappoint me, sand-worm. There is venom in your heart but your tongue lacks bite. A man who would take the place of Mr. Snow needs iron in his soul. If he cannot say or do the hard things, the clan will go under."

Cadillac searched his conscience and found what he felt was the true answer. "He who would give wise counsel must know when to take life and when to spare it. The Way of the Warrior is not drenched in blood. The strength and courage needed to kill your enemy is only the first step along the path to understanding."

Motor-Head snorted contemptuously. "I will not cross words with you, little brother. Your head holds the star-secrets, my hand holds sharp iron, but we were both born to defend the Plainfolk in the name of Talisman." He waved a finger at the fruit in Cadillac's hand. "Go! Sweeten your tongue on that yellow-fist while you wonder at the ways of the world ... and leave the cloud warrior to us."

When darkness fell, Mr. Snow's party halted. After

a brief meal around a small log fire, sentinels were posted and the rest of the party wrapped themselves in their woven straw blankets. Cadillac found it impossible to sleep. He twisted and turned restlessly, gnawed by indecision and guilt. Finally, when he could bear it no longer, he sought out the old wordsmith.

Mr. Snow was sleeping deeply and was not in the best of humor when Cadillac woke him up. "Great Sky-Mother, what is it?" he grumped. He sat up and shivered. "Talisman! It's cold! Uuughh! I'm getting too old to sleep outdoors." He pulled the straw blanket around his shoulders. "Is there any wood left to put on that fire?"

Cadillac cast around in the darkness and found a few pieces. He stirred the dying embers and blew on them till the wood burst into flame.

Mr. Snow warmed his hands. "That's better," he muttered. He studied Cadillac's face in the flickering orange glow. "You look as if the roof's fallen in."

"I have dishonored you, Old One."

Mr. Snow yawned and stretched. "Let me be the judge of that. Just start at the beginning and keep it short and simple." He dropped his eyes from Cadillac's face and stared at the flames.

Cadillac recounted his anguish at what he had seen in the stone, then took a deep breath and told Mr. Snow he had sent Motor-Head, Black-Top, and Steel-Eye to punish the cloud warrior. He sat back nervously, expecting his teacher to explode in anger.

For a while, Mr. Snow said nothing. He just stared into the fire for what seemed like a long time. When he raised his head he looked old and tired. "When did they leave?"

"Soon after we ate."

Mr. Snow let out a long, weary sigh, then rubbed his face briskly. "We'd better get going, then. . . ."

"To the settlement?" Cadillac found himself confused by Mr. Snow's low-key response.

"Where else?"

"You are not angry, Old One?"

Mr. Snow yawned again. "Angry? You bonehead! You imbecile! What you have done changes nothing! Do you think any of us can deflect the will of Talisman? You are an *instrument* of that will!"

Cadillac uncrossed his legs and knelt with his head bowed. "Forgive me, Old One, for being blind and deaf to your words."

"There's nothing to forgive," grumped Mr. Snow. "When I was your age, I also thought I could be master the world. But that's not the way it is." He got to his feet and started to roll up his blanket.

Cadillac rose. "Does that mean we must accept dishonor—take no action, do nothing?"

"Of course not!" Mr. Snow exclaimed. "You do whatever has to be done! But above all, you must try to *understand!* Come on, help me wake the others. . . ."

"But Old One . . . what is the point of going? If we can change nothing . . ."

A mischievous look crept into Mr. Snow's eyes. He chuckled and thrust a finger under Cadillac's nose. "We are going to teach *you* a lesson. Which I hope won't be wasted, because the run from here is probably going to kill me."

Clearwater found the small square package of folded red leaves lying on the talking mat outside her hut after Death-Wish had chased her two clan-sisters around the screen of yellow leaves and into the rock pool. Taking it into the hut, she opened it and found the pouch. With her hunting knife, she cut the sealed knot and peeked inside. The musty odor told her it contained Dream Cap. Pulling out the necklace, she studied the tag bearing the silent speech-signs of the sand-burrowers and recognized it as something that had been taken from Steve. And when she held it to her forehead, she knew immediately who it was from and what she was required to do. Clearwater's heart alternately leapt and quailed at the thought of going to the cloud warrior and the dread of what might happen if they were found together. She knew that Mr. Snow would not have asked her to risk death and dishonor unless it was necessary. She also knew that if she did what was required without the rest of the clan knowing, the cloud warrior would go, leaving her to face Cadillac weighed down by the shameful knowledge that she had betrayed him. And that would be like dying, too. But she was a child of the Plainfolk, of the clan M'Call, from the bloodline of the She-Kargo. And as Mr. Snow had said to Steve, the M'Calls had the courage to accept their destiny.

Death-Wish left to return to the main settlement as Clearwater prepared the evening meal she was to share with her clan-sisters. Both were unaware that their portions contained a liberal dose of Dream Cap. Cooked with food, it acted as a strong sedative, and within an hour both slipped away gently into a deep sleep.

Confident that neither would awaken until the sun was at the head of the sky on the following day, Clearwater went to the rock pool where her clan-sisters had provided Death-Wish with a frolic-some combination of sex and hygiene and carefully washed her newly patterned body. Returning to the hut, she knelt before it on the woven mats and sang to herself as she braided fresh flowers into her hair and rubbed a fragrant oil onto her arms, breasts, belly, and thighs. The song she sang was about a She-Wolf who lay with her young warrior-love through the time of the New Earth only to lose him at summer-dawn when he fell under the knives of a marauding clan. A sad, keening lament that brought tears to her eyes.

And so it was that on the last night before Cadillac and Mr. Snow returned, Steve stirred sleepily and discovered Clearwater snuggling down beside him under his wolfskins. As his eyes snapped wide open, she laid a warning finger on his lips and then embraced him. The touch of her lips on his, the electric shock that ran through him as her supple body slid sinuously against his own, nearly blew the top of his head off. It was unbelievable. Out of this world. Putting the bomb in the barrel with Lundkwist was nothing compared with this. Steve might not know what the word love meant, but he knew how it felt. It made his heart leap; made him feel he would suffocate with sheer joy. It was all coming true; it was happening; she was here—lithe, eager, vibrant, sensual, demanding—yet at the same time, it seemed totally unreal.

As they lay together in the darkness, tenderly locked in each other's arms, their lovemaking had a gentle dreamlike quality, far removed from the sweaty clash of lamp-tanned muscled limbs, the mechanical thrust and counterthrust, the feeling of disassociation that accompanied his previous sexual encounters. They were borne aloft on a wave of emotion, transported to another plane, another timeless dimension beyond the bounds of physical reality.

This isn't really happening, thought Steve. My imagination's working overtime. But no. When he awoke again in the first gray light of dawn he found Clearwater nestled sleepily against him, her legs interlocked with his. It took a few seconds to collect his thoughts, then the reality of the situation hit Steve like a sledgehammer between the eyes.

"Christopher Columbus!" he whispered to himself. What they had done was the height of folly; if discovered it would destroy the relationships he had carefully built up, demonstrate his total disregard of the clan's social values . . . and bring death to them both.

Clearwater was also full of regrets. Not for what they had done, but only because her desire for Steve had placed *his* life in jeopardy. She took his face in her hands and told him that there was only one solution to the jam they had landed themselves in. He must escape on the arrowhead he had built.

Steve gathered her into his arms. "I'm not leaving here unless you promise to come with me."

Clearwater put her hands on his chest. "That is madness. There is no place on the arrowhead for me!"

Steve knew she was right. There was no way that Blue-Bird could carry both of them. The wing area, which had been limited by the fabric he'd been able to salvage, simply would not generate enough lift. The only other alternative was suicidal, but he brushed aside all thoughts of failure and seized her firmly by the arms. "Okay, then . . . we'll go on foot."

Clearwater shook her head sadly, her eyes filled with tears. "Oh, golden one—think with your *head* not your heart. You ask the impossible! Where could we run to? Look at me! I am a Mute!"

Steve ran his hands along the black-and-brown jigsaw pattern on her forearms. "You're not! Not like the others!"

"Yes, I know. Underneath this my skin is like yours, but your people would never accept me. And even if they did, I could not live in your dark world beneath the desert."

"It's not dark!" Steve hissed. "There is no night! Even in the deepest place the light is as bright as when the sun is at the head of the sky! There is no White Death, no rain. Thousands of us spend their whole lives within the earth-shield. Happily," he added, with less than total conviction.

"I could not live in your bright burrows for a day," whispered Clearwater. "Is that what you wish to do with me—take me down there to die?"

"No, no," Steve muttered. He searched his mind desperately for a more practical solution to their predicament; a more persuasive argument.

Clearwater caressed his cheek. "Even if I agreed to come with you, we are doomed from the start. You would not be able to outrun the Bears. They would hunt us relentlessly night and day, even in their sleep."

Steve knew she was referring to the Mutes' ability to run continuously, with their characteristic loping stride, for twenty-four hours or more, sleeping on their feet like birds on the wing. He thought hard and suddenly had a brilliant idea. "What about your magic? You made that rock fly, didn't you? You can use that to protect us!"

Clearwater shook her head again. "No. It would be too dangerous. I am no match for Mr. Snow."

Steve looked at her with a surprised frown.

Clearwater looked equally surprised. "Did he not tell you he was a summoner when he spoke of the Talisman Prophecy?"

"No," said Steve flatly. "He forgot to mention it."

"There are nine Great Rings of Power," Clearwater explained. "I have barely grasped the first two. Mr. Snow has absolute mastery over the first seven."

"What about the other two?"

"Only Talisman is strong enough to wield the Nine," replied Clearwater "but no one among the Plainfolk has greater power than Mr. Snow. The seventh Ring is called the Storm-Bringer. Were you not there, aboard the iron snake, when he blinded it with mist, then brought lightning, thunder, and the floodwaters down upon it?"

"Are you telling me that that old man . . ." Steve stared at her with stunned disbelief. "He did that? Mr. *Snow* . . . made that river flood? Almost wrecked the train?"

"Yes!"

Steve tried to cope with this revelation. Incredible though it was, he did not doubt a word of it. He pictured the rock plummeting from the sky, and then he thought about the spiked heads of Fazetti and Naylor outside her hut in the forest. "And what did *you* do?"

Clearwater looked deep into his eyes and read the question in his mind before answering. "I did what had to be done. And I also saved you from Motor-Head's hammer." She sealed his lips as he went to reply, then took hold of his hands and kissed them lovingly, holding them against her face. "You must go! I beg you . . . go *now!* Don't wait until Cadillac and Mr. Snow return!"

It was against all Steve's instincts to break and run when the going was tough, but this time he knew it was the smart thing to do. There was no way he could hide what had happened—especially from Mr. Snow, who had shown himself expert at piercing the layers of guile that had hidden Steve's true intentions so well in the past. He *had* to go. Not only to protect Clearwater and himself, but also for the sake of the Federation. He had to find some way to tell them about the Talisman Prophecy. They knew about wordsmiths, but not about summoners and seers. Or that Mute magic was not a defeatist rumor but a deadly fact that could no longer be ignored. It could prove tricky to be the bearer of news no one wanted to hear. If he did it right, he could maybe earn ten promotional grades at one jump; if he did it wrong, he could find himself getting shot on the Public Service Channel for spreading alarm and despondency.

And there was also the little matter of getting even with Lundkwist, Gus White, and the others involved in the conspiracy to elbow him out of the top spot at the centenary graduation. Yeah. . . .

"It's getting light. You must go," she whispered.

"You, too. . . ." They held each other tightly in one last desperate embrace, then he began to dress with swift, practiced movements. Something he'd learned during his three years at the Academy.

"The arrowhead . . . can you prepare it by yourself?"

"Yeah, don't worry," he murmured, savoring for one last brief moment the lingering fragrance of her oiled skin, the softness of her hair, and the warmth of her body as she cradled his head between her cheek and shoulder. He pulled away, took her hands from around his neck, stole a last quick kiss, then pushed her out of reach. "Go on, get going."

Clearwater shook her head. "No. It will be safer if you leave first. Once you have gone, no one will see me."

Steve was curious to know what she meant, but this was no time for awkward questions. He peeked through the door flap. Nothing moved outside. The place was as quiet as New Deal Plaza during a First Family Inspirational. He looked back at Clearwater and saw her rummaging through the pockets of her walking-skins.

"I was given something that belongs to you." She held up the necklace bearing Steve's dog tag. "May I keep it?"

"Of course. Here . . . let me put it on for you." He took hold of the tag and showed it to her. "You see these marks? This one here is my name. 'Steven Roosevelt Brickman.' "

"That is good," said Clearwater. "It means part of you will always be with me." She swept her long hair forward over one shoulder and inclined her head in a quasi-ceremonial gesture.

Steve slipped the chain around her slim neck, adjusted the hang of it so that the tag bearing his name nestled in the cleft between her breasts, then smoothed her hair back into place and took her face in his hands. "I'll come back. I don't know when, or how, but I'll find a way. I promise." And he meant it, too. "Think of me."

"Always," whispered Clearwater. Half of her could not bear to let him go; the other, more sensible, half did not believe she would ever see him again, knew it would be better to wipe out what had happened, to erase him from her mind. Impossible. . . .

"Ciao," said Steve, using one of the Mute words for saying "goodbye." Come on, Brickman, he urged himself. Move! Hit the road! He ducked out under the door flap and turned to pick up the quarterstaff he'd left lying alongside the hut. Out of the corner of his eye he saw something leaning against the left-hand head-pole. Steve stared at it, then reached out and touched it gingerly, as if he were afraid it might vanish. It was his air rifle! The one that Cadillac had torn from the Skyhawk! Seizing it, he ran his hands over it sensuously, savoring the hard, cold feel of the barrel cluster; then he wiped off the thin film of condensation with his sleeve and quickly checked the contents of the magazine. Only three triple volleys. Shit. . . . Still, better than nothing. He looked at the air pressure gauge. More than enough. Oh, you sweet mother! He toyed briefly with the idea of saying thank you and decided it wasn't necessary. If she'd wanted a big speech she'd have brought the rifle inside. He started to get up; then, on a sudden impulse, he stopped and knelt down again. Pulling a straw mat toward him, he rolled it lengthwise around the rifle. Satisfied that it was safely hidden, he rose to his feet, tucked the mat under his arm, slung the quarterstaff over his shoulder, and strode off toward the bluff without a backward glance.

Inside the hut, Clearwater sat on her heels and bit her lip in an effort to stem the bitter tears that clouded her eyes. She fingered the dog tag and thought of the all-too-brief moment she had spent in the cloud warrior's arms. Then, with a sigh, she drew on her walking-skins. When she stepped outside she was relieved to see there was still only the faintest glimmer of light at the eastern door. Soon Steve would be winging his way toward the dawn.

Clearwater walked through the sleeping settlement to Mr. Snow's hut, laid down the talking mat she had brought with her, wrapped herself up warmly in her night fur, and squatted down to await the arrival of the two wordsmiths. She tried hard to think of Cadillac, but the power within that had made her a summoner sent her mind's eye soaring toward the bluff. And there it circled, like a wide-winged death bird. Below her she could see the arrowhead resting on its poles ... and farther away, her beloved cloud warrior making his way toward it.

But wait! What was that? ...

Eyes closed, Clearwater raised her head clear of the enveloping furs, her nostrils flared like a fast-foot doe scenting danger.

Reaching the top of the slope above the settlement, Steve was relieved to see that Blue-Bird was still there, lashed to its supporting trestles some fifty feet back from the edge of the bluff. It was also unguarded. For some peculiar reason for which Steve had never sought an explanation, Mutes did not raid rival settlements or go out looking for trouble at night. Once the sun went down, they put their knives away. The lookouts around the perimeter of the clan's turf remained in position but usually slept till dawn with only a nominal guard against four-footed predators such as wolves or mountain lions. Since the departure of Mr. Snow's party, two Mute warriors had been posted to guard Blue-Bird, but only during the day. The thought that Steve might cut and run in the middle of the night had obviously not occurred to anyone.

As he approached the craft, he saw that someone had made him a present of a red-and-white wingman's helmet. It swung gently from one of the harness straps. How odd, thought Steve. He peered into the surrounding grayness but could see nothing. Probably a stray gust of wind, eddying up over the bluff. He looked at the name on the helmet. It was Fazetti's, one of his Eagle Squadron buddies.

Tough luck, Lou. Too bad you didn't make it. . . .

Steve laid down the quarterstaff and the rolled straw mat with the rifle inside and put the helmet on. He raised the visor and fixed the neck strap so that it was a good tight fit on his head, then he loosened the ropes holding the swept-back wings onto the head-high trestles and moved the support out from under the rear-mounted motor. Drawing his combat knife, he cut one of the ropes in half and dropped the two pieces onto the rolled mat. His plan was to tie them around each end of the roll, then fasten it to the bottom section of the triangular control bar on which his hands would rest. But the same impulse that had prompted him to conceal the rifle in the mat told him to leave that particular job until the very last moment. If someone blew the whistle on him, he might need to be able to get at that rifle fast. . . .

Steve was conscious that he didn't have a moment to waste, but he found himself in something of a quandary. Up to now, all his flights had been in broad daylight, and although it was late in the year, the weather had been warm and sunny—just what was needed to charge the solar cells that delivered power from the wings to the motor. It had proved to be a fluctuating supply, but it provided a useful backup. And now here he was, in semidarkness, surrounded by cold, damp air. Even if he'd been able to salvage a static charge unit, the weight would have made its installation impractical. But no sun meant no power, and that meant instead of a motor he was loading himself down with a useless heap of junk for maybe four to six hours—more if the weather was bad. Should he take a chance and go for it with the complete rig? Or should he strip the motor off the airframe? He had the tools. It was half a dozen nuts and bolts and a few leads. It would mean kissing good-bye to all those hours of painful circuit mending and testing, but what the heck. . . .

Steve walked around Blue-Bird a couple of times, weighing up the pros and cons, squared up to it with his hands on his hips, appealed silently to the sky . . . and decided to pull the motor. Now that his mind was made up, he worked quickly, disconnecting the power leads before loosening the retaining bolts. One . . . two . . . three . . . four. Two left to go, one on either side of the motor. It was ironic. Dumping the motor had increased the potential payload of the glider. If he had considered that option before, and if Clearwater had been willing to leave, with a few last-minute adjustments to the harness he would have been able to take her with him.

Steve moved the rear trestle back in to take the weight of the motor while he pulled the last two bolts. As he reached up to fit the crude wrench onto one of the remaining nuts, he felt the skin on the back of his neck go cold. He looked over his shoulder and almost had heart failure. Motor-Head was standing right behind him, leaning casually on his quarter-staff.

"Jack me! Wow!" exclaimed Steve. "You know, for a big guy you're awful quiet on your feet."

Motor-Head bared his teeth in a grim smile.

Steve had a feeling he was in trouble. "Where are Mr. Snow and Cadillac—down in the settlement?"

"No, they're not back yet," said Motor-Head. "We came on ahead."

"Oh. . . ." Glancing around, Steve saw two shadowy figures positioned between Blue-Bird and the bluff. It didn't look good. Play it cool, Brickman. Bluff your way out.

Motor-Head looked Blue-Bird over. "Going somewhere?"

"Me? Oh, no. I was just . . . fixing a few things. Couldn't sleep, so . . . I, uh, came up to do some work on the motor."

"In the dark?"

Steve shrugged. "Just got here. It'll be light soon."

"Yes. Tell me . . . why the helmet?"

"It's to keep my ears warm," Steve said.

"Got it. . . ." The big Mute aimed a finger over Steve's shoulder. "Is that what you call the 'motor'?"

Steve eyed him warily. "Yeah."

Motor-Head put an arm through the sling of his quarterstaff, then eased Steve aside and stood with his legs astride facing the handcarved propeller. He placed his fingers on the propeller hub, then ran them out along the blades. "Why does it have my name?"

What a dummy! thought Steve. Still, better kid him along. "Ah, that's because—like you—it is strong and powerful," he said. "It makes the arrowhead fly like an eagle."

Motor-Head nodded thoughtfully. "Ah-hahh . . . interesting." Grasping the tips of the propeller, he snapped both blades off at the hub with one swift jerk of his huge hands, examined the two pieces briefly, then dropped them at Steve's feet. "Now it flies like a lump of crow-shit."

Steve looked down at the broken blades and knew that there was no chance of walking away from this one. He had one good chance. If Motor-Head didn't know what was rolled up inside the mat, he could get to his rifle and drop all three of them. He raised his head and met the Mute warrior's challenging gaze. "Well, you should know. You're full of it."

Motor-Head bared his fanglike teeth in a tight smile. How he regretted his promise not to cut open this carrion! He spat on the ground. "You have a quarter-staff. Beat it out of me!"

This could work out just fine, Steve thought. "I might just do that," he said coolly. He took a couple of steps backward, then edged sideways under the wing toward the spot where his quarterstaff lay next to the rolled straw mat.

Motor-Head pulled his staff out of its carrying sling and whirled it around in a brief, flashy display.

That's right. Come on, sucker. . . .

Steve took another couple of steps toward the hidden rifle. He looked toward the edge of the bluff and was able to recognize the two shadowy figures as Black-Top and Steel-Eye. Black-Top was holding a loaded crossbow. Steve considered his chances of grabbing his rifle and blowing them away before Black-Top nailed him with a bolt. Not good. Not good at all.

And it got worse. As if reading his mind, Motor-Head tossed his own quarterstaff toward Steve. "Take mine. Your little arms will need a big stick."

Steve caught it across his chest, conscious that the odds against him getting out alive were lengthening by the second. Motor-Head fixed him with his beady eyes, then bent down and scooped up Steve's quarterstaff. Up to now, everything had gone so wrong, he was half expecting Motor-Head to pull open the matting roll, but the bit Mute ignored it.

Steve knew he had a hope of winning, provided the fight was limited to quarterstaves. He had already beaten Motor-Head seven times in a row, and he had the ribboned plaits to prove it. Motor-Head could have dispatched him easily with a knife, but his reputation as a warrior was at stake. He *had* to win with Steve's chosen weapon to regain his position as paramount Bear. Steve now realized that for Motor-Head, swapping staves was a symbolic act through which he took some of Steve's "power" into himself. If he could hold him off long enough, the Mute's psychological need to win might make him angry. It was this aggressivity that Steve had exploited in the past. Once Motor-Head lost control it would be all over. The trouble was, Steve didn't have all day to play around. He had to floor this hulking piece of lump-shit in the next fifteen minutes. Some chance. . . .

It was one contest Steve would have been prepared to concede, but he knew that if he took a dive the result would be the same as if he were beaten to the ground. Sooner or later Motor-Head was going to kill him. It was galling to think that the speedy solution to all his problems was lying so near at hand. But the six feet that separated him from the hidden rifle might just as well have been six miles. Forget it, Brickman, he told himself. You're going to have to solve this one the hard way.

Grasping the quarterstaff firmly in both hands, Steve backed away from Blue-Bird to give himself some fighting room. A vague battle plan was beginning to coalesce in his mind. It was no good just winning. He had to finish up on his feet, fit enough to fly and within reach of the rolled-up rifle. Maybe if he could maneuver this big lump to the edge of the bluff and somehow topple him over . . .

Motor-Head threw aside the sling of his borrowed staff, flexed it to test its condition, then assumed the opening wide-legged stance. Steve faced up to him, the tip of his quarterstaff angled across that of his opponent. Black-Top and Steel-Eye split up, moved back several yards, and crouched down facing each other, halfway between Blue-Bird's wing tips and the edge of the bluff.

The use of the six-foot-long quarterstaff—or sword-stick, as it was sometimes called—went back to the Federation's third century, when it had been introduced as an exercise weapon by a member of the First Family called Bruce Lee Jefferson. As practiced by Trackers, it was a cross between the Japanese martial-art form known as *kendo*, where bamboo sword-sticks were used, and the six- to nine-foot-long oak quarterstaff wielded by popular heroes of the Middle Ages like Robin Hood. In the East, it had been used to teach budding samurai the art of swordsmanship; in the West, for training knights to use the two-handed battle sword.

In the Federation, trainees wore *kendo*-style helmets, gauntlets, and thick pads covering the target areas, with additional protection for the back, shoulders, pelvis, and thighs. Both ends of the stick could be used; and apart from the mental discipline, lightning-fast reflexes, and sheer physical stamina required, it was the dexterous manipulation of the staff, using a parrying stroke as the springboard for a scoring blow, that distinguished the true expert from the talented tyro.

According to the rules governing formal bouts, the only blows that counted were those striking the top or sides of the head, the sides of the torso, the right and left forearm, and a direct thrust to the throat. But this was no formal bout. This time around, there would be no rules.

As they faced up to each other, Steve reckoned that this might shorten the odds in his favor; the hulking Mute was sharp, but he was sneakier. He had to get in low and fast ... and not just because of the time factor. Apart from his visored helmet and his flight fatigues, his body was unprotected, whereas Motor-Head was wearing his usual stone and bone-decorated leather skull mask and body plates. Steve could afford to take a few shots to the head, but if any of Motor-Head's blows landed with full force elsewhere it could mean a broken wrist, rib, or collar bone. Even if he won, and then managed to take out Black-Top and Steel-Eye, any injury along these lines would make the task of flying Blue-Bird both difficult and extremely painful. Somehow Steve had to block every attack Motor-Head made or, at the very least, sap the force of each blow before it crashed against his unprotected body. Keeping his staff crossed with Motor-Head's, Steve circled slowly to the left. Motor-Head matched him with wide-legged mirror steps to the right.

Down in the settlement, on the mat outside Mr. Snow's hut, Clearwater saw the danger to the cloud

warrior and felt the power begin to flow through her
body from its secret source deep within the earth
below. It coursed through her veins, pierced her flesh
like thousands of tiny red-hot needles, and sent its
fire into the core of her bones. Every muscle in her
body grew taut and began to jerk spasmodically. She
fell backward, eyes still tightly shut, back arched,
legs drawn up beneath her. The power inside her
began to build with a frightening intensity, filling
her body with an explosive pressure like molten lava
inside a volcano that is about to erupt. With the
rapidly shrinking part of her mind that still remained
hers in this moment of possession, Clearwater realized she was about to become the executioner of her
clan-brothers. The thought appalled her, but she knew
Talisman would stop at nothing to protect his own.
The power doubled, tripled in strength, and offered
itself to her will. She tried to resist it; tried not to
cede to the overwhelming desire to save the cloud
warrior. One hand flew to her neck, the other clamped
itself over her mouth, fingers digging deep into the
skin in a desperate effort to hold back the death-
dealing cry that was forming in her throat.

On the bluff, the quarterstaves flashed and crashed
together as Steve and Motor-Head suddenly burst
into action. Thrust/parry/strike/parry, thrust/parry/
strike/parry, to the head, to the side, to the arm, to
the leg. Keep circling, Brickman! This lump has been
practicing. He is *fast*! Only one thing to do ... let
him lay one on you and hope it will provide a chance
to slow him down. . . .

The opportunity came. With a frightening yell,
Motor-Head brought his staff up, over, and down
toward Steve's right shoulder in a blow that, had it
been from a samurai sword, would have sliced him
open from neck to navel. Steve stepped underneath
it, robbing the blow of some of the force with his own
staff before letting it crash onto his helmet. Instead
of taking it full on the crown of the head, which
would have compacted his spine and quite possibly
broken his neck, Steve managed to turn it into a

glancing blow to the left side of the helmet, twisting his shoulder out of the way as Motor-Head's staff bounced off and swept on down. But the trap was only half-sprung. Steve staggered, knees buckling under the blow. For a fleeting instant, Motor-Head allowed his killer instinct to relax. His face lit up with a gleam of triumph. It was the break Steve needed. In that split-second celebratory pause before the follow-up blow, Steve ducked in under Motor-Head's guard, landed bone-crunching blows on both knees and ankles, then rammed the end of his staff into the point of the Mute's pelvis.

Motor-Head doubled over under the force of the blow. He staggered, trying to master the shrieking pain in his crotch, knees, and ankles. Steve sensed it was now or never. He smashed his staff down across Motor-Head's broad back, once, twice . . . then landed a third blow across the back of his neck. The blows brought the big Mute to his knees, but the armored leather body plates and the deep rim of his skull mask absorbed most of the damage.

Out of the corner of his eye, Steve saw Black-Top and Steel-Eye moving in from the sidelines. Steve hurriedly brought his staff down again on their buddy's head in an effort to take him out of the fight before they reached him. The blow would have knocked anybody else's block off, but it just seemed to bounce off Motor-Head's skull. With his quarter-staff still gripped in his hands, the big warrior rested stiff-armed on his knuckles, shook the pain out of his head like a dog shaking water from its ears, then lifted his left knee and got one foot on the ground.

Christo! thought Steve. This lump's gonna get up! His own feeling of imminent triumph rapidly faded into near panic. Black-Top and Steel-Eye were practically on top of him. He swung his staff around in a sideways arc and slammed it against Motor-Head's right arm just below the leather shoulder plate. It hit the Mute's iron-hard biceps with a dull, sickening *thwack*. Down, you jack-assed heap of lump-shit! he screamed inwardly. Go *down*! Reversing his grip,

Steve aimed a similar blow at Motor-Head's left arm, putting all his strength into a two-handed slice. To his surprise, Motor-Head threw his left arm upward and outward, stopped the blow with the palm of his hand, then closed his fingers around the thick shaft. Steve cursed and tried to pull his staff free . . . and found it was stuck fast in Motor-Head's outstretched hand.

"Gotcha. . . ." The big Mute's pain-wracked face split into a murderous grin. "Step back, brother Bears. This mother's mine. . . ." Raising his right arm, he waved Black-Top and Steel-Eye out of the way. The two Mute warriors moved back behind him toward the edge of the bluff, Black-Top cradling his loaded crossbow, Steel-Eye with his hand on the hilt of his knife. Steve tugged viciously on the Mute's quarter-staff, but Motor-Head didn't let go. It hurt when he stood up, but he hauled himself onto his feet and got a good grip on Steve's pole with his right hand. Mo-Town! That hurt, too!

Steve knew he had to do something but didn't know what. He had started out with Motor-Head's staff, but now the Mute had a grip on both of them. Steve knew that to have any chance of recovering Motor-Head's, he had to hang on to it with both hands. Which meant that he had to stay within range of his own staff—which the big Mute was about to beat him with. He could make a grab for it the way Motor-Head had, but even if he managed to catch it, he couldn't match the strength in Motor-Head's arms. The Mute would end up with both staves in about two seconds flat.

Adjusting his grip on Steve's quarterstaff, Motor-Head drove it teasingly into Steve's ribs, then cracked him over the head. Steve took one hand off Motor-Head's staff in an attempt to ward off the next blow. In a flash, the Mute slid his hand along the pole, pulling Steve another foot in toward him. Steve saw what was happening. He tried to get both hands back on the pole but was too late. Motor-Head laughed throatily and *thwacked* him hard on the outside of the thigh. If it had been a two-handed blow, it would have shattered the bone; even so, Steve, at that particular moment, felt like he might never walk again.

Triple lump-shit! he thought. I can't take much more of this! He knew Motor-Head was only taunting him. He had to do something. Motor-Head was pulling him ever closer, making it almost impossible to stay clear of the whirling quarterstaff in the Mute's right hand. Come on, Brickman! If you can get out of this, you can get out of anything! As the idea came, Motor-Head hauled in some more slack on the pole in his left hand. It was now or never. Okay, this is it, Brickman! Go for it!

As Motor-Head aimed another taunting blow, Steve threw up his left hand and caught the end of the staff as it flashed down. The impact sent a shock wave all the way down to his left foot, and his palm felt as if it had burst open. Gritting his teeth against the pain, he pulled down hard on the two poles as Motor-Head tugged in the opposite direction. For a split second, the poles were like two parallel bars. In the instant that Motor-Head won the tug-of-war and jerked the poles toward him, Steve threw his body into the air, arms straight down like a vaulting gymnast, and drove the heels of his combat boots into the Mute's face. "Heyy-*yahh!!*"

The impact knocked Motor-Head over like a felled tree. Steve's body sailed on, curving through the air to land at the feet of the startled Black-Top. Before either warrior could react, Steve tore the crossbow from Black-Top's grasp and slammed the butt against the side of the warrior's head. As Black-Top went down, Steve spun around to find Steel-Eye coming at him with a fistful of sharp iron. Unable to find the trigger in time, Steve brought one half of the sprung metal bow down onto Steel-Eye's knife-arm, then leant back, pivoted on his left heel, swung his right leg up to waist height, and snapped it straight, flattening Steel-Eye's solar plexus against his spine. The Bear went down blowing air like a ruptured pressure hose.

For a couple of seconds, Steve stood there as if mesmerized. He was shaking like a leaf. His head ached from the blow he'd let Motor-Head lay on him and his body suddenly seemed full of sharp, jabbing pains. The rifle! Get the rifle . . . and finish off these lumps before they get up again! Steve turned toward Blue-Bird, stumbled over Motor-Head's outstretched arm, and fell awkwardly to the ground, losing the crossbow as he went down. He felt a huge hand grip his ankle. Steve kicked himself free, threw himself toward the crossbow, pulled it toward him, and scrambled to his knees. With his finger now firmly on the trigger he turned toward his three fallen adversaries and was appalled to find they were all getting to their feet.

One side of Black-Top's face was swollen; Steel-Eye was half-bent and barely able to breathe; blood oozed from Motor-Head's broken nose and mouth. Motor-Head was empty-handed. The others held long Mute fighting knives with the dished-top cutting edge.

Steve stood up and backed away toward the hidden rifle as they took a step toward him. He raised the crossbow and aimed it at Motor-Head's chest. "Stay right where you are!"

Motor-Head paused and gave Steve a lopsided bloodstained grin. "You dropped something." He held up a crossbow bolt.

Steve stared at it incredulously, then glanced quickly down at the crossbow. The steel bowstring was still drawn back ready for release, but there was no bolt in the firing slot! Christo! It must have been thrown out when he'd used it to batter Black-Top and Steel-Eye to the ground, or when he'd dropped it! Shit!

Flanked by his two clan-brothers, Motor-Head broke the two quarterstaves, one over each thigh, and tossed the pieces aside. "No more games, carrion!" He took another step toward Steve and held up his huge, six-fingered paws. "Take a good look at these hands! They are going to tear your eyes and your lying tongue out of your head, then they are going to crush your sharp-edged little face like a rotten yellow-fist!"

Steve edged back toward the hidden rifle. I am not going to make it, he thought tiredly. After *all* this . . . *I am not going to make it!* Oh, sweet Christopher! . . .

In the same moment of time that encompassed Motor-Head's step toward Steve, Clearwater's hands took on a life of their own. They tore themselves away from her neck and mouth and pulled her arms outward onto the ground. Her eyes snapped open and the chilling cry of the summoner issued from her throat. The earth answered, yielding up its secret strength. The full force of the third Ring of Power flowed into her body to be shaped by her will. . . .

Below the bluff, about a mile east of the settlement, Mr. Snow and Cadillac led the homeward run across the rolling plain. Mr. Snow did not hear Clearwater's cry, but his finely attuned senses heard the earth answer. He signaled the party of warriors to halt. They crouched, listening instinctively for any sounds that signified danger. And then they all heard it. A low, distant, deep-throated rumbling. But this was not from the sky, this was earth-thunder! The ground shivered as some unseen force, like buried lightning bolts, zigzagged through the earth beneath them in the direction of the settlement. The M'Call Bears groaned and fell on their faces, seized by the paralyzing primal fear that afflicted all Mutes; a distant race memory of a time when the earth rose up and the sky exploded with blinding white rain-fire that burnt flesh from bone, the grass from the earth, and turned the world to dust.

Wordsmiths were supposed to be made of sterner stuff. Mr. Snow hauled Cadillac off his knees as he babbled a plea to Mo-Town to spare them all from the wrath of the lord Pent-Agon. "No need for that! Come one, get those legs moving! We've got to get back. . . ." Mr. Snow hurried forward, pushing Cadillac ahead of him. "Go on! Run! Run!"

Above them, in the settlement, at that selfsame instant, the rumbling earth-thunder grew louder and louder. The ground beneath Clearwater shuddered violently, rose quickly to form a hillock—overturning Mr. Snow's hut in the process—flattened itself abruptly, then split apart on either side of her body with an ear-shattering roar. All over the plateau, terrified M'Calls scrambled out of their huts and threw themselves face down—men, women, and children huddling together as they hugged the earth and begged Mo-Town to save them.

Moving with terrifying speed, a large fissure zigzagged away from Clearwater's prostrate body across the plateau toward the main cluster of huts; then, before any damage was caused, it turned sharply left and raced up the slope toward the bluff.

Once again, it was in the same moment of time that Steve decided to stake everything on one last desperate gamble. Pulling the trigger to release the taut bowstring, he hurled the crossbow at Motor-Head's chest and made a break for the rifle. As the bow flew through the air and Steve turned and ran toward Blue-Bird, the drumroll of earth-thunder shook the ridge and caused the three Mutes to become rooted to the spot. With a dry, spine-chilling cracking noise, the fissure reached the bluff as Steve reached the matting roll and got his hand on the butt of his rifle. It was as if the earth were being ripped open by a giant invisible knife. Before he could catch his breath, a narrow jagged fissure suddenly opened up right across the plateau, separating him from his now-terrified attackers. There was another deafening explosive roar of earth-thunder. The ground shook violently, throwing Steve onto his back. Rolling over onto his stomach he saw the edge of the bluff tear itself loose from the rest of the plateau. The whole strip of earth on which Motor-Head and his clan-brothers were standing just fell apart and went sliding down the steep slope, carrying the bodies of the three Mutes with it in a dust-laden torrent of rocks, pebbles, and earth.

Badly shaken, Steve got cautiously to his feet, clutching his rifle. Close! he thought. If the quake had run a few yards farther in, he and the glider would have gone the same route. He raised the visor of his helmet and made a quick inspection of Blue-Bird. The trestles under the wings and the now-useless engine had fallen over, but the craft itself was undamaged. Steve put the three trestles back in place and hurriedly loosened the last two bolts holding the engine in place. He found that his hands were shaking, and he had to stop to try and get a grip on himself. He untangled the harness straps, and satisfied himself that he was ready to go. It was much lighter now. Broad bands of purple, crimson, orange, and yellow lay along the eastern horizon. Faint, confused cries floated up from the direction of the settlement.

Within seconds of their arrival, Mr. Snow and Cadillac were quickly surrounded by a shocked and still-panicky crowd of Mutes seeking reassurance. When he had recovered his breath, Mr. Snow dealt with them firmly, telling them that if it had been the end of the world, as some of them obviously thought it was, he would have announced it in advance. If they really wished to follow his advice they should all stop running about like headless turkey-cocks and go back to the normal business of the day. That said, he brushed aside all further questions and pushed his way through the crowd, shooing away those who attempted to follow him.

Clearwater sat upright on her talking mat, her face deathly pale under the patterned blacks and browns. Her eyes were dilated, and she kept biting her lips to stop their trembling.

Mr. Snow surveyed the wreckage of his hut, his scattered possessions, and the deep, narrow fissure that ran away toward the bluff. "Was this your doing?"

Clearwater nodded silently, then found the strength to speak in a whisper. "I did not wish it. It was Talisman who called." She held out her hands to Cadillac. He put an arm around her and helped her up. She wavered slightly, then gained control of her legs and held herself erect without his support.

Mr. Snow's face softened. He placed his hands on her shoulders. "You have true power. You will make a worthy adversary of the sand-burrowers." He took hold of her elbow and gestured toward the bluff. "Come . . . walk with us."

Holding his rifle at the ready, Steve advanced to the new edge of the bluff. He wanted to make sure that, when he made his leap to freedom, there would be no last-minute surprises. He was relieved to discover that there was now a good steady breeze sweeping up from the plain. Spitting the dust from his mouth, he saw that there were two bodies lying twenty or thirty yards down the slope, half-buried under rocks and earth. He looked for the third but was unable to spot it. It went completely against his better judgment, but some perverse urge made him slither down toward the corpses in the hope of discovering that one of them was Motor-Head.

Pushing aside the rubble with the toe of his boot, Steve uncovered enough to recognize Black-Top and Steel-Eye. He looked them over but couldn't be sure if they were dead. It didn't matter. Dead or not, neither of them was going anywhere. He scrambled up on a pile of rocks and scanned the lower part of the slope. With the possibility of more after-shocks it was a crazy thing to do. It was equally crazy to hang around for one second longer, but Steve felt the need to know he'd won. If he was ever to come back for Clearwater, it would be better to fix Motor-Head *now*, once and for all.

He could see nothing, and there was no more time to look. He turned and started back up the slope. When he had gone a few yards, Steve's sixth sense sounded the alarm. Slipping his index finger onto the trigger, he turned around and saw a Mute pulling himself out of the dirt near the bottom of the slope. The distance between them was about a hundred and fifty yards. Too far away for Steve to make out the Mute's face, but it had to be Motor-Head. He gazed up the slope at Steve then started toward him.

Steve pulled his rifle into his shoulder and found

he had the shakes. He took a deep breath, aimed at the middle of the Mute's barrel chest, and squeezed off a triple volley. *Chu-witt-chu-witt-chuwitt!!*

Motor-Head kept coming.

Christo! thought Steve. Steadying himself on the shifting layer of pebbles that now coated the steep slope, he aimed again, this time at Motor-Head's belly, and fired his second volley.

Motor-Head stopped, fell over, picked himself up, and broke into a stumbling run, his powerful thighs driving him up the steep, rock-strewn slope.

Smokin' lump-shit! Steve thought. This guy is unstoppable! He scrambled back to the top of the bluff, then turned, went down on one knee to give himself a steadier firing position, and aimed for the base of Motor-Head's throat. The rifle wavered in his trembling hands. Steve took a firmer grip and squeezed off his last three rounds.

The impact jerked Motor-Head sideways but did not break his stride. He just kept on coming, powering up the slope like the Trans-Am express.

Now you're in trouble, Brickman. . . . Move! Move! *Move!!* Steve dropped the empty rifle, raced back toward Blue-Bird, kicked away the rear trestle, and started to clip himself into the harness. If the big Mute didn't slow down . . . Oh, you jackass, Brickman! You totaled out! As he fastened the straps with fumbling fingers, Steve cursed himself for his incredible foolishness. He only had seconds left in which to run Blue-Bird forward and launch himself before Motor-Head reached the top of the bluff. . . .

Seizing the sides of the triangular control bar, Steve lifted Blue-Bird clear of the trestles and ran forward. The stiffening breeze spilled over the edge of the bluff, rippled over the wing with a dry slap-snap, then put a taut curve in the fabric. Pausing about five paces from the edge, Steve leaned against the breeze, bracing himself for the run forward and leap into space. He had made dozens of successful launches from the bluff, but each time there was always an element of chance. This one *had* to be right. . . .

Check straps ... deep breath ... Okay, Brickman.
Go for it! Steve firmed up his grip on the sides of the
control bar, which at this point was bearing the weight
of the wings above him, and ran for the edge. As he
launched himself over the bluff, Motor-Head leapt up
in front of him like a killer whale coming out of the
water in a vertical climb, grabbed hold of the control
bar, and was carried out into space.

Steve fought to maintain control of the glider, but
with the big Mute hanging on the bar between his
own outstretched hands it was a near-impossible task.
Blue-Bird rocked violently, then dived to the right,
swooping dangerously close to the bluff before rising
on a strong gust of wind. They were climbing now,
but Steve knew it was only a matter of time before
they hit the deck. He looked down between his arms
and saw the crazed, murderous look on Motor-Head's
broken, bloody face. His arms and legs had been
scuffed and torn in the rock-slide, and he was bleeding from several bullet wounds. Steve hadn't missed.
It was the combination of willpower and enormous
physical strength that had kept Motor-Head going
and had led to this last-ditch attempt to block his
escape. The Mute was going to die, and he intended
to take Steve down with him.

Steve tried to pry Motor-Head's fingers loose with
one hand, but it was useless. He couldn't even budge
one little finger. Blue-Bird began to slip to the left.
Steve hauled it back on an even keel, then lost it
again as it went into a steep dive. He was out over
the plain now, about eight hundred feet up. He had
to dump the Mute before he lost any more height. He
was going to have to cut him loose.... Reaching
back with his right hand, he tried to claw his combat
knife out of the scabbard strapped to his leg. He
couldn't get a proper grip on it.

It didn't matter. The Mute was now struggling
wildly to maintain his grip on the bar.

Motor-Head's eyes widened as he realized that he
no longer had the strength to hold on. The dying
burst of energy he had summoned up in a last effort

to kill the cloud warrior ebbed away. This was the terrible moment he had often dreamed of; the unspeakable horror that had robbed him of sleep, leaving him sweating and trembling in the moon-dark. Falling. Falling from the claws of a huge bird with pointed wings, ridden by a warrior with golden hair and a face like polished stone. His fingers slowly slipped from the control bar. Hanging on with one hand he made one last effort to grab Steve by the throat; then, with a despairing cry, he dropped away, arms outstretched.

Mo-Town! Drink, sweet Mother. . . .

Steve soared upward like a bird released from a cage.

Cadillac, Clearwater, and Mr. Snow reached the edge of the bluff in time to see the figure fall away from the arrowhead. Clearwater gave a brief cry of anguish as it crashed to earth. A cry echoed by Cadillac.

"Mo-Town, forgive me! I have killed my clan-brother!"

"Not so," replied Mr. Snow quietly. "Do you not remember the answer you gave when the cloud warrior asked why Motor-Head called him the Death-Bringer?"

"Yes. I said that perhaps the death he feared was his own."

"Good. Do you now understand that in sending him here you changed nothing? In attempting to change your destiny, all you succeeded in doing was to play your part in fulfilling his."

"I shall still grieve for him, Wise One," Cadillac said.

"We all shall," Mr. Snow agreed. "His name shall stand among the greatest of the M'Calls." The old wordsmith stepped to the edge of the bluff and stood between his two young charges, his feet planted firmly astride, arms folded, his body erect.

On the far horizon, the sky was streaked with yellow and hot rose-pink as the sun nudged open the eastern door. No one spoke as the cloud warrior was borne aloft on the morning wind. They watched him rise into the sky and bank gently toward the Great Desert of the South.

Cadillac knew he would not speak to Clearwater of what he had seen in the stone regarding her desire for the sand-burrower. There would be no accusations or recriminations. The Path was drawn; the Cosmic Wheel turned. The true Warrior faced his destiny with courage; he did not allow himself to be deflected from the Path by unworthy emotions. The rising sun stretched their shadows into giants whose heads were lost in the mountains behind them.

Clearwater waited until the arrowhead had dwindled to a mere speck in the sky, then broke the silence. "Will he come back?" she asked, unsure if she really wanted to know the answer to that question.

"Yes, in the time of the New Earth," replied Cadillac. "I have seen it in the stones. He will come in the guise of a friend with Death hiding in his shadow, and he will carry you away on a river of blood."

Clearwater gazed out across the plain that descended like a rolling sea beyond the bluff and up at the clouds rimming the hills on the southern horizon. The yellowing sky above was now empty. Steve had disappeared. "Am I to die in the darkness of their world, or will I live to see the sun again?"

"You will live," said Mr. Snow quietly. He put his hands on their shoulders and drew them closer to him. "You will both live. You are the sword and shield of Talisman."

YOU

CAN WIN

$10,000

BUT ONLY IF YOU TAKE . . .

What would you do if you discovered that the President of the United States was a Soviet spy? That's the incredible situation faced by Larry Fox, lower-echelon CIA agent in Istanbul, in *Active Measures*, the first science fiction/espionage novel to offer a $10,000 prize! Complete details appear in every copy of *Active Measures*, a Baen Book by Janet Morris and David Drake. But *Active Measures* isn't just a chance to win a large cash prize—it's also a gripping, action-filled story.

Here's just a taste to get you started:

"You wanted an hour," Gallen reminded him. "You've got fifty-three minutes left." She reached up and fitted the tab of the door's chain bolt into its slot. The snick of metal on metal was no harder than her blue eyes.

"Check. I interviewed a Soviet defector who appeared to be . . . *could be*—" Fox said bluntly as he eased to the foot of the bed and sat facing the side wall rather than the woman by the door—"Abdulhamid Kunayev." The bolt above her head wouldn't hold a solid kick: it provided a symbol of the bargain Gallen had accepted; lighting a long fuze would have done the same. "In the course of the interview, the defector stated that President Crossfield is a Soviet penetration." Listening to himself, Fox realized how crazy he sounded and began quickly to explain: "He—"

She cut him off: "What evidence did this . . . defector . . . cite to support those statements?" Her voice was emotionless but it seemed to have risen an octave.

"Captain, I didn't *believe* them," Fox said despairingly in a low voice that trembled. There was a mirror over the long desk built into the wall opposite the bed; he closed his eyes rather than stare at his own face, battered by weakness and failure. The implications of the Kunayev contact were too important for validation to depend solely on him; but nobody was going to make decisions based on the information he'd collected until and unless he could convince Shai Gallen that there was some decision to make concerning Larry Fox, GS-11, Field Collector of moderate experience, beyond how deep under Langley to bury him.

He didn't know how in hell to begin doing that, but he realized as he monitored his thoughts that at least he was worried about it—human again, with human feelings, not just a computing gunsight—though somewhere in him that gunsight was locked onto his memories like a targeting array, waiting for someone to squeeze the red switch.

"Sir," Fox said a little too loudly as he attempted to override the quaver in his voice, "the defector broke contact almost at once." Gallen wasn't a girl he'd known in the Lebanon; she was his DDO—operations director for CIA; he *had* to handle this like the professional he ought to be. "He said he was afraid of the U.S. because the President was a mole, then he took off as if he saw something in the street below. I was prevented from following him by my Turkish contact. So I didn't see what happened—I lost contact with the defector."

Gallen got up from the armchair with a look of cold fury on her face. Her glasses didn't distort the glaring eyes behind them: the lenses were clear, an excuse for the heavy frames. Fox was willing to bet that the attache case beside the DDO held at least a recorder and a voice-stress analyzer. Gallen's glasses would house either an actual intercom connecting her to a crew outside the room, or an audio monitor giving her a readout from the stress analyzer. The tone in Gallen's ear would change as the level of stress in Fox's voice went up and down. There were more reasons for stress than the subject choosing to lie, however; he hoped she'd remember that.

Abruptly Gallen slammed the wall behind her with the side of her fist: "Give me some *reason* that a man with Kunayev's resources would pick a low-level line operative to tell his story to . . . some reason not to think you're feeding me crap which, based on the increased message traffic and troop movements on the Sino-Soviet and NATO borders, the Soviets know damn well that Blaustein's Assessment boys would love to believe. Come *on*, Larry—*find* something. Even you've got to realize that you're dead in the water if I can't help you and that I *won't* help you if it puts my credibility, and therefore hundreds of my field operators, in jeopardy. If anybody's going to get fucked here tonight, it's you, not me. We're not talking about flow-charts now, we're talking about extended chemical debriefing." Her fist uncurled and her hand cut a tight, angry circle in the air.

Fox looked at her and took a deep breath. . . .

VERNOR VINGE
THE PEACE WAR

55965-6 · 400 pp. · $3.50

BAEN BOOKS